SPENCE + LILA

BOBBIE ANN MASON

SPENCE + LILA

ILLUSTRATIONS BY LaNelle Mason

THE ECCO PRESS

THE ECCO PRESS
100 West Broad Street
Hopewell, New Jersey 08525

Published simultaneously in Canada by
Penguin Books Canada Ltd., Ontario
Printed in the United States of America

Library of Congress Cataloging-in-Publication Data

Mason, Bobbie Ann.-
Spence + Lila / Bobbie Ann Mason. — 1st Ecco ed.
p.   cm
ISBN 0-88001-904-2
1. Marriage—Fiction.   2. Aged—Fiction.   3. Aged—Medical care—
Fiction.   1. Title.
[PS3563.A7877S64   1998]
813'.54—dc21   97-23997

Designed by Lydia Link

9 8 7 6 5 4 3 2 1

FIRST ECCO EDITION 1998

*For my parents
and for Janice, LaNelle, Don, and Roger*

SPENCE + LILA

*O*N THE WAY to the hospital in Paducah, Spence notices the row of signs along the highway: WHERE WILL YOU BE IN ETERNITY? Each word is on a white cross. The message reminds him of the old Burma-Shave signs. His wife, Lila, beside him, has been quiet during the trip, which takes forty minutes in his Rabbit. He didn't take her car because it has a hole in the muffler, but she has complained about his car ever since he cut the seat belts off to deactivate the annoying warning buzzer.

As they pass the Lone Oak shopping center, on the outskirts of Paducah, Lila says fretfully, "I don't know if the girls will get here."

"They're supposed to be here by night," Spence reminds her. Ahead, a gas station marquee advertises a free case of Coke with a tune-up.

Catherine, their younger daughter, has gone to pick up Nancy at the airport in Nashville. Although Lila objected to the trouble and expense, Nancy is flying all the way from Boston. Cat lives nearby, and Nancy will stay with her. Nancy offered to stay with Spence, so he wouldn't be alone, but he insisted he would be all right.

When Cat brought Lila home from the doctor the day before and Lila said, "They think it's cancer," the words ran through him like electricity. She didn't cry all evening, and when he tried to hold her, he couldn't speak. They sat in the living room in their recliner chairs, silent and scared,

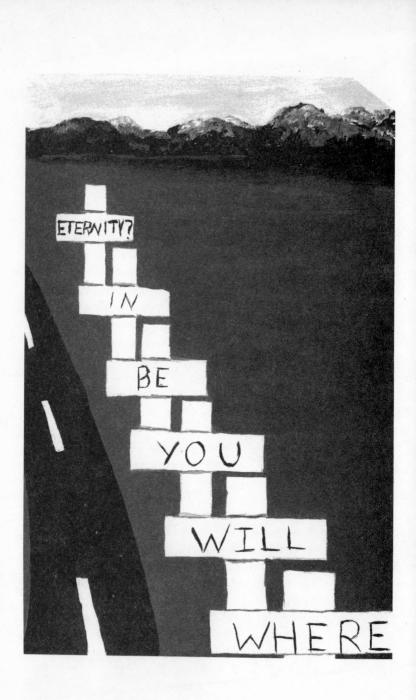

watching TV just as they usually did. Before she sat down for the evening, she worked busily in the kitchen, freezing vegetables from the garden and cooking food for him to eat during her stay in the hospital. He couldn't eat any supper except a bowl of cereal, and she picked at some ham and green beans.

He knew she had not been feeling well for months; she'd had dizzy spells and she had lost weight. The doctor at the local clinic told her to come back in three months if she kept losing weight, but Cat insisted on taking her mother to Paducah. The doctors were better there, Cat insisted, in that know-it-all manner both his daughters had. Cat, who was careless with money, didn't even think to ask what the specialists would charge. When she brought Lila home, it was late—feeding time. Spence was at the pond feeding the ducks, with Oscar, the dog. When Oscar saw the car turn into the driveway, he tore through the soybean field toward the house, as if he, too, were anxious for a verdict.

They had told Lila that her dizzy spells were tiny strokes. They also found a knot in her right breast. They wanted to take the knot out and do a test on it, and if it was cancer they would take her whole breast off, right then. It was an emergency, Lila explained. They couldn't deal with the strokes until they got the knot out. Spence imagined the knot growing so fast it would eat her breast up if she waited another day or two.

They're crawling through the traffic on the edge of Paducah. When he was younger, Spence used to come and watch the barges on the river. They glided by confidently, like miniature flattops putting out to sea. He has wanted to take Lila for a cruise on the *Delta Queen,* the luxury steamboat that paddles all the way to New Orleans, but he hasn't been able to bring himself to do it.

[15]

He turns on the radio and a Rod Stewart song blares out.

"Turn that thing off!" Lila yells.

"I thought you needed a little entertainment," he says, turning the sound down.

She rummages in her purse for a cigarette, her third on the trip. "They won't let me have any cigarettes tonight, so I better smoke while I got a chance."

"I'll take them things and throw 'em away," he says.

"You better not."

She cracks the window open at the top to let the smoke out. Her face is the color of cigarette ashes. She looks bad.

"I guess it's really cancer," she says, blowing out smoke. "The X-ray man said it was cancer."

"How would he know? He ain't even a doctor."

"He's seen so many, he would know."

"He ain't paid to draw that conclusion," Spence says. "Why did he want to scare you like that? Didn't the doctor say he'd have to wait till they take the knot out and look at it?"

"Yeah, but—" She fidgets with her purse, wadding her cigarette package back into one of the zipper pockets. "The X-ray man sees those X-rays all day long. He knows more about X-rays than a doctor does."

Spence turns into the hospital parking lot, unsure where to go. The eight-story hospital cuts through the humid, hazy sky, like a stray sprig of milo growing up in a bean field. A car pulls out in front of him. Spence's reactions are slow today, but he hits the brakes in time.

"I think I'll feel safer in the hospital," Lila says.

Walking from the parking lot, he carries the small bag she packed. He suspects there is a carton of cigarettes in it. Cat keeps trying to get Lila to quit, but Lila has no willpower. Once Cat gave her a cassette tape on how to

[16]

quit smoking, but Lila accidentally ran it through the washing machine. It was in a shirt pocket. "Accidentally on purpose," Cat accused her. Cat even told Lila once that cigarettes caused breast cancer. But Spence believes worry causes it. She worries about Cat, the way she has been running around with men she hardly knows since her divorce last year. It's a bad example for her two small children, and Lila is afraid the men aren't serious about Cat. Lila keeps saying no one will want to marry a woman with two extra mouths to feed.

Now Lila says, "I want you to supervise that garden. The girls won't know how to take care of it. That corn needs to be froze, and the beans are still coming in."

"Don't worry about your old garden," he says impatiently. "Maybe I'll mow it down."

"Spence!" Lila cries, grabbing his arm tightly. "Don't you go and mow down my garden!"

"You work too hard on it," he says. "We don't need all that grub anymore for just us two."

"The beans is about to begin a second round of blooming," she says. "I want to let most of them make into shellies and save some for seed. And I don't want the corn to get too old."

The huge glass doors of the hospital swing open, and a nurse pushes out an old woman in a wheelchair. The woman is bony and pale, with a cluster of kinfolks in bluejeans around her. Her aged hands, folded in her lap, are spotted like little bird dogs. The air-conditioning blasts Spence and Lila as they enter, and he feels as though they are walking into a meat locker.

TWO

*S*HE FELT that lump weeks ago, but she didn't mention it then. When she and Spence returned from a trip to Florida recently, she told Cat about it, and Cat started pestering her to see a specialist. The knot did feel unusual, like a piece of gristle. The magazines said you would know it was different. Lila never examined her breasts the way they said to do, because her breasts were always full of lumps anyway—from mastitis, which she had several times. Her breasts are so enormous she cannot expect to find a little knot. Spence says her breasts are like cow bags. He has funny names for them, like the affectionate names he had for his cows when they used to keep milk cows. Names like Daisy and Bossy. Petunia. Primrose. It will be harder on him if she loses one of her breasts than it will be on her. Women can stand so much more than men can.

She makes him leave the hospital early, wanting to be alone so she can smoke a cigarette in peace. After he brought her in, he paced around, then went downstairs for a Coke. Now he leaves to go home, and she watches him from behind as he trudges down the corridor, hugging himself in the cold. Lila is glad she brought her housecoat, but even with it she is afraid she will take pneumonia.

In the lounge, she smokes and plays with a picture puzzle laid out on a card table. Someone has pieced most of the red barn and pasture, and a vast blue sky remains to be done. Lila loves puzzles. When she was little, growing up at her uncle's, she had a puzzle of a lake scene with a castle. She worked that puzzle until the design was almost worn away. The older folks always kidded her, but she kept working the puzzle devotedly. She always loved the satisfying snap of two pieces going together. It was like knowing something for sure.

Her son Lee towers in the doorway of the lounge. She stands up, surprised.

"Did you get off work early?" He works at Ingersoll-Rand.

"No. I just took off an hour, and I have to go back and work till nine. They're working me overtime this month." He has lines on his face and he is only thirty-two.

He hugs her silently. He's so tall her head pokes his armpit, where he has always been ticklish.

"I didn't know you were that sick in Florida," he says. "We shouldn't have dragged you through Disney World."

"I knew something was wrong, but I didn't know what." She explains the details of the X-rays and the operation, then says, "I'm going to lose my breast, Lee."

"You are?" The lines on his face freeze. He needs a shave.

"They won't know till they get in there, but if it's cancer they'll go ahead and take it out."

"Which one?"

"This one," she says, cupping her right breast.

A woman with frizzy red hair hobbles into the lounge, her hospital gown exposing her fat, doughy knees. "I was looking for my husband," she says, "but I reckon he ain't here."

Lila waits for the woman to leave, then laughs. She's still holding her breast. "You don't remember sucking on these, do you, Lee?" She loves to tease her son. "You

sucked me dry and I had to put you on a bottle after two months. I couldn't make enough milk to feed you."

With an embarrassed grin, Lee looks out the window. "I believe you're making that up."

"You want one last tug?" She reaches up and tousles his hair. His eyes are her eyes—the same vacant blue, filled with specks, like markings on a baby bird. They both laugh, and she takes a cigarette from her housecoat pocket. Lee lights it for her, then lights his own cigarette. They share a Coke from a cooler filled with ice and free cold drinks in cans for visitors in the lounge. Lila's proud of her son. He has such a pretty wife and two smart kids, but he has to work too hard to keep up his house and car payments.

"Spence didn't know about these drinks," she says. "He went all the way down to the basement to the machine."

"He didn't stick around five minutes, I bet," Lee says, handing her the can.

"Lord, no. These places give him the heebie-jeebies."

"They do me too." Lee is playing with his lighter, flicking the flame on and off. "When's Nancy coming in?"

"I don't know. Cat called from the airport before we left home and said Nancy's airplane was late. They was supposed to get here by about four o'clock." She sips from the Coke and hands it back to Lee.

"Did Cat take off from work?"

Lila nods. "I told the girls they didn't have to go to all this trouble, but I guess they're scared I'm going to kick the bucket."

"No, you won't," Lee says. He hesitates, trying to say something, but he's exactly like Spence, bashful and silent at all the wrong moments. "What caused this?" he asks. "Do the doctors know what they're doing?"

"They're specialists," Lila says. "The woman that runs the dress store where Cat works recommended the doctor I went to yesterday. He's supposed to be good." Touching her son's knee, she says, "Promise me one thing, Lee."

He flicks ash off his cigarette by tapping it from beneath with his little finger. "What?"

"That you and Cat will start talking to one another. I can't believe my own children would hate each other."

"We don't hate each other!"

"Well, you could be nice to each other—it wouldn't hurt."

Lee stubs out his cigarette in the ashtray and nods his head thoughtfully. "I'll try," he says. "But it's up to her." He stands. "I have to get back to work."

"Are you going home for supper?"

"No. I'll grab a Big Mac or something."

Lee walks her back to her room and gives her another hug. His belt buckle presses under her breasts. When he was about fourteen, he started shooting up like a cornstalk and she thought he'd never stop. He was named after Lila's father, who abandoned her when she was four and went off to Alaska—long before it was a state. Lila was never sure it was appropriate to name her only son after him, but it's Christian to forgive. Now, as he leaves, she suddenly feels the fear she felt when Nancy left home for the first time—certain she won't see her child again.

After experimenting with the remote-control device, Lila watches television for a while. The news doesn't make any sense. The commercials are about digestion. Her digestion has always been good. Spence has heartburn and can't eat much for supper. Sometimes he has chest pains, but he says it's just heartburns. On the news, a couple about her age have won over three million dollars in a lottery. "We'll pay off the bills, I guess," the man says. "And get a new living room suit," the woman adds.

A nurse trots in with some forms for Lila to fill out.

"I can't see good enough," Lila says, searching for her glasses in her purse. "My glasses don't fit anymore, but my daughter says that's what I get for buying them at the dime store." She laughs and holds the forms at arm's length. Pointing to the blurred fine print, she asks, "What's this say?"

"It's just routine, ma'am," says the nurse. "Tonight when the doctor comes he'll give you a release form and read it to you and make sure you understand everything that's going on."

"What's going to happen to me?"

Before the nurse can answer, a girl walks in and plunks down Lila's supper tray without comment.

"My, you're getting a feast tonight," says the nurse, sending the tray toward Lila on a roller platform that fits over the bed. On the tray are dark broth, red Jell-O, black coffee.

"Couldn't I have ice tea?" Lila asks. "Coffee makes me prowl all night."

"Don't worry. We'll give you a sleeping pill."

Lila watches the sports news, something she would never do at home. When the weather comes on, she pays careful attention. The radar map shows rain everywhere in the adjoining states, but none in western Kentucky. They need rain bad. They had too much rain back in the spring. The high today was eighty-nine.

The liquid supper splashes in her stomach. From behind the curtain partition, a woman is groaning. A nurse coaxes her out of bed and helps her walk out of the room. The patient is old, her face distorted with pain as she clutches a pillow to her belly.

Lila hasn't felt so alone since Spence was in the Navy. Nancy was two, and they were still living with Spence's parents. Rosie and Amp were so quiet, their faces set like concrete as they lost themselves in their chores. Lila was awkward in Rosie's kitchen, with Rosie hovering over her. When Lila wanted to warm food for Nancy, Rosie insisted that Lila had to use a certain small aluminum pan, so they wouldn't have to wash a large one. But the food always stuck to the little pan, and it was hard to scrape clean. Rosie washed dishes in an enamel pan set on a gas ring and scalded them in another pan on another ring. The scum of the slippery lye soap never really washed off the dishes. Rosie added the dirty dishwater to the slop bucket for the hogs. Hogs liked the taste, she said. That fall, a neighbor helped Amp butcher a hog and Rosie made lye soap from the fat. Lila sewed sausage casings from flour sacks. She added flecks of dried red peppers to the ground sausage. She added more than she should have, because she knew Spence liked it extra hot, and she wanted it to be spicy for him when he came home. She knew he would come home.

Lila had to talk to somebody, so she chattered away to Nancy in their room. She was still stunned by the new experience of having a baby. Nancy kept on nursing, and Lila let her, even though her teeth made the nipples sore. She read Spence's letters aloud to her. Nancy couldn't understand the words, but Lila knew she needed her daddy, and that was the best Lila could do to help her feel his existence. Nancy listened, serious and focused, like a curious bird. There was not much to see out there, he wrote—a few birds resting on the waves like setting hens, and now and then playful porpoises that seemed to do circus tricks in the water. Spence wrote about a storm at sea, in which the boat rocked like a tire swing, the waves washing the deck. The ship stopped at an island in the Philippines and he got a twelve-hour shore leave. He wrote messages to Nancy— had she learned to milk a cow yet? was she shedding her baby teeth? Silly things, to be funny. Not until he got home did he tell about the deafening noises of the war, a racket like the end of the world.

Their room was unheated and they had a hard winter. Nancy caught cold after cold, and Lila huddled her close in the bed, under the weight of half a dozen quilts. She was afraid of rolling over on her, the way a sow sometimes mashed her pigs. One night Lila woke up and found Nancy uncovered, wet and shivering. After that, the cold went into pneumonia. Lila wanted to take her to the doctor, but Amp protested, "Why, he would charge! We can doctor her." Rosie baked onions in ashes and squeezed the juice into a spoon and fed it to her. At night Lila warmed the bed with heated bricks wrapped in newspaper, and she hardly slept, making sure she kept the child covered up; in the daytime she made a bed for her in a box close to the fireplace. She wrapped her chest in greased rags. One frightening night, when Lila prayed so hard she was almost screaming, Nancy's fever finally broke, and gradually her breathing improved. Over the following weeks, as Nancy grew stronger, Lila kept talking to her, singing and reading Spence's letters aloud, trying to find new meaning and hope in each one. Finally, there was a warm spell, when the north wind didn't blow through the cracks around the windows of their room. The yellow bushes in front of the house put out some blooms, and some geese flew over.

Uneasily, Lila and Rosie sat by the fire and pieced quilt blocks, tuning in the war news on the radio at intervals. Their shared silent worry about Spence gradually drew them together, and eventually Lila loved Spence's parents as though they were her own. That spring, during a fierce electrical storm, they gathered in Amp and Rosie's bedroom and wrapped feather bolsters around themselves. Amp said lightning wouldn't strike feathers. "Did you ever see a chicken get hit by lightning?" Rosie asked.

❊　　❊　　❊

Suddenly Lila's daughters are there, rushing to hug her. They're smiling too much. Nancy's eyes have that deep, private look Lila has often seen in them. She drops her backpack and tote bag on the bed and buries her head on Lila's shoulder. Lila's face is full of Nancy's hair, smelling faintly of shampoo. Nancy always washed her hair too much. Lila was forever warning Nancy not to go outside with a wet head or she would catch cold, but Nancy wouldn't listen, determined to do things her own way.

Cat smells like perfume, maybe the scent of irises. Lila rarely gets hugs from her, even though they are closer in some ways, because she hasn't moved away like Nancy and her comings and goings aren't such big events. Cat came running home in tears when she began having trouble with Dan, but Nancy never mentions anything wrong in her life. Nancy analyzes everything closely, passing judgment on it, the way her grandmother would have examined someone's quilt—studying and evaluating the stitching for evenness and smallness. Nancy would never make a quilt, though. But Cat would.

"My plane got fog-delayed in Boston," Nancy says, pulling back from Lila. "And instead of landing in Nashville, we flew all the way to Birmingham and then back to Nashville. How are you feeling, Mom?"

"Well, I ain't ready to go out and pick cotton," says Lila. "But you didn't have to come all this way."

"I wanted to come."

Cat says, "I ate lunch twice while I was waiting for the plane. And read two whole magazines from cover to cover. And watched people. I saw a lot of weirdos."

Nancy plops on the side of the bed. "When Cat's nervous she eats, and when I'm nervous I can't eat."

Cat, her car keys still in her hand, has on a long skirt with a flounce, from the boutique where she works. Nancy dresses like a boy most of the time and has worn the same belt on her bluejeans for years, but Cat has always been a fashion plate. In high school she was Miss Sorghum at a festival. Cat used to get exasperated with Nancy and say she didn't want to be seen in public with her, but she's finally given up on her sister. Cat always said, "Be fancy, Nancy!"

The girls run through a million questions they want to ask the doctor, but Lila cannot remember what she wants to ask. She meant to tell the doctor yesterday about her mastitis and to ask whether it causes cancer. The main thing is the cost. Cat assured her everything would be covered, but Lila doesn't believe Medicare covers everything. She heard that if it was cancer, it wouldn't be covered. Now Cat is investigating the drawers and closets in the room, checking things. Cat has always been particular. She's a fine housekeeper, something Lila never had time to be. Cat won dozens of ribbons in 4-H.

"Look what I hatched out," Lila says proudly to the nurse who comes in to take her temperature. "My little girls."

"They don't look a thing alike," the nurse says, then glances at her watch.

After the nurse removes the thermometer and leaves, Nancy says, "Robert wanted me to tell you he misses you and he's sorry he couldn't come."

Lila smiles. Her grandson is a thoughtful boy, always sending her cards on Mother's Day and her birthday.

"Jack too," Nancy says.

"Jack's awful good to let you come traipsing down here."

Nancy flinches in protest. "He didn't *let* me! He had nothing to do with it. You're my mom and I came to see you."

The bed is loaded with Nancy's things, blue pouches with zipper pockets. Lila thrives on such confusion. She teases Nancy, "I swear with all that stuff you tote around you're just like old Aunt Hattie Cross. Aunt Hattie always carried her wash pan and her toothbrush everywhere she went. We kidded her about packing her potty around. We'd say she brushed her teeth in her pot."

"I've got my toothbrush right here—somewhere," Nancy says, grinning. "I didn't bring my pot, though."

"Well, you can use mine," Lila says with a laugh. "There's one in the bathroom with my name on it!"

She tousles Nancy's hair lovingly. Lila's children are all grown, with their own families. This is what life comes down to, she realizes—replacing your own life with new ones. It's just like raising a crop. Somehow, this makes her think of prize-winning vegetables at the fair. It always made her sad to see the largest and prettiest vegetables on display. The best tomatoes and corn and broccoli sat there and ruined just so people could look at them.

"Lee was here," Lila says. "He said he'd talk to you, Cat, but it was up to you. I wish y'all would stop fussing over that air conditioner."

"It wasn't the air conditioner. It was that dumb three-wheeler!" Cat says angrily. "He never should have let Scott ride it. He was too little, and he didn't have a helmet. Those things are dangerous!"

"Where are Scott and Krystal?" Lila asks, shifting the subject.

"With Dan. They went to Hopkinsville yesterday to stay two weeks with him. I thought you knew that."

"No." Lila is puzzled. She says, "I can't keep things straight anymore. I thought Lee was mad at you over that air conditioner you gave him. I didn't know it was the three-wheeler."

Cat pats Lila's hair. "Let's don't worry about this stuff, O.K.?"

Nancy says, "The main thing right now is you."

"I think they're going to take this breast off," Lila says, placing her hand under her right breast.

"You've always been so proud of those," Cat says, reaching to touch the top of Lila's breast lightly.

"My big jugs," Lila says, smiling. "I raised three younguns on these. I guess they're give out now." She can't say what she feels—that the last thing she would have expected was to be attacked by disease in the very place she felt strongest. It seemed to suggest some basic failing, like the rotten core of a dying tree.

Nancy rests her hand on her mother's shoulder. "Is all this too fast?" she asks.

"Well, I have to get it done."

"It's up to you—if you feel it's going too far, or if you want to wait." Nancy removes her hand to smooth her hair. Lila spots a gray hair on Nancy's head and almost bursts into tears.

"No, I want to get it over with."

"We hate to see you pushed around," Cat says. "They're your breasts, and if they're worth more to you than all this—"

"It's your decision," says Nancy.

"I know what you mean," says Lila, cradling her breasts like babies. "But they ain't worth more than living."

"I think it's going to be all right, Mom," says Nancy, taking Lila's hand. "The lump isn't big and you found it early."

"I wouldn't have found it if it hadn't been for Cat." Lila starts to cry. "Don't y'all stare at me. I don't like to be stared at."

The old woman in the other bed, behind a curtain, yells at a nurse, "You can just take that thing and ram it up your butt."

Cat and Nancy start snickering. "I'll be like that tomorrow!" says Lila, laughing back her tears. "Oh, me!"

*S*PENCE can't sleep. With the frenzied urgency of a hunting dog, Oscar is barking at an animal out in the field. Spence wonders if it could be the wildcat that had screamed out by the barn one night. Wildcats scavenged at the dump beyond the industrial park, and a man had shot one there not long ago. Spence was heartsick when he heard about that. Some people would shoot anything, just to see how it killed. Last year, he saw, for perhaps ten seconds, a wildcat at the pond. It was small and scrawny, with a short, black-tipped tail and long, tufted ears. It disappeared into the scrub along the creek.

He jams pillows under his neck. They are soft like her breasts, but he doesn't want to let himself think about her body. She has been looking bad for a long time, losing weight, not eating. She kept making excuses, saying she wasn't hungry, or that she was more active than usual. In early June, when they were in Florida, she was sick. They went with Lee and his wife, Joy, and the kids, all crammed in Lee's station wagon. It was the wrong season. When Lee planned the trip, they didn't think about the season because they could only go in the summer, after Joy finished the school year. She teaches the second grade. In Florida, the temperature was already in the high nineties. They stayed in a cabin at Flamingo, the southernmost point on the U.S. mainland. When they entered the cabin, clouds of mosquitoes swarmed in through the door with them.

Afterward, they laughed at the way they had frantically slapped at the insects and sprayed each other down with insect repellent. It reminded Spence of spraying cows for flies. After they wiped out the mosquito invasion, he and Lee sat in the air-conditioning and watched TV while Lila and Joy cooked supper. The children, Jennifer and Greg, scratched their bites until they were raw. Through the night mosquitoes whined only occasionally, and then the next day the hot sun burned them off. Spence loved the heat. As they rode along the main highway, he told Lila, "I wouldn't mind having a job mowing the shoulders along the road down here."

It was his first real trip since he was in the Navy. He was surprised at how much he loved the swamp. On a lookout point, they gazed out over the endless sea of saw grass. It was studded with little rises, like islands. The Indians called them hummocks. He felt free. The sun blazed down on them, and he thought he could live there always. Lee kept apologizing for bringing them to Florida in the wrong season. Most of the migrating birds had gone north. In the winter, thousands of herons and egrets and storks and ibises gathered in the Everglades, but in the late spring the swamp was bare, with only a few birds, and the alligator hole was quiet, the alligators lying still like rotting logs in the murky water. Once, they spotted an alligator crossing the road, sluggish and lizard-like. They saw a blue racer. And several long-necked white birds. A few blue herons.

Lila didn't like Florida. Earlier in the trip, when she started having the dizzy spells and the numbness in her arm, they took her to a hospital in Orlando. The doctor—who charged sixty-five dollars for an emergency-room visit and spent only five minutes with Lila—said she had an irritated nerve and suggested she go to her own doctor when she returned home. They spent two miserable days at Disney World—the purpose of the whole trip, for the kids. Spence didn't care for it. He wanted to see snakes and birds and alligators, so Lee drove them on down to the Everglades. They had insisted Lila didn't have to go, but she said she didn't mind, that she felt better. But when they explored the trails, she stayed in the car, with the air conditioner blowing, and smoked and napped, while Spence and the others explored the boardwalk trails through the swamps. He was fascinated by the mahogany hummocks, and he read all the plaques that told about the wildlife. He liked to imagine when the Indians lived there in the swamp, venturing from hummock to hummock in their canoes, exploring. Back in the stuffy, smoky car, she was quiet and her face was pale, but she said she was all right. "It's the heat," she said. "I'm hotter than a she-wolf in a pepper patch!"

Those dizzy spells turned out to be little strokes—TIAs, the doctor in Paducah called them. The blood wasn't feeding to her brain. Now Spence shudders in the night, imagining a scene in Florida—Lila having a major stroke on one of those lonely trails. The nearest hospital was fifty miles away, and they would not have known how to find it. If something had happened to her then, he would have been to blame.

Dawn is creeping under the shades. The sheets are wadded, the quilt is lying on the rug, the cat scratching at the back door. Lila is crazy about the cat, Abraham. Spence has never seen her so crazy about a cat, the way she baby-talks to him. The morning after Spence heard that wildcat, Abraham's fur was ruffled, as though something had been chewing on him and rolling him in the dirt. Abraham has long hair and is spotted like a Guernsey. Stiff and aching, Spence gets up and watches the sun rise over the soybean fields. Oscar is out there, walking slowly, sniffing close to the ground.

While CNN blares out the latest on Iran-Iraq, Iran-contra, Nicaragua, South Africa, something in Idaho, Spence makes breakfast in the microwave. He watches the strips of bacon curl up and ooze grease down the ridges of the bacon rack. When the bacon is done, he makes scrambled eggs. He sets the dish in for twenty-five seconds, then stirs the eggs with a fork and cooks them for twenty-five more seconds. Spence bought the microwave so he could fix his meals while Lila was away on her trips with the senior citizens. She has been to Hawaii, the Badlands, Savannah and New Orleans.

He bought the microwave at a flea market, almost new. At first, he set it on top of the refrigerator, but Lila couldn't reach it. So he found a wobbly metal table at a sale and set the oven on it next to the kitchen table. The first time he tried the microwave, he cracked an egg in a dish and the egg exploded in the oven with a sound like a shotgun. He learned to punch the yolk with a fork to let the pressure out. "Crazy thing," Lila said on the telephone to one of her friends. "He never reads the directions to anything." The oven came with an incomplete set of instructions, and he had to learn how to use it by trial and error. Once, he exploded a potato, for fun.

After eating, he and Oscar head for the barn to feed the calves, five little Holsteins he is raising for beef in a pasture between the barn and the woods. The fencing is makeshift—boards and an electric wire.

"Oscar, you sure are smart," Spence says. "You learned about that electric fence in one easy lesson."

Oscar wags his tail. The calves flick flies with their tails. They amble forward, rubbing each other and gazing at Spence with liquid eyes the texture and size of fried

eggs. A horrifying image flashes through his mind—jabbing their eyes with a fork. Once he tried raising a veal calf, and every time he remembers it he hates himself. The little thing stayed in the dark stall alone, and whenever Spence came to bottle-feed him, the calf cried. When after only a few weeks Spence took him to the slaughterhouse, the calf couldn't stand up. The meat was tender and pale. He and Lila couldn't talk about it. The packages languished in the freezer, and by the time she cooked the last ones, the meat had lost its freshness.

He steadies himself against the barn door for a moment, then enters the barn, the calves following. He distributes cups of feed into the troughs, and the calves dig their heads in. He fastens their necks to the stanchions, and while they feed he talks to them.

"Sunflower," he says. "You're too skinny. Whoa, there, Mudpuddle. Watch what you're doing, Dexter. Delbert. Boss Hogg, don't get crazy now."

Always, when Spence feeds his calves, he goes through their names.

FOUR

*L*ILA SAYS, "They sure don't let you get lonesome here—all the traipsing in and out they do at all hours."

Cat and Nancy are hovering over the bed, staring at her with an unnatural sort of eagerness. "Did you sleep?" Cat asks.

"Off and on," says Lila. She tries to sit up against the pillow, but she feels woozy from this morning's medicine. "That coffee last night made me jumpy, but they give me some pills and a shot."

Nancy says, "That's outrageous! There was no good reason to give you coffee. You should have refused it."

Cat's earrings dangle in Lila's face. Lila's mind feels fuzzy, far away. She is afraid the operating room will be cold.

"Are you scared?" Nancy asks, holding Lila's hand.

"They work you over too much for you to be scared. I haven't had time to think." Lila squeezes Nancy's hand and reaches for Cat's. "You girls are being good to me," she says. "I sure am lucky."

"Well, we care about you," Cat says.

"You're going to be just fine, Mom," says Nancy. "You're tough."

"I guess I better say goodbye to my jug," Lila says, laughing and looking down at herself. "If Spence don't hurry on here, he's going to miss his chance."

Just then Spence appears, still in short sleeves. Yesterday she tried to tell him to wear long sleeves, but he wouldn't listen to her. After giving Nancy a hug, he steps back and eyes her up and down to see how much older she seems.

"You look poor as a snake," he says. "Why didn't you bring Robert?"

"He's going off to camp tomorrow. Jack's taking him up to New Hampshire. It's the same place he went last year, where they go on treks into the mountains."

"Bring him down here. I'll see that he communes with nature." Spence grins at Nancy.

"I'm sure you will. You'll have him out planting soybeans." Nancy twists out of a nurse's way.

"It would be good for him," Lila says sleepily. "Working out in the fields would teach him something."

She closes her eyes, vaguely listening to Spence and the girls talk. If this is her time to go, she should be ready. And she has her family with her, except for Lee, who had to work. She feels she is looking over her whole life, holding it up to see how it has turned out—like a piece of sewing. She can see Cat trying on a dress Lila has made for her, and Lila checks to see whether it needs taking up. She turns up the hem, jerks the top to see how it fits across the shoulders, considers an extra tuck in the waist. In a recurrent dream she has had for years, she is trying to finish a garment, sewing fast against the clock.

They are still chattering nervously around her when the surgeon appears. He's young, with sensitive hands that look skilled at delicate finger work. Lila always notices people's fingers. Nancy and Cat keep asking questions, but Lila is sleepy and can't follow all that he is saying. Then he moves closer to her and says, "If the biopsy shows a malignancy, I'm going to recommend a modified radical mastectomy. I'll remove the breast tissue and the lymph nodes under the arm. But I'll leave the chest muscles. If you follow the physical therapy, then you'll have full use of your arm and you'll be just fine." He smiles reassuringly. He resembles a cousin of Lila's—Whip Stanton, a little man with a lisp and a wife with palsy.

"How small would the lump have to be for you to recommend a lumpectomy instead?" Nancy asks the doctor.

"Infinitesimal," he says. "It's better to get it all out and be sure. This way is more certain."

"Well, more and more doctors are recommending lumpectomies instead of mastectomies," Nancy argues. "What I'm asking is, what is the dividing line? How large should the lump be for the mastectomy to be preferable?"

Lila sees Spence cringe. Nancy has always asked questions and done things differently, just to be contrary. "Nancy, Nancy, quite contrary," they used to tease her.

The doctor shrugs and leans against the wall. "It depends on a number of factors," he says. "You can't reduce it to a question of size. If it's an aggressive tumor, a fast-growing one, then a smaller lump might be more dangerous than one that has grown slowly over a longer period of time. And my suspicion is that this is an aggressive tumor. You can get a second opinion if you want to, but we've got her prepped, and if the second opinion was in favor of a lumpectomy, then wouldn't you have to go for a third opinion, so you could take two out of three? But in this case, time is of the essence." The doctor grins at Lila. "What do you think, Mrs. Culpepper? You look like a pretty smart lady."

"Why, you're just a little whippersnapper," Lila says. "All the big words make me bumfuzzled. I guess you know your stuff, but I got you beat when it comes to producing pretty daughters." She has heard he is single, and she heard the nurses joking with him. She can't keep her mind on the conversation. It's as though she's floating around the room, dipping in and out of the situation, the way the nurses do.

"That's for certain," he says, twirling his stethoscope like a toy.

"My daughters are curious, though," Lila says apologetically. Even the outfits they are wearing are curious—layers of dark, wrinkled cotton.

"They're weird," Spence says.

"No, we're not," says Cat indignantly. She's dressed up in one of her man-catching outfits, with heavy jewelry, but what man would like that getup? Cat claims women actually dress for women. Nancy was always too impatient to fool with her appearance. She's like Lila that way, wearing any old thing handy. When Nancy moved up north she stopped wearing lipstick and curling her hair, and for a while she didn't even wear a brassiere. Lila was afraid Nancy's breasts would be damaged.

"Do you have any questions, Mr. Culpepper?" the doctor asks. "Is there anything I can clarify?"

Lila senses Spence's embarrassment as he shakes his head no. The nurses are whizzing around, and the woman in the other bed is arguing with her doctor.

"What about them strokes?" Spence pipes up then.

"Well, the first priority is to deal with this lump in her breast, and later we'll check the obstructions in the carotid arteries." The doctor touches his neck, indicating the main blood vessels. He says, "It's possible that I'll recommend further surgery next week to clean out the plaque in those arteries."

"I was having strokes in Florida," Lila says. She

touches her arm, where the numbness spreads a few times a day. As they talk, she feels one of her dizzy spells coming on. She longs for a cigarette.

"How risky is that second operation?" Cat demands.

"Well, there's always the risk of death," the doctor says bluntly. He's not looking at anyone. His eyes are fixed on the doorframe. "And a carotid endarterectomy is tricky because there's always the chance the patient will have a stroke on the table. But the benefits outweigh the risks. Increase the blood supply to the brain and she'll stop having those transischemic attacks, and we'll prevent the big stroke down the road."

"The big stroke down the road," Nancy repeats, after he leaves. "It sounds like the title of a children's book."

Spence seems frozen in his position in the corner chair. His eyes stare vacantly as a nurse comes in with a syringe in her hand like a weapon. "Are you ready, Mrs. Culpepper?"

"Oh, must I?"

"It'll all be over with before you know it."

"Y'all messed up my fishing trip," Lila says crossly, trying to manage a smile. "I was aiming to go fishing this week."

"That's why we call you patients—because you have to be patient," the nurse says cheerfully. "Now you want to lie back for me? And make a fist."

From out of nowhere, Lila can hear Spence telling about the war, about a guy on his ship who went ashore one night on one of the Pacific islands and got himself tattooed. Spence wrote in his letter, "He had his whole butt tattooed with a picture of two beagles in a field—a pretty field, with green grass. And the dogs were after a rabbit that was disappearing into his crack. The next day the bos'n made him chip paint all day, and he hurt so bad he cried. It was a pretty picture, though, the grass was just as green! But I sure bet that hurt. He's a big guy too." She's about to laugh, remembering that letter.

She sees the girls whispering. The patient in the other bed is up walking again, but she refused her breakfast. Lila's breakfast was ice water. She wasn't hungry anyway. Food doesn't taste right to her anymore. The food on her trip to New Orleans back in March was unappetizing. The gumbo even had shells in it. Now Nancy is bending over her, hugging her, followed by Cat, her face close to Lila's. Cat whispers, "Hang in there, Mom." Spence is edging out the door as the orderlies appear with a bed on wheels. In their green outfits, they are leprechauns. Or men from Mars. "Are you going to give me some sugar or not?" Lila calls to Spence.

"I reckon," he says, clutching her hand and bending down to kiss her. He's self-conscious, but the nurse is busy filling out a chart and doesn't notice them.

"Take care of my babies," she says, meaning the cat and dog. "And don't forget them beans."

"I won't forget your old beans!" He chokes on his laugh.

As the leprechauns wheel her away, she sees Spence gazing after her helplessly. She has forgotten to tell Nancy and Cat something, something important she meant to say about Spence. His face disappears and she is in an elevator, with music playing, the kind of music they play in heaven.

$\mathcal{S}$PENCE can't stand hospitals. The smells make him sick. The sounds of pain hurt. In an hour, the doctor will telephone Lila's room with the biopsy report, which will determine how he should proceed with the surgery. Spence hates waiting.

He drives to a gas station that has a mini-market. There, he buys two baked potatoes with cheese topping and eats them in the car with a can of Coke. He plays the radio, his rock station. The potatoes need more pepper. Nancy and Cat urged him to eat in the cafeteria with them, but he had little appetite in a building with so many sick people and their germs. In the corridor when he arrived at the hospital that morning, Spence saw a man with a hole in his face where his nose had been. Spence knows a man who went to the cancer specialists in Memphis and had a new nose grafted on. His face doesn't look bad with the new nose, considering it came from a dead man. When Spence told Nancy about it, she didn't believe him. Nancy always believes what she wants to believe. He smiles, thinking of how the doctor outsmarted her when she tried to challenge him. Spence is proud of his daughter, though. She has an important job—something to do with computers—with a company that requires her to travel all over the United States. When Nancy married Jack Cleveland, a Yankee, Spence was sure she was making a mistake. He was afraid there wasn't a living in photography—more of a hobby than work—but the marriage has lasted, and Robert is a smart, good-looking boy. It pains Spence that Nancy lives so far away. She went up there right after college. She was always restless and adventurous, because of the books she read. When she was little, she would read the same book over and over, as if she could make it come true.

Spence finishes the potatoes, gasses up the car, then drives to an auto-supply store to buy a windshield-wiper blade refill, but he can't find the right length and he doesn't want to buy a whole new wiper. He needs to get a tune-up, but he forgot to bring the coupon he clipped from the newspaper for a free one. He tries to calculate whether he would come out ahead if he went instead to that filling station offering the free case of Coke with a tune-up. But he doesn't have time to fool with the car today anyway. Impatiently, he drives back to the hospital, the radio blasting out rock-and-roll. The music fits the urgency of his life. The music seems to organize all the noises of public places into something he can tolerate. The rhythm of driving blends with the music on the radio and the beat in his nervous system. Before the children were born, he and Lila used to go dancing at little places out in the country that people called "nigger juke joints." They went to one across the county line where they could get beer. Lila never liked beer, but she loved to dance. He can imagine her long legs now, flashing white in the dark of the dance floor. He remembers a saxophone player and a blues singer as good as Joe Williams. The real music is always hidden somewhere, off in the country, back in his head, in his memory. There are occasional echoes of that raunchy old music he always loved in some of the rock songs on the radio.

At the hospital, he is forced to park in the last row.

"Midnight Rambler" by the Rolling Stones comes on the radio then, and he sits there and listens until it is finished. His family is busting out at the seams—like the music. He can't keep track of what they are up to. When a plane crash is on the news, he's afraid Nancy was on the plane. And Cat's life is a mess. She married too young, and her husband had big ideas he couldn't follow through on. He managed a hardware store, then opened his own water-bed outlet, but it failed. Spence told Cat the day Dan leased the store that waterbeds were filled with snake oil, not water, and she was mad at him for a long time for saying that. Lila tried to talk Cat into staying with Dan, but Spence is glad she got rid of him. Lila worries about Cat and the kids alone at night, with no man around the house, but Lila isn't afraid to go gallivanting around the world herself.

When Spence's mother died a few years ago, they were free to travel. By then, they had sold off the cows and weren't tied down on the farm. Spence told Lila he was going to send her around the world. She begged him to go too, but he refused to go traveling with a bunch of old people, yammering about their ailments. "I ain't that old," he protested.

"But we couldn't light out by ourselves," she said. "We'd get knocked in the head and robbed. We'd get lost. On these tours, they take care of you."

He was afraid for her to go off, but he wanted her to have the chance. Her first trip was to Hawaii, and at home alone he imagined her out on the Pacific, in a cruise boat that stopped at Pearl Harbor. When she came home from Hawaii, she brought a certificate for a hula-dancing course (three lessons) and some ceramic pineapples. "Did you get scared?" he asked. "Not a bit," she said. "I slept good, had the biggest time of my life." The airplane, she said, was big enough to play ball in. On her second trip, a bus tour out to the Badlands, she brought him a toy rabbit with antlers—a jackelope. It was a joke present, but she wouldn't admit it, insisting she saw a jackelope cross the highway. After that, she went on two more trips, and when relatives commented snidely about how his wife was running around on him and spending all his money, it made him furious. He told them, "She took care of my mother for ten years, and she deserves to get out and have fun. If she wants to go to the moon, I'll let her. I don't care how much it costs."

While she was away in Hawaii, his memories of the Pacific grew louder, more insistent. The sounds of the antiaircraft guns echoed and reverberated below deck, where he was an ammunition passer. Storms battled the ship relentlessly, slopping the decks and plunging and hurtling the ship like a carnival ride. In the dark, cramped quarters—stinking with B.O. and puke—he tried to sleep, but he thought about Lila, nursing the baby and helping his parents get the crops in. He could see her milking the few cows they had during the war, washing the milk cans. One calm, sunny day, he carried buckets of water to swab the deck and forgot momentarily where he was, imagining he was carrying buckets of milk from the barn to the house. Then a fighter plane zoomed down low over the destroyer to land on the aircraft carrier a few hundred yards off the port bow.

When Spence enters Lila's room, the girls are reading magazines. The air-conditioning is cold. He's in a short-sleeved shirt, but they are wrapped up in layers of clothes.

"We stole her cigarettes," Cat says. "She had five packs at the bottom of her bag."

Nancy seems smaller each time he sees her, while Cat fattens up like a Butterball turkey. Cat has on a wrinkled jumpsuit with buttons and zippers all over it, and a wide belt with three buckles, and several pounds of beads. Nancy has on a sweater and a jacket and baggy pants with buttons at the ankles. This is July.

"Where did y'all get them clothes?" he says. "The rag barrel?"

Cat lets out a giggle. "One of the doctors called us 'honky Shiite terrorists.'"

Spence's daughters have never acted their age, but in a way he doesn't mind—they are still his little girls. He may burst into tears. Feeling a pang of heartburn, he sits down and grabs a section of the *Courier-Journal* from the floor. Too late, he thinks about the germs on the floor.

A nurse flies in and says to Nancy, "I'll have to ask you to get off the bed, hon. It's for the patient."

"I was warming it up for her," Nancy grumbles. She folds her reading glasses and slips them into a case.

"Y'all are always arguing with the doctors and nurses," Spence says to his daughters after the nurse leaves. "Talking back to them."

"Well, if we left it up to you, who knows what could happen to Mom!" Nancy says, sitting up on the edge of the bed and reaching for her shoes. "She could get mutilated. A lot of doctors just want to operate because they're enamored with their equipment." Nancy situates herself on a spread-out newspaper on the floor. "Let me ask you one thing, Dad. If you were in the hospital hooked up to tubes and you weren't even conscious, or maybe you were in excruciating pain—what would you want us to do?"

"I'm afraid of what y'all might have them doctors do to me." Spence shudders.

"Well, maybe you ought to think about it," Nancy says. "While you're still in charge."

"I'll solve that one," he says. "I just won't go to doctors. You're right about them anyway. They just want to work you over and take your money." He folds the newspaper and drops it to the floor. He says to Cat, "I believe your mama is more worried about you than she is about this operation."

"Well, I don't know what to do about it. She didn't see Scott laying on the ground that time. I thought he was dead!"

"He wasn't hurt."

"But Lee never should have let Scott ride that dumb three-wheeler. He was too little, and he didn't have a helmet. Those things are dangerous, the way kids ride them all over creation."

For a moment Spence sees Lila in his daughter. Lila swinging in a porch swing the night they married, her shoulder pads sticking out like scaffolding.

Cat goes on, "When I took Scott to the hospital, his fingers were numb—that's a sign of concussion. There was a kid killed just last week on a three-wheeler. Didn't you see that in the paper?"

Spence shakes his head in despair. It was an accident, and Lee was scared too. He says, "That's not what I meant. Lila's just worried about you—staying by yourself at night."

"What does she want me to do—bring some guy home with me?"

The telephone trills just then and Cat snatches it up. "Yes. Yes." She listens grimly.

"What is it?" Nancy says, motioning anxiously to Cat. "Is she O.K.?"

Cat nods. When she hangs up, she says, "The biopsy showed it was malignant, and he's going ahead with the mastectomy."

Spence's stomach lurches. "Oh, no," he says faintly.

His heart is racing. Nancy says nothing. Cat picks at her nails.

"They won't have her back up here till she gets out of the recovery room," Cat says. "It could be hours."

"Let's get out of here," Nancy says. "Let's go do something." She rolls her magazine and plunges it into her tote bag.

Cat, feeling for something in her purse, says, "I knew she had cancer when I saw her after she came back from Florida. I could see it in her face."

❀   ❀   ❀

Later, in the lounge, Spence spins through all the TV channels, but there are no ball games on today. The Cards are having a good season, especially with Joe Magrane, a Kentucky boy, pitching. Spence settles on a game show, but in his mind he sees her garden, with the corn growing full, and he sees her coming to the house early in the morning with buckets of vegetables. Her straw hat is set cockeyed on her head, and her blouse is damp. She bends over in the shade of the big oak and sorts through handfuls of shell beans, picking out some dried ones to save for seed. The cat twines himself around her ankles and she talks to him softly and sweetly, praising him for his morning's exploits. Behind her, the soybeans stretch out like a dusty green rug. The soybeans have been invaded by grasshoppers, and Spence is afraid of losing the crop. He never had a problem with grasshoppers before he switched to one-crop farming. His neighbor, Bill Belton, promised to spray the beans soon. Bill has a little crop-duster plane and won't charge Spence much. He has been kidding Spence about going up in the plane with him, but Lila won't hear of Spence going up. Spence has thought about it, though, imagining what it would be like to see

[51]

the fields from up high, with the pond like a glass eye and the buildings like dollhouses. He has never been up in an airplane.

He goes to the rest room and washes his teeth. Some of the potato is under the upper plate and starting to irritate the roof of his mouth. Earlier, he was in such a hurry to get back to Lila's room he didn't wash his teeth. On the commode, he smokes half a cigarette. For the last several years, he has limited himself to two cigarettes a day. But he can't stop Lila. She puffs away like the smoke-stack in the industrial park beyond the soybean fields. Sometimes he watches her puffing and sees the smoke-stack puffing simultaneously, and they are like coor-dinated events in his life, events he has no control over. He runs water at the sink over the cigarette butt and drops it in the waste can.

In the hall, he runs into Guy Samson, a man he sees often at the feed mill. Spence used to rent Guy's bulls.

"Spence, have you got somebody here?" Guy asks.

"My wife," Spence says, feeling himself tremble. "She's being operated on. Breast cancer."

"That's tough, Spence," Guy says, shaking his head worriedly. "My mother-in-law's here now with cancer, and she's real bad. She's hooked up to them machines in intensive care."

"They're hooking everybody up these days."

"Ain't that the truth. Does your wife have to have cobalt?"

Spence shudders. "They haven't said." He knows that with cancer they will give her cobalt treatments, and he has tried to put this out of his mind.

"That cobalt is what I'd be afraid of," Guy says, nod-ding his head sympathetically.

Spence is shivering in the cold.

"Take it easy, Spence," says Guy as they part.

The word "cobalt" stung Spence to the quick. He has known people who had cobalt. Claudine Turrell lost her hair and was sick from radiation poisoning, like the Japanese after the bomb. Claudine finally died, after suffering for weeks. The same thing happened to Bob Miller and Clancy Stone. And Lila's friend Reba died only last year, after several rounds of cobalt treatments. It occurs to Spence now that Lila has not even mentioned Reba, as if it would be bad luck to say her name. Lila visited Reba in the hospital and came home describing Reba's bald head and skinny neck—a picked chicken, Lila said sadly.

The doctors would say, "These cobalt treatments might give her a little time." There is no choice about it, really. There are no significant choices most of the time. You always have to do what has to be done. It's like milking cows. When their bags are full, they have to be milked.

SIX

L ILA FEELS a twitching on the back of her hand, like a fly that has landed, but she is unable to swat at it. Then she feels the tube hanging out of her hand. She eases open her eyes, sees blurred faces and machines with hoses—like the electric milkers they used to have for the cows. Her eyes close and she sees green beans setting on blooms again and okra poking up like hitchhikers' thumbs. A volunteer sunflower has sprung up amidst the peppers. There is a burning in her chest, a smoldering fire in a woodstove. Something bulky is there, a heavy weight holding her down. She is too weak to bring her hand up to touch it. A TV set, somewhere near, seems to be playing a story about a woman's best friend dying of cancer. The friend's name is Reba, and they play cards and go fishing together. Reba is smart and has a giggle like a little girl. One day Reba finds a lump the size of a golf ball in her breast. She claims it came there overnight, but she is lying. Reba kept it a secret, hadn't wanted to admit it was there. She had such tiny breasts, not like Lila's large, knotty breasts. A golf ball could hide in Lila's unnoticed. Reba's hair falls out and she wastes away to nothing and disappears beyond the garden.

Someone wheels a cart into the room. Lila hears tinkling glass, the sucking of rubber soles, voices bubbling. The sound of the TV story has faded away. Outlines of people grow sharper, faces peering quizzically at her. Lila does not want them staring at her. She must look awful.

SEVEN

𝒜LL THE WAY to the hospital the next day, Spence listens to tapes of the Blasters and Fleetwood Mac that Nancy brought for him. The Fleetwood Mac tape doesn't even sound like Fleetwood Mac. He wouldn't have recognized the group. The Blasters remind him of Jerry Lee Lewis. Spence saw Jerry Lee Lewis on a special recently. He looked bad—old and worn out.

He dreads seeing Lila, so he has fooled around half the morning, delaying the trip to Paducah. In Paducah, before going to the hospital, he looks for a gallon of windshield-washer fluid and has to go to a couple of places to compare prices. He pays four dollars for it. Later, in the Wal-Mart, where he stops to look for that wiper-blade replacement, he spots the same brand of washer fluid on sale for two dollars. He has blown two bucks. It makes him mad. All the coffee makers and video games and electric ice-cream parlors in the Wal-Mart are depressing. People are buying so much junk, thinking it will make them happy. And then when they can't even make a path across the floor through their possessions, they have a yard sale. Spence can't stand to waste anything. His parents never wasted a scrap. "Always be saving," Pap told his grandchildren. "Hard times might come." Cat fought him, pitching a fit once over two shelly beans left on her plate. These days, with all the new money, everyone has gone wild. Around here, there is nowhere to go, so people either get drunk or go crazy—sometimes both. Spence knows a guy whose wife left him and ran off to Biloxi, Mississippi, with a prefab-home builder whom she later shot dead. After that, the guy had a nervous breakdown and was sent off to the asylum. The children went to foster homes. Spence can't imagine what the world is coming to. Yesterday, the newspaper reported two burglaries in town—a holdup at an all-night food store and a break-in at an old widow's house.

In the Wal-Mart parking lot, he has a sudden queasy feeling. He can't remember where he is. He sees rows and rows of cars. His brain reels. He must have a car here, but he can't remember what car. He sees a Camaro, an Oldsmobile, rows of shiny silver and white cars, lined up like teeth. The vertical lines of street lamps tower in the landscape like defoliated trees. The parking lot seems slightly familiar, but he can't place it. He may be thinking of one he has seen on TV. He stumbles onward and suddenly spots his car—the Rabbit that needs a tune-up. The little car seems to have aged ten years overnight. It is parked next to a black van with round windows and a pink-and-blue mural of an angel and a Jesus with a halo. Spence wonders what loony drives such a vehicle. Spence has never been comfortable in church. He is suspicious of most preachers and believes all the evangelists on the radio and TV are con artists. The night before, when Lila came out of the recovery room and was wheeled back into Room 301, she said to him, "Did you pray for me?" Her question startled him. They never spoke of prayer, or heaven, but Spence knew she prayed for him, frequently, because she went to church and was afraid that because he didn't they wouldn't end up in heaven together. When he answered her, he felt a chill up his spine. "Sure," he

said, joking. "You know how good I am at saying grace."
She got tickled at him then but had to stop laughing
because she hurt. "I've got a long row to hoe," she said.
She wasn't fully awake.

EIGHT

*L*ILA FEELS as though she has been left
out in a field for the buzzards. The nurses are in at all
hours, making no special effort to be quiet—a nurse who
checks dressings, another one who changes dressings, a
nurse with blood-thinner shots three times a day, a nurse
with breathing-machine treatments, various nurses' aides
who check temperature and blood pressure, the cleaning
woman, the mail lady, the priest and nuns from the hospital, the girls who fill the water jugs, the woman who
brings the meal trays, the candy stripers selling toiletries
and candy and magazines from a cart. Lila can't keep track
of all the nurses who come to check her drainage tube—
squirting the murky fluid out of the plastic collection bottle, measuring the fluid intake and output, writing on
charts. The nurses walk her around the entire third floor
twice a day, accompanied by her I.V. bag, wheeling on a
stand. Spence is nervous, bursting in anxiously, unable to
stick around. And the girls are in and out, bringing her
little things—a basket of flowers from the gift shop downstairs and some perfume. Lee and Joy brought a rose in a
milk-glass bud vase. The church sent pink daisies. The old
woman in the other bed has no flowers.

The surgeon told Lila she could live without a breast.
"You couldn't live without a head, or a liver, or a heart,"
he said when he informed her in the recovery room that

he had removed her breast. "But you can live without a breast. You'll be surprised."

"It would be like living without balls," Lila replied. "You'd find that surprising too, but you could probably get along without them."

Lila is not sure she said that aloud, and remembering it now, she is embarrassed that she might have, under the influence of the drugs. She's surprised Nancy hasn't said the same thing to the doctor's face.

Lila hears the old woman in the other bed grunting and complaining. "I'll not leave here alive!" she shouted when a nurse gave her a bath. "You're wasting your time fooling with me."

By the second day after her surgery, Lila is no longer hooked to the I.V. She plucks at the hospital gown in front where her bandage itches. The drainage tubes irritate her skin. She feels weak, but restless. "I'm afraid my blood's too thin already," she tells the nurse who comes with the blood-thinner shot.

"No, this is what the doctor wanted," the nurse says.

"I'm getting poked so full of holes I'm like a sifter bottom."

Besides the shots, there are the tests. They have wheeled her into the cold basement three times to run her through their machines. They have scanned her bones, her liver, her whole body, looking for loose cancer cells. Now the cancer doctor comes in to tell Lila the results of the tests: The cancer has spread to two out of the seventeen lymph nodes that were removed. Spence isn't there yet, but Cat and Nancy fire questions at him. Lila's head spins as the doctor explains that once the cancer has reached the lymph nodes, it has gone into the bloodstream, and then it can end up anywhere. The news doesn't quite register.

"I'm recommending chemotherapy," the doctor says.

"Is that cobalt?" Lila asks weakly. The doctor is young and reminds her of the odd-looking preacher who led the revival at church last year. The preacher had a long nose and wore a gold shiny suit.

The doctor says, "No. This will be a combination of three drugs—Cytoxan, methotrexate and 5FU." He explains that she will have a chart showing two weeks of treatments, then a three-week rest period, then two weeks of treatments, and so on. She will get both pills and shots. Like dogs teaming up on a rabbit, Cat and Nancy jump on him about side effects.

"This particular treatment is tolerated very well," he says. "That's not to say there won't be side effects. A little hair loss, a little nausea. Some people react more adversely than others."

Lila can't keep her mind on what he's saying. "I've got plenty of hair," she says, tugging at her curls. "And it's coarse, like horse hair." The last permanent she got didn't take on top.

"You're going to have to lay off the smoking too," the doctor says, consulting his clipboard.

"They won't let me smoke here," Lila says. She bummed a cigarette from a visitor in the lounge the night before, but it burned her lungs and tasted bitter. She couldn't finish it.

The cancer doctor says now, "Cigarettes will interfere with the chemotherapy."

"See!" Nancy says triumphantly. "Doctor's orders. And you wouldn't listen to us."

"These girls snitched my cigarettes," Lila says to the doctor. "Is that any way to treat an old woman that's stove up in the hospital?"

"Best thing for you," the doctor says with a slight grin.

[63]

"And they're telling me I can't eat what I'm used to," Lila goes on.

"She eats a high-fat diet," Nancy says.

"Don't listen to them," the doctor says to Lila. "You eat anything you want to. If I was your age, I'd eat anything I wanted to."

Lila sees Nancy bristle. Nancy says, "She's eaten bacon and eggs every morning of her life and she has clogged arteries. What are you saying?"

"It's too late for her to do anything about her diet. Cutting back on cholesterol won't help at all. It's simply too late. And it's too late for you too," he says. "How old are you?"

"Forty-four."

"Too late." He nods at Cat. "How old are you?"

"Thirty-four."

"It might help you a little, but not much. They did autopsies on the soldiers who died in Vietnam, and those young boys—nineteen years old—already had plaque in their arteries."

"Not all doctors agree with you about cholesterol," Nancy says, shooting him a mean look.

As he scribbles on his chart, the doctor tells a complicated story about some experiments on Italian women conducted with the drugs he is prescribing. Nancy and Cat follow him out into the hall. Lila suspects they are keeping something from her. She doesn't know what to think. The doctor didn't say if she would be cured, and she was afraid to ask.

She can feel the wound draining, little drips that tickle. The nurses don't use any kind of ointment on it. When she was a child, she had an infected place where she had stuck a stob in her shin. Her aunt Dove bought some

Rosebud salve from a peddler and it healed the sore. Lila remembers when they used to rub dirt in wounds; dirt was pure, what grew things. Good dirt was precious.

In the other bed, the old woman yells at the nurse bringing her lunch tray.

"You can just take that right back, because I don't want it."

"If you don't start eating for us, we'll have to put you back on the I.V., Mrs. Wright," the nurse says in a tone one would use to a child.

The nurse disappears into the hall and comes back with Lila's dinner.

"Oh, no, not more food," Lila says.

Spence, looking tired and cold, comes in a little later. She is still picking at her dinner.

"The doctor said it spread to two out of seventeen lymp' nodes," Lila tells him. Before she can respond to Spence's shocked expression, Cat and Nancy return and tell him what the doctor said.

"He's going to try chemotherapy," Cat says.

"Cobalt?"

"No."

Spence grins, the worry on his face lifting. "I was afraid they were going to do cobalt. I couldn't sleep none all night, thinking about it."

"No. Just shots and pills."

Spence says, "What'll it do?"

"He wouldn't say."

"He was optimistic," Nancy assures Spence.

Cat repeats what the doctor said about the treatment. Lila, amazed that anyone can remember all that, notices that Cat doesn't go into detail about the discussion on fat. Spence listens without comment.

Lila shoves her tray at Spence. "Here, does anybody want some of this turkey? I can't go another bite."

"That mess looks awful." He turns up his nose.

"We're going to the cafeteria," Nancy says. "Why don't you come with us, Daddy?"

He shakes his head. "I found this place with baked taters four for a dollar."

"*Four* baked potatoes?" Cat asks.

"I just get two," he says. "And a Coke and some peanuts."

"You better go down to the cafeteria," Lila says to him, "and get you some meat and vegetables. I can't say much for their cooking, though."

"You can say that again," Mrs. Wright in the other bed says, her voice calling through the curtain partition. "They call this turkey and dressing? It ain't even Thanksgiving. We had better grub at the poorhouse when I used to work in the kitchen."

Lila says, "You better eat it, though, to keep body and soul together."

"I told 'em I wasn't eating a bite and I won't. I'll not leave this hospital alive anyway."

Spence and Cat and Nancy grin at each other. Cat whispers to Spence, "She's been going on like that all morning."

A nurse says, "I'll be back to check your drainage when you're done eating."

"They never leave you alone," says Lila. "All night long they come in. 'Mrs. Culpepper? Time to take your temperature.' 'Mrs. Culpepper? Time to check the drainage.' They come in here and wake me up just to refill the water jug."

"They go by their rules," Nancy says. "They don't care about you as a person."

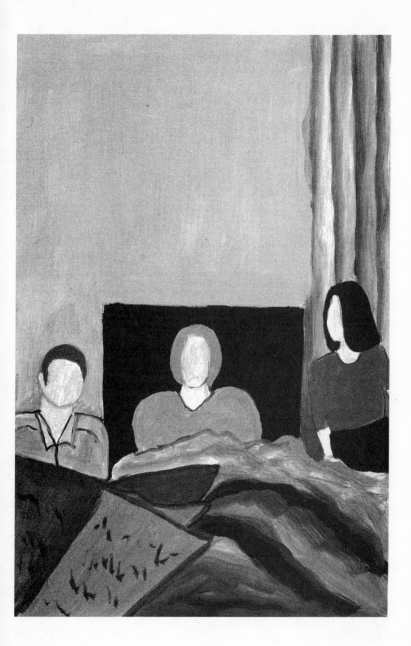

"There's one nurse that's cute as a bug's ear," Lila says. "She tickles me. She's got a cute disposition and the littlest feet."

"Isn't Mom doing great?" Cat says to Spence with a grin.

"She's got her fire back," Spence says, beaming at Lila.

"This place ain't seen nothing yet," says Lila. "I'm tough as nails and rough as a cob!" She laughs at herself and feels the bandage pull her skin. She wants to be cheerful, for the girls, but she doesn't feel cheerful.

In the afternoon, when the girls have gone, a nurse draws back the curtain partition, and the sunlight through the window next to Mrs. Wright's bed floods Lila's side of the room. The TV is playing a soap opera about a woman whose husband is having an affair with their adopted daughter.

"I hate them old stories," Mrs. Wright says. "The same thing ever' day, and it never does come to an end."

"They just want to keep you going on them," Lila says. The adopted daughter on TV is pregnant now. She has agreed to be a surrogate mother for her adoptive parents, who can't have children.

"My belly steeples is itching," says Mrs. Wright. "I feel like yanking 'em out."

"Don't you have any family close by to come and see you?" Lila asks. The woman has had no visitors.

"None except my brother, but he's in Tennessee. And he don't care a rat's behind what happens to me. There's a bunch of nieces and nephews and their littluns—just little tadpoles."

Lila says, "I've raised three fine younguns." She fumbles for the remote-control box by the bed and turns down the sound of the soap opera.

Mrs. Wright says, "I've farmed all my life except for

a year when I went to Detroit and worked during the war. I've gone out in the morning when the dew was dried off and cut hay and baled it and got it in before it rained. We'd work till ten or eleven at night."

"I always helped hay too," Lila says. "You ain't got nothing on me."

"I lifted the bales right into the truck just like a man. Did you lift bales into the truck?"

"Well, I *drove* the truck," says Lila. "They wouldn't let me lift like that—in case my insides might drop."

"That could be the cause of my trouble," Mrs. Wright says. "I wouldn't have come to this place, but they bellyached and bellyached till they got me here. I could have got along fine without them cutting me open."

"Who bellyached?"

"Oh, them people I rent my trailer from."

The woman rattles on, but Lila pretends to be falling asleep. In the TV story, the adopted daughter is driving over a bridge. The bridge railing breaks. Debris scatters, gray water rolling with bits of wreckage. Then an instant soup is steaming in a cup and a bleached-blond woman in a shiny kitchen is smiling. Lila's kitchen is not that fancy, even though they remodeled a few years ago, but she remembers how proud she was to get out of Rosie's miserable, dark kitchen, with the dishwater simmering on the gas stove. By the time Cat was born, Lila and Spence had built their own house, a hundred yards away from his parents' house, through the woods. They had two dozen cows by then, and the dairy prospered. Rosie churned butter; Lila helped with the milking and bottling; Spence made the deliveries in town; Amp and Spence raised corn and hay. In her new house, a plain four-room square, Lila had her own kitchen, with running water. With her blackberry money, she bought a pressure cooker. Later, they bought a freezer and installed indoor plumbing, and eventually they added more rooms. Lila relaxed and let things go. She didn't yell at the kids for strewing their clothes and toys everywhere. She spoiled them. Before Easter Sunday, she often found herself staying up past midnight finishing their Easter outfits. And she made so many clothes for Cat over the years she could have stocked a store. Her children were always well fed and wore good clothes.

The house she grew up in had a sort of unfinished feeling to it. Some of the rooms upstairs were bare wood walls, with the studs showing, and the family itself felt unfinished. It shot off in different directions—in-laws, cousins, widows, a cousin with an illegitimate child, an aunt whose husband had abandoned her. Uncle Mose took in strays like Lila, anybody with a pair of hands to help him work his tobacco, but Lila always felt she was just an extra mouth to feed. When she married Spence and moved in with his parents, she felt out of place. Their house was dark and filled with silences. Rosie even shelled beans with great concentration, as if chatter would be inefficient. Lila tried to fit in, as she had learned to do in a large household of grownups, but when Amp and Rosie stepped on her feelings, or made her feel unworthy because she didn't know how to do things their way, there were no aunts or cousins to run to. At Uncle Mose's, in that big clumsy bunch, she was the youngest, and she had to play by herself. She tied doll bonnets on cats and packed them, squirming, from place to place. A cat drowned in the cistern once. The men drained the cistern, and her cousin Dulcie, who bossed everybody, made Lila descend a ladder into that dark pit to get the dead cat. "You're so crazy about cats, you're the right one to send," Dulcie said in a practical tone. Lila brought the cat up in her arms, slimy and already rotting, and for a long time after that the water wasn't fit to drink, but they washed in it. Even now, whenever Lila sees a dead cat she recalls that cat in the cistern.

As Lila is waking up, later in the afternoon, Nancy appears with a cup of coffee, and the old woman says to her, "You'll be high, wide and handsome about eleven o'clock tonight if you drink that."

"How are you doing, Mrs. Wright?" Nancy asks.

"I'm still swelled, but he looked at it and said I was doing good. But I'm not."

"Did you eat your lunch?"

"No. That hospital food ain't fitten to eat—no seasoning."

"You didn't touch a bite," Lila reminds her sleepily. "So how do you know it wasn't any good?"

"I could tell by looking." Mrs. Wright heaves her heavy blue-and-white legs over the edge of the bed and faces the window. "Nobody'll ever talk me into going in the hospital again."

Nancy sets her coffee on the night table and clasps Lila's hand. Lila feels strength flowing into her arm from her daughter, and she holds Nancy's hand tightly.

"Do you want me to read to you?" Nancy asks. "Cat had to go to work. She said she'd be back at six."

"No, that's all right. I couldn't keep my mind on it."

"How do you feel?"

"There's too much commotion going on here to think," Lila says. She pulls at the front of her gown.

Nancy touches the limp curls that droop onto her mother's forehead. "I think it looks very promising," Nancy says. "They caught it early and they can do wonders nowadays."

[71]

A nurse, appearing suddenly, closes the curtain partition between the two beds. "Mrs. Culpepper? We need to check your dressing."

The nurse shoos Nancy out and pulls another curtain around the bed. She pokes at the bandage and peels it back. Lila doesn't want to look, but she glimpses a brown spot. She wonders if they saved her nipple. Cat mentioned earlier that if they saved her nipple they could rebuild her breast. The brown spot is far off center.

NINE

*T*HE WAY doctors throw their forty-dollar words around like weapons is infuriating. Spence knows big words, plenty of them. He prefers not to use his vocabulary in conversation, though, for fear of sounding pretentious. Using the right simple words at the right time requires courage enough. At times there is no way on earth he can say what he feels.

He knows what he *wants* to say, and he imagines saying it to Lila, but it takes guts to admit guilt and wrong, to express sorrow, to lavish loving feelings on someone. If only he could, he would say, "Lila, you and me have been together a long time, and we've been through a lot together." He laughs to himself. How phony that would be. It sounds like something on television. He has never said those things because he would feel as though he were speaking lines. Real love requires something else, something deeper. And sometimes a feeling just goes without saying.

Show her you love her, they say. Doesn't he show her? Everything he does is for her, even when he goes his own way and she is powerless to stop him—like the time he drove the tractor across the creek after it had washed out and she was afraid the tractor would turn over. As he headed out through the field to the creek, she called and called, but he wouldn't stop. He has always teased her about her habit of worrying herself sick over nothing.

Teasing rattles her, but it would be out of character for him to behave any other way, and she would respect him less.

He could say to Lila, "It's all right. Your breast isn't your life. You can live without it, and I'll accept that." More lines. He has to show her another way, letting her know indirectly how much he still loves her. "Our love will never die." Words are so inadequate. Phony. Nobody he knows says things like that anyway. People either lie to be nice or they say what they think. The girls used to accuse Spence of being cruel when he spoke his mind, but that is not true. He is just honest. He hates hypocrites.

The morning after her operation, when he came in so late, afraid to see her, she was sitting up in bed, gabbing with a nurse as if nothing had happened. "Where in the world have you been?" she said to him accusingly. "I thought you'd forgot about me." She had on lipstick, and her hair was pretty, the color of straw. Later, he helped her walk down the corridor, pulling her I.V. along like a child's wagon, and she joked with him about her lost breast. She said, "I didn't realize how you depend on your jugs for balance. I feel all whopper-jawed! And I have to go around holding the other one up till I can wear a brassiere." Spence told her he could rig her up a sling, like the one he fashioned for a hound dog once when she had an open wound on the bottom of her paw.

When they made a turn at the end of the hallway, Lila suddenly asked him, "Why do you think this happened to me?"

"No reason. Things just happen. What do you mean?"

"I don't know. It just don't seem right."

Spence wanders through the house now, seeing her things. The collection of dolls she laboriously sewed clothes for, the knickknacks she bought at yard sales, her closet stuffed with pants suits and flowered dresses she made for herself, the rack of quilts she spent so many winters constructing. A casserole she made for him is still in the refrigerator, as well as a ham and bowls of green beans and stock peas. Neighbors brought Spence an odd assortment of dishes—coconut pie, lima beans cooked with macaroni, stewed tomatoes, green Jell-O streaked with shredded cabbage. Spence doesn't eat much in the evenings because food at night gives him heartburn, and he is at the hospital during the day, so the food is spoiling. It is depressing. If it were Lila's funeral, the same people would bring the same food.

He is walking to the pond with Oscar, escaping the chaos in the house. Nancy and Cat have come to clean, and they're rearranging everything. They moved his outdoor clothes out of the living room—his boots, his jackets, the manure-stained pants he wore for feeding the animals. Lila always let him keep the clothes by the door, where they were handy, but Nancy and Cat dumped them all—including his boots and bootjack—in a corner of the bedroom. "Honestly, Daddy," said Cat in exasperation. She handed him a slop bucket to take to the ducks.

"What do you think, Oscar?" he says aloud. At that moment, Oscar sees the ducks and bounds forward merrily. Oscar is a small gray dog with shaggy hair down in his eyes. "Get back here. Don't chase them ducks!" Spence shouts. On the pond bank, the ducks skitter ahead of Oscar and splash into the water. Oscar tests the water, then gets distracted by a grasshopper. Spence empties the slop bucket on the bank—rotting lettuce and blackening radishes and rubbery break beans from the vegetable crisper that Cat cleaned out. The ducks paddle to the bank and dart their bills furtively at the garbage. Oscar has gone down into the creek. Spence scans the pond bank for the hoofprints of deer. Recently he saw three deer crossing the field to the pond—a doe and two young ones. Spence has never shot a deer and does not plan to.

From a rise near the pond Spence surveys the ocean of soybeans, with the dips and waves in the front fields and the stripe of corn edging the back ten. The farm has seventy-three acres. He remembers his father teaching him how to figure while they worked the fields. Pappy drilled him in the multiplication table as they cultivated the rows of corn with a mule. When Spence was eight, he realized that when he was thirty-three Pappy would be sixty-six, twice his age. Now Spence is almost sixty-six himself. His father has been dead for fifteen years. Spence is glad Pappy did not live to see the milk cows sold off.

A grasshopper shoots through the air. The soybeans are thick with them. With no-till beans, he had to use a weed-killer a week after planting, and he suspects that it killed a certain weed the grasshoppers liked, so they are eating the new bean leaves instead. Bill Belton will have to spray soon. Besides the cropduster plane, Bill is deeply in debt for a combine and a planter. Spence has never gone into debt, but he knows a couple of farmers who have lost their land after overborrowing. When he took a part-time job, driving a van during the school year for the high school, he was able to get medical benefits, which will help now with Lila's illness. But he worries about whether it is enough. He might have to cash in his certificate of deposit, which doesn't mature until October. In his worst moments, he can imagine losing his farm to doctors.

On the edge of the field, he steps across a ridge of dirt pushed up by a tractor tire. A few stray soybeans perch on the top, and the tire print beside it is dry like a scar. He thinks of the furrow the doctors may cut in Lila's neck.

When he was looking at her things, he ran across a
postcard she had written him from Savannah. It showed
a picture of a lighthouse. When he got home from the
Navy, she seemed stronger, tougher, and he felt weaker,
torn apart. After the Navy, Spence never wanted to travel
again. Home was like that lighthouse. At night on the
ocean, the exploding artillery shells kept him awake. The
seasickness was worse below deck. Swinging in his ham-
mock, slamming against metal walls and poles, he wanted
to die. The sounds down there were magnified—whistles,
loudspeakers, the big thumps bombs made hitting water,
feet running on deck, metal doors clanging shut. It was
deafening. He never saw any of the battles. He knew
when there was a battle because the lights turned red. He
threw up on a five-inch shell on its way up to the gun
turret. He never knew if the shells he touched found their
way to the heart of an enemy craft. Up on deck, it was
calmer: the fighter planes coming and going from the flat-
top; the big ship protected in the huddle like a queen bee.
It felt better out on deck, because he could see what was
going on. He was where the weather was. The fighters
landing on the carrier reminded him of snake doctors
floating through the air, alighting on a weed, flitting off.
A snake doctor touched down on his bare arm once when
he was a child and left a blister as large as a nickel. In his
nightmares out on the sea, the kamikazes made blisters on
the deck of the destroyer and the ship exploded with fire.
After he came home, he still couldn't sleep. He stayed up
late and read about the battles, wanting to find out about
the big battle he was in, but he couldn't find many books
about the Pacific. Most of them were about Germany. He
could see the battle in his mind's eye, from what he heard
afterward, but there wasn't enough information in the
books. He wanted to know how his destroyer fit in the

larger picture, a whole world at war. He had so many questions about the Japanese, the islands, the atom bomb. He wanted to know every detail of what happened, how it happened, why. But the more he read, the more confusing it became, the larger it grew. He couldn't keep up the reading at night because he always had to get up so early to milk, and after that he faced a long day in the fields. Eventually, his eyes went bad and reading gave him terrible headaches. "Forget about that war," Lila told him. "It's over."

Last night he had a nightmare about Godzilla invading his soybeans. Now he imagines his fields barren and swampy, like the Everglades. He has heard that when the big earthquake expected in the Mississippi River Valley hits, everything for miles will turn to liquid clay.

✻   ✻   ✻

By the time Spence returns to the house, the girls have finished cleaning, and now they are freezing corn. Nancy is cutting corn off the cob, and Cat stirs corn in a skillet on the stove. Cookie pans spread with cooked corn are cooling in front of the air conditioner. The kitchen is steamy. Freezer bags litter the table.

"Ain't it too late in the day to pick corn?" he asks.

"We couldn't wait till tomorrow. It's getting too old," Cat says.

Nancy cuts the corn off the cob the way her mother taught her to do it years ago—first halfway through the kernels, then all the way, then scraping the cob for the juice. It has been years since Nancy has done this, and there is a frown on her face.

"Mom took the news about the chemotherapy real well," says Cat.

"She's more scared than she admits," Nancy says.

"She's really brave," Cat says. "But she's being extra brave for us."

"I'd go to pieces," Nancy says, viciously scraping the cob with the knife.

"I hope she stays off the cigarettes," Cat says.

"The cigarette tax is going up," Nancy says. "Reagan will just send the money to the contras."

Trying to stay busy, Spence collects the trash from the basement and starts burning it in the trash barrel behind the old milkhouse. The cloud of black smoke blows south, toward the smokestack of the industrial park. Spence likes that—he's sending the park a message, like Indians with smoke signals. Suddenly Nancy, the corn knife still in her hand, is standing there yelling at him.

"You're not supposed to burn those plastic Coke bottles!"

"But how am I going to get rid of them?"

"You'll have to dump them. You shouldn't buy that kind."

He throws some boxes on the fire, and angry, dark smoke boils up.

"Plastic releases polyvinyl chloride," she says. "It's a deadly pollutant."

"I don't want to dump too much trash in the creek."

Nancy runs inside the house, holding her nose, and he tosses the remaining plastic bottles onto the fire. The two-liter size is ninety-nine cents, a savings of a dollar-eleven over Coke in cans. He feels helpless. Nancy is so much like Lila. He remembers Lila chasing him with a mop all the way to the railroad track once. They were very young, and she was mad at him for tracking his muddy boots on the floor she had just mopped. He can still see her short, loose dress, her breasts swinging like fruit on a branch in a strong breeze.

[79]

TEN

*L*ILA FEELS the arteries in her neck throbbing, heavy with blood trying to reach her brain. Nancy claimed the blood vessels were stopped up with bacon grease. The bacon that comes with the hospital breakfast is usually burned, and Lila still has no appetite, but she tries to eat because it is wrong to waste food. She hasn't smoked. The thought of cigarettes makes her gag.

She doesn't believe the cancer has spread. She can't feel it anywhere. The doctor said the knot was only the size of a lima bean. She is self-conscious about the emptiness on her right front. The bandage itches, and the drainage tube irritates her. The tube coils out of the wound and connects to the plastic drainage bottle taped to her stomach, close to her shaved groin. She does not know why they had to shave her there. With the bottle flapping as she walks down the hall, she imagines that this is what a man's balls must be like. She pulls at the hospital gown, filling it out with air so she won't appear so lopsided. With the drainage bottle and her flattened chest, she might have had a sex-change operation. Her mind still seems cloudy at times, and then sometimes all the recent events come at her in a rush. She probably shouldn't have gone to Florida. She recalls Cat saying, "Lee and Daddy never should have taken you to the Everglades when it was off-season—ninety-eight degrees and wall-to-wall mosquitoes." Lila told Cat, "That cloud of mosquitoes was purely black!"

Losing her breast feels something like giving birth. Part of her that used to bulge out is now vacant, the familiar growth gone. It's an empty sensation, but not exceptionally painful. Now that she has been thinking about it, it seems natural, after all, that disease should attack her there, that she should be most vulnerable there. Probably she strained her breasts; they were too large; and she has had so much mastitis. It makes sense. When Lee was born, she was tired and overworked. During the winter she had been working at the clothing factory, and that summer she made several premature trips to the hospital, returning home empty-handed. It was frustrating, and when Lee was finally born, the other children stood beside her hospital bed accusingly, as if she had done something peculiar for her age. She was only thirty-two, but seeing Nancy, who was already twelve, made her feel old. Nancy pleaded, "Come home soon, because nobody will do what I say and I hate to cook." They didn't tell Lila until later about the scare with Cathy—as she was called then. She wasn't called Cat until that movie *Cat Ballou*. Cathy had disappeared, and they didn't find her for over two hours. She was walking down the railroad tracks, her face stained purple—probably from eating poisonous pokeberries. She was sick all night.

After Lila came home from the hospital with the baby, he cried so much at night that Spence started sleeping on his parents' screened-in porch. Lila realized Lee was hungry for solid food. She began feeding him baby food, as well as cow's milk in a bottle. For the only time in her life, Lila could barely manage. Vegetables from the garden were coming in, the blackberries were ripe, and Cat was still so little she had to be watched every minute. Nancy was becoming difficult—moody and resentful of her chores. She played loud music on the radio. Lila got no sleep those first few months. But a few years later, they bought their first television, and an unexpected harmony filled the house. They gathered in the living room with a dishpan full of popcorn. Their favorite show was *I Love Lucy*. When Lucy broke into one of her childish bawls, Lee would pucker up and pretend to bawl too. "A great sense of humor for a kid," Nancy said. Lila recalled long winter nights at Uncle Mose's, when there was no entertainment to work by. There was only the bickering of her older cousins over the ironing and sewing, with Uncle Mose in his rocking chair, reading the Bible and farting, seemingly at will. Behind his back, they called him Old Whistle-britches.

Nancy is waving a large envelope in Lila's face. "Mom, I have something wonderful to show you. Jack just sent some new pictures of Robert."

"He's going to be a ladykiller," Cat says. "Nancy, I wish you'd brought him with you!"

"Oh, let me get my glasses," says Lila eagerly. She doesn't see her oldest grandchild often, but in the pictures Nancy frequently sends, Lila has watched him grow, like that kitten in the television commercial who changes into a grown cat in just a few seconds.

Nancy, removing the pictures from the envelope, says, "Jack sent them Federal Express to me at Cat's. He sent them last night and they got here this morning."

"I can't get over that," says Cat. "Anymore, everything's so fast."

Lila adjusts her glasses and examines the pictures as Nancy hands them to her one by one. They are large black-and-white pictures on thick paper, unlike the little snapshots the drugstore develops.

[83]

"He's filled out a lot," Lila says. "He don't look like a starved chicken anymore."

Robert seems confident and grown. In one picture, he's holding something, maybe keys, and in his sunglasses he's in a playful pose, pretending he's somebody famous. He's in dark pants and a T-shirt with faint writing on it.

"Isn't he darling?" Cat says. "I could just eat him up."

"He's about five-ten now," says Nancy. "Look at this one."

"That's my favorite," Cat says. "He looks like Daddy."

"Why, he does!" Lila studies the picture closely. She can see Spence hiding there—the firm lines of the jaw, the clenched teeth, the concealed beginning of a grin. Spence wasn't much older than Robert is now when she first saw him. He was riding a mule down Wolf Creek Road. His mother had cut his hair, causing his cowlick to shoot up like a tuft of grass on top of a stump, but it only accentuated his good looks. Lila gets tickled and laughs at Robert's hair. "I sure didn't know he had a cowlick," she says.

"It's not a cowlick. It's spiked," Nancy explains. "It's what kids do to their hair these days."

"Robert has your eyes," Lila says, noticing the dark glint in Nancy's eyes. "I always said he had your eyes."

Lila remembers the time Lee cut his foot on the jagged edge of a rusted coffee can that had been opened by one of those old-timey can openers. Lila knew from Nancy's scared eyes as she ran toward the house with Lee in her arms that something terrible had happened, even before she saw the blood from Lee's foot.

"And now for the prize." Nancy is hiding the last picture against her chest. "This is Robert at the end of the school year. They didn't have a prom. They had what they call a 'superlative.' It's an honors thing, where they celebrate their achievements."

"I can't believe this," says Cat as Nancy turns the picture face forward.

Robert, in a tuxedo, is standing against a doorway next to a pretty girl in a long dress with a ruffle around the neck. Both of them have that wild hair, standing up as if electrified.

"He's girlfriending already!" Lila cries. "Law, that hair."

"Her name is Amy," says Nancy. "Her mother is our accountant."

"I bet all the girls are crazy about him," says Cat. "Look at that sexy grin."

Nancy says, "They're just friends, or so I'm told. Amy's dress is pink, and he has a pink cummerbund to match."

"Everything is pink now," says Cat.

"Why don't Jack ever take anything in color?" Lila asks. "I have to use my imagination."

"I guess that's the idea," says Nancy. She laughs. "Jack didn't want to send this picture earlier, but I guess he changed his mind. He thought you might have a fit over the hair."

Smiling, Lila lays her glasses on the nightstand. "Well, I'm mighty proud," she says. "You sure did put out a fine youngun, and stayed married—for how long now?"

"Almost twenty years. It was twenty years ago today—"

"Today?"

"No, not today. That's a song allusion. Not till this fall."

"That's a record," Cat says in a flat tone.

Lila realizes the sadness in Cat's voice. She is certain Cat could have patched it up with Dan. Quickly, Lila says, with deep pride, "All of my children have given me some mighty fine grandchildren."

"Krystal and Scott both asked about you on the phone, Mom," Cat says. "Krystal hates it in Hopkinsville and wants to come home."

Nancy gathers up the photographs, promising to leave them for Lila to look at again later.

"Y'all don't have to be here every minute," Lila insists to Cat and Nancy.

"We're here because we care about you," says Cat.

"Well, you're showing it," Lila says. A sudden swell of emotion rises in her throat. The tugging sensation of nursing them as babies is as clear as yesterday. Nancy liked to bite. Cat was always hungry. Nancy wasn't weaned until she was two and a half. Rosie would say, "You're giving that youngun too much peezootie." That was a word of Rosie's Lila never heard anyone else use.

"Is there anything you want us to do?" Nancy asks.

With a little catch in her voice, Lila says, "There's something I wanted you to promise me. I didn't get to say it before."

They listen, like a pair of young cats fixed on a squirrel. Lila says, without her voice breaking, "I want you to take care of your daddy if something happens to me. He won't be able to take care of hisself."

"Don't worry, Mom. We'll take care of him." Cat caresses Lila's hand, picking at a cuticle where nail polish has smeared.

Lila says, "I don't want to be buried in that Spring Valley mausoleum. It's on the side of the road on a curve, and a truck could come along and bust it open."

"Don't think that way!" Nancy says.

Cat leans forward to give Lila a hug. "We'd never leave you by the side of the road. You know that."

"I wouldn't have found that knot if it hadn't been for you. In the old days, people didn't get breast cancer. Or they didn't know they had it. They just got sick and died."

"Well, science can do amazing things nowadays," Nancy says. "And the chemotherapy is going to work."

"You just don't realize how far we've come," says Lila, squeezing Nancy's hand.

"Yes, I do. I would have died at age ten of pneumonia if it hadn't been for penicillin."

Nancy always has an answer. But she seems not to realize she had survived pneumonia another time, when she was two. That was before penicillin. The memory jolts Lila.

"Times are better now," she insists to her daughters. "You don't know how good you've got it."

Nowadays, Lila thinks, young people expect to have everything right at the start. House and car, washer and dryer. They're not patient. When she worked at the clothing factory, she earned enough money to make life a little easier. In the few years she worked there, she bought a steam iron, an electric mixer, an electric stove, a set of steak knives, a dinette set. Spence never wanted her to go to work, but after Nancy started to school, and before Cat and Lee came along, the factory was hiring. Excitedly, Lila applied for the job, wearing a suit she had made. The hiring man admired her sewing and gave her the job. She sat at a large machine, stitching in collars or cuffing pants. She put on weight, sitting long hours on the high stool, but her arms grew strong from pushing and pulling the heavy suit material through her machine. The oiled wood floors were sticky with clumps of thread, and the air was stifling, despite the overhead fans. She carried her dinner—pimiento or tuna-fish sandwiches, with the lettuce wrapped separately; and sometimes a tomato, and salt and pepper folded in little pieces of waxed paper. She usually carried cake or cookies. On her breaks and lunch period, it was a deep pleasure to drink a cold, slippery bottle of Coca-Cola from the large cooler in the hallway. Lila loved the people, the talk that went on above the noise. She bragged on her child and listened to others brag on theirs; they swapped pictures and stories. The woman at the machine next to hers had asthma attacks from the wool dust in the air, and they had to carry her outside occasionally. A man working at the end of her row always entertained the hands with songs popular on the radio. She can still hear him singing "Slow Boat to China." Recently someone told her he had left his wife and died of a brain tumor in Arizona, alone. Another woman was always called "Miss Gregory" instead of her first name because she always dressed so elegantly for such rough work. They would say, "Miss Gregory sets on a pillow sewing a fine seam." Lila felt that way too, proud and alive. It was piecework, and sometimes she could make nearly ninety cents an hour, she was so fast.

Later, Cat has gone down the hall to the bathroom and Nancy is reading. Lila is telling Mrs. Wright she doesn't think her cancer has spread, when Cat returns, excited. "Did you see that prisoner on this floor? There's a guy with a guard from the state penitentiary. He's two rooms down the hall. He looks really sick, like he couldn't crawl an inch even if he tried to escape."

Lila shudders. "I hope that guard don't fall asleep. That's all I need, to be held hostage in the hospital!"

Mrs. Wright says, "It won't make me one bit of difference."

ELEVEN

O N SUNDAY Lila's half-sister, Glenda, and her husband, Bill, stop by the hospital with a basket of artificial violets. It has a little ceramic rabbit in it, nibbling at the leaves. Lila is wearing her good blue gown and a bed jacket. Cat put Lila's makeup on her that morning and fixed her hair. Lila's scalp itches, but she doesn't want to wash her hair for fear of catching cold.

"Well, Lila, are you going to have to have cobalt?" Glenda asks. Glenda is overweight, with baby-fine light hair that used to be a pretty blond.

"No, I'm not," says Lila happily. "Just shots and pills for six months, and then they do all the tests again to see if it spread."

"I told Bill I didn't think you'd have to have cobalt," says Glenda.

Bill is a red-faced, deliberate sort of man, a retired farmer. He says defensively, "Well, seems like they want to put everybody through that."

"I don't think it spread very much," Lila says. "I could feel it in those leaders under my arms, but they think they got it all out." She runs her hand down her arm, which is stiffening up. The physical therapist has been there, instructing her how to work her arm. Lila has to grasp a yardstick, one hand on each end, and slowly raise it above her head, then lower it and swing it from side to side.

Glenda says, "We heard you're going to be operated on again, Lila."

Lila nods. "Depends on what they find out with my neck." She scrapes her fingers down her throat. "The blood ain't going through good."

Glenda says brightly, "Bob Barber had *his* veins cleaned out and he said it was like getting new glasses. He could think better after they operated."

"Are they going to do that test where they shoot you with the dye?" asks Bill.

"Uh-huh. I purely dread it too."

"They say that really hurts," Bill says. "They shoot it in your leg and it works its way up to your head and burns."

"They told me I had to lay real still for eight hours after they do it," Lila says. "If I turn over it might be dangerous."

"A clot might go to your brain," Glenda says.

"How have y'all been?" Lila asks, changing the subject. If Spence were here, he would be furious at them.

"All right, I reckon," says Glenda. "Bill here has to go in for his checkup—he has sugar—and he has to have tests for that spasmatic colon he's got."

Bill, hacking at a cough, says, "I told them I wasn't going to have that test where you drank that drank again. I had that last year, and my bowels backed up and didn't move for three months. It made a knot as big as my fist. It stayed there and everything went around it. I liked to died."

Glenda laughs. "He sure was something to live with while that was going on."

"Lila, you look like a spring chicken," says Bill. "Why, your hide won't hold you when you get home!" He offers to get Cokes for everyone.

"You can get a free drink in the lounge," Lila says.

[90]

After he leaves, Lila says, "I'm so proud to see you, Glenda!"

Glenda was eight and Lila was four when their mother died. Lila has one memory of her: a chubby little woman with dark hair, saying "fried pies" out on a porch, with a dog running up from a field—somewhere Lila could never identify. Her mother was only about twenty-eight when she died, of childbed fever. Glenda, who remembered her better, told Lila once, "She was light-complected and had pretty teeth. She liked to ride horses, and they say that's why she died. She rode a horse when she shouldn't have." The baby died too. Lila had been told it was a girl. Lila's father left Lila at Uncle Mose's and disappeared. Glenda went to live with her real daddy and his second wife in a little place down below Wolf Creek.

Lila didn't see Glenda again until after she married Spence and the war was over. Lila and Spence visited Glenda one Sunday afternoon. They sat on Glenda and Bill's porch and watched the traffic go by. Lila remembers her happiness that day—Glenda's daughter, Laura Jean, teaching Nancy how to ride a little red scooter; a dusty driveway; a setting hen; a can of sorghum Bill gave them. She remembers Glenda shooing flies from the apple slices spread out on a screen door to dry in the sun. Glenda was fat. That day she told Lila the baby their mother died with was a boy, not a girl.

"Lila, how are those daughters of yours treating you?" Glenda asks now.

"Oh, they've been awful good to me. They've been here every minute." Lila laughs. "They froze my corn the other evening. They should have done it in the morning when the dew's wet."

"It won't be crisp," Glenda says, nodding. "It'll be tough."

"I hope I'm out of here in time to do all the pickles. They'll draw the line at pickles."

"Nobody can do dill pickles like you can, Lila. You've got a secret recipe, I believe. One of these days I'm going to get you down and mash that recipe out of you."

"I just do it by guess. Last year I got them too sour. They was sour enough to make a pig squeal!" Lila laughs, then hiccups.

The old woman's voice booms through the curtain. "Who's got the he-cups over there?"

"Me," says Lila. She can't get comfortable, and the little jolts hurt her incision.

"You're a-growing," Mrs. Wright says. "That's what that means."

"I hope so," Lila says, pulling at her gown. "I wish I could grow a new jug."

"You can't get no sleep around here to save your neck," Mrs. Wright says. "They come in here late last night and started burning the house down!"

Lila sees the prisoner trudging past the door, clinging to his uniformed guard. His gown gapes open in the back, exposing his hairy rear end. He shuffles along, his head bent. Lila feels a sudden foreboding of death. This is all there is left to life: lying here in a hospital gown with her breast amputated, watching a bare-butt criminal go by and listening to a nutty old woman griping behind a curtain. Days ago, Lila told herself she was ready to go, that she had made her peace with the world, that she had had a good life and she was grateful. But now she revolts. She doesn't want to give up. She swings out of bed a little too quickly, and a pain shoots through her arm. But that's O.K. It will go away.

"Walk me down the hall," she says to Glenda. "I ain't ready to die yet."

TWELVE

"Y<small>OU'RE NOT EATING</small> for us, Mrs. Wright," the nurse says disapprovingly. This nurse is the cute one, with the tiny feet. She's the only nurse who bothers to chat with the old woman.

"She made a little sign on it," says Lila.

"I like broccoli cooked *done,*" says Mrs. Wright, sitting up against her pillows defiantly and pushing her tray trolley forward. "I like all kinds of greens. I could eat my weight in asparagus. But not raw."

It's time for Lila to breathe oxygen. The nurse's aide hauls the breathing contraption to Lila's bedside and pulls the curtain between the beds. She aims the blue mask at Lila's face.

"I believe my lungs is clearing up," Lila says to her.

"Well, they ought to be if you keep off them cigarettes," the girl says.

"Woman!" Mrs. Wright booms through the curtain. "I did something for sixty-five years and then quit—and you can too."

"What's that—smoking?" asks Lila.

"Naw—chewing tobacco. I started in the first grade, but since I was operated on four days ago I haven't wanted a chew. Got a bad taste in my mouth."

Lila can't reply because she is holding her breath. The girl says, "You're doing good. Just hold it two more seconds. There."

Lila says, rubbing her neck, "These veins need oxygen."

"That smoking was closing them down," the girl says.

"I'm worried about that test they're going to run on my neck. They don't want to operate on both sides at once. They need to keep one vein open to feed the brain in case I have a stroke on the operating table." The words rush out. Lila can talk to the nurses about her fears, but doctors make her flustered.

"I'm sure they know what's best for you," the nurse's aide says. "Now breathe in again. The test will tell them which way to go."

"I'm more scared of that test than I am of the operation," Lila says. She sucks in air, feeling her face go red, her stitches tickling.

As the girl leaves, she rips open the curtain again, and Mrs. Wright says, "I'll be glad when I get back to my cat."

"Well, that's the first I heard you were going to leave the hospital!" says Lila. "I thought you wasn't aiming to leave here alive."

Mrs. Wright grumbles and works at her short-tailed gown, which has ridden up. "The doctor didn't say nothing about going home, but he said something about getting these belly steeples out. I feel like jerking 'em out myself. They put a screw in and some plastic. I had this herny for five or six years, and I was doing just fine with it till they started in bellyaching about it."

"Is somebody feeding your cat?" Lila misses Abraham. Spence won't give him enough attention.

Mrs. Wright shakes her head. "I guess she'll find something. That cat—she's a beautiful cat. Calico. She has the prettiest face. Where she's white she's *white*, and where she's black she's *black*, and where she's red she's *red!* She ain't got no tail. When she was a kitten she got in the hay baler and got her tail cut off. And she got her ears snipped off too somehow. She's crippled up in one paw. But she can catch mice. She catches 'em with one paw and stuffs 'em in her mouth and reaches out and hooks another one. That cat sleeps with me in the house every night in the world!"

"My cat doesn't come in the house," Lila says. "Spence never did like cats in the house."

"I'd tease the menfolks and offer 'em a chaw of tobacco straight out of the tobacco barn. I'd say you ain't a man if you can't chew that." Mrs. Wright laughs, a man's grunt. "If you chew tobacco, you won't never have worms. Lands, I ain't worked tobacco in ten years! That's how I ruptured myself, lifting a ten-by-twenty-five presser of tobacco."

"We never raised tobacco. I've got corn coming in and my girls don't know how to do it right."

"Honey, there ain't a soul to tend to my garden. I've got bell peppers and okry and Kentucky Wonders. Everything will ruin."

The TV news comes on, and the old woman says, "The politicians send all our money overseas, where all they do is fight and all they ever *will* do is fight."

The hospital routines are becoming too familiar—the florist's delivery cart passing by the door, the physical therapist who comes in each morning to help Lila work her arm to keep it from freezing up, the boy who sweeps the floors every afternoon, the night nurse with the cold hands and the way she has of popping the thermometer in Lila's mouth just as though she were using a dipstick to check the oil level in a car engine. When Lila asked the night nurse about the prisoner, she said, "I don't know what happened to him, but I sure wouldn't want to meet him in a dark alley."

[95]

Lila tries to read recipes in *Family Circle,* but her eyes blur and her glasses don't help. She would like to read from the Bible in the drawer of the nightstand, but the print is too fine. The preacher is supposed to come by, but he hasn't.

THIRTEEN

$\mathcal{S}$ITTING IN THE LOUNGE while Lila naps, Spence is surrounded by worried-looking strangers, most of them overweight. Human beings come in such freakish forms, it always surprises him to be in a crowd of them. His nerves are bad. He can't sit still. Downstairs, he saw a woman in a wheelchair; evidently she was too fat to walk. She was the fattest woman he'd ever seen outside a circus. He works a Coke out of the ice in the cooler and lifts the tab. He takes a long drink and belches. Heartburn. The night before, it woke him up at two-thirty and he couldn't go back to sleep. His head whirled, catching memories of recent events until he was brought up to date, to the awful present. If Lila didn't make it through the second operation, her funeral could be as early as next weekend. In the dark, tossing in bed, he imagined her funeral. He couldn't stop whole scenes from playing in his head, like a TV documentary. The sermon, the flowers, perfunctory conversations with the kinfolks at the funeral home, coming home with his children and solemnly feasting on that food the neighbors brought.

If this is going to be her time, then what he and Lila should do is have a last fling together. But he can't go in her room and make love to her. He can't even talk to her or tell her how he feels while she's lying there in that white-cold bed with the nurses bumbling around the room like doodlebugs working on a cowpile. And now it seems likely that the doctors will get hold of her again, with their knives and scissors, probing violently in another place precious to him—her rugged throat, always tanned and healthy. The surgeons in masks will probably laugh and joke while they work, probably because they're making so much money. They must feel immense power, like presidents and TV executives. Spence's stomach turns over as a cloud of cigarette smoke fills the room. Someone switches the TV from a fishing show to the Nashville channel. Spence hates hillbilly music.

Lee and the kids came to see Lila earlier that afternoon. Now Lee joins Spence in the lounge, drinking a Sprite and gazing vacantly at the TV while Jennifer and Greg explore the hospital. Lee always seems tired. He didn't want to learn farming because he didn't want to get up at four to milk, but he has to work even harder at his factory job. He owes the bank almost four hundred dollars a month for a squatty little brick ranch house on a hundred-foot lot in town with no trees. It makes Spence sick.

The prisoner enters the lounge with the guard, who walks him around the room as if on an inspection tour. He is huge and young, with short blond hair and freckles. He looks as though he might have been a nice boy who turned bad. His dark eyes somehow don't fit his physique—a clue, Spence thinks, to why he turned bad. Something about his body isn't quite right. The sight of him is jarring. The guy has probably known that all his life, and the conflict made him mean. The criminal's I.V. rolls along with him like an obedient dog on a rope.

"I bet he got stabbed," Lee says. "All those prisoners want to do is cut on each other when they get the chance."

Spence says, "When the guard has to go to the bathroom, he chains that guy to the bed. I saw him."

"He don't look strong enough to get very far."

Spence asks, "How does she seem to you?"

"Mom? Oh, she's bearing up. She almost seems like her old self." Lee stares at his lap. "I feel terrible that we dragged her to Florida."

"She worries," Spence says. "She gets something in her head. Like that deal with you and Cat over the air conditioner."

"Mom didn't have anything to do with that."

Spence rubs his hands against his jeans. "I thought Cat give you that air conditioner."

"I told you how it was." Lee takes his time lighting a cigarette. "Cat said I could have the air conditioner, so I went and got it and installed it, and then she changed her mind and wanted it back, but I already had it in the window. I had to rework the frame to get it set right. It would have been easier for her to get a secondhand air conditioner than to fool with this one. She got mad because I wouldn't let her have it back."

"She claims she just meant to let you borrow it."

"She said I could have it, and I took her at her word."

Words. Lila's kinfolks deliberately tried to hurt her with words. They put him in a sour mood. And her friends chattered about diseases. Lila ate it up. His daughters embarrassed him. They even complained to the doctors about the hospital food, but the doctors had nothing to do with it. When Lila's first meal after surgery was a hamburger with pickles and potato chips, Nancy said it wasn't nutritious, especially for someone with carotid-artery disease. "A greasy old hamburger!" Nancy snapped at the doctor. Spence wanted to spank her. He can remember when he and Lila were courting, and they went out for hamburgers. A hamburger and Coke at Fred and Sue's Drive-in was the most delicious meal they had ever had. Even after they were married, they looked forward to going out for hamburgers almost as much as they looked forward to making love. His mother was stingy with meat and cooked the same plain grub day in and day out.

Lee is speaking to him about subdivisions. Lee brings up subdivisions about once a month, trying to convince Spence that since his land is close to town it will be worth something someday.

"Why don't you sell off some frontage and get a start on a development?" Lee asks.

"What would I want to do that for?"

"You're setting on a gold mine."

"Good. You can come over and dig in it."

"You could sell one lot and get enough to build a house on another lot and then sell it at a profit."

"Why didn't Joy come today?" Spence asks.

"She went to Mister Sun. Her and her sister go to the tanning booth every chance they get. I gave her a membership for her birthday." Lee stands to go, as Jennifer and Greg appear in the lounge. "I have to get home and finish paneling the den. The wallpaper's peeling off, and Joy's having a fit."

"You're going to do that on Sunday?" asks Spence, surprised. "I thought your mama taught you not to work on Sunday."

"I don't have time during the week, with overtime."

"Why don't you repaper? Ain't that cheaper?"

"No. I'd have to put up some new gypsum board, and by the time you get gypsum board and tape it and paint an undercoat, it's cheaper to panel." Lee clutches his Sprite can, crumpling it, left-handed.

"Paneling's got formaldehyde in it," says Spence. "It causes cancer. Ask Nancy. Nancy can explain it to you."

"Nancy's got an explanation for everything," Lee says

with a laugh. "What does she say caused Mom to get cancer?"

"Bacon grease. She says them veins in her neck is stopped up with bacon grease."

"Bacon grease in her neck?" asks Jennifer, Lee's seven-year-old.

"Come on, Goofus," says Lee to Greg, who is punching on Lee, trying to get his attention. "Let me know if there's anything I can do," Lee says to Spence.

After Lee leaves, Spence goes to check on Lila one more time before he heads home for the evening. He runs into Cat in the hall. She's wearing some kind of pink getup with a green-flowered ruffle at the bottom.

"Hi, kid," he says. "Where you been all day?"

"I went to the River Days Festival. They had a flea market and a fiddle contest."

"Fiddles ought to be outlawed."

"Why?"

"They make too much noise. The way they screak gives me a rigor."

She ignores him. "Did you see how pretty Mom looked? I fixed her hair and painted her fingernails this morning before her company came."

He nods. "You look pretty too. Except your ears look like some tobacco worms are sucking on 'em." Her earrings are fat and pale green and hang down past her chin line.

Cat slaps at his arm playfully. "I don't know how Mom put up with you all these years," she says.

"Where are you going?" he asks when Cat turns toward the elevator.

"I have a date to go out to eat."

"With that guy that took you up to Carbondale and left you that time?"

"No. He was a jerk."

"I thought you had more sense than that."

"Well, sometimes you just get in a fix and you don't know how you got there."

The elevator doors open and she steps on, waving goodbye. As the doors close, he remembers the time Cat was coming down the lane to meet him in the field. She was only about three. She crawled under the fence and started across the pasture toward him when a bull saw her and headed her way. "Go back, Cathy," he cried. "Get under the fence!" He never saw such a calm, smart child. She purposefully turned and sped toward the fence and crawled under. He was always proud of that, of how smart she was.

A WOMAN from the mastectomy sup-
port group arrives the next afternoon, bringing Lila a temporary pad to stuff in her brassiere until she can be measured for a permanent one. Lila feels embarrassed because
both her daughters and Spence are right there. Spence is
reading the newspaper noisily, rattling the pages and jerking them out smooth. Lila worries about his nerves.

"It's called a prosthesis," the woman explains. Lila did
not catch her name. Cheerful and little, pert as a wren, she
stands beside the bed, speaking to Lila like a school-
teacher. She presents Lila with the object, which is in a
plastic bag.

"Law," says Lila. "That weighs a ton." It reminds her
of those sandbags used to hold down temporary signs on
the highway.

"I can tell you're surprised," the woman chirps. "We
don't realize the weight we're carrying around. You can
put a strain on your back if you don't get properly fitted.
So don't just stuff your bra with any old thing to make it
look right. It's got to feel right and it's got to be the right
weight, or you can run into serious problems."

The woman says she has had a mastectomy herself,
and presumably she is wearing one of these sandbags in
her brassiere. Lila notices Spence squirming. Nancy and
Cat don't jump on this woman the way they did on the

doctors. Cat is playing solitaire and Nancy is reading a book. Mrs. Wright is asleep.

The woman tells a long tale about her own mastectomy. "I was worried about recurrence," she says. "And I did have a lump to come in the other breast. It was tested and it was benign, but I made the decision to have the second breast removed too. I just didn't want to take the chance of having cancer again. Now that may sound extreme to you, but it was just the way I felt. So I'm free from worry, and the prosthesis works just fine."

The woman's little points are as perky as her personality. If the originals were that small, she probably doesn't miss them, Lila thinks. The woman talks awhile about balance, and then she talks about understanding. She has a packet of materials for Lila to read. "You may get depressed over losing part of your femininity," she says. "And we want you to know we're available to help." Lila listens carefully, but she can't think of anything to say.

"The doctors were skeptical when we started our organization," the woman says, leaning toward Lila and speaking in a confidential half-whisper. "But after we advertised, we had fifty women come to the first meeting. There was a great need for this, and we want you to know that we're there to serve you."

"Would I have to come all the way to Paducah?"

"Yes. That's where we hold our meetings, on the first Monday night of each month."

"Well, I don't get out much at night. And I don't like to drive on that Paducah highway."

"Let me urge you just to try it and see what it does for you. I'll give you the names of some people to contact." She talks on and on, about how the family should be understanding. In the packet are letters to daughters and sons and husbands. Spence and the girls are pretending they aren't there. "The letters say things that you may be uncomfortable saying, things you might be afraid to say, but they will explain your feelings at this delicate time when you need emotional support. All you have to do is send the appropriate letter to your daughters and your husband and to your sons, if you have any. It will be a nice surprise for them if you just send them in the mail. It's a much easier way for you to communicate your feelings."

"My girls have stood by me," Lila says, nodding proudly at Cat and Nancy. "And my boy works long hours and can't come as often, but he does when he can. Nancy flew all the way down here from New York."

"Boston," Nancy says, peering over her reading glasses.

"That's the same thing to us down here," the woman says with an apologetic smile.

"How much will this thing cost?" Lila asks. "If you charge by the pound, it might be high." She laughs at herself. She wonders why the woman didn't replace her breasts with big ones. Small-breasted women were always envious of Lila.

"The important thing is to get the proper fitting. With your fitting, and the bra and the prosthesis, the package comes to about a hundred and fifty dollars."

"Good night!" Lila and Spence cry simultaneously.

"But it's an important investment."

After the woman has gone, Spence says, "Will Medicare cover that?"

"I doubt it," Lila says. "I failed to ask her. Law, I hope I don't have to have false teeth anytime soon! I won't be able to keep track of that much stuff."

"You don't need that thing. We can rig you up something."

"Why, shoot, yes," Lila says. "I ain't spending a hundred and fifty dollars for a falsie."

Nancy laughs. "I read about a woman who stuffed her bra with buckshot, and she got stopped at the airport by the metal detector."

Cat says, "I heard about a woman who had an inflatable bra, and she went up in an airplane, and with the change in air pressure they exploded!"

They're all laughing, and Lila spontaneously tosses the prosthesis to Spence. "Catch!" she cries. Spence snatches it out of the air and flings it to Nancy and Nancy tosses it to Cat. Cat starts to throw it to Lila but stops herself, probably realizing Lila's right arm is weak. Lila is laughing so much her stitches hurt. Cat hands her the little sandbag and Lila says, "Well, it'll make a good pincushion."

They all laugh even harder then because Lila is in the habit of keeping stray straight pins and safety pins fastened to her blouse, and more than once in her life she has accidentally jabbed her breast with a pin.

FIFTEEN

"WELL, so long," says Lila to Mrs. Wright, who is riding out the door in a wheelchair. She's going home.

The old woman crouches, her eyes aimed at her belly. She's in a print dress, lavender and green. She doesn't look up, but grunts faintly. Lila hopes she never develops such an attitude.

"I bet she can't wait till she gets back to her trailer so she can fix her up a mess of hog jaws and turnip greens," she says to her friends Mattie and Eunice, who are visiting. "She wouldn't eat a bite here."

Mattie and Eunice are in Lila's card-playing group. Last year, Reba was the fourth, and this year the fourth is Addie Mae Smith. But now Addie Mae is visiting her daughter in Florida and doesn't know Lila is in the hospital. "The flowers are from all of us, though," Mattie says, giving Lila a bowl of houseplants. "Addie Mae can go in on them when she gets back."

"I had a big crowd Sunday," says Lila. "Cat fixed my hair, but the curl's fell out now." She tugs at some stray sprigs. Cat took such care with her, fluffing her hair expertly with the plastic pick, like a hen pecking fondly at her chicks. When Cat was fussing with her, she said, out of the blue, "Mom, I know I didn't do the right things the right way. I should have gone to college and not married so young. But everything's different now, and you don't know how hard it is to work it all out. Things aren't the way they used to be—if they ever *were.*" She sounded bitter, but then she said, "It's not your fault I didn't turn out right. You're the sweetest mother in the world, and I'll never be as good as you." They had cried together for a moment, until they were interrupted by a nurse with a blood-thinner shot.

Mattie and Eunice won't let Lila say anything bad about herself. They tell her how good she looks. They chatter about their families and events at church. The conversation works around to the weather occasionally, and that prompts them to tell her again how good she's looking. They bring her a nightgown—store-wrapped in pink flowered paper. Lila can tell that it won't hang right over her new bustline, but it's the thought that counts. Mattie and Eunice haven't mentioned her breast. No one mentions Reba and her months of suffering. It's as though Reba never existed. Lila folds the gown and places it inside the tissue in the box. She smooths out the wrapping paper and folds it to save.

"It's freezing in here," Mattie says.

"I've been cold as a frog," Lila says. "Nancy and Cat had to bring me an undershirt and this sweater." She has on a blue cardigan of Cat's. "In here, I can't tell what the weather is."

Mattie has to get up and stir for her circulation. She sets the gift box on a shelf in the closet. Restlessly, she pokes in Lila's things, while Eunice flips through one of Cat's magazines. Mattie pats her little gray curls, flashing her rainbow of rings. Her rings and brooches and beads overwhelm her small frame. She has a whole houseful of doodads she collects from yard sales, and she spends half her time dusting. Lila wouldn't have the patience.

Eunice is sitting close to the bed so Lila can see the

pictures in the magazine. Eunice pauses over a picture of a handsome young man in his underwear.

"Look at all that going to waste," Lila says to Eunice.

"Are you sure that ain't stuffing?" says Eunice, examining the picture carefully.

"No, that ain't stuffing! That's the real thing!"

Eunice begins giggling and then Lila starts. Her breast jiggles and pulls across at her stitches. Eunice's face is red.

"I'm liable to say anything," Lila says. "This place is making me goofy. The nurses think I'm nuts."

Mattie looks disapproving, but Lila loves to watch Eunice laugh at a sexy joke. Eunice is a widow. Her husband, Herbert Wall, was big and fat, and Eunice once said he had such a load of "equipment" that it gave him a hernia. That remark made Lila think of a sheep, its swinging sack the size of a mushmelon. The boy in the underwear ad is young enough to be Lila's grandson, but he makes her feel a twinge of desire. She wishes she could go home right now and get in bed with Spence. One of the magazines Cat brought mentioned that men lose their desire for women who have had mastectomies. The thought hurt her and made her feel an anxiety like the urges she used to feel when she was working tobacco and she first knew Spence. He lived five miles down the road, and he would walk past the field where she worked after school and dawdle there. Lila's uncle found out he was hanging around and tried to scare him away, but Spence was daresome and he flirted openly with her, slowing down her work. Whenever she broke a tobacco plant by mistake she buried it so Uncle Mose wouldn't find out. She used to meet Spence at the edge of the tobacco field, down in the creek. They chewed gum from the black gum tree. It made their teeth black and their breath fresh, and when they kissed it was like a cool, sweet breeze.

Mattie walks over to the bed and stares closely at Lila. "When are they going to operate on your neck?"

"I have that test tomorrow, and they'll operate a-Thursday, depending on what they find out." She closes her fist and opens it. It feels slightly numb.

"Are you scared, dear?" Eunice asks.

"I didn't have time to get scared the first operation, and now there's so much going on I can't think. My brain was addled anyway." Lila laughs. "Probably from being out in the hot sun."

"All that gardening you do, Lila," says Mattie kindly.

"I've never seen anybody do as much yard work as you do," says Eunice. "You've got a lot to be proud of. You've got the prettiest yard."

"Well, I sure am lucky, with my children, my family, the things I've done. All the trips I got to go on." Lila is growing sleepy. Her arm feels numb, the way it did in Florida.

"That's something to be thankful for, Lila," says Mattie, and Eunice nods.

"Spence would hate all the noise and waiting in line. He'd rather be home digging taters!" Lila laughs at the thought of Spence on a bus tour with the senior citizens. Abruptly, she says, "The doctor said I could live without a breast. He said I'd be surprised."

"My sister told me about a woman she works with who had her breast takened out," says Mattie, who has been standing by the crucifix on the wall, studying it as if it were for sale. "She was a terminal case. The cancer had spread to ninety percent of her lymp' nodes."

"It just spread to two of mine, but they takened them out," Lila says, touching her right armpit.

Mattie doesn't seem to hear Lila. She's wound up, like the musical doll Cat gave Lila once for Mother's Day. "But come to find out—this woman lived!" Mattie continues. "She had chemotherapy five years and she had cobalt, but the cobalt burned a hole in her heart and gave her heart trouble, and so she had to have her chest wall replaced. She waited too late to sue, because her husband thought she was going to die and he didn't think they could do anything. But she got better and then all of a sudden her husband died of a brain tumor, and then six months after that her son was killed in a car wreck! But *she's* still a-kicking."

"I never heard of so many things happening to one woman," says Eunice.

"It's a miracle she bore up under all that," Lila says.

"Well, Lila, the Lord never gives us more than we can bear," says Mattie.

"Yes," Lila says, gazing at the underwear ad.

One summer night shortly before her eighteenth birthday, she ran away with Spence and they were married. She brought her few possessions in a bag she had sewed out of sacking. She didn't even have a Bible. They drove across the state line, not really knowing if they would go through with the plan. It seemed outrageous, like something the old folks told about in one of their stories of the pioneers. Spence promised her a good life. He already had a start, on his father's farm. "I don't ask for much," he said. "Just to have my clothes kept up and food on the table." He drove an old Ford with a door that rattled and headlights that sometimes blinked out. While searching for the justice of the peace, they got lost on a back road, which ended in a woods across from a cornfield. Spence persuaded her to have the honeymoon first and then look for the justice of the peace later, arguing that they'd never find this perfect, peaceful place again. Lila was always a practical person and she could see his line of reasoning. When they finally arrived at the justice of the peace, the man had already gone to bed, but he obligingly got up, tied his barking dog, and performed the service for them on his front porch. In the dim porch light, neither he nor his wife, who acted as the witness, in her curlers and housecoat, could tell how wrinkled Lila's clothes were. She had on a new suit she had made, with shoulder pads, and Spence told her she was the most beautiful girl in the world. They sneaked into his house before daylight, and at milking time he brought her out of his room to meet his astonished parents. She was tall and thin, but even then her breasts were large, and they jutted forward into the surprised line of sight of her new mother-in-law.

The artificial breast is in the drawer. The pamphlets are hard to read, and the letters don't say the right things—not the things she would say to her husband, her daughters, her son. The girls have read through the packet, and Lila thinks it would be even more embarrassing to send letters than to say what she felt. The letters wouldn't sound like her. One of the pamphlets says, "Women usually go through periods of depression after a mastectomy. They equate their femininity and their sexuality with the lost breast." Lila is so confused, with so many people telling her what to think, that she can't quite grasp her own thoughts.

Last week, the day she was operated on, she remembers waking up in a fog, wanting to turn over onto her side, but something held her flat. The room was extremely cold. Her feet were numb. And then she felt her habitual cough grab her and shake her out like a dust mop. She wondered, even then, before she was sure they had removed her breast, how they disposed of it: Did it all come out in one hunk, or did they hack it out? She thought about dressing a chicken, the way she cut out the extra fat and pulled out the entrails. She thought of how it was so easy to rip raw chicken breasts.

SIXTEEN

ILL BELTON's brick ranch house, just down the road from Spence, is only a few years old, but the plastic shutters are warped and one of the downspouts is crooked. In the backyard, a wash line runs between the house and Bill's dish antenna. The dish has a happy-face painted on it. Bill's tobacco barn sags, the paint worn off years ago. Bill hasn't grown tobacco since the bottom fell out of the burley market. Now he has a hundred acres in soybeans and a crop-dusting plane. Spence often sees Bill's plane above the countryside—flying low, aggravating cows and horses.

"Ho, there, Spence," says Bill, who is down by his dilapidated barn, working on his tractor. The airplane is parked under a makeshift carport shelter on the side of the barn.

"When do you aim to dust my beans?" asks Spence. "The grasshoppers is eating 'em up. In the middle of the night I can hear 'em gnawing. I'm afraid I'll wake up one morning and the fields will be bare."

"I been meaning to get over there, Spence," says Bill, picking up an oilcan from a rickety table of rusted tools.

The outside wall of the barn is decorated with squirrel tails, snakeskins, and a coon skin. Memories of dead animals jam Spence's mind: a butchered hog, a cat smashed under the car's tire, a crippled dog slowly dying of a fes-

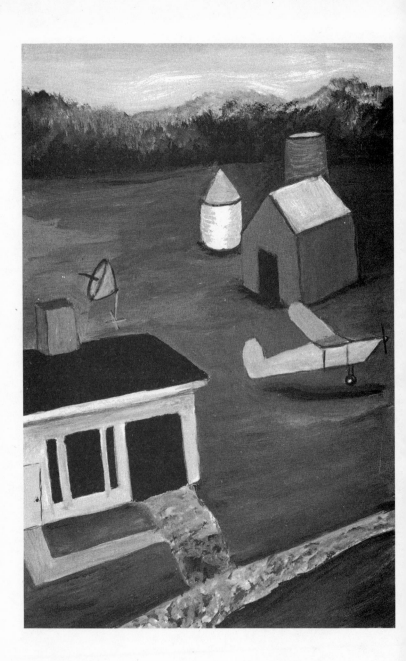

tering wound, a cow that was down and had to be shot, a bird with a wing shot to shreds.

"How's Lila doing?" Bill asks.

"She's fussing at me, as usual." Spence grins. "But she's getting some tests done today, and I'm afraid she'll have to be operated on again tomorrow—this time on her neck." He touches his neck and can almost feel it being slashed.

"The one where they go in and clean out your veins?"

Spence nods.

"Seems like everybody and his dog's having that one. Is Medicare going to cover all that, Spence?"

Spence shakes his head worriedly. "I doubt it. I heard if it's cancer they won't pay it all."

"Well, at least you've got some benefits from driving that van for the school. Me, I don't got nothing. I was in a mess here while back when Mozelle had colon trouble." He toys with the oilcan, as if he has forgotten what he meant to do with it. "They come at me to the tune of three thousand dollars. And I already owed fifty thousand on this machinery."

"So how did you manage? How'd you buy that airplane?" A few years ago, Bill had splurged on his combine—soon after building his house.

Bill just gazes off over the barn roof at some blackbirds wheeling around in the sky. Nothing but blackbirds swarm over anymore, Spence has noticed. Most of the songbirds have disappeared since the industrial park was built. Bill says, "You want some coffee, Spence? Want to come on in the house? Mozelle's gone to get her hair fixed, but I think I know how to run that coffee machine."

"No, I ain't got time. And coffee jags me out." Spence doesn't want to start in on his coffee spiel, about imports

[117]

versus domestic crops. He thinks the coffee habit is a conspiracy—to get people addicted to a luxury that comes from a foreign country.

"Since when do you drink coffee?" asks Spence as they walk toward the car.

Bill shrugs. "I got to be nearly this old before I found out it can keep you awake when you need to be awake. All that business about how you don't need as much sleep when you get old ain't true. It was just a story they told." He opens the screen to the porch and says, "Come on indoors. I want to show you something."

Bill's den wall is covered with what Spence calls "gimme caps"—caps with ads on them. Massey-Ferguson, Budweiser, John Deere, Black & Decker, Strong Feed Co. The wall is full of colors, reminding Spence of a game at a carnival where you throw darts at a wall of balloons. Bill shows Spence a green cap that says, "Hickman County Stud." Bill laughs. "A guy had this made up special for me, just for a joke."

Bill takes out a coffee can from a cabinet under the TV set. Spence remembers the rusty coffee-can lid that Lee stepped on when he was little. He was running in the grass and cut his foot open. Nancy panicked. She ran to the house packing him in her arms, her words streaming out incoherently, like the blood from Lee's foot. Nancy panics easily; that's why she thinks the world is going to be ruined by poisons and nuclear bombs and fat, anything she hears on the news.

"I don't want no coffee," Spence says.

"Hold your horses, Spence. This ain't coffee." Bill removes the plastic top from the can and pulls out a handful of pale, round seeds—like mustard seeds. "I'll sell you these babies for ten dollars a teaspoon," he says.

"Where'd you get those?" Spence knows what they

are—marijuana seeds. He recognizes them from something he has seen on TV.

"A guy gave 'em to me and I planted some of them." Bill dribbles the seeds back into the can. "You know how many I set out last year?"

"How would I know? I don't come over and count your crops."

"Twenty. Guess what I made off of 'em."

"I don't know. A thousand dollars?" Spence always exaggerates guesses like this to undercut the other guy's joke.

Bill laughs. "I set out about twenty slips, back in the cornfield. I had twenty acres in corn last year, so I strewed 'em out." He flings his arm toward his south fields. "These things grow like weeds, but you need to water 'em good. They need a lot of water the first two weeks. After that, they just grow like burdock. They do better if you sucker 'em. At the end of the summer, when they started turning, I cut the stalks off and packed 'em to the barn in a gunnysack and cured 'em. Then I put 'em in a big bed sheet and rolled it with a rolling pin and pounded the stalks good. I didn't want to take a chance on losing a smidgen of that leaf. Then I took the stalks out and packaged up the leaves in those little plastic zipper bags. And I took 'em up to the truck stop in Newton and sold 'em to a fellow I know. Them suckers brought twenty thousand dollars."

"Gah!" says Spence, his mouth open.

"A thousand bucks *apiece,* Spence." He shook the coffee can. "Look at these babies," he says gleefully. "My millions."

"Pretty soon you'll be sowing an acre of this stuff and then you'll get caught."

"Hell, Spence, I ain't talking acres. This is the small farmer you're talking to. I ain't no goddamn corporation."

[119]

Spence turns to go, and Bill says, "I figure there ain't nothing wrong with it. I don't sell it to kids."

"Yeah, but you sold it to truckers, and then they get out on the road, high on dope."

"Nah! They take it home. It ain't like tobacco, Spence. You don't smoke it all the time. You wait till you're setting around watching television or something."

"Sounds like you know what you're talking about."

"I'm just being a good farmer, Spence. Knowing my product. Now I'm ahead on my payments and I've got that airplane that can pull in the cash."

"Then I reckon you can give me a cut rate."

Bill grins. "For you, Spence, good buddy. I'll come early in the morning if it ain't windy. Better fasten up your calves tonight." He returns the coffee can to the cabinet under the TV. Jokingly, he says, "Why don't we go sow some of these seeds up along the railroad track?"

"I don't have time to get involved in organized crime," Spence says with a grin.

"You know what, Spence? You ought to go take a walk back to your back fencerow and see what's growing there."

"Why?"

"Those boys on the old Folsom place are liable to be growing something on your side of the line and you not know it. And then if the law was to find out—why, it's on your property, not theirs."

"I hadn't thought of that," Spence says, alarmed. "You reckon?"

"I wouldn't put it past 'em. They've got that new truck and I didn't see soybeans doing that good last year, and they've got that combine to pay for and they had a new pond bulldozed. They're really turning it on over there."

The Frost brothers—a bachelor and a widower—

bought out the old Folsom farm, the property behind Spence's, but they don't know how to farm it. They came from down in Mississippi and aren't used to Kentucky soil. Lila was upset with them once for running over her petunias when they came to bring some firewood from a dead post-oak tree they had sawed down on the fence line. Spence was surprised they had let him have the wood.

As Spence opens his car door, Bill calls after him, "Let me take you up for a ride in the airplane, Spence."

"I don't even like to ride in your truck with you, Bill. You're too reckless."

"Got to live dangerously, Spence!"

"Well, you seem to be doing that. You'll get cancer breathing them bug-killer fumes."

"Oh, go up with me sometime just for a ride. We don't have to spray when we go. I'll show you what your place looks like from the air."

Spence starts up his Rabbit. He would like to fly. He wishes he could just get in that flimsy little plane and fly off somewhere.

SEVENTEEN

*S*PENCE hates the familiar smells, the cold temperature, the sounds of the scurrying nurses. The sight of the old people being led for their walks down the corridor bothers him most. They clutch pillows to hold their insides in.

That morning Lila had the test she dreaded, and now she has to lie quietly all day, without turning or raising her legs. "It wasn't as bad as they said it would be," she says when Spence comes in. "It felt warm in my head, like it was going to blow up, but it didn't hurt that awful much."

"All that worry for nothing," he says, squeezing her hand. "That's the way you always do. You listen to them old women talk."

"The doctor says he wants to operate on the left side."

"Tomorrow?"

"Tomorrow about one o'clock." Her new roommate is staggering out the door with a nurse. "She had her gall bladder takened out," Lila explains to Spence.

"Where's the girls?"

"Cat had to go to work and Nancy's gone to see about the garden. Didn't you pass her on the road?"

"I didn't notice." Nancy has been driving Lila's car, even though the muffler is growing louder.

"All those machines they've got in the basement for the tests—it was the space age down there! I felt like I was on television, with all those gadgets they used." Lila shivers. "I'm taking cold. They tried to tell me they keep it cold to keep the germs down, but I always take cold when my neck gets chilled."

Her hand works away from his and grabs at the air. "Reach me some water," she says.

He pours water from her water jug into a paper cup and holds it close to her face. She can't raise her head and he has to bend the flexi-neck straw and aim it at her mouth. This is the extent of his ability to deal with the sick.

She says, "If I don't make it, I don't want to be stuck in that mausoleum. A truck could come along and bust that thing open."

"Don't worry about that," Spence says with a grin. "We'll put you back in the field where you can keep an eye on the corn crop."

She starts to laugh and is stopped by her cough. A pretty but snaggletoothed nurse materializes beside the bed. "How are we doing?" she asks.

"We're doing fine," says Spence.

"Let me sleep," Lila says. "I've had enough torture for one day."

"Honey, I just have to check one thing," the nurse says.

"Won't y'all ever leave me alone?"

"You're being so good we just don't want to let you go home," says the nurse cheerfully. "We're just trying to keep you here 'cause we like you so much. Sir, would you step outside?"

Spence waits in the hall, lost in a memory of Lila feeding a calf formula from a bucket with a nipple. The cow, Honey Bunch, had calved down near the creek, below the pond. When Spence brought the calf to the barn, the cow tagged along, nudging his elbow, making soft noises. The next day, Lila noticed her returning to the creek, confused. Lila followed her and found a second calf there, nestled beneath a hickory tree on the creek bank, too weak to follow its mother to the house. Lila said the cow had strained her milk by running back to the creek, trying to nurse both calves. Patiently, Lila hand-fed the calves and talked to them, even getting up in the night to go to the barn to tend them. She would do the same with wild rabbits, kittens, anything. Spence feels helpless. What if he had to feed her? Change her bed?

The surgeon arrives, in his green garb. Spence is relieved that Cat and Nancy aren't there to pounce on him.

"We have the results of the angiogram," the doctor says, glancing at his clipboard. "She's sixty percent blocked on the left side and forty percent on the other one. My recommendation is to open up that artery on the left side and pull out that plaque, and then see how she does. I don't want to do them both at once because of ·her weakened condition. And there's a chance she'll do so well she won't need the other one done."

The thought of opening an artery makes Spence picture skinning a snake. He tries to think of what to ask. "She complained about that dizziness down in Florida," he says.

"The blood flow was impaired," the doctor says. He has a complexion like canned wienies and seems as delicate as a woman. He says, "We have to be careful removing the plaque, because if a fragment gets into the bloodstream it could flow to the brain and cause damage. And of course the angiogram doesn't show us everything. It doesn't show if there's blockage around her heart, for example."

Nancy and Cat would have thrown questions at him about her heart, but Spence doesn't want to ask about that. He says goodbye to the doctor, sees that Lila is trying to sleep, and leaves the hospital, glad to be out in the hot July sun. He spends the afternoon running errands—picking up bulk feed from the feed mill, paying the electric bill, gassing up his Rabbit. He has that coupon for the free tune-up, but the line at the gas station is too long, and he'd rather do it himself anyway.

When he gets home, Nancy is there, bringing a bucket of cucumbers and tomatoes from the garden. She's in shorts and a T-shirt, looking sixteen. He remembers her at that age, sitting on the corn planter behind him as he drove the tractor. She complained because she got so bored, sitting there all day in order to close up the seed bins at the end of each row while he turned the tractor. As they worked, she kept coming up with schemes for mechanical inventions to eliminate her job. "You're just not paying attention," he insisted to her. "There's everything here if you just notice." Weeds, the patterns of the rows, the language of the birds overhead, moisture levels inside the soil the harrow turned up. He felt free on his tractor. He could ride a tractor from now to the end of the world, rejoicing in the pleasure of his independence.

Now Nancy sets the bucket under a shade tree and he tells her what the doctor said.

"I know," she says, pulling her long bangs out of her eyes. "I talked to him before I left."

"The test wasn't as bad as she expected."

"No. She was scared of it, but it wasn't bad."

Indoors, he changes clothes and puts on his boots. He can't get used to keeping his clothes in the bedroom, instead of near the door, where they were handy.

"Where are you going?" she asks when he goes out again.

"Back in the field."

"I'll come with you."

They walk down the lane to the pond, Oscar bounding ahead, then occasionally racing back. Abraham follows them, his fluffy tail held high. At the pond, the ducks swim away from Oscar. Spence stoops to pet Abraham's head, but he slinks away from him and leaps into the soybeans after a grasshopper. The grasshoppers are jumping among the beans like giddy children on trampolines.

"Mom really loves that cat," says Nancy, who is playing with a sprig of dried grass, trying to get Abraham interested.

Spence says, "Do you know what old Cousin Dulcie said to Lila?"

"No, what?"

"She told Lila about some woman who had that operation and then went home and died."

"Dulcie has the sensitivity of a turnip."

Spence nods. "Do you think she's too weak to go through with another operation?"

"I don't know. She was always so strong it's hard to tell."

"Oscar!" Spence calls. The dog is onto a trail, his nose to the ground. "Oscar, don't you go scaring up them rabbits."

Nancy says, "Mom doesn't want us to think she's not strong and positive. It's her maternal instinct. She can't stop protecting us, even when she has been violated in the worst way—" She breaks off, as if she thinks Spence might not understand her words. He's embarrassed. She tosses the sprig of grass toward the pond and the ducks look up. "Is the water O.K. now?" she asks.

When the tobacco warehouse up on the highway caught fire last fall, the blackened, tar-stained water from the fire hoses ran down into the creek and emptied into the pond. The water was hot, and the heat killed the fish. The tobacco company official who investigated assured them the tar was harmless and offered them two thousand dollars compensation. It was twice as much money as they had invested bulldozing and stocking the pond, so they had to accept it, but Spence and Lila grieved, seeing the fish floating in the water, then massing on the bank. They had to bury them.

"It seems all right now," he says. "When it happened, the frogs was as thick as them grasshoppers on the beans out here. So all the frogs died, and all the fish. I even found a big mud turtle in with all them fish."

"Did you have the water tested?"

He shakes his head no. "It's O.K. There's a runoff, and the water keeps running in from the creek."

He can feel Nancy tense up, wanting to lecture him on how he should have sued. But Spence doesn't trust lawyers any more than he trusts the company officials. The two thousand was a good deal. Kicking at a shampoo bottle that has washed out of the creek, he says, "She's worried herself sick over first one thing and then another. The pond and losing them fish. And she worries about Cat being by herself at night and what it's doing to the kids. And then that business with Cat and Lee."

"I think Cat's sorry about that," Nancy says.

"Have you talked to her about it?"

"Not much."

"Have you seen Lee?"

"A couple of times, but we didn't talk about it. Cat was mad at Lee for taking Mom to Florida when she wasn't feeling well."

I can't live without Lila, Spence thinks suddenly. Somewhere from the depths of his memory sprouts an old scene of her milking a cow named Turnipseed. The flies

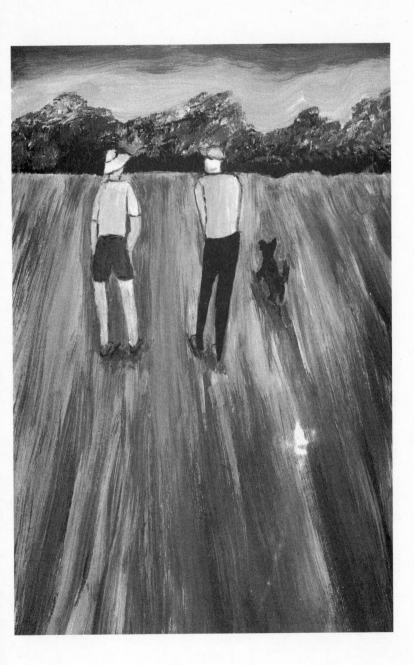

were bad. Lila tied Turnipseed's tail to the stanchion to keep it from switching her in the face as she milked. He can even remember the polka-dotted dress she was wearing on that particular day. There she is, sitting on the milk stool, splotches of lime on her heavy brown shoes. When the cows were all milked and turned out, she scraped the manure off the floor and scattered lime all over the concrete. That scene happened thousands of times; it is strange that one stands out—Turnipseed's tail, the spots on her shoes like the dots on the dress.

"What's going to happen to this farm?" Nancy is asking.

Spence is struck by how old he is, so old even his children are aging. "I'll leave it for you kids to fight over," he says. "I can't keep up this place much longer—I'm about give out. I can't keep the gullies filled up. The whole farm's going to wash away if I don't keep at it."

"It'll become a subdivision like that monstrosity down the road," Nancy says. "It makes me sad that we can't carry it on."

"Well, we had two strikes against us," Spence says. "Starting out with two girls." He grins at her, imagining Nancy as a farm wife instead of an adventurer.

"Why didn't you teach Lee how to farm?" she asks. "It's a shame he has to work such long hours at that factory."

"He makes a better living at what he's doing than he ever would on a farm these days."

"It still would have been good for him to know," Nancy argues. Back when she was in college, she would have argued the opposite. He remembers a time when she tried to persuade them to move to town and open a grocery store.

"I always made good, and we never had to do without," Spence says. "But nowadays a young couple would have to borrow too much to start out. There wouldn't be a living in it anymore—not in a place this size."

They head down the lane into the creek below the pond. A gap in the bank is stopped up with layers of rusted car parts, old bedsprings, chair frames—all filled in with piles of leaves. An enamel coffeepot and some rubber tubing have washed out of the trash. Oscar paddles in the creek, slopping his big paws through the shallow puddles. Nancy skips across on some flat rocks and Spence strides right through the mud and gravel. On the other side, Nancy stops and turns to face Spence.

"Daddy, do you remember one day when we rode the hay wagon across the creek? You were driving the tractor and Mom and I rode on top of the hay all the way back to the house."

Spence shook his head. "We did that every year."

"It felt like riding an elephant when the wagon bobbed down into the creek. Granny sent back our dinner at noon and we ate on the creek bank at the back field. She sent fried chicken and biscuits and ham and those white peas I like and slaw and sliced tomatoes and onions and a jug of iced tea."

"How do you remember all that?"

"I don't know. I just remember being happy that day."

A car horn sounds in the driveway, across the field. "That's Cat," Nancy says. "We've got to do corn again." But she doesn't leave immediately. She says, "That day Mom was so pretty. It was before she got worn down taking care of Granny. I thought then that she'd live forever." Nancy, suddenly fighting back tears, says, "When I was little, I don't think it ever once occurred to me that I might lose one of you."

Spence is too choked up to speak. Nancy crosses the

flat rocks again, her shoe sinking into some soft gravel, and when she reaches the other side, she says, "Cat came back here that day with the hired hand and the dinner, and she rode back with us. I remember that now. We found a bird's nest in a cedar tree, and down in the creek we saw some footprints of a raccoon. Cat tore her dress on the fence and cried. That was the summer you bought me a cowboy hat."

Nancy leaves, following the path along the upper creek, which feeds the pond. He's not sure he remembers that day, but he can see Lila riding on top of the load of hay as clearly in his imagination as he could in memory. Lila and the girls in straw hats, Lila in some of his old pants and a long-sleeved shirt with a rip in the sleeve. As the picture grows clearer in his mind, Nancy's straw hat changes to a cowboy hat, Cat's dress to a robin's-egg blue—the same as her car in the driveway now. He smiles, remembering the cowboy hat. He had to hunt all over town to find one Nancy's size.

He follows the creek line down toward the back fields. In the center of one of the middle fields is a rise with a large, brooding old oak tree surrounded by a thicket of blackberry briers. From the rise, he looks out over his place. This is it. This is all there is in the world—it contains everything there is to know or possess, yet everywhere people are knocking their brains out trying to find something different, something better. His kids all scattered, looking for it. Everyone always wants a way out of something like this, but what he has here is the main thing there is—just the way things grow and die, the way the sun comes up and goes down every day. These are the facts of life. They are so simple they are almost impossible to grasp. It's like looking up at the stars at night, seeing them strung out like seed corn, sprinkled randomly across the sky. Stars seem simple, even monotonous, because there's no way to understand them. The ocean was like that too, blank and deep and easy.

Spence moves on. Above, a jet plane flies over, leaving a white scar. At the back of the farm the creek joins another creek, a twisted gully that cuts through several farms before joining Wolf Creek. Oscar has strayed momentarily, but comes rushing up to lap at the water in the creek. The water is very clear, the pebbles shining. It is rarely deeper than Spence's knees, and in summer it is just patchy puddles, but sometimes Spence has dreams about swimming in this clear, shallow water. He dreams of the knock and dash of waves high as buildings.

The back field holds the ten acres of corn. It's tall, and the ears are fattening up. Oscar threads his way through the rows of corn, and Spence follows the narrow edge next to the fencerow. He reaches the back line just as Oscar rouses a cottontail, which bounds erratically along the path, then disappears into the blackberry briers. Perplexed, Oscar roots around, then gives up, coming to Spence as if to win approval for his restraint.

"Oscar, you know I don't want you catching them rabbits."

In Spence's opinion, dogs and cats should have amusing, old-fashioned names—Buford, Brutus, Nebuchadnezzar, Abraham. He doesn't like names like Fluffy and Fifi or names from television, like Mr. T. He knows a man with two Boston bull terriers named Cagney and Lacey. Spence never watches that show because Lacey's New York accent grates on his nerves.

There they are. It is true. A scattering of marijuana plants, thriving on the fertilizer he used on his corn. The plants grow in amongst the cornstalks of the first three rows, like inseparable companions. He wouldn't have guessed what pretty plants they are. The lacy leaves are almost tropical, like the vegetation he vaguely recalls from the islands in the Pacific. These plants are strong, with the unmistakable nature of weeds—hardy, tenacious, stubborn.

He counts thirteen of the plants. He suspects Bill knows about them, because it is odd that Bill mentioned the possibility. Bill's land joins Spence's on one edge, across the creek. Spence figures that Bill, not the Frost boys, planted them himself and decided to let Spence in on the joke, before Spence either got in trouble or missed out on the harvest. Bill and Spence have always played tricks on each other. Once some puppies showed up at the house. They had been dropped on the road. But Spence recognized the puppies—a litter from Bill's hound. Spence packed up the puppies in a box and dropped them back at Bill's house. The next time he saw Bill, the subject of the puppies didn't come up.

Lila often teased Spence about the way his pranks sometimes backfired—such as the time he got his eyes tested, part of the physical exam he had to take in order to drive the school van. The doctor positioned him in the chair but then left the room and jabbered with another patient about some designer glasses frames for such a long time that Spence grew irritated. He walked over to the eye chart across the room and memorized the last line, the finest print. Later, during the eye examination, Spence reeled off the last line. "That's amazing," the eye doctor said. "Read that again." Spence repeated the line of meaningless letters. "That's truly amazing," the eye doctor said. "For a man your age! Now, let's see you read it backwards."

A sound in the creek startles him. It's just a bird squabble. A blue jay soars out of a scaly-bark hickory. Spence gazes back over the field, taking in where he has been.

He can visualize that battle he was in as clearly as if it's happening now. He was below deck, frantically passing the five-inch shells to the main guns above, and then he could hear the one-point-ones—the dive-bombers were closer, heading for the capital ships. He could hear the antiaircraft guns going faster, sharper, the boom-boom-boom overlaid with bah-bah-bah-bop, then the rat-tat-tat chatter of machine guns. Sailors who had been on duty above deck told him later that radar had picked up six Japanese dive-bombers heading toward the carrier. The fleet shot down three of them, but the other three were closing in on their target. Suddenly several American fighter planes appeared, to finish up the job the ships failed to do. Like sparrows teasing a hawk, the fighters began swirling up and down and over and around each of the bombers. They shot down two of them, but the remaining bomber penetrated the defenses and was closing in on the big ship. The fighters swirled in all directions and then one fighter got on the bomber's tail, in the right position to shoot it down. The Japanese plane was already swooping toward the carrier, and the American fighter flew straight at him, like a mad bumblebee. Instead of shooting him down, the fighter rammed him from above and behind, just as crazily and fearlessly as the kamikazes nose-dived into the American decks. The explosion sent both planes cartwheeling, on fire, into the sea. It was impossible to believe, the crew said. He flew right up the Jap's ass. His guns must have jammed. They were sure his guns jammed, and there were just a couple of seconds to go before the enemy plane would have released the bomb. The fighter, in position, made an on-the-spot decision to die, to save the carrier. It was a moment frozen forever. The sailors talked about it all the way to Guam. They knew their ship might have to do something like that. At any moment their captain could whip the ship into the path of a torpedo. They might have to take a torpedo, the same way that fighter rammed the bomber. That's what they were there for.

Spence was sure the pilot's name would be in all the books he read later, but he couldn't find it. He was just another anonymous hero.

EIGHTEEN

*H*ER HEAD is clearing and she can turn over now and stir her limbs. She feels warmer. It is night, and a glow from the hall shines on the crucifix, highlighting it like a Christmas display.

The woman in the other bed has four visitors. Her family has paraded past the foot of Lila's bed all day: kids of all ages, uncles, aunts, parents, in-laws. The smallest child, the patient's little boy, seems to feel neglected and confused by his mother's illness. He slams the plastic bedpan on the bathroom floor deliberately, and when he's scolded he bursts into tears and says everybody's picking on him. His aunt takes his side. Lila would hate to have to cook for that bunch. They seem helpless without the woman at home to take care of them. They had gone to eat at the Cracker Barrel, reporting back to the sick woman every single thing they ate and how much it cost. Several times they got a laugh out of how the oldest boy spilled iced tea in his pie and ruined it. The little boy's grandmother said she had to cut up his ham for him and then he refused to eat it. She said she hated to waste ham, hogs were so high. The woman in bed is barely awake after her surgery, and the kinfolks are talking, talking, talking, laughing, telling stories. The noise competes with the television. Lila tries to watch *Family Feud,* but she has *Family Feud* right here, live.

She might die tomorrow.

Spence left soon after they brought her supper—broth and Jell-O and coffee, the same meal she had the night before her mastectomy. She didn't drink the coffee. When he left, abruptly, she felt so much was left unsaid. Lee and Joy and their children were there, as well as the crowd by the other bed, and Lila knew Spence's nerves couldn't bear the commotion for long. She imagined him going home, feeding the calves and the ducks, talking to Oscar, fixing some cereal, maybe eating a tomato, watching TV all evening—mumbling to himself the way he had started doing the last few years. She imagined that routine continuing. Tonight, tomorrow night, more nights, alone, for years.

When Spence's father died, Lila and Spence had talked about what each would do if the other went first. Spence was only fifty then, but he said he had just realized he would die someday, had never believed it before. But Amp was so old. His passing seemed natural. Much later, after Rosie had gone too, and Spence and Lila were alone together for the first time in their marriage, they felt as though they would live forever. They could never imagine one of them without the other.

If Spence went first, her life would change as much as it changed when she was eighteen and married him. She would be afraid to stay on the farm alone, with all the crime spreading out from town into the country these days. But she wouldn't want to have to move in with Cat or Lee and be a burden to them, the way Rosie was to her. Rosie lived on for ten years after Amp died, moving in with Spence and Lila toward the end. She was unhappy in their house. She would get up from a nap in the afternoon and eat breakfast, swearing the sun came up at three-thirty that morning. She thought the people on TV were in the room with them. "I want to go home," she'd say repeatedly, and sometimes she would go back, wandering up to the old house in her gown. But strangers lived in her house; they had rented the place. One night it burned down—a cigarette on the couch. After that, Rosie gave up her sewing and spent her days playing with scraps of material and pieces of paper, sorting them in boxes like a half-witted child. When she died, Lila found boxes and boxes of nothing but smaller boxes, and plastic bags stuffed with more bags and twist ties. She found strings and a lifetime's collection of greeting cards. Rosie even saved name tags from Christmas in a hosiery box. To Granny from Catherine. To Granddaddy from Lee.

Lila can't sleep. Random scenes pass before her eyes. The strong, comfortable smells of cows in the barn waiting to be milked, the steamy air in winter. Gathering in tomatoes before a frost. Sprinkling lime on the potatoes spread out on the ground in a stall of the barn. Laying the onions on screen-door racks above. An electrical storm scattering black tree limbs across the yard. Rosie's foot clamping down on the step-pedal of her slop bucket. Life has turned out so differently from anything she could have imagined at Uncle Mose's. The world has changed so much: cars, airplanes, television. She can't complain. She tries to go along with anything new, but she is afraid that inside she hasn't changed at all. It still hurts her to see liquor kept in a house where there are children, to see farmers out spreading manure on their fields on Sundays, to see young people fall away from the church.

Her innocence has always embarrassed her. Her children went away and came back with such strange knowledge she can't fathom. Nancy makes her feel dumb, with that bossy way she's always had of bringing home new ideas—cholesterol, women's rights. What Nancy knows is from books, but Cat knows people. She knows instinctively what looks good on her customers and knows how to compliment them. Cat can make people feel beautiful. But Cat would rather spend money on expensive outfits than take the time to sew. Cat is never satisfied. Lila always says, "The more you get, the more you want." Lila never wanted much. But on Waikiki Beach, she felt thrilled and grateful for the chance to see what was out there. And she thought she would never get enough. She was seeing what Spence saw in the Navy, and maybe seeing what Nancy was looking for when she left home.

Growing into old age toward death is like shifting gears in a car; now she's going into high gear, plowing out onto one of those interstates, racing into the future, where all her complicated thoughts that she has never been able to express will be clear and understandable. Her mind cannot grasp these thoughts exactly, but there is something important about movement that she wants to tell. The way corn will shoot up after a rain. The way a baby chicken's feathers start showing. The way a pair of wrens will worry and worry with a pile of sticks, determined that the place they have chosen is the right one for a nest—the ledge over the door that gets disturbed every morning at milking time, or a pocket in a pair of overalls hanging on the wash line. A baby's tooth appearing like a shining jewel.

When her children were babies, Lila used to powder their bottoms and then kiss them right between the legs before she pinned on the diapers. They would squeal with pleasure. Nancy saw her do that to Cat and Lee when they were babies, and she was appalled. Lila said, "You don't see how I can do that, do you?" It was such overwhelming, simple love, there was nothing wrong with it. As they grew bigger and bigger, Lila couldn't tear herself away from them. She always wanted to pet them, though it embarrassed them. Even now she likes to kiss them on their lips. Lee turns red. Nancy is stiff, Cat more receptive. Cat is more like Lila, with the need to keep hugging her children, touching and holding.

After Spence came home from the Navy and began to build up the dairy again, they were happy, beginning to get a little ahead. One morning Spence had gone into town to deliver the milk and Lila was scrubbing overalls on the washboard out in the wash house. Rosie was adding coal to the fire under the wash kettle. Suddenly they heard Nancy crying indoors. When Lila rushed up the steps to the porch and to the kitchen to see if Nancy had fallen, she found Amp with the razor strop, whipping Nancy on the legs. Lila screamed at him to stop, but he kept on, aiming the strop precisely and fiercely. Nancy was howling, her legs already black with bruises. Like someone rushing into a jump-rope game, Lila ran through the flailing razor strop and snatched up Nancy, fleeing with her to their bedroom. "She climbed up on the table after I told her not to," Amp explained, following them. "She wouldn't *mind*. She has to learn to mind."

"Don't you never do that again!" Lila shouted. Her rage against his authority shocked her. She slammed the door and clung to Nancy on the bed, both of them crying until Nancy's sobs finally subsided into hiccups. Lila bathed the poor legs in Epsom salts, soaking the bruises. When Spence found out, he threatened his father, saying he would leave the farm, leave him without any hands to work it. But Spence was immobilized. There was nowhere to go, no way to get their own land. Lila doesn't believe Nancy remembers. She always loved her grandfather, and he never hurt her again. But she always clung to Lila for protection. Strangers frightened her, and she would look up at Lila, waiting for her mother to speak for her. Lila felt like an old mother hen holding out her wing. Even now,

Nancy's strange, frightened expressions remind Lila of that incident, and she doesn't have the heart to bring it up again. She never understood why Amp did that to Nancy. Men, Lila believed, had a secret, awful power. She was always taught not to hang around the men when they got together, when one came to visit and they would talk out at the stable. Rosie cautioned her about that.

A nurse interrupts Lila's thoughts, bringing her a pill. Lila doesn't ask what it is. She swallows it with a sip of water. The new roommate is getting some kind of midnight treatment, and she gives out a burst of little pup yelps.

There are loose ends: things Lila can't get out of her mind. The yellow bushes by the house that would bloom so pretty in the spring, with their sweeping arms. Spence cut them back so he could paint the side of the house and they grew bigger the next year, even more beautiful. Eventually, they died back, and for many years Lila longed to see those bushes again, but they were in the past. As you grow older, you give up things, hand things over to the younger generation. You plant a smaller garden. Instead of accumulating, you start giving away, having a yard sale. But Lila never felt she was growing old, until just a few months ago, when she started getting so tired. When she had babies she never slept. She remembers the years at the factory, when she worked from eight until six and still managed to cook, wash, iron, clean, sew, garden, can, even help with the crops and cows. She never knew when to stop.

When she eloped with Spence, she brought something with her that has lasted to this day—a handful of dried field peas, a special variety that her cousins told her that her mother had raised. Lila kept the peas going in the garden year after year, always saving out some seed. They weren't brown and ordinary. They were white, plumper than most field peas, and she never saw that kind anywhere else. She always called them "our peas."

You grow older, you start reversing direction. Old people draw up in a knot like a baby in the womb. Rosie died curled like a grubworm. Tell Nancy about the peas.

Her mind fights the tranquilizer. She'll fight to the end. I'm stubborn as a Missouri mule, she thinks. I'll accept things up to a point, and then I won't budge.

The way her kids turned out. What will happen to her garden. What they will do with her things. She doesn't care about her things. Junk. She'd rather be outdoors. She never cared about housekeeping.

Playing in her uncle's creek when she was little . . . meeting Spence down in that creek . . . years later when his tractor got stuck in their own creek, hauling him out with the truck. The way he plows her garden lickety-split, clumsily uprooting the precious new slips. She and Spence have spent a lifetime growing things together.

On the wall, the crucifix goes out like a light and there's a strange calm in the corridor, like the hush in church before the preacher begins.

NINETEEN

*I*N THE growing morning light, Spence can hear the airplane coming, a little chug like a hummingbird's surprising motorcycle rumble. He fastened up the calves last night. He hasn't seen Abraham this morning, but Oscar is on the porch with Spence. The tiny single-engine plane flying along the creek line appears so light Spence is sure a good tail wind could make it do a somerset. He watches as Bill flies up and down the largest field, trailing brownish clouds behind him. The wind is from the south, blowing away from the house, so Spence cannot smell the spray. His head is stuffed up from the air-conditioning in the hospital. The plane lifts above the first tree line, barely missing it, then dips down into the second field. At the back, just before reaching the corn, the plane turns and plows back into its own trails of fumes. If Lila dies from that operation and her funeral is Sunday, he could go up in that plane Monday, and if it crashed he would spare Nancy from having to make a separate trip home for his funeral. He had a bad night.

The telephone is ringing. Spence runs inside and grabs the phone, expecting bad news. He has never gotten over the early association between bad news and the telephone.

"Well, how's Lila doing?" a shrill-voiced woman asks. She must be someone Lila knows from her trips with the senior citizens. "They said she was having her neck operated on," the woman continues.

"Yeah. Today—about one o'clock," Spence says, longing for whole minutes of blissful forgetting.

"Lila was looking bad," she says.

You old bat, he thinks, wishing the doctors would saw on *her* neck.

He tells the woman, "Lila's sassing the doctors. Can't nothing hold her down. She's raring to get home and do up her pickles."

"Well, I just wanted to know how she was," the woman says, hanging up abruptly.

It is past seven o'clock. Spence takes a capsule the doctor prescribed for Lila when she had bronchitis back in the winter. The bottle says, "Take one capsule after supper for breathing." The steam from his shaving water helps clear his nose. In the refrigerator, tan beads of glistening moisture dot the sinking meringue of the coconut pie. Nancy and Cat didn't take much of the food. Spence lays four strips of bacon on the bacon rack in the microwave and punches the time buttons. He watches the bacon curl, like time-lapse photography of flowers blooming and dying that he has seen on TV. He stops the oven just before the bell rings. He hates the sound—ping!—like a pebble from a slingshot hitting a hubcap. In the distance, the airplane's engine is receding. Through the window, Spence sees Abraham on the porch licking orange dust from his fur.

After breakfast, he pauses in the doorway of the spare room to look at some of Lila's things—a row of old dolls on a quilt. She bought old dolls at yard sales and cleaned them up and sewed clothes for them. She found a porcelain doll head in the junkhouse behind the barn and made a body for it. Lila can take a scrap of anything and work it into something pretty. The day before, while the girls were freezing the corn, he thought he heard her call him, but it was Cat, and he realized that if Lila died he would hear the girls talking and he would catch an echo of her voice in theirs and think it was her.

❊   ❊   ❊

At the hospital, she says, "I had a hard night. I didn't sleep a week." She meant wink. She's silly from the drugs. "I'm drunker'n a two-tailed tom," she says, trying to raise her head. After they wheel her away to surgery, Spence strides down the corridor toward the elevator, passing a young woman who says to an older woman, "He wants to get Stevie one of them three-wheelers, but Renée don't want him to have it." A man in a hospital gown trudges down the hall alone, wheeling his I.V. and carrying his piss bag in his hands, carefully, like a baby. The prisoner is out walking too, pressing a folded blanket against his stomach, as if he has had surgery again. He is pale and weak, his eyes buried under those brows that jut out like awnings. He looks half dead.

Downstairs, Spence buys a Coke from the machine and sits at a table by a window in a corner of the cafeteria. Coke always settles his stomach, and the Coke acid helps clean his dentures. The window opens onto a little gray enclosed area—a triangle of grass framed by the angles of the two wings of the building. An updraft suddenly catches some trash and begins spinning it up in the air. A plastic bag and a foil potato-chip bag are dancing and circling, battling each other. As they rise in the updraft, they seem like cartoon characters. They seem alive, a young courting couple chasing and pursuing each other,

[147]

then falling exhausted to the grass before rising up with renewed energy for the chase again. The dance keeps going on for so long Spence sits there, mesmerized.

He loses track of time, and Nancy and Cat find him there.

"Come on, let's eat," says Cat. "When I'm nervous, I have to eat."

Nancy grabs his elbow. "Come on, Dad, they have a lot of food you like. They have corn bread and green beans."

Nancy and Cat travel through the line, knowing exactly what they are doing. Spence hates cafeterias. There are too many choices. As they approach the cashier, he regards with chagrin what he has taken from the salad bar: corn bread, salad with bacon bits, cottage cheese, pineapple, peppers, shredded cheese, cherry tomatoes, dill pickles, crackers.

They sit at a table near the back of the cafeteria, away from the crowd.

"Do you want some of these tommytoes?" he asks Nancy, shoving the cherry tomatoes at her.

"No. I like those fresh tomatoes from Mom's garden. We brought her some the other day, with an onion."

"She saved some of it in a drawer for supper, and you could smell that onion all over the hospital," says Cat with a laugh. "Hey, there's Mom's preacher, Dad."

Spence spots the preacher from Lila's church speaking with a man on the far side of the cafeteria.

"Tell me something, Dad," Nancy says. "I remember the Pentecostals around here never would wear jewelry and makeup. But the PTL Club is Pentecostal, and they decorate themselves like Christmas trees. Why is that?"

"TV commercials," he says.

"I guess so."

"That reminds me. I heard a great joke, Dad," says Cat. "If you scrape off all of Tammy Bakker's makeup, do you know what's underneath?"

"What?"

"Jimmy Hoffa."

Spence can hardly eat. Cat is eating out of nervousness, not missing a bite. Nancy is picking at salad.

"Where do you hear jokes like that, Cat?" asks Nancy. "I never hear jokes."

Cat shrugs. The preacher is headed their way. He stops at their table and lays his hand on Spence's shoulder, saying, "I've got some sick here to look after, but I want you to call me this evening and tell me how she's doing."

"All right," says Spence, cringing. He hates to use the telephone.

The preacher's hand is still on Spence's shoulder, and now the man starts working the muscle. It's supposed to be a friendly and caring gesture, Spence figures, but it makes him nervous. He has never known a man who caressed anybody's shoulder that way. Cat and Nancy are staring at the way the preacher is rubbing on Spence's shoulder.

"I'll be praying real hard for Mrs. Culpepper," the preacher says. He is a young fellow who reminds Spence of the Cards' utility infielder. Spence can't remember the player's name.

TWENTY

ITH HIS CHILDREN, Spence sits in the second-floor waiting room, a small corner area with a Coke machine and a telephone and a TV. The Cards are playing the Astros, and Lee seems absorbed in the game. Nancy is reading a book. Nancy would probably read a book during a nuclear attack. Cat would reach for food, and Lee would go to sleep. Lee always slept when something was bothering him. He would sleep so long it was like a deep illness.

"Dad, what size bra does Mom wear?" asks Cat, who is filling out a form.

"I don't know. Big ones." Five-pound flour sacks.

Nancy says, "When that phone rings, I'm going to jump out of my skin."

Cat folds the form and picks up a women's magazine. A red-white-and-blue Fourth of July cake is on the front. She says to Nancy, "Look at this article, 'How to Warn Your Children About Strangers Without Scaring Them.' I'm at the point where I'm going to have to trust Krystal to know what goes on. I think she's smart. I think she knows what goes on."

In a TV commercial for *Time* magazine, the Pope appears momentarily, holding a strange animal Spence can't identify. "I didn't know the Pope was allowed to have pets," he says.

"He probably needs *some*thing," says Lee, dragging on his cigarette.

A couple about Spence's age enter the waiting area and sit down on a vinyl couch. They stare at the TV. The woman's eyes, with sagging pouches under them, are red from crying. She holds her pocketbook like a lap cat and rubs the material of her skirt nervously. The man, in short sleeves, seems cold. Spence can see the goose pimples on the man's arms.

"Is Joe Magrane pitching today?" the man asks.

"Yeah. He's starting," says Lee, not taking his eyes from the screen.

The man says, "Saint Louis sure goes for those lefties."

"The Cards wouldn't know a right-handed pitcher if he knocked 'em in the head," says Lee.

Jack Clark is up, and he hits a double for the Cards. Spence tries to lose himself in the slow, careful movements of the game. Baseball is the same situations over and over, but no two turn out alike. Like crops and the weather. Life.

When the telephone rings, Cat grabs it. Nancy shuts her book on her thumb and lowers her reading glasses. Spence sees Cat's intake of breath, then her affirmative nod toward them.

"She's O.K.," Cat says, hanging up. "But he thought at first she might have had a slight stroke. When he woke her up, her speech was a little slurred for a minute."

"Her words are always slurred when she's sleepy," Spence says. "That ain't nothing."

"Well, he decided she was all right. He wanted to wake her up as soon as he could, just to see if she had any nerve damage."

"She's O.K. then," Nancy says, breaking into a smile.

"God, I'm relieved!" She holds her book at arm's length. "Look how I'm shaking."

Spence realizes he is shaking too—all the way to his knees.

"Thank God," says Lee. He jams his cap down on his head and turns toward the elevator. "I have to get back to work," he says. "I'll see y'all tonight."

Lila will be in intensive care that night, and they will have to wait until nine o'clock to see her. They will be allowed to see her for fifteen minutes—no more than two persons at a time. Spence decides to go home for a few hours.

In the car, the radio plays "Hearts on Fire" and he sings along with it. Then Phil Collins comes on. Spence can't stand Phil Collins, with his high-pitched yapping, like a pup fastened up in a shed. He turns the radio down. When he drove to the hospital that morning, his head had been full of intolerable imaginings—a funeral in two days. Now his relief empties out his mind, and he drives all the way home as if in a dream.

At home, a loaf of homemade bread wrapped in tinfoil sits on the deck, with a note, "From Hattie Goebel." It is still warm. He stuffs the loaf in a kitchen cabinet, then goes out and cranks up the push mower. He mows the patch around the orchard that he missed a few days before. The mower needs oiling. It keeps sputtering. He's proud of the appearance of his place—well cared for and not trashy. The new siding on the house looks good. After mowing, he reads the newspaper and tries to take a nap, but he can't get to sleep. He gets up and puts on his boots and heads for the back field with a tow sack and a bucket and a shovel.

"Come on, Oscar," he says. "We've got work to do."

For half an hour, he works at transplanting the marijuana plants from the corn row over to the back edge of
Bill's land across the creek. He doesn't want to get in
trouble with the Frost boys. Maybe Bill thought he was
being neighborly, telling Spence about the plants when he
might need help with his hospital bills, but it makes
Spence angry. He doesn't want a handout. He has never
borrowed, and he has always made good on his farm. But
the plants in his corn have been bothering him—not the
risk, so much. He doubts if the law would find these few
plants; they go after major offenders, and he could always
claim the seeds strayed from Bill's crop. And it's not that
he is being especially virtuous. There's just something
about growing them that seems out of character for him.
Instead of being an outlaw, he would actually be in fashion, and he never wanted to follow the crowd. It would
be like borrowing to buy a combine, or spraying his fields,
or getting a credit card, or mortgaging his house—getting
in deeper and deeper, like everyone else. He felt helpless
when Nancy lectured him about the plastic bottles, but at
the moment he feels he can do something. He can imagine
the whole farm planted in this stuff someday; it could take
over, like jimsonweed and burdock. But not yet.

He waters the plants with buckets of water from the
creek. He props a drooping plant against a cornstalk.
Oscar, wet and muddy from splashing in the creek, flops
down at Spence's feet, spraying water on him.

"Oscar, you sure love to work, don't you, boy?"
Spence says, pulling a cocklebur from the dog's shaggy
chin.

Spence walks back to the barn in a state of suspen-
sion—the worst over but an air of uncertainty remaining,
like waiting out a drought.

After feeding the calves, he eats a bowl of cereal and

a piece of baloney and drinks a glass of milk. The news is on. He washes his teeth and runs the dishwasher. He waters the hanging plants on the deck. He feeds Abraham a can of turkey and giblets. Spence dreads calling the preacher.

When he returns to the hospital, Lee is waiting for him in the lounge.

"They moved her to the fourth floor, to the intensive care ward in the heart unit," Lee says.

"What's wrong with her heart?" His own heart somer-sets.

"Nothing. They just didn't have enough beds in the main unit."

"Oh. You liked to scared me there for a minute."

They crowd into the elevator. There is a hush and a giggle when three more people squeeze in. "The limit's sixteen!" cries a nervous woman in lime-green pants. "Reckon it'll quit on us?" someone asks. Spence squirms. "We've got too many overweight folks in here!" another woman says cheerfully.

In the corridor, Spence asks Lee, "Could you do me a favor and call the preacher?"

"What for?"

"He wanted to know how she was."

"Why can't you call him?"

"He makes me nervous."

The walls of the fourth floor are painted shades of pink, light tones of blood, like blood you spit out when brushing your teeth. As they walk down the hall, Spence says, "Preachers have this act they go into—one for the sick, one for the grief-stricken, one for weddings. They just switch from one to another like they was dialing a TV channel. And then the bull they start in on is like those get-well cards."

"That's their job," says Lee.

Nancy was right. Spence should have taught Lee to farm. If he spent some time out in the fields, he might have a chance to think about things and he wouldn't make so many excuses. Lee's always taking up for the wrong people.

Nancy and Cat are already in the lounge. "She's doing fine," Nancy says. "A nurse just told us she's awake."

Cat's hair is swept up on one side and fastened with an old-fashioned turtle-shell comb. "Did you eat supper?" Cat asks Spence.

"Some cereal and a piece of baloney."

"We went to that new Italian restaurant by the mall," Cat says, making a face at Spence's supper. "It was real good."

"I don't like Italian food," said Spence, wrinkling his nose back at her. "Pizza. Ugh!"

"Heartburn City," says Lee to Spence with a grin.

"We didn't have pizza," says Cat. "We had calamari."

"What's that?"

"Squid," Cat says, eyeing Lee. "I'm surprised I had the nerve to eat it, but I decided to go for it."

The waiting room of the heart unit is large and pleasant, with comfortable chairs and a huge television—a thirty-six-inch, Spence guesses. There is probably more money in heart bypasses than other kinds of surgery, he realizes. People with money probably have more heart trouble because making money is so stressful. The people with stomach problems on the second floor seemed poorer than the people on the fourth floor. A nun slips past the door, almost a hallucination—a penguin. Spence has seen very few nuns, except on TV, but once he saw a nun driving a tractor along a main road, and he puzzled about that for years, inventing histories for her.

He sits there, the music from a rock-and-roll program on TV going through his veins. No one else is watching except him and Cat. If Lila had died during the operation, he thinks now, he would hear rock-and-roll at her funeral. It would be in his head. Lee laughs at him for listening to rock music, but Spence doesn't care. He doesn't really care what people think most of the time. Yet he knows he couldn't have that music at her funeral because of what people would think. If she gets through this illness he might take her dancing again—if his back doesn't act up.

Cat says, "I've got this record. This group is great."

Some long-haired group is swinging bright-colored guitars flamboyantly.

"Their hair looks like they've been rolling around in cow mess," says Spence. Nancy has plunged into her book again, oblivious. "Is your book good?" he asks.

She nods. "Uh-huh."

He should read more, but reading gives him bad headaches. Since he got cable, though, watching TV is an education. When the news shows people in a foreign country, you can tell what the weather is like by what they are wearing. His favorite show is *National Geographic*. He gets to see places he'd never go to—the ocean floor, the North Pole, Siberia, Australia. He loves seeing unusual animals from all over the world. His grandchildren are smart because of all they are exposed to on TV. Sometimes he is flabbergasted by how much they know. They know about dinosaurs, the Japanese yen, satellite communications— the most unlikely subjects.

At nine o'clock a nurse says, "Two of you can go in for ten minutes and then the other two can go in."

"Come on, Lee," Cat says. "Let's you and me go first."

They follow the nurse, and Spence says to Nancy,

"She'll be half asleep, on them tubes. She won't even know they're there."

A moment later he says, "You're right. I should have learnt Lee to farm."

When Nancy and Spence take Cat and Lee's places at nine-fifteen, Lila is awake but too weak to raise her head. She smiles faintly.

"Get out of that bed and rattle them pots and pans!" Spence bellows at her. "We've got to go milk."

"Oh, shoot! I ain't about to get up and go milk," she says. "I've milked enough cows in my time."

She groans and he keeps teasing her, while Nancy places a washrag on Lila's forehead and gives her some water to sip. Her hair is tousled, and she has on no makeup. Tubes are taped to her wrist, and down her neck is the fresh wound, a long slash clamped together with metal staples. The loose flesh under her chin is pulled tight.

Suddenly Cat rushes into the room. "You're missing Mick and Tina!" she says, turning on the small TV that extends from the wall on a long metal neck. She pulls the set toward Lila's bed. "Mick Jagger and Tina Turner!"

"Oh, you don't want to miss Mick and Tina!" Spence says to Lila, clasping her arm.

On the flickering screen, Mick Jagger and Tina Turner are dancing a sexy dance, each singing to the other in a taunting but strangely loving way.

"Look at 'em!" Spence cries, excited by their movements.

"I can't see." As she turns, Lila's tubes dangle before her face. Spence pushes the tubes aside and tilts the TV closer.

"Look at 'em go!" he says gleefully, watching Tina's heavy black body—her big boobs and long legs and wide hips. She's wearing a black leather skirt and fishnet tights. She stomps around in high heels, with her pelvis thrust out. She's like a pickup truck, Spence thinks. Jagger, in contrast, is a lanky beanpole. His big rubbery lips remind Spence of a cow's screw hole.

"Who are they?" says Lila groggily.

"Mick Jagger and Tina Turner," says Nancy.

Spence has a sudden memory—dancing with Cat to Ike and Tina Turner and the Ikettes on the radio. Cat must have been no more than nine.

"How can she be so sexy?" Cat says. "She's no taller than I am and look how wide her hips are."

Tina Turner turns Spence on, the way Lila does—Lila's large, warm, sexy body. Tina is wearing a crazy Halloween fright wig. Her boobs shaking on the screen make him want to cry.

"Hand me that water," Lila says. "I can suck a little ice."

Spence pushes bits of crushed ice between her lips and she crunches it. Then her I.V. unit starts beeping. The fluid isn't getting through the tubes. Nancy fiddles with the tubes, but the machine keeps beeping.

"Where's the nurse?" Spence says impatiently.

Cat goes to look for her. If Lila were a heart patient and the beep signaled danger, she could be dead by now. Intensive care doesn't mean what Spence thought it meant. The nurse ambles in, punches some buttons and jerks the tubes.

"Just two of you are supposed to be in here," she says.

"I'm leaving," Cat says, but her eyes are still stuck to the TV screen.

The amazing thing, Spence realizes now, is that Lila's color has returned. Her face is rosy and full, lighting up every blemish of her complexion, each freckle and age mark and wrinkle. Her face is restored, the way raisins plump up in water.

"Your color looks good," Spence says, holding her hand. She moans a little, a seductive moan, out of place here in the hospital. He is too happy to speak.

He takes the washrag from Nancy and lays it on Lila's forehead. She gazes at the TV. "Who are they?" she says.

And then an incredible thing happens. Mick Jagger grabs Tina Turner's skimpy black leather skirt and rips it off of her and throws it across the stage. There she is in her fishnet tights and black panties, still dancing as if nothing has fazed her. Spence's mouth drops open. "Did you see that?" he says.

"Uh-huh," Lila says. "A colored woman showing her butt." She tries to laugh and her hand goes to her throat, to the ridge of stapled flesh down her neck.

Lila's color looks so good, her face warm and full like a ripe peach. The blood is flowing to her face again. He keeps gazing at her, and she says, "I'll be glad when I get home and don't have everybody staring at me all the time."

Her words sound right. She's not paralyzed. The stuff didn't flow to her brain and damage it.

The nurse reappears, her arm bent so that her watch faces them. "It's been fifteen minutes," she says.

Spence squeezes Lila's hand, and he touches her face. "Your color looks good," he says. The nurse switches off the TV. Mick and Tina have finished their wild dance, and Spence turns to go. "See you tomorrow," he says happily to his wife.

TWENTY-ONE

*T*HE AIRPLANE rumbles and shakes, the propeller whisking the dirt from the airstrip along the edge of Bill's pasture. Spence holds his ears as Bill urges him to climb in. Bill has an oil-stained satchel with him—probably tools to fix the airplane in case it conks out in midair.

"Buckle up, Spence."

"A lot of good that'll do!" yells Spence, fumbling with the seat belt. He's sitting in front, just behind the nose, and Bill is in back, with the dashboard and controls. This is like horse-and-buggy days, with Spence as the horse.

The takeoff reminds Spence of the stock car races at the fairgrounds. Somewhere, Spence heard that certain racing cars were so fast they had to have a parachute in the back to help them brake, and Spence figured it also kept them from taking off into the air.

The airstrip is bumpy with stubble. The plane buckjumps. "Shake, rattle and roll," Spence sings to himself, feeling a new meaning in that song.

"Here we go!" Bill cries as he points the nose up.

Spence is out of his head to go up with Bill. But it's a joyride. Lila is out of danger, and she will be home on Friday, two days from now. The inspiration came to Spence at 3 A.M. two nights ago. He was dreaming about flying. Enemy planes were spraying the whole ocean with a deadly poison to kill the ships. He was in a Navy fighter, having to decide in a split second whether to live or die.

In the dream, he was brave, as fearless and determined as those pilots in the war. He woke up, shaking with the horror of it, but he thought if you knew you were going to die, you should soar. It's true, he realized. We know we're going to die—sooner or later. He felt he had to go up in Bill's plane then, to prove he could face the possibility of death as bravely as Lila had. Of course, when Lila hears about this little adventure, she'll kill him.

Up in the air, it's a little smoother. The trees shrink, the fences become lines, the highway a ribbon. A school bus creeps along the highway like an inchworm. Then the airplane dips down and flies lower.

"There's your place, Spence." Bill is shouting, but Spence can barely make out his words above the engine's noise.

They are just above the tree line at the back, where Bill's property joins Spence's farm. To the left is the Frost place. They are flying so low Spence can almost spot the marijuana plants he transplanted into Bill's corn. They cross the line and gain altitude. Spence's farm lies before them. The house squats at the far end. It's pale green with brown shingles. The colors blend into the ground and the grass. The corncrib is barely visible through the woods; the barn sags; the old, unused henhouse seems out of place, parked in the center of the orchard.

All his life, Spence has had a conception of the size and shape and contours of his farm, but whenever he studies the topographical map, it seems somewhat off, not exactly what he knows to be true. Now, above the place, seeing it whole, he realizes it resembles the map after all. The twists and turns of the creek surprise him, though he knows every feature by heart—the little plum tree on a triangular island, the stand of scaly-bark hickory near the crossing, the cluster of birches, the honeysuckle vines that

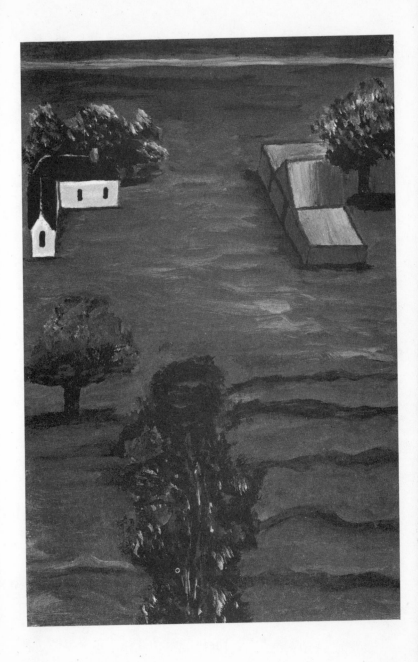

stay green all winter—all the particulars. But up above, they lose definition and become small parts of something much bigger. His children used to paint pictures by the numbers, and now the farm looks to him like a large design for paint-by-the-numbers. The lone oak tree in the middle field was always so majestic, but now it seems small, a weed. The soybeans are a rich green rug. He is reminded of those giant designs the ancient Indians made in South America. He saw them on a special last year and couldn't get them out of his mind. Those Indians could never have seen their designs whole—big frogs and turtles and cats—yet the outlines were laid out perfectly.

The plane rides rough, but Spence doesn't care. He loves it, the way he used to love riding a cranky mule. Below, the calves are frisking through the pasture, running at the sound of the plane. From up above, they are like puppies playing. Spence smiles. He feels great. Calves playing have always been one of his favorite sights. A surprise for Lila forms in his mind. It's time to stock the pond again. He'll slip some large catfish, two- or three-pounders, in with the little fingerlengths. He wants to see the look on her face when she catches such a big one. She won't expect that. He loves to see her when she's happily surprised. She always laughs so big.

Bill turns the plane and swoops back down over the farm. Spence gazes at his land, his seventy-three acres—cut through by the creek and a stand of trees—and suddenly he sees something new about the layout. The woods are like hair, the two creeks like the parting of a woman's legs, the house and barn her nipples. Spence laughs to himself. He has been sending out a cosmic message to alien explorers and didn't even know it. He wonders if Bill has noticed this configuration—probably not, or he would have pointed it out. Spence wonders if he's losing his mind. Maybe seeing the land that way only means that his mind is on Lila coming home.

At the edge of the upper bean field, Spence notices something else—a tinge of brown. The row of trees at the edge of the field is turning brown. Spence realizes the trees must have been burned by the pesticide. Bill must have flown too low over those trees, or failed to turn off the nozzles when he flew over them, or miscalculated the wind and the distance. The leaves are burnt, the trees endangered. Spence feels sickened, and for a moment he can taste those fumes. He notices the tall oak barked up by lightning in an electrical storm last year. It is dead.

Bill banks the plane and Spence's stomach flips. Then Bill straightens out of the turn and heads toward the largest bean field.

"Hey, Spence!" yells Bill.

Spence turns and sees Bill fumbling at the buckles on the satchel he brought. He's not even steering the plane.

"Hey, watch what you're doing!" Spence cries. They're flying over the creek.

But there are no other planes in the air, not even any birds. The plane is up high enough that they won't crash if they hit a bump of air. It feels like driving down an immense, vacant highway—fast and wild because there is nothing to hit. Then from the satchel Bill takes out something familiar—a coffee can. It's that can of seeds. With a grin, Bill snaps the top off the can and pinches some seeds between his finger and thumb. The seeds fly out the window into Spence's soybeans. The first thought that goes through Spence's mind is that he can't strangle Bill here on the spot because they have to get the plane down.

"You crazy idiot!" Spence yells. "You're the one that planted those things in my back field, not the Frost boys!"

"Can't hear you, Spence!" Bill flings out some more

seeds into the field, and the plane zooms on, aiming at some target of its own.

"Stop it. I'll turn you in!"

Cackling with laughter, Bill shouts something Spence can't make out.

Spence yells back, "Well, they won't grow! I'll pull 'em up. You said they need a lot of water." The forecast that morning called for rain. They are due for a good soaking rain, at last. Bill is laughing so much he's paying no attention to flying. They are diving down, heading for the tree line near the barn.

"I'll get you back for this," Spence says. "Set this thing down."

Bill doesn't hear him over the noise of the airplane, but he cuts back on the throttle and the engine seems to stop. He makes a broad swoop just above the trees, then begins turning, heading back, aiming for his airstrip. Below, a herd of Guernseys at the Campbell farm scatters like pieces of a breaking dish.

TWENTY-TWO

"I'M REAL PROUD of you for quitting those cigarettes," says Cat as she combs Lila's curls.

"I'm not coughing anymore. I can't get over that." Lila plucks at her blouse, holding the material out on the right side.

"If you do that, people will notice it more," says Cat, slapping at Lila's hand. "Stop it! Don't do that."

"I can't help it. I feel so self-conscious."

"You look pretty, Mom," says Nancy, who is gathering up Lila's things.

Lila is in pants and a blouse for the first time in two weeks. She feels warmer with something on her legs. Cat is wearing a wrinkled white cotton dress with a dropped waistline and patch pockets. The dress has threads hanging from the hem and Lila wants to snatch at them.

"That dress needs ironing," she says.

"It's supposed to look wrinkled."

Lila laughs. "All those years I spent ironing. I could have just let y'all go out in wrinkled clothes."

"When you get healed up you can start wearing this." Cat holds up the sample prosthesis that woman left.

"The sandbag," Lila says with a grin. It's still in its plastic envelope, with the pamphlets and letters.

"Here, Nancy, let's don't forget this," says Cat, tossing the package to Nancy. Cat lifts Lila's overnight bag and says, "I'll go get the car and bring it around to the front.

[167]

When the nurse gets here to check you out, I guess we'll be ready to go."

Nancy stuffs the package into a paper sack with the water jug, the lotion, the extra Kleenex, all the items that came with the room. She sets the bowl of houseplants from Mattie and Eunice and the basket of artificial violets from Glenda on top of the other things in the sack.

"Do you want to keep these get-well cards, Mom?" she asks.

"Yes. I didn't get to read all the verses."

"People send these cards because they can't think of what to say on their own."

"Well, it's the thought that counts."

But it occurs to Lila how true it is that people either won't or can't come out with their feelings. She appreciates all the cards and the visits from the preacher and the kinfolks and her friends. But there's something wrong, like a wall she's slamming against, like those ocean waves Spence sometimes dreams about. She recalls Rosie clamming up and hiding in herself, for years, where nobody could get to her. Lila married into a family that never knew what to say. Spence is all bottled up and Lee and Nancy are just like him. All those books Nancy reads, and she never has much to say about what she really feels.

Lila says, "You girls sure have been good to me."

"You've been through a lot, Mom," says Nancy, curving her arm around Lila, giving her a tender hug. Lila holds on to Nancy, clutching her close.

"I can't say what I want to say," Lila says. "Maybe I should mail those letters that woman left."

"You don't have to do that, Mom. We understand."

"I never would have thought you all would care this much about me as you've shown," Lila says. "I was always used to doing for y'all, and I never expected you to do for me this way."

"But you deserve it."

It's not words Lila wants. Holding her child is enough, and Nancy is clinging to her, the way Lila once held her baby and read her those meaningless words, those letters from the ocean.

"I guess Spence figured he could get out of coming to the hospital this time," Lila says after Nancy lets go.

"He's busy with a surprise for you," Nancy says, rubbing away a tear. "We offered to come and get you." She glances at her watch. "I'll go find the nurse. This is ridiculous."

It is strange how happy one can be at the worst times. When Spence was on leave from the Navy, before he was sent overseas, Lila felt happy just to be able to see him once more, knowing she might never see him again. Now she feels exhilarated. When the cleaning woman comes in with a cart of equipment and starts talking about her son whose wife suddenly left him, Lila listens eagerly, as if it were the most fascinating story she'd ever heard. The cleaning woman, who is fat, with hair that sprouts out in tufts, says, "His wife left the kitchen in such a mess he had to get me over there to help clean it up! She'd spilled the meat-grease can all over the stove and it was all down in the burners."

The woman begins swabbing the commode with a rag, using her bare hand. Spence would gag if he saw that.

The woman says, "He was in shock. He thought she cared about him, and then she just up and left."

"It can be the other way around too," Lila says happily. "You think your family takes you for granted and then you find out they care a whole lot more than you thought they did."

[169]

"I bet that criminal down the hall don't have no family that's standing behind him," the cleaning woman says.

"Wonder what's wrong with him."

"I heard 'em a-talking and they said he swallowed razor blades, and they went in and didn't get 'em all and had to go back in again."

"Law! And I thought I had troubles!"

"What did they do to you here?" the woman asks, as she swishes her rag in a bucket.

"Oh, I've been through the wringer!" Lila cries. "I've had my tit cut off and my neck gouged out and steeples put in, and I've been stuck with needles all over like a pincushion and put down in cold storage long enough to get pneumonia. And they stole my cigarettes—I ain't had one in two weeks. Did I leave anything out? Oh, and I need new glasses!" Lila pauses to laugh. "I'll be glad when I get out of this place!"

"We sure are going to miss your laugh," a nurse says.

She backs the wheelchair into the room, and Lila sits down. The nurse buckles Lila in, and she feels as if she is in that airplane taking off for Hawaii. As she goes wheeling down the hallway, for some reason she remembers playing ball with the neighbor boys on Sunday afternoons at Uncle Mose's. They liked to pick fights with her, teasing her so much she would beat them up. Her breasts had gone through a short growing season, like something shooting out fast after a long, wet spring. "Been eating sassafras buds, Lila?" they would say, and she would fly into them. She could beat those boys to pieces. She loved that.

TWENTY-THREE

"I CAN'T GO TO BED," Lila protests to Spence that afternoon at home. "I don't care how weak I am. I'm sick of laying."

"You've got to build your strength up," Spence says. He didn't go to the hospital that morning because the man was coming to deliver the fish he had ordered. He stocked the pond with fifty fingerlength catfish and twenty-five crappie and an extra twenty-five two-pound catfish, barely finishing before Cat and Nancy got home with Lila. The girls have left but will be back soon. Lila was mad at him for not coming to the hospital to get her. "Was a ball game on?" she accused him. He feels clumsy and nervous with her at home, as if she must be expecting more than just ordinary life now, after her ordeal.

Lila has just discovered the state of the refrigerator and she is ready to clean his plow. "You didn't even touch any of those vegetables I cooked! And I reckon that ham's ruined."

"No, it's not! We eat on it and Lee took some ham and tater salad and half of a cake. And Nancy and Cat eat some when they were here. There was too much grub—we couldn't make away with all of it."

"Who made this coconut pie?"

"I don't remember."

"I love coconut pie better than anything, but that one looks like a tire gone flat."

She opens the back door and steps onto the deck.

"Where are you going?"

"Out here in the sun. I'm glad I'm back here where I can get warm. I've been cold as a well-digger's butt for two weeks."

"We could go to Florida," he says, following her. "Back to the Everglades."

"No, I ain't never going down there again! That's where I got sick."

"The sun was warm there. It dried out my sinuses and I didn't have any trouble breathing."

"It made me dizzy," she says.

Abraham jumps onto the deck from the milkhouse roof, landing at Lila's feet. He immediately rolls over onto his back, curling his paws and looking at her upside down.

"Well, there's my youngun!" cries Lila, sitting down in the slatted deck chair. "Come here, baby!"

The cat jumps into her lap, purring, and she hugs him. He wriggles away and turns circles in her lap, then jumps down again and rolls over.

"That means he's happy to see me," says Lila proudly. "Did you miss me, Abraham? Law, you've fallen off. You ain't nothing but skin and bones."

"He's been busy," Spence says. "Catching grasshoppers and mice. I see him out in the beans early in the dew, and he comes in looking like a drownded rat."

"He loves them mouses, don't you, Abraham," Lila baby-talks.

The night before, Oscar woke Spence up, barking ferociously at something. From the thrilling sounds of the barks, Spence knew Oscar was excited over an animal, not a human intruder. He wondered if it could be the wildcat.

As he lay awake, he thought with pleasure about the fish he was going to put in the pond. He remembered that the first time he ever laid eyes on Lila was at her uncle's pond. She was fishing. Her bare legs were long, like a crane's. Now he's nervous about his surprise and longs to tell her about it, but he has to save it.

Suddenly Lila is down the steps and striding along the driveway. He has to hurry to catch up with her.

"Where do you think you're going? You're not able to be going out for a hike."

"I'm going to check on the garden," she says, picking up speed. "I just want to see it."

He walks along with her, her legs working fast—her dancing legs. Abraham trots along with them, his tail a bottle brush sticking straight up. Oscar joins them then, scooting out from his dust hole under the car. When Lila arrived from the hospital, they had to hold him to keep him from jumping on her.

"Them vines are firing up," she says.

Despite the recent rain, the garden is drying up in the midsummer heat. Some of the Kentucky Wonder vines have dried up, and the corn is starting to turn brown, but the field peas are thriving among the corn. Lila plunges into the garden, between the okra and the peppers, and leans over to check a pepper.

"That one's ready to pick," she says, snapping it off. She straightens up and twists off a sharp-pointed okra from a stalk. Suddenly Spence realizes she is yanking up weeds and fishing out dirty, stunted cucumbers from beneath dying vines. She snaps off another fuzzy okra, grabs tomatoes.

"Check that corn, Spence. I bet it's hard. It's overgrown, but the field peas look nice."

"What do you think you're doing!" cries Spence. "You ain't got no business out here working in the garden."

"The girls didn't do a thing about those beans like I told 'em to."

"You don't have no gloves on! The doctor said you couldn't handle dirt without gloves. You might get a sore infected and then your arm'll fall off without those lymph nodes."

Lila's hands are full of vegetables, and she cradles them in her left arm. Beads of sweat have popped out on her forehead. She's smiling. "Look at that punkin, would you!" she cries, pointing. "That's going to be the biggest one we ever had! Well, I'll say!" She lets out a big laugh. "That's going to be one for Cinderella!"

Spence stands there, while the sweat on her forehead changes from drops to a moist, smooth layer. Her face is rosy, all the furrows and marks thrusting upward with her smile the way the okra on the stalk reach upward to the sun. Her face is as pretty as freshly plowed ground, and the scar on her neck is like a gully washed out but filling in now. He thinks about the way the soybeans are going to grow those little islands of marijuana, like lacy palm trees waving above the beans, hummocks like those in the Everglades, mounds like breasts. And then he imagines the look on Lila's face when she catches one of those oversized catfish he has slipped into the pond.

"These cucumbers is ready for pickling," Lila says.

"You sure were gone an awful long time," Spence says, his lips puckering up. "I thought to my soul you never *was* going to come home." He takes some of the vegetables from her. "I've got a cucumber that needs pickling," he says.

The way she laughs is the moment he has been waiting for. She rares her head back and laughs steadily, her throat working and her eyes flashing. Her cough catches her finally and slows her down, but her face is dancing like pond water in the rain, all unsettled and stirring with aroused possibility.

BOBBIE ANN MASON is the author of numerous short stories and the novels *Feather Crowns* and *In Country*. A collection of her short stories, *Midnight Magic: Selected Stories of Bobbie Ann Mason*, is available from Ecco. Mason lives in her native Kentucky.

EICHMANN IN JERUSALEM

Also by Hannah Arendt

ON VIOLENCE

MEN IN DARK TIMES

* ON REVOLUTION

* BETWEEN PAST AND FUTURE

THE HUMAN CONDITION

THE ORIGINS OF TOTALITARIANISM

* Available in a Viking Compass edition

REVISED AND ENLARGED EDITION

EICHMANN
in Jerusalem

A REPORT
ON THE BANALITY OF EVIL

BY

Hannah Arendt

THE VIKING PRESS
NEW YORK

Originally published in 1963
Revised and enlarged edition published in 1965 by
The Viking Press, Inc., 625 Madison Avenue, New York, N.Y. 10022
Viking Compass edition issued in 1965

Thirteenth printing March 1973

Published simultaneously in Canada by
The Macmillan Company of Canada Limited

SBN 670-29038-6 (hardbound)
SBN 670-00165-1 (paperbound)

Library of Congress catalog card number: 64-25532
Printed in U.S.A.

The contents of the original edition of this book, in slightly abbreviated
and otherwise slightly different form, originally appeared as a series of
articles in *The New Yorker*.

Note to the Reader

This is a revised and enlarged edition of the book which first appeared in May, 1963. I covered the Eichmann trial at Jerusalem in 1961 for *The New Yorker*, where this account, slightly abbreviated, was originally published in February and March, 1963. The book was written in the summer and fall of 1962, and finished in November of that year during my stay as a Fellow of the Center for Advanced Studies at Wesleyan University.

The revisions for this edition concern about a dozen technical errors, none of which has any bearing on the analysis or argument of the original text. The factual record of the period in question has not yet been established in all its details, and there are certain matters on which an informed guess will probably never be superseded by completely reliable information. Thus the total number of Jewish victims of the Final Solution is a guess—between four and a half and six million—that has never been verified, and the same is true of the totals for each of the countries concerned. Some new material, especially on Holland, came to light after the publication of this book, but none of it was important for the event as a whole.

Most of the additions are also of a technical nature, clarifying a particular point, introducing new facts, or, in some instances, quotations from different sources. These new sources have been added to the Bibliography and are discussed in the new Postscript, which deals with the controversy that followed the original publication. Apart from the Postscript, the only non-technical addition concerns the German anti-Hitler conspiracy of July 20, 1944, which I had mentioned only incidentally in the original version. The character of the book as a whole is completely unaltered.

Thanks are due to Richard and Clara Winston for their help in preparing the text of the Postscript for this edition.

HANNAH ARENDT

June, 1964

O Germany—
Hearing the speeches that ring from your house,
one laughs.
But whoever sees you, reaches for his knife.

—BERTOLT BRECHT

Contents

Note to the Reader   v

I: The House of Justice   3

II: The Accused   21

III: An Expert on the Jewish Question   36

IV: The First Solution: Expulsion   56

V: The Second Solution: Concentration   68

VI: The Final Solution: Killing   83

VII: The Wannsee Conference, or Pontius Pilate   112

VIII: Duties of a Law-Abiding Citizen   135

IX: Deportations from the Reich—Germany, Austria, and the Protectorate   151

X: Deportations from Western Europe—France, Belgium, Holland, Denmark, Italy   162

XI: Deportations from the Balkans—Yugoslavia, Bulgaria, Greece, Rumania   181

XII: Deportations from Central Europe—Hungary and Slovakia   194

XIII: The Killing Centers in the East   206

XIV: Evidence and Witnesses   220

XV: Judgment, Appeal, and Execution   234

Epilogue   253

Postscript   280

Bibliography   299

Index   304

EICHMANN IN JERUSALEM

I: *The House of Justice*

"*Beth Hamishpath*"—the House of Justice: these words shouted by the court usher at the top of his voice make us jump to our feet as they announce the arrival of the three judges, who, bareheaded, in black robes, walk into the courtroom from a side entrance to take their seats on the highest tier of the raised platform. Their long table, soon to be covered with innumerable books and more than fifteen hundred documents, is flanked at each end by the court stenographers. Directly below the judges are the translators, whose services are needed for direct exchanges between the defendant or his counsel and the court; otherwise, the German-speaking accused party, like almost everyone else in the audience, follows the Hebrew proceedings through the simultaneous radio transmission, which is excellent in French, bearable in English, and sheer comedy, frequently incomprehensible, in German. (In view of the scrupulous fairness of all technical arrangements for the trial, it is among the minor mysteries of the new State of Israel that, with its high percentage of German-born people, it was unable to find an adequate translator into the only language the accused and his counsel could understand. For the old prejudice against German Jews, once very pronounced in Israel, is no longer strong enough to account for it. Remains as explication the even older and still very powerful "Vitamin P," as the Israelis call protection in government circles and the bureaucracy.) One tier below the translators, facing each other and hence with their profiles turned to the audience, we see the glass booth of the accused and the witness box. Finally, on the bottom tier, with their backs to the audience, are the prosecutor with his staff of four assistant attorneys, and the counsel for the defense, who during the first weeks is accompanied by an assistant.

At no time is there anything theatrical in the conduct of the judges. Their walk is unstudied, their sober and intense attention, visibly stiffening under the impact of grief as they listen to the tales of suffering, is natural; their impatience with the prosecutor's attempt to drag out these hearings forever is spontaneous and refreshing, their attitude to the defense perhaps a shade over-polite, as though they had always in mind that "Dr. Servatius stood almost alone in this strenuous battle, in an unfamiliar environment," their manner toward the accused always beyond reproach. They are so obviously three good and honest men that one is not surprised that none of them yields to the greatest temptation to playact in this setting—that of pretending that they, all three born and educated in Germany, must wait for the Hebrew translation. Moshe Landau, the presiding judge, hardly ever withholds his answer until the translator has done his work, and he frequently interferes in the translation, correcting and improving, evidently grateful for this bit of distraction from an otherwise grim business. Months later, during the cross-examination of the accused, he will even lead his colleagues to use their German mother tongue in the dialogue with Eichmann—a proof, if proof were still needed, of his remarkable independence of current public opinion in Israel.

There is no doubt from the very beginning that it is Judge Landau who sets the tone, and that he is doing his best, his very best, to prevent this trial from becoming a show trial under the influence of the prosecutor's love of showmanship. Among the reasons he cannot always succeed is the simple fact that the proceedings happen on a stage before an audience, with the usher's marvelous shout at the beginning of each session producing the effect of the rising curtain. Whoever planned this auditorium in the newly built *Beth Ha'am*, the House of the People (now surrounded by high fences, guarded from roof to cellar by heavily armed police, and with a row of wooden barracks in the front courtyard in which all comers are expertly frisked), had a theater in mind, complete with orchestra and gallery, with proscenium and stage, and with side doors for the actors' entrance. Clearly, this courtroom is not a bad place for the show trial David Ben-Gurion, Prime Minister of Israel, had in mind when he decided to have Eichmann kidnaped in Argentina and brought to the District Court of Jerusalem to stand trial for his role in the "final solution of the Jewish question." And Ben-Gurion, rightly called the "architect of the state," remains the invisible stage manager of the proceedings. Not once does he attend a session; in the courtroom he speaks with the voice of Gideon Hausner, the Attorney General, who, representing the government, does his best, his very best, to obey his master. And if, fortunately, his best often turns out not to be good enough, the reason is that the trial is presided over by someone who serves Justice as faithfully as Mr. Hausner serves the State of Israel. Justice demands that the accused be prosecuted, defended, and judged, and that all the other questions of seemingly greater import—of "How could it happen?" and "Why did it happen?," of "Why the Jews?" and "Why the Germans?," of "What was the role of other nations?" and "What was the extent of co-responsibility on the side of the Allies?," of "How could the Jews through their own leaders cooperate in their own destruction?" and "Why did they go to their death like lambs to the slaughter?"—be left in abeyance. Justice insists on the importance of Adolf Eichmann, son of Karl Adolf Eichmann, the man in the glass booth built for his protection: medium-sized, slender, middle-aged, with receding hair, ill-fitting teeth, and nearsighted eyes, who throughout the trial keeps craning his scraggy neck toward the bench (not once does he face the audience), and who desperately and for the most part successfully maintains his self-control despite the nervous tic to which his mouth must have become subject long before this trial started. On trial are his deeds, not the sufferings of the Jews, not the German people or mankind, not even anti-Semitism and racism.

And Justice, though perhaps an "abstraction" for those of Mr. Ben-Gurion's turn of mind, proves to be a much sterner master than the Prime Minister with all his power. The latter's rule, as Mr. Hausner is not slow in demonstrating, is permissive; it permits the prosecutor to give press-conferences and interviews for television during the trial (the American program, sponsored by the Glickman Corporation, is constantly interrupted—business as usual—by real-estate advertising), and even "spontaneous" outbursts to reporters in the court building—he is sick of cross-examining Eichmann, who answers all questions with lies; it permits frequent side glances into the audience, and the theatrics characteristic of a more than ordinary vanity, which finally achieves its triumph in the White House with a compliment on "a job well done" by the President of the United States. Justice does not permit anything of the sort; it demands seclusion, it permits sorrow rather than anger, and it prescribes the most careful abstention from all the nice pleasures of putting oneself in the limelight. Judge Landau's visit to this country shortly after the trial was not publicized, except among the Jewish organizations for which it was undertaken.

Yet no matter how consistently the judges shunned the limelight, there they were, seated at the top of the raised platform, facing the audience as from the stage in a play. The audience was supposed to represent the whole world, and in the first few weeks it indeed consisted chiefly of newspapermen and magazine writers who had flocked to Jerusalem from the four corners of the earth. They were to watch a spectacle as sensational as the Nuremberg Trials, only this time "the tragedy of Jewry as a whole was to be the central concern." For "if we shall charge [Eichmann] also with crimes against non-Jews, . . . this is" not because he committed them, but, surprisingly, *"because we make no ethnic distinctions."* Certainly a remarkable sentence for a prosecutor to utter in his opening speech; it proved to be the key sentence in the case for the prosecution. For this case was built on what the Jews had suffered, not on what Eichmann had done. And, according to Mr. Hausner, this distinction would be immaterial, because "there was only one man who had been concerned almost entirely with the Jews, whose business had been their destruction, whose role in the establishment of the iniquitous regime had been limited to them. That was Adolf Eichmann." Was it not logical to bring before the court all the facts of Jewish suffering (which, of course, were never in dispute) and then look for evidence which in one way or another would connect Eichmann with what had happened? The Nuremberg Trials, where the defendants had been "indicted for crimes against the members of various nations," had left the Jewish tragedy out of account for the simple reason that Eichmann had not been there.

Did Mr. Hausner really believe the Nuremberg Trials would

have paid greater attention to the fate of the Jews if Eichmann
had been in the dock? Hardly. Like almost everybody else in
Israel, he believed that only a Jewish court could render justice
to Jews, and that it was the business of Jews to sit in judgment
on their enemies. Hence the almost universal hostility in Israel
to the mere mention of an international court which would have
indicted Eichmann, not for crimes "against the Jewish people,"
but for crimes against mankind committed on the body of the
Jewish people. Hence the strange boast: "We make no ethnic
distinctions," which sounded less strange in Israel, where rabbinical law rules the personal status of Jewish citizens, with the
result that no Jew can marry a non-Jew; marriages concluded
abroad are recognized, but children of mixed marriages are
legally bastards (children of Jewish parentage born out of wed-
lock are legitimate), and if one happens to have a non-Jewish
mother he can neither be married nor buried. The outrage in
this state of affairs has become more acute since 1953, when a
sizable portion of jurisdiction in matters of family law was
handed over to the secular courts. Women can now inherit
property and in general enjoy equal status with men. Hence it
is hardly respect for the faith or the power of the fanatically
religious minority that prevents the government of Israel from
substituting secular jurisdiction for rabbinical law in matters of
marriage and divorce. Israeli citizens, religious and nonreligious,
seem agreed upon the desirability of having a law which pro-
hibits intermarriage, and it is chiefly for this reason—as Israeli
officials outside the courtroom were willing to admit—that they
are also agreed upon the undesirability of a written constitution
in which such a law would embarrassingly have to be spelled
out. ("The argument against civil marriage is that it would split
the House of Israel, and would also separate Jews of this country
from Jews of the Diaspora," as Philip Gillon recently put it in
Jewish Frontier.) Whatever the reasons, there certainly was
something breathtaking in the naïveté with which the prosecution
denounced the infamous Nuremberg Laws of 1935, which had
prohibited intermarriage and sexual intercourse between Jews
and Germans. The better informed among the correspondents
were well aware of the irony, but they did not mention it in
their reports. This, they figured, was not the time to tell the

Jews what was wrong with the laws and institutions of their own country.

If the audience at the trial was to be the world and the play the huge panorama of Jewish sufferings, the reality was falling short of expectations and purposes. The journalists remained faithful for not much more than two weeks, after which the audience changed drastically. It was now supposed to consist of Israelis, of those who were too young to know the story or, as in the case of Oriental Jews, had never been told it. The trial was supposed to show them what it meant to live among non-Jews, to convince them that only in Israel could a Jew be safe and live an honorable life. (For correspondents, the lesson was spelled out in a little booklet on Israel's legal system, which was handed to the press. Its author, Doris Lankin, cites a Supreme Court decision whereby two fathers who had "abducted their children and brought them to Israel" were directed to send them back to their mothers who, living abroad, had a legal right to their custody. And this, adds the author—no less proud of such strict legality than Mr. Hausner of his willingness to prosecute murder even when the victims were non-Jews— "despite the fact that to send the children back to maternal custody and care would be committing them to waging an unequal struggle against the hostile elements in the Diaspora.") But in this audience there were hardly any young people, and it did not consist of Israelis as distinguished from Jews. It was filled with "survivors," with middle-aged and elderly people, immigrants from Europe, like myself, who knew by heart all there was to know, and who were in no mood to learn any lessons and certainly did not need this trial to draw their own conclusions. As witness followed witness and horror was piled upon horror, they sat there and listened in public to stories they would hardly have been able to endure in private, when they would have had to face the storyteller. And the more "the calamity of the Jewish people in this generation" unfolded and the more grandiose Mr. Hausner's rhetoric became, the paler and more ghostlike became the figure in the glass booth, and no finger-wagging: "And there sits the monster responsible for all this," could shout him back to life.

It was precisely the play aspect of the trial that collapsed under the weight of the hair-raising atrocities. A trial resembles a play in that both begin and end with the doer, not with the victim. A show trial needs even more urgently than an ordinary trial a limited and well-defined outline of what was done and how it was done. In the center of a trial can only be the one who did—in this respect, he is like the hero in the play—and if he suffers, he must suffer for what he has done, not for what he has caused others to suffer. No one knew this better than the presiding judge, before whose eyes the trial began to degenerate into a bloody show, "a rudderless ship tossed about on the waves." But if his efforts to prevent this were often defeated, the defeat was, strangely, in part the fault of the defense, which hardly ever rose to challenge any testimony, no matter how irrelevant and immaterial it might be. *Dr.* Servatius, as everybody invariably addressed him, was a bit bolder when it came to the submission of documents, and the most impressive of his rare interventions occurred when the prosecution introduced as evidence the diaries of Hans Frank, former Governor General of Poland and one of the major war criminals hanged at Nuremberg. "I have only one question. Is the name Adolf Eichmann, the name of the accused, mentioned in those twenty-nine volumes [in fact, there were thirty-eight]? . . . The name Adolf Eichmann is not mentioned in all those twenty-nine volumes. . . . Thank you, no more questions."

Thus, the trial never became a play, but the show Ben-Gurion had had in mind to begin with did take place, or, rather, the "lessons" he thought should be taught to Jews and Gentiles, to Israelis and Arabs, in short, to the whole world. These lessons to be drawn from an identical show were meant to be different for the different recipients. Ben-Gurion had outlined them before the trial started, in a number of articles designed to explain why Israel had kidnaped the accused. There was the lesson to the non-Jewish world: "We want to establish before the nations of the world how millions of people, because they happened to be Jews, and one million babies, because they happened to be Jewish babies, were murdered by the Nazis." Or, in the words of *Davar*, the organ of Mr. Ben-Gurion's Mapai party: "Let world opinion know this, that not only Nazi Germany was responsible for the destruction of six million Jews of Europe." Hence, again in Ben-Gurion's own words, "We want the nations of the world to know . . . and they should be ashamed." The Jews in the Diaspora were to remember how Judaism, "four thousand years old, with its spiritual creations and its ethical strivings, its Messianic aspirations," had always faced "a hostile world," how the Jews had degenerated until they went to their death like sheep, and how only the establishment of a Jewish state had enabled Jews to hit back, as Israelis had done in the War of Independence, in the Suez adventure, and in the almost daily incidents on Israel's unhappy borders. And if the Jews outside Israel had to be shown the difference between Israeli heroism and Jewish submissive meekness, there was a lesson for those inside Israel too: "the generation of Israelis who have grown up since the holocaust" were in danger of losing their ties with the Jewish people and, by implication, with their own history. "It is necessary that our youth remember what happened to the Jewish people. We want them to know the most tragic facts in our history." Finally, one of the motives in bringing Eichmann to trial was "to ferret out other Nazis— for example, the connection between the Nazis and some Arab rulers."

If these had been the only justifications for bringing Adolf Eichmann to the District Court of Jerusalem, the trial would have been a failure on most counts. In some respects, the lessons were superfluous, and in others positively misleading. Anti-Semitism has been discredited, thanks to Hitler, perhaps not forever but certainly for the time being, and this not because the Jews have become more popular all of a sudden but because, in Mr. Ben-Gurion's own words, most people have "realized that in our day the gas chamber and the soap factory are what anti-Semitism may lead to." Equally superfluous was the lesson to the Jews in the Diaspora, who hardly needed the great catastrophe in which one-third of their people perished to be convinced of the world's hostility. Not only has their conviction of the eternal and ubiquitous nature of anti-Semitism been the most potent ideological factor in the Zionist movement since the Dreyfus Affair; it was also the cause of the otherwise inexplicable readiness of the German Jewish community to negotiate with the Nazi authorities during the early stages of the regime.

(Needless to say, these negotiations were separated by an abyss from the later collaboration of the *Judenräte*. No moral questions were involved yet, only a political decision whose "realism" was debatable: "concrete" help, thus the argument ran, was better than "abstract" denunciations. It was *Realpolitik* without Machiavellian overtones, and its dangers came to light years later, after the outbreak of the war, when these daily contacts between the Jewish organizations and the Nazi bureaucracy made it so much easier for the Jewish functionaries to cross the abyss between helping Jews to escape and helping the Nazis to deport them.) It was this conviction which produced the dangerous inability of the Jews to distinguish between friend and foe; and German Jews were not the only ones to underestimate their enemies because they somehow thought that all Gentiles were alike. If Prime Minister Ben-Gurion, to all practical purposes the head of the Jewish State, meant to strengthen this kind of "Jewish consciousness," he was ill advised; for a change in this mentality is actually one of the indispensable prerequisites for Israeli statehood, which by definition has made of the Jews a people among peoples, a nation among nations, a state among states, depending now on a plurality which no longer permits the age-old and, unfortunately, religiously anchored dichotomy of Jews and Gentiles.

The contrast between Israeli heroism and the submissive meekness with which Jews went to their death—arriving on time at the transportation points, walking on their own feet to the places of execution, digging their own graves, undressing and making neat piles of their clothing, and lying down side by side to be shot—seemed a fine point, and the prosecutor, asking witness after witness, "Why did you not protest?," "Why did you board the train?," "Fifteen thousand people were standing there and hundreds of guards facing you—why didn't you revolt and charge and attack?," was elaborating it for all it was worth. But the sad truth of the matter is that the point was ill taken, for no non-Jewish group or people had behaved differently. Sixteen years ago, while still under the direct impact of the events, David Rousset, a former inmate of Buchenwald, described what we know happened in all concentration camps: "The triumph of the S.S. demands that the tortured victim allow himself to be led to the noose without protesting, that he renounce and abandon himself to the point of ceasing to affirm his identity. And it is not for nothing. It is not gratuitously, out of sheer sadism, that the S.S. men desire his defeat. They know that the system which succeeds in destroying its victim before he mounts the scaffold . . . is incomparably the best for keeping a whole people in slavery. In submission. Nothing is more terrible than these processions of human beings going like dummies to their deaths" (*Les Jours de notre mort*, 1947). The court received no answer to this cruel and silly question, but one could easily have found an answer had he permitted his imagination to dwell for a few minutes on the fate of those Dutch Jews who in 1941, in the old Jewish quarter of Amsterdam, dared to attack a German security police detachment. Four hundred and thirty Jews were arrested in reprisal and they were literally tortured to death, first in Buchenwald and then in the Austrian camp of Mauthausen. For months on end they died a thousand deaths, and every single one of them would have envied his brethren in Auschwitz and even in Riga and Minsk. There exist many things considerably worse than death, and the S.S. saw to it that none of them was ever very far from their victims' minds and imagination. In this respect, perhaps even more significantly than in others, the deliberate attempt at the trial to tell only the Jewish side of the story distorted the truth, even the Jewish truth. The glory of the uprising in the Warsaw ghetto and the heroism of the few others who fought back lay precisely in their having refused the comparatively easy death the Nazis offered them—before the firing squad or in the gas chamber. And the witnesses in Jerusalem who testified to resistance and rebellion, to "the small place [it had] in the history of the holocaust," confirmed once more the fact that only the very young had been capable of taking "the decision that we cannot go and be slaughtered like sheep."

In one respect, Mr. Ben-Gurion's expectations for the trial were not altogether disappointed; it did indeed become an important instrument for ferreting out other Nazis and criminals, but not in the Arab countries, which had openly offered refuge to hundreds of them. The Grand Mufti's connections with the Nazis during the war were no secret; he had hoped they would help him in the implementation of some "final solution" in the Near East. Hence, newspapers in Damascus and Beirut, in Cairo and Jordan, did not hide their sympathy for Eichmann or their regret that he "had not finished the job"; a broadcast from Cairo on the day the trial opened even injected a slightly anti-German note into its comments, complaining that there was not "a single incident in which one German plane flew over one Jewish settlement and dropped one bomb on it throughout the last world war." That Arab nationalists have been in sympathy with Nazism is notorious, their reasons are obvious, and neither Ben-Gurion nor this trial was needed "to ferret them out"; they never were in hiding. The trial revealed only that all rumors about Eichmann's connection with Haj Amin el Husseini, the former Mufti of Jerusalem, were unfounded. (He had been introduced to the Mufti during an official reception, along with all other departmental heads.) The Mufti had been in close contact with the German Foreign Office and with Himmler, but this was nothing new.

If Ben-Gurion's remark about "the connection between Nazis and some Arab rulers" was pointless, his failure to mention present-day West Germany in this context was surprising. Of course, it was reassuring to hear that Israel does "not hold Adenauer responsible for Hitler," and that "for us a decent German, although he belongs to the same nation that twenty years ago helped to murder millions of Jews, is a decent human being." (There was no mention of decent Arabs.) The German Federal Republic, although it has not yet recognized the State of Israel—presumably out of fear that the Arab countries might recognize Ulbricht's Germany—has paid seven hundred and thirty-seven million dollars in reparation to Israel during the last ten years; these payments will soon come to an end, and Israel is now trying to negotiate a long-term loan from West Germany. Hence, the relationship between the two countries, and particularly the personal relationship between Ben-Gurion and Adenauer, has been quite good, and if, as an aftermath of the trial, some deputies in the Knesset, the Israeli Parliament, succeeded in imposing certain restraints on the cultural-exchange program with West Germany, this certainly was neither foreseen nor hoped for by Ben-Gurion. It is more noteworthy that he had not foreseen, or did not care to mention, that Eichmann's capture would trigger the first serious effort made by Germany to bring to trial at least those who were directly implicated in murder. The Central Agency for the Investigation of Nazi Crimes, belatedly founded by the West German state in 1958 and headed by Prosecutor Erwin Schüle, had run into all kinds of difficulties, caused partly by the unwillingness of German witnesses to cooperate and partly by the unwillingness of the local courts to prosecute on the basis of the material sent them from the Central Agency. Not that the trial in Jersusalem produced any important new evidence of the kind needed for the discovery of Eichmann's associates; but the news of Eichmann's sensational capture and of the impending trial had sufficient impact to persuade the local courts to use Mr. Schüle's findings, and to overcome the native reluctance to do anything about "murderers in our midst" by the time-honored means of posting rewards for the capture of well-known criminals.

The results were amazing. Seven months after Eichmann's arrival in Jerusalem—and four months before the opening of the trial—Richard Baer, successor to Rudolf Höss as Commandant of Auschwitz, could finally be arrested. In rapid succession, most of the members of the so-called Eichmann Commando—Franz Novak, who lived as a printer in Austria; Dr. Otto Hunsche, who had settled as a lawyer in West Germany; Hermann Krumey, who had become a druggist; Gustav Richter, former "Jewish adviser" in Rumania; and Willi Zöpf, who had filled the same post in Amsterdam— were arrested also; although evidence against them had been published in Germany years before, in books and magazine articles, not one of them had found it necessary to live under an assumed name. For the first time since the close of the war, German newspapers were full of reports on the trials of Nazi criminals, all of them mass murderers (after May, 1960, the month of Eichmann's capture, only first-degree murder could be prosecuted; all other offenses were wiped out by the statute of limitations, which is twenty years for murder), and the reluctance of the local courts to prosecute these crimes showed itself only in the fantastically lenient sentences meted out to the accused. (Thus, Dr. Otto Bradfisch, of the *Einsatzgruppen,* the mobile killing units of the S.S. in the East, was sentenced to ten years of hard labor for the killing of fifteen thousand Jews; Dr. Otto Hunsche, Eichmann's legal expert and personally responsible for a last-minute deportation of some twelve hundred Hungarian Jews, of whom at least six hundred were killed, received a sentence of five years of hard labor; and Joseph Lechthaler, who had "liquidated" the Jewish inhabitants of Slutsk and Smolevichi in Russia, was sentenced to three years and six months.) Among the new arrests were people of great prominence under the Nazis, most of whom had already been denazified by the German courts. One of them was S.S. General Karl Wolff, former chief of Himmler's personal staff, who, according to a document submitted in 1946 at Nuremberg, had greeted "with particular joy" the news that "for two weeks now a train has been carrying, every day, five thousand members of the Chosen People" from Warsaw to Treblinka, one of the Eastern killing centers. Another was Wilhelm Koppe, who had at first managed the gassing in Chelmno and then become successor to Friedrich-Wilhelm Krüger in Poland. One of the most prominent among the Higher S.S. Leaders whose task it had been to make Poland *judenrein,* in postwar Germany Koppe was director of a chocolate factory. Harsh sentences were occasionally meted out, but were even less reassuring when they went to such offenders as Erich von dem Bach-Zelewski, former General of the Higher S.S. and Police Leader Corps. He had been tried in 1961 for his participation in the Röhm rebellion in 1934 and sentenced to three and one half years; he was then indicted again in 1962 for the killing of six German Communists in 1933, tried before a jury in Nuremberg, and sentenced to life. Neither indictment mentioned that Bach-Zelewski had been antipartisan chief on the Eastern front or that he had participated in the Jewish massacres at Minsk and Mogilev, in White Russia. Should German courts, on the pretext that war crimes are no crimes, make "ethnic distinctions"? Or is it possible that what was an unusually harsh sentence, at least in German postwar courts, was arrived at because Bach-Zelewski was among the very few who actually had suffered a nervous breakdown after the mass killings, had tried to protect Jews from the *Ein-satzgruppen*, and had testified for the prosecution at Nuremberg? He was also the only one in this category who in 1952 had denounced himself publicly for mass murder, but he was never prosecuted for it.

There is little hope that things will change now, even though the Adenauer administration has been forced to weed out of the judiciary more than a hundred and forty judges and prosecutors, along with many police officers with more than ordinarily compromising pasts, and to dismiss Wolfgang Immerwahr Fränkel, the chief prosecutor of the Federal Supreme Court, because, his middle name notwithstanding, he had been less than candid when asked about his Nazi past. It has been estimated that of the eleven thousand five hundred judges in the *Bundesrepublik*, five thousand were active in the courts under the Hitler regime. In November, 1962, shortly after the purging of the judiciary and six months after Eichmann's name had disappeared from the news, the long awaited trial of Martin Fellenz took place at Flensburg in an almost empty courtroom. The former Higher S.S. and Police Leader, who had been a prominent member of the Free Democratic Party in Adenauer's Germany, was arrested in June, 1960, a few weeks after Eichmann's capture. He was accused of participation in and partial responsibility for the murder of forty thousand Jews in Poland. After more than six weeks of detailed testimony, the prosecutor demanded the maximum penalty—a life sentence of hard labor. And the court sentenced Fellenz to four years, two and a half of which he had already served while waiting in jail to be tried. Be that as it may, there is no doubt that the Eichmann trial had its most far-reaching consequences in Germany. The attitude of the German people toward their own past, which all experts on the German question had puzzled over for fifteen years, could hardly have been more clearly demonstrated: they themselves did not much care one way or the other, and did not particularly mind the presence of murderers at large in the country, since none of them were likely to commit murder of their own free will; however, if world opinion—or rather, what the Germans called *das Ausland*, collecting all countries outside Germany into a singular noun—became obstinate and demanded that these people be punished, they were perfectly willing to oblige, at least up to a point.

Chancellor Adenauer had foreseen embarrassment and voiced his apprehension that the trial would "stir up again all the horrors" and produce a new wave of anti-German feeling throughout the world, as indeed it did. During the ten months that Israel needed to prepare the trial, Germany was busy bracing herself against its predictable results by showing an unprecedented zeal for searching out and prosecuting Nazi criminals within the country. But at no time did either the German authorities or any significant segment of public opinion demand Eichmann's extradition, which seemed the obvious move, since every sovereign state is jealous of its right to sit in judgment on its own offenders. (The official position of the Adenauer government that this was not possible because there existed no extradition treaty between Israel and Germany is not valid; that meant only that Israel could not have been forced to extradite. Fritz Bauer, Attorney General of Hessen, saw the point and applied to the federal government in Bonn to start extradition proceedings. But Mr. Bauer's feelings in this matter were the feelings of a German Jew, and they were not shared by German public opinion; his application was not only refused by Bonn, it was hardly noticed and remained totally unsupported. Another argument against extradition, offered by the observers the West German government sent to Jerusalem, was that Germany had abolished capital punishment and hence was unable to mete out the sentence Eichmann deserved. In view of the leniency shown by German courts to Nazi mass murderers, it is difficult not to suspect bad faith in this objection. Surely, the greatest political hazard of an Eichmann trial in Germany would have been acquittal for lack of *mens rea,* as J. J. Jansen pointed out in the *Rheinischer Merkur* [August 11, 1961].)

There is another, more delicate, and politically more relevant, side to this matter. It is one thing to ferret out criminals and murderers from their hiding places, and it is another thing to find them prominent and flourishing in the public realm—to encounter innumerable men in the federal and state administrations and, generally, in *public* office whose careers had bloomed under the Hitler regime. True, if the Adenauer administration had been too sensitive about employing officials with a compromising Nazi past, there might have been no administration at all. For the truth is, of course, the exact opposite of Dr. Adenauer's assertion that only "a relatively small percentage" of Germans had been Nazis, and that a "great majority [had been] happy to help their Jewish fellow-citizens when they could." (At least one German newspaper, the *Frankfurter Rundschau*, asked itself the obvious question, long overdue— why so many people who must have known, for instance, the record of the chief prosecutor had kept silent—and then came up with the even more obvious answer: "Because they themselves felt incriminated.") The logic of the Eichmann trial, as Ben-Gurion conceived of it, with its stress on general issues to the detriment of legal niceties, would have demanded exposure of the complicity of all German offices and authorities in the Final Solution—of all civil servants in the state ministries, of the regular armed forces, with their General Staff, of the judiciary, and of the business world. But although the prosecution as conducted by Mr. Hausner went as far afield as to put witness after witness on the stand who testified to things that, while gruesome and true enough, had no or only the slightest connection with the deeds of the accused, it carefully avoided touching upon this highly explosive matter—upon the almost ubiquitous complicity, which had stretched far beyond the ranks of Party membership. (There were widespread rumors prior to the trial that Eichmann had named "several hundred prominent personalities of the Federal Republic as his accomplices," but these rumors were not true. In his opening speech, Mr. Hausner mentioned Eichmann's "accomplices in the crime who were neither gangsters nor men of the underworld," and promised that we should "encounter them—doctors and lawyers, scholars, bankers, and economists—in those councils that resolved to exterminate the Jews." This promise was not kept, nor could it have been kept in the form in which it was made. For there never existed a "council that resolved" anything, and the "robed dignitaries with academic degrees" never decided on the extermination of the Jews, they only came together to plan the necessary steps in carrying out an order given by Hitler.) Still, one such case was brought to the attention of the

court, that of Dr. Hans Globke, one of Adenauer's closest advisers, who, more than twenty-five years ago, was co-author of an
infamous commentary on the Nuremberg Laws and, somewhat
later, author of the brilliant idea of compelling all German Jews
to take "Israel" or "Sarah" as a middle name. But Mr.
Globke's name—and only his name—was inserted into the
District Court proceedings by the defense, and probably only
in the hope of "persuading" the Adenauer government to start
extradition proceedings. At any rate, the former *Ministerialrat*
of the Interior and present *Staatssekretär* in Adenauer's Chancellery doubtless had more right than the ex-Mufti of Jerusalem
to figure in the history of what the Jews had actually suffered
from the Nazis.

For it was history that, as far as the prosecution was concerned, stood in the center of the trial. "It is not an individual
that is in the dock at this historic trial, and not the Nazi
regime alone, but anti-Semitism throughout history." This was
the tone set by Ben-Gurion and faithfully followed by Mr.
Hausner, who began his opening address (which lasted through
three sessions) with Pharaoh in Egypt and Haman's decree "to
destroy, to slay, and to cause them to perish." He then proceeded to quote Ezekiel: "And when I [the Lord] passed by thee,
and saw thee polluted in thine own blood, I said unto thee: In
thy blood, live," explaining that these words must be understood
as "the imperative that has confronted this nation ever since its
first appearance on the stage of history." It was bad history and
cheap rhetoric; worse, it was clearly at cross-purposes with putting Eichmann on trial, suggesting that perhaps he was only an
innocent executor of some mysteriously foreordained destiny, or,
for that matter, even of anti-Semitism, which perhaps was necessary to blaze the trail of "the bloodstained road traveled by
this people" to fulfill its destiny. A few sessions later, when
Professor Salo W. Baron of Columbia University had testified
to the more recent history of Eastern European Jewry, Dr.
Servatius could no longer resist temptation and asked the obvious questions: "Why did all this bad luck fall upon the Jewish
people?" and "Don't you think that irrational motives are at the
basis of the fate of this people? Beyond the understanding of a
human being?" Is not there perhaps something like "the spirit of

history, which brings history forward . . . without the influence of men?" Is not Mr. Hausner basically in agreement with "the school of historical law"—an allusion to Hegel—and has he not shown that what "the leaders do will not always lead to the aim and destination they wanted? . . . Here the intention was to destroy the Jewish people and the objective was not reached and a new flourishing State came into being." The argument of the defense had now come perilously close to the newest anti-Semitic notion about the Elders of Zion, set forth in all seriousness a few weeks earlier in the Egyptian National Assembly by Deputy Foreign Minister Hussain Zulficar Sabri: Hitler was innocent of the slaughter of the Jews; he was a victim of the Zionists, who had "compelled him to perpetrate crimes that would eventually enable them to achieve their aim—the creation of the State of Israel." Except that Dr. Servatius, following the philosophy of history expounded by the prosecutor, had put History in the place usually reserved for the Elders of Zion.

Despite the intentions of Ben-Gurion and all the efforts of the prosecution, there remained an individual in the dock, a person of flesh and blood; and if Ben-Gurion did "not care what verdict is delivered against Eichmann," it was undeniably the sole task of the Jerusalem court to deliver one.

II : *The Accused*

Otto Adolf, son of Karl Adolf Eichmann and Maria née Schefferling, caught in a suburb of Buenos Aires on the evening of May 11, 1960, flown to Israel nine days later, brought to trial in the District Court in Jerusalem on April 11, 1961, stood accused on fifteen counts: "together with others" he had committed crimes against the Jewish people, crimes against humanity, and war crimes during the whole period of the Nazi regime and especially during the period of the Second World War. The Nazis and Nazi Collaborators (Punishment) Law of 1950, under which he was tried, provides that "a person who has committed one of these . . . offenses . . . is liable to the death penalty." To each count Eichmann pleaded: "Not guilty in the sense of the indictment."

In what sense then did he think he was guilty? In the long cross-examination of the accused, according to him "the longest ever known," neither the defense nor the prosecution nor, finally, any of the three judges ever bothered to ask him this obvious question. His lawyer, Robert Servatius of Cologne, hired by Eichmann and paid by the Israeli government (following the precedent set at the Nuremberg Trials, where all attorneys for the defense were paid by the Tribunal of the victorious powers), answered the question in a press interview: "Eichmann feels guilty before God, not before the law," but this answer remained without confirmation from the accused himself. The defense would apparently have preferred him to plead not guilty on the grounds that under the then existing Nazi legal system he had not done anything wrong, that what he was accused of were not crimes but "acts of state," over which no other state has jurisdiction (*par in parem imperium non habet*), that it had been his duty to obey and that, in Servatius' words, he had

committed acts "for which you are decorated if you win and go
to the gallows if you lose." (Thus Goebbels had declared in
1943: "We will go down in history as the greatest statesmen of
all times or as their greatest criminals.") Outside Israel (at a
meeting of the Catholic Academy in Bavaria, devoted to what
the *Rheinischer Merkur* called "the ticklish problem" of the
"possibilities and limits in the coping with historical and political
guilt through criminal proceedings"), Servatius went a step
farther, and declared that "the only legitimate criminal problem
of the Eichmann trial lies in pronouncing judgment against his
Israeli captors, which so far has not been done"—a statement,
incidentally, that is somewhat difficult to reconcile with his
repeated and widely publicized utterances in Israel, in which he
called the conduct of the trial "a great spiritual achievement,"
comparing it favorably with the Nuremberg Trials.

Eichmann's own attitude was different. First of all, the indictment for murder was wrong: "With the killing of Jews I had
nothing to do. I never killed a Jew, or a non-Jew, for that matter
—I never killed any human being. I never gave an order to kill
either a Jew or a non-Jew; I just did not do it," or, as he was later
to qualify this statement, "It so happened . . . that I had not
once to do it"—for he left no doubt that he would have killed
his own father if he had received an order to that effect. Hence
he repeated over and over (what he had already stated in the
so-called Sassen documents, the interview that he had given in
1955 in Argentina to the Dutch journalist Sassen, a former S.S.
man who was also a fugitive from justice, and that, after Eichmann's capture, had been published in part by *Life* in this
country and by *Der Stern* in Germany) that he could be accused
only of "aiding and abetting" the annihilation of the Jews, which
he declared in Jerusalem to have been "one of the greatest
crimes in the history of Humanity." The defense paid no attention to Eichmann's own theory, but the prosecution wasted much
time in an unsuccessful effort to prove that Eichmann had once,
at least, killed with his own hands (a Jewish boy in Hungary),
and it spent even more time, and more successfully, on a note
that Franz Rademacher, the Jewish expert in the German
Foreign Office, had scribbled on one of the documents dealing
with Yugoslavia during a telephone conversation, which read:

"Eichmann proposes shooting." This turned out to be the only "order to kill," if that is what it was, for which there existed even a shred of evidence.

The evidence was more questionable than it appeared to be during the trial, at which the judges accepted the prosecutor's version against Eichmann's categorical denial—a denial that was very ineffective, since he had forgotten the "brief incident [a mere eight thousand people] which was not so striking," as Servatius put it. The incident took place in the autumn of 1941, six months after Germany had occupied the Serbian part of Yugoslavia. The Army had been plagued by partisan warfare ever since, and it was the military authorities who decided to solve two problems at a stroke by shooting a hundred Jews and Gypsies as hostages for every dead German soldier. To be sure, neither Jews nor Gypsies were partisans, but, in the words of the responsible civilian officer in the military government, a certain Staatsrat Harald Turner, "the Jews we had in the camps [anyhow]; after all, they too are Serb nationals, and besides, they have to disappear" (quoted by Raul Hilberg in *The Destruction of the European Jews,* 1961). The camps had been set up by General Franz Böhme, military governor of the region, and they housed Jewish males only. Neither General Böhme nor Staatsrat Turner waited for Eichmann's approval before starting to shoot Jews and Gypsies by the thousand. The trouble began when Böhme, without consulting the appropriate police and S.S. authorities, decided to *deport* all his Jews, probably in order to show that no special troops, operating under a different command, were required to make Serbia *judenrein.* Eichmann was informed, since it was a matter of deportation, and he refused approval because the move would interfere with other plans; but it was not Eichmann but Martin Luther, of the Foreign Office, who reminded General Böhme that "In other territories [meaning Russia] other military commanders have taken care of considerably greater numbers of Jews without even mentioning it." In any event, if Eichmann actually did "propose shooting," he told the military only that they should go on doing what they had done all along, and that the question of hostages was entirely in their own competence. Obviously, this was an Army affair, since only males were involved. The implementation of the Final

Solution in Serbia started about six months later, when women and children were rounded up and disposed of in mobile gas vans. During cross-examination, Eichmann, as usual, chose the most complicated and least likely explanation: Rademacher had needed the support of the Head Office for Reich Security, Eichmann's outfit, for his own stand on the matter in the Foreign Office, and therefore had forged the document. (Rademacher himself explained the incident much more reasonably at his own trial, before a West German court in 1952: "The Army was responsible for order in Serbia and had to kill rebellious Jews by shooting." This sounded more plausible but was a lie, for we know—from Nazi sources—that the Jews were not "rebellious.") If it was difficult to interpret a remark made over the phone as an order, it was more difficult to believe that Eichmann had been in a position to give orders to the generals of the Army.

Would he then have pleaded guilty if he had been indicted as an accessory to murder? Perhaps, but he would have made important qualifications. What he had done was a crime only in retrospect, and he had always been a law-abiding citizen, because Hitler's orders, which he had certainly executed to the best of his ability, had possessed "the force of law" in the Third Reich. (The defense could have quoted in support of Eichmann's thesis the testimony of one of the best-known experts on constitutional law in the Third Reich, Theodor Maunz, currently Minister of Education and Culture in Bavaria, who stated in 1943 [in *Gestalt und Recht der Polizei*]: "The command of the Führer . . . is the absolute center of the present legal order.") Those who today told Eichmann that he could have acted differently simply did not know, or had forgotten, how things had been. He did not want to be one of those who now pretended that "they had always been against it," whereas in fact they had been very eager to do what they were told to do. However, times change, and he, like Professor Maunz, had "arrived at different insights." What he had done he had done, he did not want to deny it; rather, he proposed "to hang myself in public as a warning example for all anti-Semites on this earth." By this he did not mean to say that he regretted anything: "Repentance is for little children." (*Sic!*)

Even under considerable pressure from his lawyer, he did not change this position. In a discussion of Himmler's offer in 1944 to exchange a million Jews for ten thousand trucks, and his own role in this plan, Eichmann was asked: "Mr. Witness, in the negotiations with your superiors, did you express any pity for the Jews and did you say there was room to help them?" And he replied: "I am here under oath and must speak the truth. Not out of mercy did I launch this transaction"—which would have been fine, except that it was not Eichmann who "launched" it. But he then continued, quite truthfully: "My reasons I explained this morning," and they were as follows: Himmler had sent his own man to Budapest to deal with matters of Jewish emigration. (Which, incidentally, had become a flourishing business: for enormous amounts of money, Jews could buy their way out. Eichmann, however, did not mention this.) It was the fact that "here matters of emigration were dealt with by a man who did not belong to the Police Force" that made him indignant, "because I had to help and to implement deportation, and matters of emigration, on which I considered myself an expert, were assigned to a man who was new to the unit. . . . I was fed up. . . . I decided that I had to do something to take matters of emigration into my own hands."

Throughout the trial, Eichmann tried to clarify, mostly without success, this second point in his plea of "not guilty in the sense of the indictment." The indictment implied not only that he had acted on purpose, which he did not deny, but out of base motives and in full knowledge of the criminal nature of his deeds. As for the base motives, he was perfectly sure that he was not what he called an *innerer Schweinehund,* a dirty bastard in the depths of his heart; and as for his conscience, he remembered perfectly well that he would have had a bad conscience only if he had not done what he had been ordered to to— to ship millions of men, women, and children to their death with great zeal and the most meticulous care. This, admittedly, was hard to take. Half a dozen psychiatrists had certified him as "normal"—"More normal, at any rate, than I am after having examined him," one of them was said to have exclaimed, while another had found that his whole psychological outlook, his attitude toward his wife and children, mother and father, brothers, sisters, and friends, was "not only normal but most desirable"—and finally the minister who had paid regular visits to him in prison after the Supreme Court had finished hearing his appeal reassured everybody by declaring Eichmann to be "a man with very positive ideas." Behind the comedy of the soul experts lay the hard fact that his was obviously no case of moral let alone legal insanity. (Mr. Hausner's recent revelations in the *Saturday Evening Post* of things he "could not bring out at the trial" have contradicted the information given informally in Jerusalem. Eichmann, we are now told, had been alleged by the psychiatrists to be "a man obsessed with a dangerous and insatiable urge to kill," "a perverted, sadistic personality." In which case he would have belonged in an insane asylum.) Worse, his was obviously also no case of insane hatred of Jews, of fanatical anti-Semitism or indoctrination of any kind. He — "personally" never had anything whatever against Jews; on the contrary, he had plenty of "private reasons" for not being a Jew hater. To be sure, there were fanatic anti-Semites among his closest friends, for instance Lászlo Endre, State Secretary in Charge of Political (Jewish) Affairs in Hungary, who was hanged in Budapest in 1946; but this, according to Eichmann, was more or less in the spirit of "some of my best friends are anti-Semites."

Alas, nobody believed him. The prosecutor did not believe him, because that was not his job. Counsel for the defense paid no attention because he, unlike Eichmann, was, to all appearances, not interested in questions of conscience. And the judges did not believe him, because they were too good, and perhaps also too conscious of the very foundations of their profession, to admit that an average, "normal" person, neither feeble-minded nor indoctrinated nor cynical, could be perfectly incapable of telling right from wrong. They preferred to conclude from occasional lies that he was a liar—and missed the greatest moral and even legal challenge of the whole case. Their case rested on the assumption that the defendant, like all "normal persons," must have been aware of the criminal nature of his acts, and Eichmann was indeed normal insofar as he was "no exception within the Nazi regime." However, under the conditions of the Third Reich only "exceptions" could be expected to react "normally." This simple truth of the matter created a dilemma for the judges which they could neither resolve nor escape.

He was born on March 19, 1906, in Solingen, a German town in the Rhineland famous for its knives, scissors, and surgical instruments. Fifty-four years later, indulging in his favorite pastime of writing his memoirs, he described this memorable event as follows: "Today, fifteen years and a day after May 8, 1945, I begin to lead my thoughts back to that nineteenth of March of the year 1906, when at five o'clock in the morning I entered life on earth in the aspect of a human being." (The manuscript has not been released by the Israeli authorities. Harry Mulisch succeeded in studying this autobiography "for half an hour," and the German-Jewish weekly *Der Aufbau* was able to publish short excerpts from it.) According to his religious beliefs, which had not changed since the Nazi period (in Jerusalem Eichmann declared himself to be a *Gottgläubiger*, the Nazi term for those who had broken with Christianity, and he refused to take his oath on the Bible), this event was to be ascribed to "a higher Bearer of Meaning," an entity somehow identical with the "movement of the universe," to which human life, in itself devoid of "higher meaning," is subject. (The terminology is quite suggestive. To call God a *Höheren Sinnesträger* meant linguistically to give him some place in the military hierarchy, since the Nazis had changed the military "recipient of orders," the *Befehlsempfänger*, into a "bearer of orders," a Befehls*träger*, indicating, as in the ancient "bearer of ill tidings," the burden of responsibility and of importance that weighed supposedly upon those who had to execute orders. Moreover, Eichmann, like everyone connected with the Final Solution, was officially a "bearer of secrets," a *Geheimnisträger,* as well, which as far as self-importance went certainly was nothing to sneeze at.) But Eichmann, not very much interested in metaphysics, remained singularly silent on any more intimate relationship between the Bearer of Meaning and the bearer of orders, and proceeded to a consideration of the other possible cause of his existence, his parents: "They would hardly have been so overjoyed at the arrival of their first-born had they been able to watch how in the hour of my birth the Norn of misfortune, to spite the Norn of good fortune, was already spinning threads of grief and sorrow into my life. But a kind, impenetrable veil kept my parents from seeing into the future."

The misfortune started soon enough; it started in school. Eichmann's father, first an accountant for the Tramways and Electricity Company in Solingen and after 1913 an official of the same corporation in Austria, in Linz, had five children, four sons and a daughter, of whom only Adolf, the eldest, it seems, was unable to finish high school, or even to graduate from the vocational school for engineering into which he was then put. Throughout his life, Eichmann deceived people about his early "misfortunes" by hiding behind the more honorable financial misfortunes of his father. In Israel, however, during his first sessions with Captain Avner Less, the police examiner who was to spend approximately 35 days with him and who produced 3,564 typewritten pages from 76 recorder tapes, he was in an ebullient mood, full of enthusiasm about this unique opportunity "to pour forth everything . . . I know" and, by the same token, to advance to the rank of the most cooperative defendant ever. (His enthusiasm was soon dampened, though never quite extinguished, when he was confronted with concrete questions based on irrefutable documents.) The best proof of his initial boundless confidence, obviously wasted on Captain Less (who said to Harry Mulisch: "I was Mr. Eichmann's father confessor"), was that for the first time in his life he admitted his early disasters, although he must have been aware of the fact that he thus contradicted himself on several important entries in all his official Nazi records.

Well, the disasters were ordinary: since he "had not exactly been the most hard-working" pupil—or, one may add, the most gifted—his father had taken him first from high school and then from vocational school, long before graduation. Hence, the profession that appears on all his official documents: construction engineer, had about as much connection with reality as the statement that his birthplace was Palestine and that he was fluent in Hebrew and Yiddish—another outright lie Eichmann had loved to tell both to his S.S. comrades and to his Jewish victims. It was in the same vein that he had always pretended he had been dismissed from his job as salesman for the Vacuum

Oil Company in Austria because of membership in the National Socialist Party. The version he confided to Captain Less was less dramatic, though probably not the truth either: he had been fired because it was a time of unemployment, when unmarried employees were the first to lose their jobs. (This explanation, which at first seems plausible, is not very satisfactory, because he lost his job in the spring of 1933, when he had been engaged for two full years to Veronika, or Vera, Liebl, who later became his wife. Why had he not married her before, when he still had a good job? He finally married in March, 1935, probably because bachelors in the S.S., as in the Vacuum Oil Company, were never sure of their jobs and could not be promoted.) Clearly, bragging had always been one of his cardinal vices.

While young Eichmann was doing poorly in school, his father left the Tramway and Electricity Company and went into business for himself. He bought a small mining enterprise and put his unpromising youngster to work in it as an ordinary mining laborer, but only until he found him a job in the sales department of the Oberösterreichischen Elektrobau Company, where Eichmann remained for over two years. He was now about twenty-two years old and without any prospects for a career; the only thing he had learned, perhaps, was how to sell. What then happened was what he himself called his first break, of which, again, we have two rather different versions. In a handwritten biographical record he submitted in 1939 to win a promotion in the S.S., he described it as follows: "I worked during the years of 1925 to 1927 as a salesman for the Austrian Elektrobau Company. I left this position of my own free will, as the Vacuum Oil Company of Vienna offered me the representation for Upper Austria." The key word here is "offered," since, according to the story he told Captain Less in Israel, nobody had offered him anything. His own mother had died when he was ten years old, and his father had married again. A cousin of his stepmother—a man he called "uncle"—who was president of the Austrian Automobile Club and was married to the daughter of a Jewish businessman in Czechoslovakia, had used his connection with the general director of the Austrian Vacuum Oil Company, a Jewish Mr. Weiss, to obtain for his unfortunate relation a job as traveling salesman. Eichmann was properly grateful; the Jews in his family were among his "private reasons" for not hating Jews. Even in 1943 or 1944, when the Final Solution was in full swing, he had not forgotten: "The daughter of this marriage, half-Jewish according to the Nuremberg Laws, . . . came to see me in order to obtain my permission for her emigration into Switzerland. Of course, I granted this request, and the same uncle came also to see me to ask me to intervene for some Viennese Jewish couple. I mention this only to show that I myself had no hatred for Jews, for my whole education through my mother and my father had been strictly Christian; my mother, because of her Jewish relatives, held different opinions from those current in S.S. circles."

He went to considerable lengths to prove his point: he had never harbored any ill feelings against his victims, and, what is more, he had never made a secret of that fact. "I explained this to Dr. Löwenherz [head of the Jewish Community in Vienna] as I explained it to Dr. Kastner [vice-president of the Zionist Organization in Budapest]; I think I told it to everybody, each of my men knew it, they all heard it from me sometime. Even in elementary school, I had a classmate with whom I spent my free time, and he came to our house; a family in Linz by the name of Sebba. The last time we met we walked together through the streets of Linz, I already with the Party emblem of the N.S.D.A.P. [the Nazi Party] in my buttonhole, and he did not think anything of it." Had Eichmann been a bit less prim or the police examination (which refrained from cross-examination, presumably to remain assured of his cooperation) less discreet, his "lack of prejudice" might have shown itself in still another aspect. It seems that in Vienna, where he was so extraordinarily successful in arranging the "forced emigration" of Jews, he had a Jewish mistress, an "old flame" from Linz. *Rassenschande,* sexual intercourse with Jews, was probably the greatest crime a member of the S.S. could commit, and though during the war the raping of Jewish girls became a favorite pastime at the front, it was by no means common for a Higher S.S. officer to have an affair with a Jewish woman. Thus, Eichmann's repeated violent denunciations of Julius Streicher, the insane and obscene editor of *Der Stürmer,* and of his pornographic anti-

Semitism, were perhaps personally motivated, and the expression of more than the routine contempt an "enlightened" S.S. man was supposed to show toward the vulgar passions of lesser Party luminaries.

The five and a half years with the Vacuum Oil Company must have been among the happier ones in Eichmann's life. He made a good living during a time of severe unemployment, and he was still living with his parents, except when he was out on the road. The date when this idyll came to an end—Pentecost, 1933—was among the few he always remembered. Actually, things had taken a turn for the worse somewhat earlier. At the end of 1932, he was unexpectedly transferred from Linz to Salzburg, very much against his inclinations: "I lost all joy in my work, I no longer liked to sell, to make calls." From such sudden losses of *Arbeitsfreude* Eichmann was to suffer throughout his life. The worst of them occurred when he was told of the Führer's order for the "physical extermination of the Jews," in which he was to play such an important role. This, too, came unexpectedly; he himself had "never thought of . . . such a solution through violence," and he described his reaction in the same words: "I now lost everything, all joy in my work, all initiative, all interest; I was, so to speak, blown out." A similar blowing out must have happened in 1932 in Salzburg, and from his own account it is clear that he cannot have been very surprised when he was fired, though one need not believe his saying that he had been "very happy" about his dismissal.

For whatever reasons, the year 1932 marked a turning point of his life. It was in April of this year that he joined the National Socialist Party and entered the S.S., upon an invitation of Ernst Kaltenbrunner, a young lawyer in Linz who later became chief of the Head Office for Reich Security (the *Reichssicherheitshauptamt* or R.S.H.A., as I shall call it henceforth), in one of whose six main departments—Bureau IV, under the command of Heinrich Müller—Eichmann was eventually employed as head of section B-4. In court, Eichmann gave the impression of a typical member of the lower middle classes, and this impression was more than borne out by every sentence he spoke or wrote while in prison. But this was misleading; he was rather the *déclassé* son of a solid middle-class family, and it was indicative of his comedown in social status that while his father was a good friend of Kaltenbrunner's father, who was also a Linz lawyer, the relationship of the two sons was rather cool: Eichmann was unmistakably treated by Kaltenbrunner as his social inferior. Before Eichmann entered the Party and the S.S., he had proved that he was a joiner, and May 8, 1945, the official date of Germany's defeat, was significant for him mainly because it then dawned upon him that thenceforward he would have to live without being a member of something or other. "I sensed I would have to live a leaderless and difficult individual life, I would receive no directives from anybody, no orders and commands would any longer be issued to me, no pertinent ordinances would be there to consult—in brief, a life never known before lay before me." When he was a child, his parents, uninterested in politics, had enrolled him in the Young Men's Christian Association, from which he later went into the German youth movement, the *Wandervogel.* During his four unsuccessful years in high school, he had joined the *Jungfront-kämpfeverband,* the youth section of the German-Austrian organ-zation of war veterans, which, though violently pro-German and anti-republican, was tolerated by the Austrian government. When Kaltenbrunner suggested that he enter the S.S., he was just on the point of becoming a member of an altogether different outfit, the Freemasons' Lodge Schlaraffia, "an association of businessmen, physicians, actors, civil servants, etc., who came together to cultivate merriment and gaiety. . . . Each member had to give a lecture from time to time whose tenor was to be humor, refined humor." Kaltenbrunner explained to Eichmann that he would have to give up this merry society because as a Nazi he could not be a Freemason—a word that at the time was unknown to him. The choice between the S.S. and Schlaraffia (the name derives from *Schlaraffenland,* the gluttons' Cloud-Cuckoo Land of German fairy tales) might have been hard to make, but he was "kicked out" of Schlaraffia anyhow; he had committed a sin that even now, as he told the story in the Israeli prison, made him blush with shame: "Contrary to my upbringing, I had tried, though I was the youngest, to invite my companions to a glass of wine."

A leaf in the whirlwind of time, he was blown from

Schlaraffia, the Never-Never Land of tables set by magic and roast chickens that flew into your mouth—or, more accurately, from the company of respectable philistines with degrees and assured careers and "refined humor," whose worst vice was probably an irrepressible desire for practical jokes—into the marching columns of the Thousand-Year Reich, which lasted exactly twelve years and three months. At any rate, he did not enter the Party out of conviction, nor was he ever convinced by it—whenever he was asked to give his reasons, he repeated the same embarrassed clichés about the Treaty of Versailles and unemployment; rather, as he pointed out in court, "it was like being swallowed up by the Party against all expectations and without previous decision. It happened so quickly and suddenly." He had no time and less desire to be properly informed, he did not even know the Party program, he never read *Mein Kampf*. Kaltenbrunner had said to him: Why not join the S.S.? And he had replied, Why not? That was how it had happened, and that was about all there was to it.

Of course, that was not all there was to it. What Eichmann failed to tell the presiding judge in cross-examination was that he had been an ambitious young man who was fed up with his job as traveling salesman even before the Vacuum Oil Company was fed up with him. From a humdrum life without significance and consequence the wind had blown him into History, as he understood it, namely, into a Movement that always kept moving and in which somebody like him—already a failure in the eyes of his social class, of his family, and hence in his own eyes as well—could start from scratch and still make a career. And if he did not always like what he had to do (for example, dispatching people to their death by the trainload instead of forcing them to emigrate), if he guessed, rather early, that the whole business would come to a bad end, with Germany losing the war, if all his most cherished plans came to nothing (the evacuation of European Jewry to Madagascar, the establishment of a Jewish territory in the Nisko region of Poland, the experiment with carefully built defense installations around his Berlin office to repel Russian tanks), and if, to his greatest "grief and sorrow," he never advanced beyond the grade of S.S. *Obersturmbann-führer* (a rank equivalent to lieutenant colonel)—in short, if, with the exception of the year in Vienna, his life was beset with frustrations, he never forgot what the alternative would have been. Not only in Argentina, leading the unhappy existence of a refugee, but also in the courtroom in Jerusalem, with his life as good as forfeited, he might still have preferred—if anybody had asked him—to be hanged as *Obersturmbannführer a.D.* (in retirement) rather than living out his life quietly and normally as a traveling salesman for the Vacuum Oil Company.

The beginnings of Eichmann's new career were not very promising. In the spring of 1933, while he was out of a job, the Nazi Party and all its affiliates were suspended in Austria, because of Hitler's rise to power. But even without this new calamity, a career in the Austrian Party would have been out of the question: even those who had enlisted in the S.S. were still working at their regular jobs; Kaltenbrunner was still a partner in his father's law firm. Eichmann therefore decided to go to Germany, which was all the more natural because his family had never given up German citizenship. (This fact was of some relevance during the trial. Dr. Servatius had asked the West German government to demand extradition of the accused and, failing this, to pay the expenses of the defense, and Bonn refused, on the grounds that Eichmann was not a German national, which was a patent untruth.) At Passau, on the German border, he was suddenly a traveling salesman again, and when he reported to the regional leader, he asked him eagerly "if he had perhaps some connection with the Bavarian Vacuum Oil Company." Well, this was one of his not infrequent relapses from one period of his life into another; whenever he was confronted with tell-tale signs of an unregenerate Nazi outlook, in his life in Argentina and even in the Jerusalem jail, he excused himself with "There I go again, the old song and dance [*die alte Tour*]." But his relapse in Passau was quickly cured; he was told that he had better enlist for some military training—"All right with me, I thought to myself, why not become a soldier?"—and he was sent in quick succession to two Bavarian S.S. camps, in Lechfeld and in Dachau (he had nothing to do with the concentration camp there), where the "Austrian Legion in exile" received its training. Thus he did become an Austrian after a fashion, despite his German passport. He remained in these military camps from

August, 1933, until September, 1934, advanced to the rank of *Scharführer* (corporal) and had plenty of time to reconsider his willingness to embark upon the career of a soldier. According to his own account, there was but one thing in which he distinguished himself during these fourteen months, and that was punishment drill, which he performed with great obstinacy, in the wrathful spirit of "Serves my father right if my hands freeze, why doesn't he buy me gloves." But apart from such rather dubious pleasures, to which he owed his first promotion, he had a terrible time: "The humdrum of military service, that was something I couldn't stand, day after day always the same, over and over again the same." Thus bored to distraction, he heard that the Security Service of the Reichsführer S.S. (Himmler's *Sicherheitsdienst*, or S.D., as I shall call it henceforth) had jobs open, and applied immediately.

In 1934, when Eichmann applied successfully for a job, the S.D. was a relatively new apparatus in the S.S., founded two years earlier by Heinrich Himmler to serve as the Intelligence service of the Party and now headed by Reinhardt Heydrich, a former Navy Intelligence officer, who was to become, as Gerald Reitlinger put it, "the real engineer of the Final Solution" (*The Final Solution*, 1961). Its initial task had been to spy on Party members, and thus to give the S.S. an ascendancy over the regular Party apparatus. Meanwhile it had taken on some additional duties, becoming the information and research center for the Secret State Police, or Gestapo. These were the first steps toward the merger of the S.S. and the police, which, however, was not carried out until September, 1939, although Himmler held the double post of Reichsführer S.S. and Chief of the German Police from 1936 on. Eichmann, of course, could not have known of these future developments, but he seems to have known nothing either of the nature of the S.D. when he entered it; this is quite possible, because the operations of the S.D. had always been top secret. As far as he was concerned, it was all a misunderstanding and at first "a great disappointment. For I thought this was what I had read about in the *Münchener Illustrierten Zeitung*; when the high Party officials drove along, there were commando guards with them, men standing on the running boards of the cars. . . . In short, I had mistaken the Security Service of the Reichsführer S.S. for the Reich Security Service . . . and nobody set me right and no one told me anything. For I had had not the slightest notion of what now was revealed to me." The question of whether he was telling the truth had a certain bearing on the trial, where it had to be decided whether he had volunteered for his position or had been drafted into it. His misunderstanding, if such it was, is not inexplicable; the S.S. or *Schutzstaffeln* had originally been established as special units for the protection of the Party leaders.

His disappointment, however, consisted chiefly in that he had to start all over again, that he was back at the bottom, and his only consolation was that there were others who had made the same mistake. He was put into the Information department, where his first job was to file all information concerning Freemasonry (which in the early Nazi ideological muddle was somehow lumped with Judaism, Catholicism, and Communism) and to help in the establishment of a Freemasonry museum. He now had ample opportunity to learn what this strange word meant that Kaltenbrunner had thrown at him in their discussion of Schlaraffia. (Incidentally, an eagerness to establish museums commemorating their enemies was very characteristic of the Nazis. During the war, several services competed bitterly for the honor of establishing anti-Jewish museums and libraries. We owe to this strange craze the salvage of many great cultural treasures of European Jewry.) The trouble was that things were again very, very boring, and he was greatly relieved when, after four or five months of Freemasonry, he was put into the brand-new department concerned with Jews. This was the real beginning of the career which was to end in the Jerusalem court.

It was the year 1935, when Germany, contrary to the stipulations of the Treaty of Versailles, introduced general conscription and publicly announced plans for rearmament, including the building of an air force and a navy. It was also the year when Germany, having left the League of Nations in 1933, prepared neither quietly nor secretly the occupation of the demilitarized zone of the Rhineland. It was the time of Hitler's peace speeches —"Germany needs peace and desires peace," "We recognize Poland as the home of a great and nationally conscious people," "Germany neither intends nor wishes to interfere in the internal affairs of Austria, to annex Austria, or to conclude an *Anschluss*"—and, above all, it was the year when the Nazi regime won general and, unhappily, genuine recognition in Germany and abroad, when Hitler was admired everywhere as a great national statesman. In Germany itself, it was a time of transition. Because of the enormous rearmament program, unemployment had been liquidated, the initial resistance of the working class was broken, and the hostility of the regime, which had at first been directed primarily against "anti-Fascists"— Communists, Socialists, left-wing intellectuals, and Jews in prominent positions—had not yet shifted entirely to persecution of the Jews qua Jews.

To be sure, one of the first steps taken by the Nazi government, back in 1933, had been the exclusion of Jews from the Civil Service (which in Germany included all teaching positions, from grammar school to university, and most branches of the entertainment industry, including radio, the theater, the opera, and concerts) and, in general, their removal from public offices. But private business remained almost untouched until 1938, and even the legal and medical professions were only gradually abolished, although Jewish students were excluded from most universities and were nowhere permitted to graduate. Emigration of Jews in these years proceeded in a not unduly accelerated and generally orderly fashion, and the currency restrictions that made it difficult, but not impossible, for Jews to take their money, or at least the greater part of it, out of the country were the same for non-Jews; they dated back to the days of the Weimar Republic. There were a certain number of *Einzelaktionen*, individual actions putting pressure on Jews to sell their property at often ridiculously low prices, but these usually occurred in small towns and, indeed, could be traced to the spontaneous, "individual" initiative of some enterprising Storm Troopers, the so-called S.A. men, who, except for their officer corps, were mostly recruited from the lower classes. The police, it is true, never stopped these "excesses," but the Nazi authorities were not too happy about them, because they affected the value of real estate all over the country. The emigrants, unless they were political refugees, were young people who realized that there was no future for them in Germany. And since they soon found out that there was hardly any future for them in other European countries either, some Jewish emigrants actually returned during this period. When Eichmann was asked how he had reconciled his personal feelings about Jews with the outspoken and violent anti-Semitism of the Party he had joined, he replied with the proverb: "Nothing's as hot when you eat it as when it's being cooked"—a proverb that was then on the lips of many Jews as well. They lived in a fool's paradise, in which, for a few years, even Streicher spoke of a "legal solution" of the Jewish problem. It took the organized pogroms of November, 1938, the so-called *Kristallnacht* or Night of Broken Glass, when seventy-five hundred Jewish shop windows were broken, all synagogues went up in flames, and twenty thousand Jewish men were taken off to concentration camps, to expel them from it.

The frequently forgotten point of the matter is that the famous Nuremberg Laws, issued in the fall of 1935, had failed to do the trick. The testimony of three witnesses from Germany, high-ranking former officials of the Zionist organization who left Germany shortly before the outbreak of the war, gave only the barest glimpse into the true state of affairs during the first five years of the Nazi regime. The Nuremberg Laws had deprived the Jews of their political but not of their civil rights; they were no longer citizens (*Reichsbürger*), but they remained members of the German state (*Staatsangehörige*). Even if they emigrated, they were not automatically stateless. Sexual intercourse between Jews and Germans, and the contraction of mixed marriages, were forbidden. Also, no German woman under the age of forty-five could be employed in a Jewish household. Of these stipulations, only the last was of practical significance; the others merely legalized a *de facto* situation. Hence, the Nuremberg Laws were felt to have stabilized the new situation of Jews in the German Reich. They had been second-class citizens, to put it mildly, since January 30, 1933; their almost complete separation from the rest of the population had been achieved in a matter of weeks or months—through terror but also through the more than ordinary connivance of those around them. "There was a wall between Gentiles and Jews," Dr. Benno Cohn of Berlin testified. "I cannot remember speaking to a Christian during all my journeys over Germany." Now, the Jews felt, they had received laws of their own and would no longer be outlawed. If they kept to themselves, as they had been forced to do anyhow, they would be able to live unmolested. In the words of the *Reichsvertretung* of the Jews in Germany (the national association of all communities and organizations, which had been founded in September, 1933, on the initiative of the Berlin community, and was in no way Nazi-appointed), the intention of the Nuremberg Laws was "to establish a level on which a bearable relationship between the German and the Jewish people [became] possible," to which a member of the Berlin community, a radical Zionist, added: "Life is possible under every law. However, in complete ignorance of what is permitted and what is not one cannot live. A useful and respected citizen one can also be as a member of a minority in the midst of a great people" (Hans Lamm, *Über die Entwicklung des deutschen Judentums*, 1951). And since Hitler, in the Röhm purge in 1934, had broken the power of the S.A., the Storm Troopers in brown shirts who had been almost exclusively responsible for the early pogroms and atrocities, and since the Jews were blissfully unaware of the growing power of the black-shirted S.S., who ordinarily abstained from what Eichmann contemptuously called the "*Stürmer* methods," they generally believed that a *modus vivendi* would be possible; they even offered to cooperate in "the solution of the Jewish question." In short, when Eichmann entered upon his apprenticeship in Jewish affairs, on which, four years later, he was to be the recognized "expert," and when he made his first contacts with Jewish functionaries, both Zionists and Assimilationists talked in terms of a great "Jewish revival," a "great constructive movement of German Jewry," and they still quarreled among themselves in ideological terms about the desirability of Jewish emigration, as though this depended upon their own decisions.

Eichmann's account during the police examination of how he was introduced into the new department—distorted, of course, but not wholly devoid of truth—oddly recalls this fool's paradise. The first thing that happened was that his new boss, a certain von Mildenstein, who shortly thereafter got himself transferred to Albert Speer's *Organisation Todt,* where he was in charge of highway construction (he was what Eichmann pretended to be, an engineer by profession), required him to read Theodor Herzl's *Der Judenstaat,* the famous Zionist classic, which converted Eichmann promptly and forever to Zionism. This seems to have been the first serious book he ever read and it made a lasting impression on him. From then on, as he repeated over and over, he thought of hardly anything but a "political solution" (as opposed to the later "physical solution," the first meaning expulsion and the second extermination) and how to "get some firm ground under the feet of the Jews." (It may be worth mentioning that, as late as 1939, he seems to have protested against desecrators of Herzl's grave in Vienna, and there are reports of his presence in civilian clothes at the commemoration of the thirty-fifth anniversary of Herzl's death. Strangely enough, he did not talk about these things in Jerusalem, where he continuously boasted of his good relations with Jewish officials.) In order to help in this enterprise, he began spreading the gospel among his S.S. comrades, giving lectures and writing pamphlets. He then acquired a smattering of Hebrew, which enabled him to read haltingly a Yiddish newspaper—not a very difficult accomplishment, since Yiddish, basically an old German dialect written in Hebrew letters, can be understood by any German-speaking person who has mastered a few dozen Hebrew words. He even read one more book, Adolf Böhm's *History of Zionism* (during the trial he kept confusing it with Herzl's *Judenstaat*), and this was perhaps a considerable achievement for a man who, by his own account, had always been utterly reluctant to read anything except newspapers, and who, to the distress of his father, had never availed himself of the books in the family library. Following up Böhm, he studied the organizational setup of the Zionist movement, with all its parties, youth groups, and different programs. This did not yet make him an "authority," but it was enough to earn him an assignment as official spy on the Zionist offices and on their meetings; it is worth noting that his schooling in Jewish affairs was almost entirely concerned with Zionism.

His first personal contacts with Jewish functionaries, all of them well-known Zionists of long standing, were thoroughly satisfactory. The reason he became so fascinated by the "Jewish question," he explained, was his own "idealism"; these Jews, unlike the Assimilationists, whom he always despised, and unlike Orthodox Jews, who bored him, were "idealists," like him. An "idealist," according to Eichmann's notions, was not merely a man who believed in an "idea" or someone who did not steal or accept bribes, though these qualifications were

indispensable. An "idealist" was a man who *lived* for his idea—
hence he could not be a businessman—and who was prepared
to sacrifice for his idea everything and, especially, everybody.
When he said in the police examination that he would have
sent his own father to his death if that had been required, he did
not mean merely to stress the extent to which he was under
orders, and ready to obey them; he also meant to show what an
"idealist" he had always been. The perfect "idealist," like everybody else, had of course his personal feelings and emotions, but
he would never permit them to interfere with his actions if they
came into conflict with his "idea." The greatest "idealist"
Eichmann ever encountered among the Jews was Dr. Rudolf
Kastner, with whom he negotiated during the Jewish deportations from Hungary and with whom he came to an agreement
that he, Eichmann, would permit the "illegal" departure of a
few thousand Jews to Palestine (the trains were in fact guarded
by German police) in exchange for "quiet and order" in the
camps from which hundreds of thousands were shipped to
Auschwitz. The few thousand saved by the agreement, prominent
Jews and members of the Zionist youth organizations, were, in
Eichmann's words, "the best biological material." Dr. Kastner,
as Eichmann understood it, had sacrificed his fellow-Jews to his
"idea," and this was as it should be. Judge Benjamin Halevi,
one of the three judges at Eichmann's trial, had been in charge
of the Kastner trial in Israel, at which Kastner had to defend
himself for his cooperation with Eichmann and other high-
ranking Nazis; in Halevi's opinion, Kastner had "sold his soul
to the devil." Now that the devil himself was in the dock he
turned out to be an "idealist," and though it may be hard to
believe, it is quite possible that the one who sold his soul had
also been an "idealist."

Long before all this happened, Eichmann was given his first
opportunity to apply in practice what he had learned during his
apprenticeship. After the *Anschluss* (the incorporation of Austria into the Reich), in March, 1938, he was sent to Vienna to
organize a kind of emigration that had been utterly unknown
in Germany, where up to the fall of 1938 the fiction was maintained that Jews if they so desired were permitted, but were not
forced, to leave the country. Among the reasons German Jews

believed in the fiction was the program of the N.S.D.A.P., formulated in 1920, which shared with the Weimar Constitution the curious fate of never being officially abolished; its Twenty-Five Points had even been declared "unalterable" by Hitler. Seen in the light of later events, its anti-Semite provisions were harmless indeed: Jews could not be full-fledged citizens, they could not hold Civil Service positions, they were to be excluded from the press, and all those who had acquired German citizenship after August 2, 1914—the date of the outbreak of the First World War—were to be denaturalized, which meant they were subject to expulsion. (Characteristically, the denaturalization was carried out immediately, but the wholesale expulsion of some fifteen thousand Jews, who from one day to the next were shoved across the Polish border at Zbaszyn, where they were promptly put into camps, took place only five years later, when no one expected it any longer.) The Party program was never taken seriously by Nazi officials; they prided themselves on belonging to a movement, as distinguished from a party, and a movement could not be bound by a program. Even before the Nazis' rise to power, these Twenty-Five Points had been no more than a concession to the party system and to such prospective voters as were old-fashioned enough to ask what was the program of the party they were going to join. Eichmann, as we have seen, was free of such deplorable habits, and when he told the Jerusalem court that he had not known Hitler's program he very likely spoke the truth: "The Party program did not matter, you knew what you were joining." The Jews, on the other hand, were old-fashioned enough to know the Twenty-Five Points by heart and to believe in them; whatever contradicted the legal implementation of the Party program they tended to ascribe to temporary, "revolutionary excesses" of undisciplined members or groups.

But what happened in Vienna in March, 1938, was altogether different. Eichmann's task had been defined as "forced emigration," and the words meant exactly what they said: all Jews, regardless of their desires and regardless of their citizenship, were to be forced to emigrate—an act which in ordinary language is called expulsion. Whenever Eichmann thought back to the twelve years that were his life, he singled out his

year in Vienna as head of the Center for Emigration of Austrian Jews as its happiest and most successful period. Shortly
before, he had been promoted to officer's rank, becoming an
Untersturmführer, or lieutenant, and he had been commended
for his "comprehensive knowledge of the methods of organization and ideology of the opponent, Jewry." The assignment in
Vienna was his first important job, his whole career, which had
progressed rather slowly, was in the balance. He must have been
frantic to make good, and his success was spectacular: in eight
months, forty-five thousand Jews left Austria, whereas no more
than nineteen thousand left Germany in the same period; in less
than eighteen months, Austria was "cleansed" of close to a hundred and fifty thousand people, roughly sixty per cent of its
Jewish population, all of whom left the country "legally"; even
after the outbreak of the war, some sixty thousand Jews could
escape. How did he do it? The basic idea that made all this
possible was of course not his but, almost certainly, a specific
directive by Heydrich, who had sent him to Vienna in the first
place. (Eichmann was vague on the question of authorship,
which he claimed, however, by implication; the Israeli authorities, on the other hand, bound [as Yad Vashem's *Bulletin* put it]
to the fantastic "thesis of the all-inclusive responsibility of
Adolf Eichmann" and the even more fantastic "supposition that
one [i.e., his] mind was behind it all," helped him considerably
in his efforts to deck himself in borrowed plumes, for which he
had in any case a great inclination.) The idea, as explained by
Heydrich in a conference with Göring on the morning of the
Kristallnacht, was simple and ingenious enough: "Through the
Jewish community, we extracted a certain amount of money
from the rich Jews who wanted to emigrate. By paying this
amount, and an additional sum in foreign currency, they made
it possible for poor Jews to leave. The problem was not to make
the rich Jews leave, but to get rid of the Jewish mob." And this
"problem" was not solved by Eichmann. Not until the trial was
over was it learned from the Netherlands State Institute for War
Documentation that Erich Rajakowitsch, a "brilliant lawyer"
whom Eichmann, according to his own testimony, "employed
for the handling of legal questions in the central offices for
Jewish emigration in Vienna, Prague, and Berlin," had origi-

nated the idea of the "emigration funds." Somewhat later, in April, 1941, Rajakowitsch was sent to Holland by Heydrich in order to "establish there a central office which was to serve as a model for the 'solution of the Jewish question' in all occupied countries in Europe."

Still, enough problems remained that could be solved only in the course of the operation, and there is no doubt that here Eichmann, for the first time in his life, discovered in himself some special qualities. There were two things he could do well, better than others: he could organize and he could negotiate. Immediately upon his arrival, he opened negotiations with the representatives of the Jewish community, whom he had first to liberate from prisons and concentration camps, since the "revolutionary zeal" in Austria, greatly exceeding the early "excesses" in Germany, had resulted in the imprisonment of practically all prominent Jews. After this experience, the Jewish functionaries did not need Eichmann to convince them of the desirability of emigration. Rather, they informed him of the enormous difficulties which lay ahead. Apart from the financial problem, already "solved," the chief difficulty lay in the number of papers every emigrant had to assemble before he could leave the country. Each of the papers was valid only for a limited time, so that the validity of the first had usually expired long before the last could be obtained. Once Eichmann understood how the whole thing worked, or, rather, did not work, he "took counsel with himself" and "gave birth to the idea which I thought would do justice to both parties." He imagined "an assembly line, at whose beginnings the first document is put, and then the other papers, and at its end the passport would have to come out as the end product." This could be realized if all the officers concerned—the Ministry of Finance, the income tax people, the police, the Jewish community, etc.—were housed under the same roof and forced to do their work on the spot, in the presence of the applicant, who would no longer have to run from office to office and who, presumably, would also be spared having some humiliating chicaneries practiced on him, and certain expenses for bribes. When everything was ready and the assembly line was doing its work smoothly and quickly, Eichmann "invited" the Jewish functionaries from Berlin to inspect it. They were appalled: "This is like an automatic factory, like a flour mill connected with some bakery. At one end you put in a Jew who still has some property, a factory, or a shop, or a bank account, and he goes through the building from counter to counter, from office to office, and comes out at the other end without any money, without any rights, with only a passport on which it says: 'You must leave the country within a fortnight. Otherwise you will go to a concentration camp.' "

This, of course, was essentially the truth about the procedure, but it was not the whole truth. For these Jews could not be left "without any money," for the simple reason that without it no country at this date would have taken them. They needed, and were given, their *Vorzeigegeld,* the amount they had to show in order to obtain their visas and to pass the immigration controls of the recipient country. For this amount, they needed foreign currency, which the Reich had no intention of wasting on its Jews. These needs could not be met by Jewish accounts in foreign countries, which, in any event, were difficult to get at because they had been illegal for many years; Eichmann therefore sent Jewish functionaries abroad to solicit funds from the great Jewish organizations, and these funds were then sold by the Jewish community to the prospective emigrants at a considerable profit—one dollar, for instance, was sold for 10 or 20 marks when its market value was 4.20 marks. It was chiefly in this way that the community acquired not only the money necessary for poor Jews and people without accounts abroad, but also the funds it needed for its own hugely expanded activities. Eichmann did not make possible this deal without encountering considerable opposition from the German financial authorities, the Ministry and the Treasury, which, after all, could not remain unaware of the fact that these transactions amounted to a devaluation of the mark.

Bragging was the vice that was Eichmann's undoing. It was sheer rodomontade when he told his men during the last days of the war: "I will jump into my grave laughing, because the fact that I have the death of five million Jews [or "enemies of the Reich," as he always claimed to have said] on my conscience gives me extraordinary satisfaction." He did not jump, and if he had anything on his conscience, it was not murder but, as it turned out, that he had once slapped the face of Dr. Josef Löwenherz, head of the Vienna Jewish community, who later became one of his favorite Jews. (He had apologized in front of his staff at the time, but this incident kept bothering him.) To claim the death of five million Jews, the approximate total of losses suffered from the combined efforts of all Nazi offices and authorities, was preposterous, as he knew very well, but he had kept repeating the damning sentence *ad nauseam* to everyone who would listen, even twelve years later in Argentina, because it gave him "an extraordinary sense of elation to think that [he] was exiting from the stage in this way." (Former Legationsrat Horst Grell, a witness for the defense, who had known Eichmann in Hungary, testified that in his opinion Eichmann was boasting. That must have been obvious to everyone who heard him utter his absurd claim.) It was sheer boasting when he pretended he had "invented" the ghetto system or had "given birth to the idea" of shipping all European Jews to Madagascar. The Theresienstadt ghetto, of which Eichmann claimed "paternity," was established years after the ghetto system had been introduced into the Eastern occupied territories, and setting up a special ghetto for certain privileged categories was, like the ghetto system, the "idea" of Heydrich. The Madagascar plan seems to have been "born" in the bureaus of the German Foreign Office, and Eichmann's own contribution to it turned out to owe a good deal to his beloved Dr. Löwenherz, whom he had drafted to put down "some basic thoughts" on how about four million Jews might be transported from Europe after the war—presumably to Palestine, since the Madagascar project was top secret. (When confronted at the trial with the Löwenherz report, Eichmann did not deny its authorship; it was one of the few moments when he appeared genuinely embarrassed.) What eventually led to his capture was his compulsion to talk big—he was "fed up with being an anonymous wanderer between the worlds"—and this compulsion must have grown considerably stronger as time passed, not only because he had nothing to do that he could consider worth doing, but also because the postwar era had bestowed so much unexpected "fame" upon him.

But bragging is a common vice, and a more specific, and also more decisive, flaw in Eichmann's character was his almost total inability ever to look at anything from the other fellow's point of view. Nowhere was this flaw more conspicuous than in his account of the Vienna episode. He and his men and the Jews were all "pulling together," and whenever there were any difficulties the Jewish functionaries would come running to him "to unburden their hearts," to tell him "all their grief and sorrow," and to ask for his help. The Jews "desired" to emigrate, and he, Eichmann, was there to help them, because it so happened that at the same time the Nazi authorities had expressed a desire to see their Reich *judenrein*. The two desires coincided, and he, Eichmann, could "do justice to both parties." At the trial, he never gave an inch when it came to this part of the story, although he agreed that today, when "times have changed so much," the Jews might not be too happy to recall this "pulling together" and he did not want "to hurt their feelings."

The German text of the taped police examination, conducted from May 29, 1960, to January 17, 1961, each page corrected and approved by Eichmann, constitutes a veritable gold mine for a psychologist—provided he is wise enough to understand that the horrible can be not only ludicrous but outright funny. Some of the comedy cannot be conveyed in English, because it lies in Eichmann's heroic fight with the German language, which invariably defeats him. It is funny when he speaks, *passim*, of "winged words" (*geflügelte Worte*, a German colloquialism for famous quotes from the classics) when he means stock phrases, *Redensarten*, or slogans, *Schlagworte*. It was funny when, during the cross-examination on the Sassen documents, conducted in German by the presiding judge, he used the phrase *"kontra geben"* (to give tit for tat), to indicate that he had resisted Sassen's efforts to liven up his stories; Judge Landau, obviously ignorant of the mysteries of card games, did not understand, and Eichmann could not think of any other way to put it. Dimly aware of a defect that must have plagued him even in school—it amounted to a mild case of aphasia—he apologized, saying, "Officialese [*Amtssprache*] is my only language." But the point here is that officialese became his language because he was genuinely incapable of uttering a single sentence that was not a cliché. (Was it these clichés that the psychiatrists thought so "normal" and "desirable"? Are these the "positive ideas" a clergyman hopes for in those to whose souls he ministers? Eichmann's best opportunity to show this positive side of his character in Jerusalem came when the young police officer in charge of his mental and psychological well-being handed him *Lolita* for relaxation. After two days Eichmann returned it, visibly indignant; "Quite an unwholesome book"—*"Das ist aber ein sehr unerfreuliches Buch"*—he told his guard.) To be sure, the judges were right when they finally told the accused that all he had said was "empty talk"—except that they thought the emptiness was feigned, and that the accused wished to cover up other thoughts which, though hideous, were not empty. This supposition seems refuted by the striking consistency with which Eichmann, despite his rather bad memory, repeated word for word the same stock phrases and self-invented clichés (when he did succeed in constructing a sentence of his own, he repeated it until it became a cliché) each time he referred to an incident or event of importance to him. Whether writing his memoirs in Argentina or in Jerusalem, whether speaking to the police examiner or to the court, what he said was always the same, expressed in the same words. The longer one listened to him, the more obvious it became that his inability to speak was closely connected with an inability to *think,* namely, to think from the standpoint of somebody else. No communication was possible with him, not because he lied but because he was surrounded by the most reliable of all safeguards against the words and the presence of others, and hence against reality as such.

Thus, confronted for eight months with the reality of being examined by a Jewish policeman, Eichmann did not have the slightest hesitation in explaining to him at considerable length, and repeatedly, why he had been unable to attain a higher grade in the S.S., that this was not his fault. He had done everything, even asked to be sent to active military duty—"Off to the front, I said to myself, then the *Standartenführer* [colonelcy] will come quicker." In court, on the contrary, he pretended he had asked to be transferred because he wanted to escape his murderous duties. He did not insist much on this, though, and, strangely, he was not confronted with his utterances to Captain Less, whom he also told that he had hoped to be

nominated for the *Einsatzgruppen*, the mobile killing units in
the East, because when they were formed, in March, 1941, his
office was "dead"—there was no emigration any longer and
deportations had not yet been started. There was, finally, his
greatest ambition—to be promoted to the job of police chief in
some German town; again, nothing doing. What makes these
pages of the examination so funny is that all this was told in
the tone of someone who was sure of finding "normal, human"
sympathy for a hard-luck story. "Whatever I prepared and
planned, everything went wrong, my personal affairs as well
as my years-long efforts to obtain land and soil for the Jews. I
don't know, everything was as if under an evil spell; whatever
I desired and wanted and planned to do, fate prevented it
somehow. I was frustrated in everything, no matter what." When
Captain Less asked his opinion on some damning and possibly
lying evidence given by a former colonel of the S.S., he
exclaimed, suddenly stuttering with rage: "I am very much
surprised that this man could ever have been an S.S. *Standartenführer*, that surprises me very much indeed. It is altogether,
altogether unthinkable. I don't know what to say." He never
said these things in a spirit of defiance, as though he wanted,
even now, to defend the standards by which he had lived in the
past. The very words "S.S.," or "career," or "Himmler" (whom
he always called by his long official title: Reichsführer S.S. and
Chief of the German Police, although he by no means admired
him) triggered in him a mechanism that had become completely
unalterable. The presence of Captain Less, a Jew from Germany
and unlikely in any case to think that members of the S.S.
advanced in their careers through the exercise of high moral qualities, did not for a moment throw this mechanism out of gear.

Now and then, the comedy breaks into the horror itself, and
results in stories, presumably true enough, whose macabre
humor easily surpasses that of any Surrealist invention. Such
was the story told by Eichmann during the police examination
about the unlucky Kommerzialrat Storfer of Vienna, one of the
representatives of the Jewish community. Eichmann had received
a telegram from Rudolf Höss, Commandant of Auschwitz, telling
him that Storfer had arrived and had urgently requested to see
Eichmann. "I said to myself: O.K., this man has always behaved

well, that is worth my while . . . I'll go there myself and see what is the matter with him. And I go to Ebner [chief of the Gestapo in Vienna], and Ebner says—I remember it only vaguely—'If only he had not been so clumsy; he went into hiding and tried to escape,' something of the sort. And the police arrested him and sent him to the concentration camp, and, according to the orders of the Reichsführer [Himmler], no one could get out once he was in. Nothing could be done, neither Dr. Ebner nor I nor anybody else could do anything about it. I went to Auschwitz and asked Höss to see Storfer. 'Yes, yes [Höss said], he is in one of the labor gangs.' With Storfer afterward, well, it was normal and human, we had a normal, human encounter. He told me all his grief and sorrow: I said: 'Well, my dear old friend [*Ja, mein lieber guter Storfer*], we certainly got it! What rotten luck!' And I also said: 'Look, I really cannot help you, because according to orders from the Reichsführer nobody can get out. I can't get you out. Dr. Ebner can't get you out. I hear you made a mistake, that you went into hiding or wanted to bolt, which, after all, *you* did not need to do.' [Eichmann meant that Storfer, as a Jewish functionary, had immunity from deportation.] I forget what his reply to this was. And then I asked him how he was. And he said, yes, he wondered if he couldn't be let off work, it was heavy work. And then I said to Höss: 'Work—Storfer won't have to work!' But Höss said: 'Everyone works here.' So I said: 'O.K.,' I said, 'I'll make out a chit to the effect that Storfer has to keep the gravel paths in order with a broom,' there were little gravel paths there, 'and that he has the right to sit down with his broom on one of the benches.' [To Storfer] I said: 'Will that be all right, Mr. Storfer? Will that suit you?' Whereupon he was very pleased, and we shook hands, and then he was given the broom and sat down on his bench. It was a great inner joy to me that I could at least see the man with whom I had worked for so many long years, and that we could speak with each other." Six weeks after this normal human encounter, Storfer was dead—not gassed, apparently, but shot.

Is this a textbook case of bad faith, of lying self-deception combined with outrageous stupidity? Or is it simply the case of the eternally unrepentant criminal (Dostoevski once mentions in his diaries that in Siberia, among scores of murderers, rapists, and burglars, he never met a single man who would admit that he had done wrong) who cannot afford to face reality because his crime has become part and parcel of it? Yet Eichmann's case is different from that of the ordinary criminal, who can shield himself effectively against the reality of a non-criminal world only within the narrow limits of his gang. Eichmann needed only to recall the past in order to feel assured that he was not lying and that he was not deceiving himself, for he and the world he lived in had once been in perfect harmony. And that German society of eighty million people had been shielded against reality and factuality by exactly the same means, the same self-deception, lies, and stupidity that had now become ingrained in Eichmann's mentality. These lies changed from year to year, and they frequently contradicted each other; moreoever, they were not necessarily the same for the various branches of the Party hierarchy or the people at large. But the practice of self-deception had become so common, almost a moral prerequisite for survival, that even now, eighteen years after the collapse of the Nazi regime, when most of the specific content of its lies has been forgotten, it is sometimes difficult not to believe that mendacity has become an integral part of the German national character. During the war, the lie most effective with the whole of the German people was the slogan of "the battle of destiny for the German people" [*der Schicksalskampf des deutschen Volkes*], coined either by Hitler or by Goebbels, which made self-deception easier on three counts: it suggested, first, that the war was no war; second, that it was started by destiny and not by Germany; and, third, that it was a matter of life and death for the Germans, who must annihilate their enemies or be annihilated.

Eichmann's astounding willingness, in Argentina as well as in Jerusalem, to admit his crimes was due less to his own criminal capacity for self-deception than to the aura of systematic mendacity that had constituted the general, and generally accepted, atmosphere of the Third Reich. "Of course" he had played a role in the extermination of the Jews; of course if he "had not transported them, they would not have been delivered to the butcher."

"What," he asked, "is there to 'admit'?" Now, he proceeded, he "would like to find peace with [his] former enemies"—a sentiment he shared not only with Himmler, who had expressed it during the last year of the war, or with the Labor Front leader Robert Ley (who, before he committed suicide in Nuremberg, had proposed the establishment of a "conciliation committee" consisting of the Nazis responsible for the massacres and the Jewish survivors) but also, unbelievably, with many ordinary Germans, who were heard to express themselves in exactly the same terms at the end of the war. This outrageous cliché was no longer issued to them from above, it was a self-fabricated stock phrase, as devoid of reality as those clichés by which the people had lived for twelve years; and you could almost see what an "extraordinary sense of elation" it gave to the speaker the moment it popped out of his mouth.

Eichmann's mind was filled to the brim with such sentences. His memory proved to be quite unreliable about what had actually happened; in a rare moment of exasperation, Judge Landau asked the accused: "What *can* you remember?" (if you don't remember the discussions at the so-called Wannsee Conference, which dealt with the various methods of killing) and the answer, of course, was that Eichmann remembered the turning points in his own career rather well, but that they did not necessarily coincide with the turning points in the story of Jewish extermination or, as a matter of fact, with the turning points in history. (He always had trouble remembering the exact date of the outbreak of the war or of the invasion of Russia.) But the point of the matter is that he had not forgotten a single one of the sentences of his that at one time or another had served to give him a "sense of elation." Hence, whenever, during the cross-examination, the judges tried to appeal to his conscience, they were met with "elation," and they were outraged as well as disconcerted when they learned that the accused had at his disposal a different elating cliché for each period of his life and each of his activities. In his mind, there was no contradiction between "I will jump into my grave laughing," appropriate for the end of the war, and "I shall gladly hang myself in public as a warning example for all anti-Semites on this earth," which now, under vastly different circumstances, fulfilled exactly the same function of giving him a lift.

These habits of Eichmann's created considerable difficulty during the trial—less for Eichmann himself than for those who had come to prosecute him, to defend him, to judge him, and to report on him. For all this, it was essential that one take him seriously, and this was very hard to do, unless one sought the easiest way out of the dilemma between the unspeakable horror of the deeds and the undeniable ludicrousness of the man who perpetrated them, and declared him a clever, calculating liar—which he obviously was not. His own convictions in this matter were far from modest: "One of the few gifts fate bestowed upon me is a capacity for truth insofar as it depends upon myself." This gift he had claimed even before the prosecutor wanted to settle on him crimes he had not committed. In the disorganized, rambling notes he made in Argentina in preparation for the interview with Sassen, when he was still, as he even pointed out at the time, "in full possession of my physical and psychological freedom," he had issued a fantastic warning to "future historians to be objective enough not to stray from the path of this truth recorded here"— fantastic because every line of these scribblings shows his utter ignorance of everything that was not directly, technically and bureaucratically, connected with his job, and also shows an extraordinarily faulty memory.

Despite all the efforts of the prosecution, everybody could see that this man was not a "monster," but it was difficult indeed not to suspect that he was a clown. And since this suspicion would have been fatal to the whole enterprise, and was also rather hard to sustain in view of the sufferings he and his like had caused to millions of people, his worst clowneries were hardly noticed and almost never reported. What could you do with a man who first declared, with great emphasis, that the one thing he had learned in an ill-spent life was that one should never take an oath ("Today no man, no judge could ever persuade me to make a sworn statement, to declare something under oath as a witness. I refuse it, I refuse it for moral reasons. Since my experience tells me that if one is loyal to his oath, one day he has to take the consequences, I have made up my mind once and for all that no judge in the world or any other authority will ever be capable of making me swear an oath, to give sworn testimony. I won't do it voluntarily and no one will be able to force me"), and then, after being told explicitly that if he wished to testify in his own defense he might "do so under oath or without an oath," declared without further ado that he would prefer to testify under oath? Or who, repeatedly and with a great show of feeling, assured the court, as he had assured the police examiner, that the worst thing he could do would be to try to escape his true responsibilities, to fight for his neck, to plead for mercy—and then, upon instruction of his counsel, submitted a handwritten document, containing his plea for mercy?

As far as Eichmann was concerned, these were questions of changing moods, and as long as he was capable of finding, either in his memory or on the spur of the moment, an elating stock phrase to go with them, he was quite content, without ever becoming aware of anything like "inconsistencies." As we shall see, this horrible gift for consoling himself with clichés did not leave him in the hour of his death.

IV : *The First Solution: Expulsion*

Had this been an ordinary trial, with the normal tug of war between prosecution and defense to bring out the facts and do justice to both sides, it would be possible to switch now to the version of the defense and find out whether there was not more to Eichmann's grotesque account of his activities in Vienna than meets the eye, and whether his distortions of reality could not really be ascribed to more than the mendacity of an individual. The facts for which Eichmann was to hang had been established "beyond reasonable doubt" long before the trial started, and they were generally known to all students of the Nazi regime. The additional facts that the prosecution tried to establish were, it is true, partly accepted in the judgment, but they would never have appeared to be "beyond reasonable doubt" if the defense had brought its own evidence to bear upon the proceedings. Hence, no report on the Eichmann case, perhaps as distinguished from the Eichmann trial, could be complete without paying some attention to certain facts that are well enough known but that Dr. Servatius chose to ignore.

This is especially true of Eichmann's muddled general outlook and ideology with respect to "the Jewish question." During cross-examination, he told the presiding judge that in Vienna he "regarded the Jews as opponents with respect to whom a mutually acceptable, a mutually fair solution had to be found. . . . That solution I envisaged as putting firm soil under their feet so that they would have a place of their own, soil of their own. And I was working in the direction of that solution joyfully. I cooperated in reaching such a solution, gladly and joyfully, because it was also the kind of solution that was approved by movements among the Jewish people themselves, and I regarded this as the most appropriate solution to this matter."

This was the true reason they had all "pulled together," the reason their work had been "based upon mutuality." It was in the interest of the Jews, though perhaps not all Jews understood this, to get out of the country; "one had to help them, one had to help these functionaries to act, and that's what I did." If the Jewish functionaries were "idealists," that is, Zionists, he respected them, "treated them as equals," listened to all their "requests and complaints and applications for support," kept his "promises" as far as he could—"People are inclined to forget that now." Who but he, Eichmann, had saved hundreds of thousands of Jews? What but his great zeal and gifts of organization had enabled them to escape in time? True, he could not foresee at the time the coming Final Solution, but he had saved them, that was a "fact." (In an interview given in this country during the trial, Eichmann's son told the same story to American reporters. It must have been a family legend.)

In a sense, one can understand why counsel for the defense did nothing to back up Eichmann's version of his relations with the Zionists. Eichmann admitted, as he had in the Sassen interview, that he "did not greet his assignment with the apathy of an ox being led to his stall," that he had been very different from those colleagues "who had never read a basic book [i.e., Herzl's *Judenstaat*], worked through it, absorbed it, absorbed it with interest," and who therefore lacked "inner rapport with their work." They were "nothing but office drudges," for whom everything was decided "by paragraphs, by orders, who were interested in nothing else," who were, in short, precisely such "small cogs" as, according to the defense, Eichmann himself had been. If this meant no more than giving unquestioning obedience to the Führer's orders, then they had all been small cogs—even Himmler, we are told by his masseur, Felix Kersten, had not greeted the Final Solution with great enthusiasm, and Eichmann assured the police examiner that his own boss, Heinrich Müller, would never have proposed anything so "crude" as "physical extermination." Obviously, in Eichmann's eyes the small-cog theory was quite beside the point. Certainly he had not been as big as Mr. Hausner tried to make him; after all, he was not Hitler, nor, for that matter, could he compare himself in importance, as far as the "solution" of the Jewish question was concerned, with Müller, or Heydrich, or Himmler; he was no megalomaniac. But neither was he as small as the defense wished him to be.

Eichmann's distortions of reality were horrible because of the horrors they dealt with, but in principle they were not very different from things current in post-Hitler Germany. There is, for instance, Franz-Josef Strauss, former Minister of Defense, who recently conducted an election campaign against Willy Brandt, now mayor of West Berlin, but a refugee in Norway during the Hitler period. Strauss asked a widely publicized and apparently very successful question of Mr. Brandt—"What were you doing those twelve years outside Germany? We know what we were doing here in Germany"—with complete impunity, without anybody's batting an eye, let alone reminding the member of the Bonn government that what Germans in Germany were doing during those years has become notorious indeed. The same "innocence" is to be found in a recent casual remark by a respected and respectable German literary critic, who was probably never a Party member; reviewing a study of literature in the Third Reich, he said that its author belonged with "those intellectuals who at the outbreak of barbarism deserted us without exception." This author was of course a Jew, and he was expelled by the Nazis and himself deserted by Gentiles, people like Mr. Heinz Beckmann of the *Rheinischer Merkur*. Incidentally, the very word "barbarism," today frequently applied by Germans to the Hitler period, is a distortion of reality; it is as though Jewish and non-Jewish intellectuals had fled a country that was no longer "refined" enough for them.

Eichmann, though much less refined than statesmen and literary critics, could, on the other hand, have cited certain indisputable facts to back up his story if his memory had not been so bad, or if the defense had helped him. For "it is indisputable that during the first stages of their Jewish policy the National Socialists thought it proper to adopt a pro-Zionist attitude" (Hans Lamm), and it was during these first stages that Eichmann learned his lessons about Jews. He was by no means alone in taking this "pro-Zionism" seriously; the German Jews themselves thought it would be sufficient to undo "assimilation" through a new process of "dissimilation," and flocked into the ranks of the Zionist movement. (There are no reliable statistics on this development, but it is estimated that the circulation of the Zionist weekly *Die Jüdische Rundschau* increased in the first months of the Hitler regime from approximately five to seven thousand to nearly forty thousand, and it is known that the Zionist fund-raising organizations received in 1935-36, from a greatly diminished and impoverished population, three times as much as in 1931-32.) This did not necessarily mean that the Jews wished to emigrate to Palestine; it was more a matter of pride: "Wear it with Pride, the Yellow Star!," the most popular slogan of these years, coined by Robert Weltsch, editor-in-chief of the *Jüdische Rundschau*, expressed the general emotional atmosphere. The polemical point of the slogan, formulated as a response to Boycott Day, April 1, 1933—more than six years before the Nazis actually forced the Jews to wear a badge, a six-pointed yellow star on a white ground—was directed against the "assimilationists" and all those people who refused to be reconciled to the new "revolutionary development," those who "were always behind the times" (*die ewig Gestrigen*). The slogan was recalled at the trial, with a good deal of emotion, by witnesses from Germany. They forgot to mention that Robert Weltsch himself, a highly distinguished journalist, had said in recent years that he would never have issued his slogan if he had been able to foresee developments.

But quite apart from all slogans and ideological quarrels, it was in those years a fact of everyday life that only Zionists had any chance of negotiating with the German authorities, for the simple reason that their chief Jewish adversary, the Central Association of German Citizens of Jewish Faith, to which ninety-five per cent of organized Jews in Germany then belonged, specified in its bylaws that its chief task was the "fight against anti-Semitism"; it had suddenly become by definition an organization "hostile to the State," and would indeed have been persecuted—which it was not—if it had ever dared to do what it was supposed to do. During its first few years, Hitler's rise to power appeared to the Zionists chiefly as "the decisive defeat of assimilationism." Hence, the Zionists could, for a time, at least, engage in a certain amount of non-criminal cooperation with the Nazi authorities; the Zionists too believed that "dissimilation," combined with the emigration to Palestine of Jewish youngsters and, they hoped, Jewish capitalists, could be a "mutually fair solution." At the time, many German officials held this opinion, and this kind of talk seems to have been quite common up to the end. A letter from a survivor of Theresienstadt, a German Jew, relates that all leading positions in the Nazi-appointed *Reichsvereinigung* were held by Zionists (whereas the authentically Jewish *Reichsvertretung* had been composed of both Zionists and non-Zionists), because Zionists, according to the Nazis, were "the 'decent' Jews since they too thought in 'national' terms." To be sure, no prominent Nazi ever spoke publicly in this vein; from beginning to end, Nazi propaganda was fiercely, unequivocally, uncompromisingly anti-Semitic, and eventually nothing counted but what people who were still without experience in the mysteries of totalitarian government dismissed as "mere propaganda." There existed in those first years a mutually highly satisfactory agreement between the Nazi authorities and the Jewish Agency for Palestine—a *Ha'avarah*, or Transfer Agreement, which provided that an emigrant to Palestine could transfer his money there in German goods and exchange them for pounds upon arrival. It was soon the only legal way for a Jew to take his money with him (the alternative then being the establishment of a blocked account, which could be liquidated abroad only at a loss of between fifty and ninety-five per cent). The result was that in the thirties, when American Jewry took great pains to organize a boycott of German merchandise, Palestine, of all places, was swamped with all kinds of goods "made in Germany."

Of greater importance for Eichmann were the emissaries from Palestine, who would approach the Gestapo and the S.S. on their own initiative, without taking orders from either the German Zionists or the Jewish Agency for Palestine. They came in order to enlist help for the illegal immigration of Jews into British-ruled Palestine, and both the Gestapo and the S.S. were helpful. They negotiated with Eichmann in Vienna, and they reported that he was "polite," "not the shouting type," and that he even provided them with farms and facilities for setting up vocational training camps for prospective immigrants. ("On one occasion, he expelled a group of nuns from a convent to provide a training farm for young Jews," and on another "a special train [was made available] and Nazi officials accompanied" a group of emigrants, ostensibly headed for Zionist training farms in Yugoslavia, to see them safely across the border.) According to the story told by Jon and David Kimche, with "the full and generous cooperation of all the chief actors" (*The Secret Roads: The "Illegal" Migration of a People, 1938-1948*, London, 1954), these Jews from Palestine spoke a language not totally different from that of Eichmann. They had been sent to Europe by the communal settlements in Palestine, and they were not interested in rescue operations: "That was not their job." They wanted to select "suitable material," and their chief enemy, prior to the extermination program, was not those who made life impossible for Jews in the old countries, Germany or Austria, but those who barred access to the new homeland; that enemy was definitely Britain, not Germany. Indeed, they were in a position to deal with the Nazi authorities on a footing amounting to equality, which native Jews were not, since they enjoyed the protection of the mandatory power; they were probably among the first Jews to talk openly about mutual interests and were certainly the first to be given permission "to pick young Jewish pioneers" from among the Jews in the concentration camps. Of course, they were unaware of the sinister implications of this deal, which still lay in the future; but they too somehow believed that if it was a question of selecting Jews for survival, the Jews should do the selecting themselves. It was this fundamental error in judgment that eventually led to a situation in which the non-selected majority of Jews inevitably found themselves confronted with two enemies—the Nazi authorities and the Jewish authorities. As far as the Viennese episode is concerned, Eichmann's preposterous claim to have saved hundreds of thousands of Jewish lives, which was laughed out of court, finds strange support in the considered judgment of the Jewish historians, the Kimches: "Thus what must have been one of the most paradoxical episodes of the entire period of the Nazi regime began: the man who was to go down in history as one of the arch-murderers of the Jewish people entered the lists as an active worker in the rescue of Jews from Europe."

Eichmann's trouble was that he remembered none of the

facts that might have supported, however faintly, his incredible
story, while the learned counsel for the defense probably did not
even know that there was anything to remember. (Dr. Servatius
could have called as witnesses for the defense the former
agents of Aliyah Beth, as the organization for illegal immigration into Palestine was called; they certainly still remembered
Eichmann, and they were now living in Israel.) Eichmann's
memory functioned only in respect to things that had had a direct
bearing upon his career. Thus, he remembered a visit he had
received in Berlin from a Palestinian functionary who told him
about life in the collective settlements, and whom he had twice
taken out to dinner, because this visit ended with a formal
invitation to Palestine, where the Jews would show him the
country. He was delighted; no other Nazi official had been able
to go "to a distant foreign land," and he received permission
to make the trip. The judgment concluded that he had been
sent "on an espionage mission," which no doubt was true, but
this did not contradict the story Eichmann had told the police.
(Practically nothing came of the enterprise. Eichmann, together
with a journalist from his office, a certain Herbert Hagen, had
just enough time to climb Mount Carmel in Haifa before the
British authorities deported both of them to Egypt and denied
them entry permits for Palestine; according to Eichmann, "the
man from the Haganah"—the Jewish military organization
which became the nucleus of the Israeli Army—came to see
them in Cairo, and what he told them there became the subject
of a "thoroughly negative report" Eichmann and Hagen were
ordered by their superiors to write for propaganda purposes;
this was duly published.)

Apart from such minor triumphs, Eichmann remembered only
moods and the catch phrases he made up to go with them; the
trip to Egypt had been in 1937, prior to his activity in Vienna,
and from Vienna he remembered no more than the general
atmosphere and how "elated" he had felt. In view of his
astounding virtuosity in never discarding a mood and its catch
phrase once and for all when they became incompatible with
a new era, which required different moods and different "elating"
phrases—a virtuosity that he demonstrated over and over during
the police examination—one is tempted to believe in his sincerity

when he spoke of the time in Vienna as an idyll. Because of the complete lack of consistency in his thoughts and sentiments, this sincerity is not even undermined by the fact that his year in Vienna, from the spring of 1938 to March, 1939, came at a time when the Nazi regime had abandoned its pro-Zionist attitude. It was in the nature of the Nazi movement that it kept moving, became more radical with each passing month, but one of the outstanding characteristics of its members was that psychologically they tended to be always one step behind the movement—that they had the greatest difficulty in keeping up with it, or, as Hitler used to phrase it, that they could not "jump over their own shadow."

More damning, however, than any objective fact was Eichmann's own faulty memory. There were certain Jews in Vienna whom he recalled very vividly—Dr. Löwenherz and Kommerzialrat Storfer—but they were not those Palestinian emissaries, who might have backed up his story. Josef Löwenherz, who after the war wrote a very interesting memorandum about his negotiations with Eichmann (one of the few new documents produced by the trial, it was shown in part to Eichmann, who found himself in complete agreement with its main statements), was the first Jewish functionary actually to organize a whole Jewish community into an institution at the service of the Nazi authorities. And he was one of the very, very few such functionaries to reap a reward for his services—he was permitted to stay in Vienna until the end of the war, when he emigrated to England and the United States; he died shortly after Eichmann's capture, in 1960. Storfer's fate, as we have seen, was less fortunate, but this certainly was not Eichmann's fault. Storfer had replaced the Palestinian emissaries, who had become too independent, and his task, assigned to him by Eichmann, was to organize some illegal transports of Jews into Palestine without the help of the Zionists. Storfer was no Zionist and had shown no interest in Jewish matters prior to the arrival of the Nazis in Austria. Still, with the help of Eichmann he succeeded in getting some thirty-five hundred Jews out of Europe, in 1940, when half of Europe was occupied by the Nazis, and it seems that he did his best to clear things with the Palestinians. (That is probably what Eichmann had in mind when he added to his story about

Storfer in Auschwitz the cryptic remark: "Storfer never betrayed Judaism, not with a single word, not Storfer.") A third Jew, finally, whom Eichmann never failed to recall in connection with his prewar activities was Dr. Paul Eppstein, in charge of emigration in Berlin during the last years of the *Reichsvereinigung*—a Nazi-appointed Jewish central organization, not to be confused with the authentically Jewish *Reichsvertretung*, which was dissolved in July, 1939. Dr. Eppstein was appointed by Eichmann to serve as *Judenältester* (Jewish Elder) in Theresienstadt, where he was shot in 1944.

In other words, the only Jews Eichmann remembered were those who had been completely in his power. He had forgotten not only the Palestinian emissaries but also his earlier Berlin acquaintances, whom he had known well when he was still engaged in intelligence work and had no executive powers. He never mentioned, for instance, Dr. Franz Meyer, a former member of the Executive of the Zionist Organization in Germany, who came to testify for the prosecution about his contacts with the accused from 1936 to 1939. To some extent, Dr. Meyer confirmed Eichmann's own story: in Berlin, the Jewish functionaries could "put forward complaints and requests," there was a kind of cooperation. Sometimes, Meyer said, "we came to ask for something, and there were times when he demanded something from us"; Eichmann at that time "was genuinely listening to us and was sincerely trying to understand the situation"; his behavior was "quite correct"—"he used to address me as 'Mister' and to offer me a seat." But in February, 1939, all this had changed. Eichmann had summoned the leaders of German Jewry to Vienna to explain to them his new methods of "forced emigration." And there he was, sitting in a large room on the ground floor of the Rothschild Palais, recognizable, of course, but completely changed: "I immediately told my friends that I did not know whether I was meeting the same man. So terrible was the change. . . . Here I met a man who comported himself as a master of life and death. He received us with insolence and rudeness. He did not let us come near his desk. We had to remain standing." Prosecution and judges were in agreement that Eichmann underwent a genuine and lasting personality change when he was promoted to a post with executive powers. But the trial showed that here, too, he had "relapses," and that the matter could never have been as simple as that. There was the witness who testified to an interview with him at Theresienstadt in March, 1945, when Eichmann again showed himself to be very interested in Zionist matters—the witness was a member of a Zionist youth organization and held a certificate of entry for Palestine. The interview was "conducted in very pleasant language and the attitude was kind and respectful." (Strangely, counsel for the defense never mentioned this witness's testimony in his *plaidoyer.*)

Whatever doubts there may be about Eichmann's personality change in Vienna, there is no doubt that this appointment marked the real beginning of his career. Between 1937 and 1941, he won four promotions; within fourteen months he advanced from *Untersturmführer* to *Hauptsturmführer* (that is, from second lieutenant to captain); and in another year and a half he was made *Obersturmbannführer*, or lieutenant colonel. That happened in October, 1941, shortly after he was assigned the role in the Final Solution that was to land him in the District Court of Jerusalem. And there, to his great grief, he "got stuck"; as he saw it, there was no higher grade obtainable in the section in which he worked. But this he could not know during the four years in which he climbed quicker and higher than he had ever anticipated. In Vienna, he had shown his mettle, and now he was recognized not merely as an expert on "the Jewish question," the intricacies of Jewish organizations and Zionist parties, but as an "authority" on emigration and evacuation, as the "master" who knew how to make people move. His greatest triumph came shortly after the *Kristallnacht,* in November, 1938, when German Jews had become frantic in their desire to escape. Göring, probably on the initiative of Heydrich, decided to establish in Berlin a Reich Center for Jewish Emigration, and in the letter containing his directives Eichmann's Viennese office was specifically mentioned as the model to be used in the setting up of a central authority. The head of the Berlin office was not to be Eichmann, however, but his later greatly admired boss Heinrich Müller, another of Heydrich's discoveries. Heydrich had just taken Müller away from his job as a regular Bavarian police officer (he was not even a member of the Party and had been an opponent until 1933), and called him to the Gestapo in Berlin, because he was known to be an authority on the Soviet Russian police system. For Müller, too, this was the beginning of his career, though he had to start with a comparatively small assignment. (Müller, incidentally, not prone to boasting like Eichmann and known for his "sphinxlike conduct," succeeded in disappearing altogether; nobody knows his whereabouts, though there are rumors that first East Germany and now Albania have engaged the services of the Russian-police expert.)

In March, 1939, Hitler moved into Czechoslovakia and erected a German protectorate over Bohemia and Moravia. Eichmann was immediately appointed to set up another emigration center for Jews in Prague. "In the beginning I was not too happy to leave Vienna, for if you have installed such an office and if you see everything running smoothly and in good order, you don't like to give it up." And indeed, Prague was somewhat disappointing, although the system was the same as in Vienna, for "The functionaries of the Czech Jewish organizations went to Vienna and the Viennese people came to Prague, so that I did not have to intervene at all. The model in Vienna was simply copied and carried to Prague. Thus the whole thing got started automatically." But the Prague center was much smaller, and "I regret to say there were no people of the caliber and the energy of a Dr. Löwenherz." But these, as it were, personal reasons for discontent were minor compared to mounting difficulties of another, entirely objective nature. Hundreds of thousands of Jews had left their homelands in a matter of a few years, and millions waited behind them, for the Polish and Rumanian governments left no doubt in their official proclamations that they, too, wished to be rid of their Jews. They could not understand why the world should get indignant if they followed in the footsteps of a "great and cultured nation." (This enormous arsenal of potential refugees had been revealed during the Evian Conference, called in the summer of 1938 to solve the problem of German Jewry through intergovernmental action. It was a resounding fiasco and did great harm to German Jews.) The avenues for emigration overseas now became clogged up, just as the escape possibilities within Europe had been exhausted earlier, and even under the best of circumstances, if war had not interfered with his program, Eichmann would hardly have been able to repeat the Viennese "miracle" in Prague.

He knew this very well, he really had become an expert on matters of emigration, and he could not have been expected to greet his next appointment with any great enthusiasm. War had broken out in September, 1939, and one month later Eichmann was called back to Berlin to succeed Müller as head of the Reich Center for Jewish Emigration. A year before, this would have been a real promotion, but now was the wrong moment. No one in his senses could possibly think any longer of a solution of the Jewish question in terms of forced emigration; quite apart from the difficulties of getting people from one country to another in wartime, the Reich had acquired, through the conquest of Polish territories, two or two and a half million more Jews. It is true that the Hitler government was still willing to let its Jews go (the order that stopped all Jewish emigration came only two years later, in the fall of 1941), and if any "final solution" had been decided upon, nobody had as yet given orders to that effect, although Jews were already concentrated in ghettos in the East and were also being liquidated by the *Einsatzgruppen*. It was only natural that emigration, however smartly organized in Berlin in accordance with the "assembly line principle," should peter out by itself—a process Eichmann described as being "like pulling teeth . . . listless, I would say, on both sides. On the Jewish side because it was really difficult to obtain any emigration possibilities to speak of, and on our side because there was no bustle and no rush, no coming and going of people. There we were, sitting in a great and mighty building, amid a yawning emptiness." Evidently, if Jewish matters, his specialty, remained a matter of emigration, he would soon be out of a job.

V : *The Second Solution: Concentration*

It was not until the outbreak of the war, on September 1, 1939, that the Nazi regime became openly totalitarian and openly criminal. One of the most important steps in this direction, from an organizational point of view, was a decree, signed by Himmler, that fused the Security Service of the S.S., to which Eichmann had belonged since 1934, and which was a Party organ, with the regular Security Police of the State, in which the Secret State Police, or Gestapo, was included. The result of the merger was the Head Office for Reich Security (R.S.H.A.), whose chief was first Reinhardt Heydrich; after Heydrich's death in 1942, Eichmann's old acquaintance from Linz, Dr. Ernst Kaltenbrunner, took over. All officials of the police, not only of the Gestapo but also of the Criminal Police and the Order Police, received S.S. titles corresponding to their previous ranks, regardless of whether or not they were Party members, and this meant that in the space of a day a most important part of the old civil services was incorporated into the most radical section of the Nazi hierarchy. No one, as far as I know, protested, or resigned his job. (Though Himmler, the head and founder of the S.S., had since 1936 been Chief of the German Police as well, the two apparatuses had remained separate until now.) The R.S.H.A., moreover, was only one of twelve Head Offices in the S.S., the most important of which, in the present context, were the Head Office of the Order Police, under General Kurt Daluege, which was responsible for the rounding up of Jews, and the Head Office for Administration and Economy (the *S.S.-Wirtschafts-Verwaltungshauptamt,* or W.V.H.A.), headed by Oswald Pohl, which was in charge of concentration camps and was later to be in charge of the "economic" side of the extermination.

This "objective" attitude—talking about concentration camps in terms of "administration" and about extermination camps in terms of "economy"—was typical of the S.S. mentality, and something Eichmann, at the trial, was still very proud of. By its "objectivity" (*Sachlichkeit*), the S.S. dissociated itself from such "emotional" types as Streicher, that "unrealistic fool," and also from certain "Teutonic-Germanic Party bigwigs who behaved as though they were clad in horns and pelts." Eichmann admired Heydrich greatly because he did not like such nonsense at all, and he was out of sympathy with Himmler because, among other things, the Reichsführer S.S. and Chief of the German Police, though boss of all the S.S. Head Offices, had permitted himself "at least for a long time to be influenced by it." During the trial, however, it was not the accused, S.S. *Obersturmbannführer a.D.*, who was to carry off the prize for "objectivity"; it was Dr. Servatius, a tax and business lawyer from Cologne who had never joined the Nazi Party and who nevertheless was to teach the court a lesson in what it means not to be "emotional" that no one who heard him is likely to forget. The moment, one of the few great ones in the whole trial, occurred during the short oral *plaidoyer* of the defense, after which the court withdrew for four months to write its judgment. Servatius declared the accused innocent of charges bearing on his responsibility for "the collection of skeletons, sterilizations, killings by gas, and *similar medical matters,*" whereupon Judge Halevi interrupted him: "Dr. Servatius, I assume you made a slip of the tongue when you said that killing by gas was a medical matter." To which Servatius replied: "It was indeed a medical matter, since it was prepared by physicians; *it was a matter of killing, and killing, too, is a medical matter.*" And, perhaps to make absolutely sure that the judges in Jerusalem would not forget how Germans—ordinary Germans, not former members of the S.S. or even of the Nazi Party—even today can regard acts that in other countries are called murder, he repeated the phrase in his "Comments on the Judgment of the First Instance," prepared for the review of the case before the Supreme Court; he said again that not Eichmann, but one of his men, Rolf Günther, "was always engaged in medical matters." (Dr. Servatius is well acquainted with "medical matters" in the Third Reich. At Nuremberg he defended Dr. Karl Brandt, Hitler's personal physician, Plenipotentiary for "Hygiene and Health," and chief of the euthanasia program.)

Each of the Head Offices of the S.S., in its wartime organization, was divided into sections and subsections, and the R.S.H.A. eventually contained seven main sections. Section IV was the bureau of the Gestapo, and it was headed by Gruppenführer (major general) Heinrich Müller, whose rank was the one he had held in the Bavarian police. His task was to combat "opponents hostile to the State," of which there were two categories, to be dealt with by two sections: Subsection IV-A handled "opponents" accused of Communism, Sabotage, Liberalism, and Assassinations, and Subsection IV-B dealt with "sects," that is, Catholics, Protestants, Freemasons (the post remained vacant), and Jews. Each of the categories in these subsections received an office of its own, designated by an arabic numeral, so that Eichmann eventually—in 1941—was appointed to the desk of IV-B-4 in the R.S.H.A. Since his immediate superior, the head of IV-B, turned out to be a nonentity, his real superior was always Müller. Müller's superior was Heydrich, and later Kaltenbrunner, each of whom was, in his turn, under the command of Himmler, who received his orders directly from Hitler.

In addition to his twelve Head Offices, Himmler presided over an altogether different organizational setup, which also played an enormous role in the execution of the Final Solution. This was the network of Higher S.S. and Police Leaders who were in command of the regional organizations; their chain of command did not link them with the R.S.H.A., they were directly responsible to Himmler, and they always outranked Eichmann and the men at his disposal. The *Einsatzgruppen*, on the other hand, were under the command of Heydrich and the R.S.H.A.— which, of course, does not mean that Eichmann necessarily had anything to do with them. The commanders of the *Einsatzgruppen* also invariably held a higher rank than Eichmann. Technically and organizationally, Eichmann's position was not very high; his post turned out to be such an important one only because the Jewish question, for purely ideological reasons, acquired a greater importance with every day and week and month of the war, until, in the years of defeat—from 1943 on—it had grown to fantastic proportions. When that happened, his was still the only office that officially dealt with nothing but "the opponent, Jewry," but in fact he had lost his monopoly, because by then all offices and apparatuses, State and Party, Army and S.S., were busy "solving" that problem. Even if we concentrate our attention only upon the police machinery and disregard all the other offices, the picture is absurdly complicated, since we have to add to the *Einsatzgruppen* and the Higher S.S. and Police Leader Corps the Commanders and the Inspectors of the Security Police and the Security Service. Each of these groups belonged in a different chain of command that ultimately reached Himmler, but they were equal with respect to each other and no one belonging to one group owed obedience to a superior officer of another group. The prosecution, it must be admitted, was in a most difficult position in finding its way through this labyrinth of parallel institutions, which it had to do each time it wanted to pin some specific responsibility on Eichmann. (If the trial were to take place today, this task would be much easier, since Raul Hilberg in his *The Destruction of the European Jews* has succeeded in presenting the first clear description of this incredibly complicated machinery of destruction.)

Furthermore, it must be remembered that all these organs, wielding enormous power, were in fierce competition with one another—which was no help to their victims, since their ambition was always the same: to kill as many Jews as possible. This competitive spirit, which, of course, inspired in each man a great loyalty to his own outfit, has survived the war, only now it works in reverse: it has become each man's desire "to exonerate his own outfit" at the expense of all the others. This was the explanation Eichmann gave when he was confronted with the memoirs of Rudolf Höss, Commander of Auschwitz, in which Eichmann is accused of certain things that he claimed he never did and was in no position to do. He admitted easily enough that Höss had no personal reasons for saddling him with acts of which he was innocent, since their relations had been quite friendly; but he insisted, in vain, that Höss wanted to exculpate his own outfit, the Head Office for Administration and Economy, and to put all the blame on the R.S.H.A. Something of the same sort happened at Nuremberg, where the various accused presented a nauseating spectacle by accusing each other—though none of them blamed Hitler! Still, no one did this merely to save his own neck at the expense of somebody else's; the men on trial there represented altogether different organizations, with long-standing, deeply ingrained hostility to one another. Dr. Hans Globke, whom we met before, tried to exonerate his own Ministry of the Interior at the expense of the Foreign Office, when he testified for the prosecution at Nuremberg. Eichmann, on the other hand, always tried to shield Müller, Heydrich, and Kaltenbrunner, although the latter had treated him quite badly. No doubt one of the chief objective mistakes of the prosecution at Jerusalem was that its case relied too heavily on sworn or unsworn affidavits of former high-ranking Nazis, dead or alive; it did not see, and perhaps could not be expected to see, how dubious these documents were as sources for the establishment of facts. Even the judgment, in its evaluation of the damning testimonies of other Nazi criminals, took into account that (in the words of one of the defense witnesses) "it was customary at the time of the war-crime trials to put as much blame as possible on those who were absent or believed to be dead."

When Eichmann entered his new office in Section IV of the R.S.H.A., he was still confronted with the uncomfortable dilemma that on the one hand "forced emigration" was the official formula for the solution of the Jewish question, and, on the other hand, emigration was no longer possible. For the first (and almost the last) time in his life in the S.S., he was compelled by circumstances to take the initiative, to see if he could not "give birth to an idea." According to the version he gave at the police examination, he was blessed with three ideas. All three of them, he had to admit, came to naught; everything he tried on his own invariably went wrong—the final blow came when he had "to abandon" his private fortress in Berlin before he could try it out against Russian tanks. Nothing but frustration; a hard luck story if there ever was one. The inexhaustible source of trouble, as he saw it, was that he and his men were never left alone, that all these other State and Party offices wanted their share in the "solution," with the result that a veritable army of "Jewish experts" had cropped up everywhere and were falling over themselves in their efforts to be first in a field of which they knew nothing. For these people, Eichmann had the greatest contempt, partly because they were Johnnies-come-lately, partly because they tried to enrich themselves, and often succeeded in getting quite rich in the course of their work, and partly because they were ignorant, they had not read the one or two "basic books."

His three dreams turned out to have been inspired by the "basic books," but it was also revealed that two of the three were definitely not his ideas at all, and with respect to the third—well, "I do not know any longer whether it was Stahlecker [his superior in Vienna and Prague] or myself who gave birth to the idea, anyhow the idea was born." This last idea was the first, chronologically; it was the "idea of Nisko," and its failure was for Eichmann the clearest possible proof of the evil of interference. (The guilty person in this case was Hans Frank, Governor General of Poland.) In order to understand the plan, we must remember that after the conquest of Poland and prior to the German attack on Russia, the Polish territories were divided between Germany and Russia; the German part consisted of the Western Regions, which were incorporated into the Reich, and the so-called Eastern Area, including Warsaw, which was known as the General Government. For the time being, the Eastern Area was treated as occupied territory. As the solution of the Jewish question at this time was still "forced emigration," with the goal of making Germany *judenrein,* it was natural that Polish Jews in the annexed territories, together with the remaining Jews in other parts of the Reich, should be shoved into the General Government, which, whatever it may have been, was not considered to be part of the Reich. By December, 1939, evacuations eastward had started and roughly one million Jews—six hundred thousand from the incorporated area and four hundred thousand from the Reich—began to arrive in the General Government.

If Eichmann's version of the Nisko adventure is true—and there is no reason not to believe him—he or, more likely, his Prague and Vienna superior, Brigadeführer (brigadier general) Franz Stahlecker must have anticipated these developments by several months. This *Dr.* Stahlecker, as Eichmann was careful

to call him, was in his opinion a very fine man, educated, full
of reason, and "free of hatred and chauvinism of any kind"—
in Vienna, he used to shake hands with the Jewish functionaries.
A year and a half later, in the spring of 1941, this educated
gentleman was appointed Commander of *Einsatzgruppe* A, and
managed to kill by shooting, in little more than a year (he
himself was killed in action in 1942), two hundred and fifty
thousand Jews—as he proudly reported to Himmler himself,
although the chief of the *Einsatzgruppen*, which were police
units, was the head of the Security Police and the S.D., that is,
Reinhardt Heydrich. But that came later, and now, in September,
1939, while the German Army was still busy occupying the
Polish territories, Eichmann and Dr. Stahlecker began to think
"privately" about how the Security Service might get its share
of influence in the East. What they needed was "an area as
large as possible in Poland, to be carved off for the erection
of an autonomous Jewish state in the form of a protectorate.
. . . This could be *the* solution." And off they went, on their
own initiative, without orders from anybody, to reconnoiter.
They went to the Radom District, on the San River, not far
from the Russian border, and they "saw a huge territory, villages, market places, small towns," and "we said to ourselves:
that is what we need and why should one not resettle Poles
for a change, since people are being resettled everywhere"; this
will be "the solution of the Jewish question"—firm soil under
their feet—at least for some time.

Everything seemed to go very well at first. They went to
Heydrich, and Heydrich agreed and told them to go ahead.
It so happened—though Eichmann, in Jerusalem, had com-
pletely forgotten it—that their project fitted very well in
Heydrich's over-all plan at this stage for the solution of the
Jewish question. On September 21, 1939, he had called a
meeting of the "heads of departments" of the R.S.H.A. and
the *Einsatzgruppen* (operating already in Poland), at which
general directives for the immediate future had been given:
concentration of Jews in ghettos, establishment of Councils of
Jewish Elders, and the deportation of all Jews to the General
Government area. Eichmann had attended this meeting setting
up the "Jewish Center of Emigration"—as was proved at the

trial through the minutes, which Bureau 06 of the Israeli police had discovered in the National Archives in Washington. Hence, Eichmann's, or Stahlecker's, initiative amounted to no more than a concrete plan for carrying out Heydrich's directives. And now thousands of people, chiefly from Austria, were deported helter-skelter into this God-forsaken place which, an S.S. officer —Erich Rajakowitsch, who later was in charge of the deportation of Dutch Jews—explained to them, "the Führer has promised the Jews as a new homeland. There are no dwellings, there are no houses. If you build, there will be a roof over your heads. There is no water, the wells all around carry disease, there is cholera, dysentery, and typhoid. If you bore and find water, you will have water." As one can see, "everything looked marvelous," except that the S.S. expelled some of the Jews from this paradise, driving them across the Russian border, and others had the good sense to escape of their own volition. But then, Eichmann complained, "the obstructions began on the part of Hans Frank," whom they had forgotten to inform, although this was "his" territory. "Frank complained in Berlin and a great tug of war started. Frank wanted to solve his Jewish question all by himself. He did not want to receive any more Jews in his General Government. Those who had arrived should disappear immediately." And they did disappear; some were even repatriated, which had never happened before and never happened again, and those who returned to Vienna were registered in the police records as "returning from vocational training"— a curious relapse into the pro-Zionist stage of the movement.

Eichmann's eagerness to acquire some territory for "his" Jews is best understood in terms of his own career. The Nisko plan was "born" during the time of his rapid advancement, and it is more than likely that he saw himself as the future Governor General, like Hans Frank in Poland, or the future Protector, like Heydrich in Czechoslovakia, of a "Jewish State." The utter fiasco of the whole enterprise, however, must have taught him a lesson about the possibilities and the desirability of "private" initiative. And since he and Stahlecker had acted within the framework of Heydrich's directives and with his explicit consent, this unique repatriation of Jews, clearly a temporary defeat for the police and the S.S., must also have taught him that the steadily increasing power of his own outfit did not amount to omnipotence, that the State Ministries and the other Party institutions were quite prepared to fight to maintain their own shrinking power.

Eichmann's second attempt at "putting firm ground under the feet of the Jews" was the Madagascar project. The plan to evacuate four million Jews from Europe to the French island off the southeast coast of Africa—an island with a native population of 4,370,000 and an area of 227,678 square miles of poor land—had originated in the Foreign Office and was then transmitted to the R.S.H.A. because, in the words of Dr. Martin Luther, who was in charge of Jewish affairs in the Wilhelmstrasse, only the police "possessed the experiences and the technical facilities to execute an evacuation of Jews *en masse* and to guarantee the supervision of the evacuees." The "Jewish State" was to have a police governor under the jurisdiction of Himmler. The project itself had an odd history. Eichmann, confusing Madagascar with Uganda, always claimed to having dreamed "a dream once dreamed by the Jewish protagonist of the Jewish State idea, Theodor Herzl," but it is true that his dream had been dreamed before—first by the Polish government, which in 1937 went to much trouble to look into the idea, only to find that it would be quite impossible to ship its own nearly three million Jews there without killing them, and, somewhat later, by the French Foreign Minister Georges Bonnet, who had the more modest plan of shipping France's foreign Jews, numbering about two hundred thousand, to the French colony. He even consulted his German opposite number, Joachim von Ribbentrop, on the matter in 1938. Eichmann at any rate was told in the summer of 1940, when his emigration business had come to a complete standstill, to work out a detailed plan for the evacuation of four million Jews to Madagascar, and this project seems to have occupied most of his time until the invasion of Russia, a year later. (Four million is a strikingly low figure for making Europe *judenrein*. It obviously did not include three million Polish Jews who, as everybody knew, had been being massacred ever since the first days of the war.) That anybody except Eichmann and some other lesser luminaries ever took the whole thing seriously seems unlikely, for—

apart from the fact that the territory was known to be unsuitable, not to mention the fact that it was, after all, a French possession —the plan would have required shipping space for four million in the midst of a war and at a moment when the British Navy was in control of the Atlantic. The Madagascar plan was always meant to serve as a cloak under which the preparations for the physical extermination of all the Jews of Western Europe could be carried forward (no such cloak was needed for the extermination of Polish Jews!), and its great advantage with respect to the army of trained anti-Semites, who, try as they might, always found themselves one step behind the Führer, was that it familiarized all concerned with the preliminary notion that nothing less than complete evacuation from Europe would do—no special legislation, no "dissimilation," no ghettos would suffice. When, a year later, the Madagascar project was declared to have become "obsolete," everybody was psychologically, or rather, logically, prepared for the next step: since there existed no territory to which one could "evacuate," the only "solution" was extermination.

Not that Eichmann, the truth-revealer for generations to come, ever suspected the existence of such sinister plans. What brought the Madagascar enterprise to naught was lack of time, and time was wasted through the never-ending interference from other offices. In Jerusalem, the police as well as the court tried to shake him out of his complacency. They confronted him with two documents concerning the meeting of September 21, 1939, mentioned above; one of them, a teletyped letter written by Heydrich and containing certain directives to the *Einsatzgruppen,* distinguished for the first time between a "final aim, requiring longer periods of time" and to be treated as "top secret," and "the stages for achieving this final aim." The phrase "final solution" did not yet appear, and the document is silent about the meaning of a "final aim." Hence, Eichmann could have said, all right, the "final aim" was his Madagascar project, which at this time was being kicked around all the German offices; for a mass evacuation, the concentration of all Jews was a necessary preliminary "stage." But Eichmann, after reading the document carefully, said immediately that he was convinced that "final aim" could only mean "physical extermination," and concluded

that "this basic idea was already rooted in the minds of the
higher leaders, or the men at the very top." This might indeed
have been the truth, but then he would have had to admit
that the Madagascar project could not have been more than a
hoax. Well, he did not; he never changed his Madagascar story,
and probably he just could not change it. It was as though
this story ran along a different tape in his memory, and it was
this taped memory that showed itself to be proof against reason
and argument and information and insight of any kind.

His memory informed him that there had existed a lull in
the activities against Western and Central European Jews between
the outbreak of the war (Hitler, in his speech to the Reichstag
of January 30, 1939, had "prophesied" that war would bring
"the annihilation of the Jewish race in Europe") and the invasion of Russia. To be sure, even then the various offices in
the Reich and in the occupied territories were doing their best
to eliminate "the opponent, Jewry," but there was no unified
policy; it seemed as though every office had its own "solution"
and might be permitted to apply it or to pit it against the
solutions of its competitors. Eichmann's solution was a police
state, and for that he needed a sizable territory. All his "efforts
failed because of the lack of understanding of the minds concerned," because of "rivalries," quarrels, squabbling, because
everybody "vied for supremacy." And then it was too late; the
war against Russia "struck suddenly, like a thunderclap." That
was the end of his dreams, as it marked the end of "the era
of searching for a solution in the interest of both sides." It was
also, as he recognized in the memoirs he wrote in Argentina,
"the end of an era in which there existed laws, ordinances,
decrees for the treatment of individual Jews." And, according
to him, it was more than that, it was the end of his career,
and though this sounded rather crazy in view of his present
"fame," it could not be denied that he had a point. For his
outfit, which either in the actuality of "forced emigration" or
in the "dream" of a Nazi-ruled Jewish State had been the final
authority in all Jewish matters, now "receded into the second
rank so far as the Final Solution of the Jewish question was
concerned, for what was now initiated was transferred to different
units, and negotiations were conducted by another Head Office,

under the command of the former Reichsführer S.S. and Chief of the German Police." The "different units" were the picked groups of killers, who operated in the rear of the Army in the East, and whose special duty consisted of massacring the native civilian population and especially the Jews; and the other Head Office was the W.V.H.A., under Oswald Pohl, to which Eichmann had to apply to find out the ultimate destination of each shipment of Jews. This was calculated according to the "absorptive capacity" of the various killing installations and also according to the requests for slave workers from the numerous industrial enterprises that had found it profitable to establish branches in the neighborhood of some of the death camps. (Apart from the not very important industrial enterprises of the S.S., such famous German firms as I.G. Farben, the Krupp Werke, and Siemens-Schuckert Werke had established plants in Auschwitz as well as near the Lublin death camps. Cooperation between the S.S. and the businessmen was excellent; Höss of Auschwitz testified to very cordial social relations with the I.G. Farben representatives. As for working conditions, the idea was clearly to kill through labor; according to Hilberg, at least twenty-five thousand of the approximately thirty-five thousand Jews who worked for one of the I.G. Farben plants died.) As far as Eichmann was concerned, the point was that evacuation and deportation were no longer the last stages of the "solution." His department had become merely instrumental. Hence he had every reason to be very "embittered and disappointed" when the Madagascar project was shelved; and the only thing he had to console him was his promotion to *Obersturmbannführer,* which came in October, 1941.

The last time Eichmann recalled having tried something on his own was in September, 1941, three months after the invasion of Russia. This was just after Heydrich, still chief of the Security Police and the Security Service, had become Protector of Bohemia and Moravia. To celebrate the occasion, he had called a press conference and had promised that in eight weeks the Protectorate would be *judenrein.* After the conference, he discussed the matter with those who would have to make his word good—with Franz Stahlecker, who was then local commander of the Security Police in Prague, and with the Undersecretary of State, Karl Hermann Frank, a former Sudeten leader who soon after Heydrich's death was to succeed him as *Reichsprotektor*. Frank, in Eichmann's opinion, was a low type, a Jew-hater of the "Streicher kind" who "didn't know a thing about political solutions," one of those people who, "autocratically and, let me say, in the drunkenness of their power simply gave orders and commands." But otherwise the conference was enjoyable. For the first time, Heydrich showed "a more human side" and admitted, with beautiful frankness, that he had "allowed his tongue to run away with him"—"no great surprise to those who knew Heydrich," an "ambitious and impulsive character," who "often let words slip through the fence of his teeth more quickly than he later might have liked." So Heydrich himself said: "There is the mess, and what are we going to do now?" Whereupon Eichmann said: "There exists only one possibility, if you cannot retreat from your announcement. Give enough room into which to transfer the Jews of the Protectorate, who now live dispersed." (A Jewish homeland, a gathering-in of the exiles in the Diaspora.) And then, unfortunately, Frank—the Jew-hater of the Streicher kind—made a concrete proposal, and that was that the room be provided at Theresienstadt. Whereupon Heydrich, perhaps also in the drunkenness of his power, simply ordered the immediate evacuation of the native Czech population from Theresienstadt, to make room for the Jews.

Eichmann was sent there to look things over. Great disappointment: the Bohemian fortress town on the banks of the Eger was far too small; at best, it could become a transfer camp for a certain percentage of the ninety thousand Jews in Bohemia and Moravia. (For about fifty thousand Czech Jews, Theresienstadt indeed became a transfer camp on the way to Auschwitz, while an estimated twenty thousand more reached the same destination directly.) We know from better sources than Eichmann's faulty memory that Theresienstadt, from the beginning, was designed by Heydrich to serve as a special ghetto for certain privileged categories of Jews, chiefly, but not exclusively, from Germany—Jewish functionaries, prominent people, war veterans with high decorations, invalids, the Jewish partners of mixed marriages, and German Jews over sixty-five years of age (hence the nickname *Altersghetto*). The town proved too small even for these restricted categories, and in 1943, about a year after its establishment, there began the "thinning out" or "loosening up" (*Auflockerung*) processes by which overcrowding was regularly relieved—by means of transport to Auschwitz. But in one respect, Eichmann's memory did not deceive him. Theresienstadt was in fact the only concentration camp that did not fall under the authority of the W.V.H.A. but remained his own responsibility to the end. Its commanders were men from his own staff and always his inferiors in rank; it was the only camp in which he had at least some of the power which the prosecution in Jerusalem ascribed to him.

Eichmann's memory, jumping with great ease over the years—he was two years ahead of the sequence of events when he told the police examiner the story of Theresienstadt—was certainly not controlled by chronological order, but it was not simply erratic. It was like a storehouse, filled with human-interest stories of the worst type. When he thought back to Prague, there emerged the occasion when he was admitted to the presence of the great Heydrich, who showed himself to have a "more human side." A few sessions later, he mentioned a trip to Bratislava, in Slovakia, where he happened to be at the time when Heydrich was assassinated. What he remembered was that he was there as the guest of Sano Mach, Minister of the Interior in the German-established Slovakian puppet government. (In that strongly anti-Semitic Catholic government, Mach represented the German version of anti-Semitism; he refused to allow exceptions for baptized Jews and he was one of the persons chiefly responsible for the wholesale deportation of Slovak Jewry.) Eichmann remembered this because it was unusual for him to receive social invitations from members of governments; it was an honor. Mach, as Eichmann recalled, was a nice, easygoing fellow who invited him to bowl with him. Did he really have no other business in Bratislava in the middle of the war than to go bowling with the Minister of the Interior? No, absolutely no other business; he remembered it all very well, how they bowled, and how drinks were served just before the news of the attempt on Heydrich's life arrived. Four months and fifty-five tapes later, Captain Less, the Israeli examiner, came back to this point, and

Eichmann told the same story in nearly identical words, adding that this day had been "unforgettable," because his "superior had been assassinated." This time, however, he was confronted with a document that said he had been sent to Bratislava to talk over "the current evacuation action against Jews from Slovakia." He admitted his error at once: "Clear, clear, that was an order from Berlin, they did not send me there to go bowling." Had he lied twice, with great consistency? Hardly. To evacuate and deport Jews had become routine business; what stuck in his mind was bowling, being the guest of a Minister, and hearing of the attack on Heydrich. And it was characteristic of his kind of memory that he could absolutely not recall the year in which this memorable day fell, on which "the hangman" was shot by Czech patriots.

Had his memory served him better, he would never have told the Theresienstadt story at all. For all this happened when the time of "political solutions" had passed and the era of the "physical solution" had begun. It happened when, as he was to admit freely and spontaneously in another context, he had already been informed of the Führer's order for the Final Solution. To make a country *judenrein* at the date when Heydrich promised to do so for Bohemia and Moravia could mean only concentration and deportation to points from which Jews could easily be shipped to the killing centers. That Theresienstadt actually came to serve another purpose, that of a showplace for the outside world—it was the only ghetto or camp to which representatives of the International Red Cross were admitted—was another matter, one of which Eichmann at that moment was almost certainly ignorant and which, anyhow, was altogether outside the scope of his competence.

V I : *The Final Solution: Killing*

On June 22, 1941, Hitler launched his attack on the Soviet Union, and six or eight weeks later Eichmann was summoned to Heydrich's office in Berlin. On July 31, Heydrich had received a letter from Reichsmarschall Hermann Göring, Commander-in-Chief of the Air Force, Prime Minister of Prussia, Pleinipotentiary for the Four-Year-Plan, and, last but not least, Hitler's Deputy in the State (as distinguished from the Party) hierarchy. The letter commissioned Heydrich to prepare "the general solution [*Gesamtlösung*] of the Jewish question within the area of German influence in Europe," and to submit "a general proposal . . . for the implementation of the desired final solution [*Endlösung*] of the Jewish question." At the time Heydrich received these instructions, he had already been—as he was to explain to the High Command of the Army in a letter dated November 6, 1941—"entrusted for years with the task of preparing the final solution of the Jewish problem" (Reitlinger), and since the beginning of the war with Russia, he had been in charge of the mass killings by the *Einsatzgruppen* in the East.

Heydrich opened his interview with Eichmann with "a little speech about emigration" (which had practically ceased, though Himmler's formal order prohibiting all Jewish emigration except in special cases, to be passed upon by him personally, was not issued until a few months later), and then said: *"The Führer has ordered the physical extermination of the Jews."* After which, "very much against his habits, he remained silent for a long while, as though he wanted to test the impact of his words. I remember it even today. In the first moment, I was unable to grasp the significance of what he had said, because he was so careful in choosing his words, and then I understood, and didn't say anything, because there was nothing to say any more. For I had never thought of such a thing, such a solution through violence. I now lost everything, all joy in my work, all initiative, all interest; I was, so to speak, blown out. And then he told me: 'Eichmann, you go and see Globocnik [one of Himmler's Higher S.S. and Police Leaders in the General Government] in Lublin, the Reichsführer [Himmler] has already given him the necessary orders, have a look at what he has accomplished in the meantime. I think he uses the Russian tank trenches for the liquidation of the Jews.' I still remember that, for I'll never forget it no matter how long I live, those sentences he said during that interview, which was already at an end." Actually—as Eichmann still remembered in Argentina but had forgotten in Jerusalem, much to his disadvantage, since it had bearing on the question of his own authority in the actual killing process—Heydrich had said a little more: he had told Eichmann that the whole enterprise had been "put under the authority of the S.S. Head Office for Economy and Administration"—that is, not of his own R.S.H.A. —and also that the official code name for extermination was to be "Final Solution."

Eichmann was by no means among the first to be informed of Hitler's intention. We have seen that Heydrich had been working in this direction for years, presumably since the beginning of the war, and Himmler claimed to have been told (and to have protested against) this "solution" immediately after the defeat of France in the summer of 1940. By March, 1941, about six months before Eichmann had his interview with Heydrich, "it was no secret in higher Party circles that the Jews were to be exterminated," as Viktor Brack, of the Führer's Chancellery, testified at Nuremberg. But Eichmann, as he vainly tried to explain in Jerusalem, had never belonged to the higher Party circles; he had never been told more than he needed to know in order to do a specific, limited job. It is true that he was one of the first men in the lower echelons to be informed of this "top secret" matter, which remained top secret even after the news had spread throughout all the Party and State offices, all business enterprises connected with slave labor, and the entire officer corps (at the very least) of the Armed Forces. Still, the secrecy did have a practical purpose. Those who were told explicitly of the Führer's order were no longer mere "bearers of orders," but were advanced to "bearers of secrets," and a special oath was administered to them. (The members of the Security Service, to which Eichmann had belonged since 1934, had in any case taken an oath of secrecy.)

Furthermore, all correspondence referring to the matter was subject to rigid "language rules," and, except in the reports from the *Einsatzgruppen*, it is rare to find documents in which such bald words as "extermination," "liquidation," or "killing" occur. The prescribed code names for killing were "final solution," "evacuation" (*Aussiedlung*), and "special treatment" (*Sonderbehandlung*); deportation—unless it involved Jews directed to Theresienstadt, the "old people's ghetto" for privileged Jews, in which case it was called "change of residence"—received the names of "resettlement" (*Umsiedlung*) and "labor in the East" (*Arbeitseinsatz im Osten*), the point of these latter names being that Jews were indeed often temporarily resettled in ghettos and that a certain percentage of them were temporarily used for labor. Under special circumstances, slight changes in the language rules became necessary. Thus, for instance, a high official in the Foreign Office once proposed that in all correspondence with the Vatican the killing of Jews be called the "radical solution"; this was ingenious, because the Catholic puppet government of Slovakia, with which the Vatican had intervened, had not been, in the view of the Nazis, "radical enough" in its anti-Jewish legislation, having committed the "basic error" of excluding baptized Jews. Only among themselves could the "bearers of secrets" talk in uncoded language, and it is very unlikely that they did so in the ordinary pursuit of their murderous duties—certainly not in the presence of their stenographers and other office personnel. For whatever other reasons the language rules may have been devised, they proved of enormous help in the maintenance of order and sanity in the various widely diversified services whose cooperation was essential in this matter. Moreover, the very term "language rule" (*Sprachregelung*) was itself a code name; it meant what in ordinary language would be called a lie. For when a "bearer of secrets" was sent to meet someone from the outside world—as when Eichmann was sent to show the Theresienstadt ghetto to International Red Cross representatives from Switzerland—he received, together with his orders, his "language rule," which in this instance consisted of a lie about a nonexistent typhus epidemic in the concentration camp of Bergen-Belsen, which the gentlemen also wished to visit. The net effect of this language system was not to keep these people ignorant of what they were doing, but to prevent them from equating it with their old, "normal" knowledge of murder and lies. Eichmann's great susceptibility to catch words and stock phrases, combined with his incapacity for ordinary speech, made him, of course, an ideal subject for "language rules."

The system, however, was not a foolproof shield against reality, as Eichmann was soon to find out. He went to Lublin to see Brigadeführer Odilo Globocnik, former Gauleiter of Vienna— though not, of course, despite what the prosecution maintained, "to convey to him personally the secret order for the physical extermination of the Jews," which Globocnik certainly knew of before Eichmann did—and he used the phrase "Final Solution" as a kind of password by which to identify himself. (A similar assertion by the prosecution, which showed to what degree it had got lost in the bureaucratic labyrinth of the Third Reich, referred to Rudolf Höss, Commander of Auschwitz, who it believed had also received the Führer's order through Eichmann. This error was at least mentioned by the defense as being "without corroborative evidence." Actually, Höss himself testified at his own trial that he had received his orders directly from Himmler, in June, 1941, and added that Himmler had told him Eichmann would discuss with him certain "details." These details, Höss claimed in his memoirs, concerned the use of gas—something Eichmann strenuously denied. And he was probably right, for all other sources contradict Höss's story and maintain that written or oral extermination orders in the camps always went through the W.V.H.A. and were given either by its chief, Obergruppenführer [lieutenant general] Oswald Pohl, or by Brigadeführer Richard Glücks, who was Höss's direct superior. (Concerning the doubtful reliability of Höss's testimony see also R. Pendorf, *Mörder und Ermordete,* 1961.) And with the use of gas Eichmann had nothing whatever to do. The "details" that he went to discuss with Höss at regular intervals concerned the killing capacity of the camp—how many shipments per week it could absorb—and also, perhaps, plans for expansion.) Globocnik, when Eichmann arrived at Lublin, was very obliging, and showed him around with a subordinate. They came to a road through a forest, to the right of which there was an ordinary house where workers lived. A captain of the Order Police (perhaps Kriminalkommissar Christian Wirth himself, who had been in charge of the technical side of the gassing of "incurably sick people" in Germany, under the auspices of the Führer's Chancellery) came to greet them, led them to a few small wooden bungalows, and began, "in a vulgar uneducated harsh voice," his explanations: "how he had everything nicely insulated, for the engine of a Russian submarine will be set to work and the gases will enter this building and the Jews will be poisoned. For me, too, this was monstrous. I am not so tough as to be able to endure something of this sort without any reaction. . . . If today I am shown a gaping wound, I can't possibly look at it. I am that type of person, so that very often I was told that I couldn't have become a doctor. I still remember how I pictured the thing to myself, and then I became physically weak, as though I had lived through some great agitation. Such things happen to everybody, and it left behind a certain inner trembling."

Well, he had been lucky, for he had still seen only the preparations for the future carbon-monoxide chambers at Treblinka, one of the six death camps in the East, in which several hundred thousand people were to die. Shortly after this, in the autumn of the same year, he was sent by his direct superior Müller to inspect the killing center in the Western Regions of Poland that had been incorporated into the Reich, called the Warthegau. The death camp was at Kulm (or, in Polish, Chelmno), where, in 1944, over three hundred thousand Jews from all over Europe, who had first been "resettled" in the Lódz ghetto, were killed. Here things were already in full swing, but the method was different; instead of gas chambers, mobile gas vans were used. This is what Eichmann saw: The Jews were in a large room; they were told to strip; then a truck arrived, stopping directly before the entrance to the room, and the naked Jews were told to enter it. The doors were closed and the truck started off. "I cannot tell [how many Jews entered], I hardly looked. I could not; I could not; I had had enough. The shrieking, and . . . I was much too upset, and so on, as I later told Müller when I reported to him; he did not get much profit out of my report. I then drove along after the van, and then I saw the most horrible sight I had thus far seen in my life. The truck was making for an open ditch, the doors were opened, and the corpses were thrown out, as though they were still alive, so smooth were their limbs. They were hurled into the ditch, and I can still see a civilian extracting the teeth with tooth pliers. And then I was off—jumped into my car and did not open my mouth any more. After that time, I could sit for hours beside my driver without exchanging a word with him. There I got enough. I was finished. I only remember that a physician in white overalls told me to look through a hole into the truck while they were still in it. I refused to do that. I could not. I had to disappear."

Very soon after that, he was to see something more horrible. This happened when he was sent to Minsk, in White Russia, again by Müller, who told him: "In Minsk, they are killing Jews by shooting. I want you to report on how it is being done." So he went, and at first it seemed as though he would be lucky, for by the time he arrived, as it happened, "the affair had almost been finished," which pleased him very much. "There were only a few young marksmen who took aim at the skulls of dead people in a large ditch." Still, he saw, "and that was quite enough for me, a woman with her arms stretched backward, and then my knees went weak and off I went." While driving back, he had the notion of stopping at Lwów; this seemed a good idea, for Lwów (or Lemberg) had been an Austrian city, and when he arrived there he "saw the first friendly picture after the horrors. That was the railway station built in honor of the sixtieth year of Franz Josef's reign"—a period Eichmann had always "adored," since he had heard so many nice things about it in his parents' home, and had also been told how the relatives of his stepmother (we are made to understand that he meant the Jewish ones) had enjoyed a comfortable social status and had made good money. This sight of the railway station drove away all the horrible thoughts, and he remembered it down to its last detail—the engraved year of the anniversary, for instance. But then, right there in lovely Lwów, he made a big mistake. He went to see the local S.S. commander, and told him: "Well, it is horrible what is being done around here; I said young people are being made into sadists.

How can one do that? Simply bang away at women and children? That is impossible. Our people will go mad or become insane, our own people." The trouble was that at Lwów they were doing the same thing they had been doing in Minsk, and his host was delighted to show him the sights, although Eichmann tried politely to excuse himself. Thus, he saw another "horrible sight. A ditch had been there, which was already filled in. And there was, gushing from the earth, a spring of blood like a fountain. Such a thing I had never seen before. I had had enough of my commission, and I went back to Berlin and reported to Gruppenführer Müller."

This was not yet the end. Although Eichmann told him that he was not "tough enough" for these sights, that he had never been a soldier, had never been to the front, had never seen action, that he could not sleep and had nightmares, Müller, some nine months later, sent him back to the Lublin region, where the very enthusiastic Globocnik had meanwhile finished his preparations. Eichmann said that this now was the most horrible thing he had ever seen in his life. When he first arrived, he could not recognize the place, with its few wooden bungalows. Instead, guided by the same man with the vulgar voice, he came to a railway station, with the sign "Treblinka" on it, that looked exactly like an ordinary station anywhere in Germany—the same buildings, signs, clocks, installations; it was a perfect imitation. "I kept myself back, as far as I could, I did not draw near to see all that. Still, I saw how a column of naked Jews filed into a large hall to be gassed. There they were killed, as I was told, by something called cyanic acid."

The fact is that Eichmann did not see much. It is true, he repeatedly visited Auschwitz, the largest and most famous of the death camps, but Auschwitz, covering an area of eighteen square miles, in Upper Silesia, was by no means only an extermination camp; it was a huge enterprise with up to a hundred thousand inmates, and all kinds of prisoners were held there, including non-Jews and slave laborers, who were not subject to gassing. It was easy to avoid the killing installations, and Höss, with whom he had a very friendly relationship, spared him the gruesome sights. He never actually attended a mass execution by shooting, he never actually watched the gassing process, or the selection

of those fit for work—about twenty-five per cent of each shipment, on the average—that preceded it at Auschwitz. He saw just
enough to be fully informed of how the destruction machinery
worked: that there were two different methods of killing, shooting
and gassing; that the shooting was done by the *Einsatzgruppen*
and the gassing at the camps, either in chambers or in mobile
vans; and in the camps elaborate precautions were taken to fool
the victims right up to the end.

The police tapes from which I have quoted were played in
court during the tenth of the trial's hundred and twenty-one sessions, on the ninth day of the almost nine months it lasted.
Nothing the accused said, in the curiously disembodied voice
that came out of the tape-recorder—doubly disembodied, because
the body that owned the voice was present but itself also appeared strangely disembodied through the thick glass walls surrounding it—was denied either by him or by the defense. Dr.
Servatius did not object, he only mentioned that "later, when the
defense will rise to speak," he, too, would submit to the court
some of the evidence given by the accused to the police; he never
did. The defense, one felt, could rise right away, for the criminal
proceedings against the accused in this "historic trial" seemed
complete, the case for the prosecution established. The facts of the
case, of what Eichmann had done—though not of everything the
prosecution wished he had done—were never in dispute; they
had been established long before the trial started, and had
been confessed to by him over and over again. There was more
than enough, as he occasionally pointed out, to hang him. ("Don't
you have enough on me?" he objected, when the police examiner
tried to ascribe to him powers he never possessed.) But since
he had been employed in transportation and not in killing, the
question remained, legally, formally, at least, of whether he had
known what he was doing; and there was the additional question
of whether he had been in a position to judge the enormity of his
deeds—whether he was legally responsible, apart from the fact
that he was medically sane. Both questions now were answered
in the affirmative: he had seen the places to which the shipments
were directed, and he had been shocked out of his wits. One last
question, the most disturbing of all, was asked by the judges,

and especially by the presiding judge, over and over again: Had the killing of Jews gone against his conscience? But this was a moral question, and the answer to it may not have been legally relevant.

But if the facts of the case were now established, two more legal questions arose. First, could he be released from criminal responsibility, as Section 10 of the law under which he was tried provided, because he had done his acts "in order to save himself from the danger of immediate death"? And, second, could he plead extenuating circumstances, as Section 11 of the same law enumerated them: had he done "his best to reduce the gravity of the consequences of the offense" or "to avert consequences more serious than those which resulted"? Clearly, Sections 10 and 11 of the Nazis and Nazi Collaborators (Punishment) Law of 1950 had been drawn up with Jewish "collaborators" in mind. Jewish *Sonderkommandos* (special units) had everywhere been employed in the actual killing process, they had committed criminal acts "in order to save themselves from the danger of immediate death," and the Jewish Councils and Elders had cooperated because they thought they could "avert consequences more serious than those which resulted." In Eichmann's case, his own testimony supplied the answer to both questions, and it was clearly negative. It is true, he once said his only alternative would have been suicide, but this was a lie, since we know how surprisingly easy it was for members of the extermination squads to quit their jobs without serious consequences for themselves; but he did not insist on this point, he did not mean to be taken literally. In the Nuremberg documents "not a single case could be traced in which an S.S. member had suffered the death penalty because of a refusal to take part in an execution" [Herbert Jäger, "Betrachtungen zum Eichmann-Prozess," in *Kriminologie und Strafrechtsreform*, 1962]. And in the trial itself there was the testimony of a witness for the defense, von dem Bach-Zelewski, who declared: "It was possible to evade a commission by an application for transfer. To be sure, in individual cases, one had to be prepared for a certain disciplinary punishment. A danger to one's life, however, was not at all involved." Eichmann knew quite well that he was by no means in the classical "difficult position" of a soldier who may "be liable to be shot by a court-martial if he disobeys an order, and to be hanged by a judge and jury if he obeys it"—as Dicey once put it in his famous *Law of the Constitution*—if only because as a member of the S.S. he had never been subject to a military court but could only have been brought before a Police and S.S. Tribunal. In his last statement to the court, Eichmann admitted that he could have backed out on one pretext or another, and that others had done so. He had always thought such a step was "inadmissible," and even now did not think it was "admirable"; it would have meant no more than a switch to another well-paying job. The postwar notion of open disobedience was a fairy tale: "Under the circumstances such behavior was impossible. Nobody acted that way." It was "unthinkable." Had he been made commander of a death camp, like his good friend Höss, he would have had to commit suicide, since he was incapable of killing. (Höss, incidentally, had committed a murder in his youth. He had assassinated a certain Walter Kadow, the man who had betrayed Leo Schlageter—a nationalist terrorist in the Rhineland whom the Nazis later made into a national hero—to the French Occupation authorities, and a German court had put him in jail for five years. In Auschwitz, of course, Höss did not have to kill.) But it was very unlikely that Eichmann would have been offered this kind of a job, since those who issued the orders "knew full well the limits to which a person can be driven." No, he had not been in "danger of immediate death," and since he claimed with great pride that he had always "done his duty," obeyed all orders as his oath demanded, he had, of course, always done his best to aggravate "the consequences of the offense," rather than to reduce them. The only "extenuating circumstance" he cited was that he had tried to "avoid unnecessary hardships as much as possible" in carrying out his work, and, quite apart from the question of whether this was true, and also apart from the fact that if it was, it would hardly have been enough to constitute extenuating circumstances in this particular case, the claim was not valid, because "to avoid unnecessary hardships" was among the standard directives he had been given.

Hence, after the tape-recorder had addressed the court, the death sentence was a foregone conclusion, even legally, except for the possibility that the punishment might be mitigated for acts done under superior orders—also provided for in Section 11 of the Israeli law, but this was a very remote possibility in view of the enormity of the crime. (It is important to remember that counsel for the defense pleaded not superior orders but "acts of state," and asked for acquittal on that ground—a strategy Dr. Servatius had already tried unsuccessfully at Nuremberg, where he defended Fritz Sauckel, Plenipotentiary for Labor Allocation in Göring's Office of the Four-Year Plan, who had been responsible for the extermination of tens of thousands of Jewish workers in Poland and who was duly hanged in 1946. "Acts of state," which German jurisprudence even more tellingly calls *gerichtsfreie* or *justizlose Hoheitsakte*, rest on "an exercise of sovereign power" [E. C. S. Wade in the *British Year Book for International Law,* 1934] and hence are altogether outside the legal realm, whereas all orders and commands, at least in theory, are still under judicial control. If what Eichmann did had been acts of state, then none of his superiors, least of all Hitler, the head of state, could be judged by any court. The "act of state" theory agreed so well with Dr. Servatius' general philosophy that it was perhaps not surprising that he should have tried it out again; what was surprising was that he did not fall back on the argument of superior orders as an extenuating circumstance after the judgment had been read and before the sentence was pronounced.) At this point, one was perhaps entitled to be glad that this was no ordinary trial, where statements without bearing on the criminal proceedings must be thrown out as irrelevant and immaterial. For, obviously, things were not so simple as the framers of the laws had imagined them to be, and if it was of small legal relevance, it was of great political interest to know how long it takes an average person to overcome his innate repugnance toward crime, and what exactly happens to him once he has reached that point. To this question, the case of Adolf Eichmann supplied an answer that could not have been clearer and more precise.

In September, 1941, shortly after his first official visits to the killing centers in the East, Eichmann organized his first mass deportations from Germany and the Protectorate, in accordance with a "wish" of Hitler, who had told Himmler to make the

Reich *judenrein* as quickly as possible. The first shipment contained twenty thousand Jews from the Rhineland and five
thousand Gypsies, and in connection with this first transport a
strange thing happened. Eichmann, who never made a decision
on his own, who was extremely careful always to be "covered"
by orders, who—as freely given testimony from practically all
the people who had worked with him confirmed—did not even
like to volunteer suggestions and always required "directives,"
now, "for the first and last time," took an initiative contrary to
orders: instead of sending these people to Russian territory, Riga
or Minsk, where they would have immediately been shot by the
Einsatzgruppen, he directed the transport to the ghetto of Łódz,
where he knew that no preparations for extermination had yet
been made—if only because the man in charge of the ghetto, a
certain Regierungspräsident Uebelhör, had found ways and
means of deriving considerable profit from "his" Jews. (Łódz, in
fact, was the first ghetto to be established and the last to be
liquidated; those of its inmates who did not succumb to disease
or starvation survived until the summer of 1944.) This decision
was to get Eichmann into considerable trouble. The ghetto was
overcrowded, and Mr. Uebelhör was in no mood to receive
newcomers and in no position to accommodate them. He was
angry enough to complain to Himmler that Eichmann had deceived him and his men with "horsetrading tricks learned from the
Gypsies." Himmler, as well as Heydrich, protected Eichmann
and the incident was soon forgiven and forgotten.

Forgotten, first of all, by Eichmann himself, who did not once
mention it either in the police examination or in his various memoirs. When he had taken the stand and was being examined by
his lawyer, who showed him the documents, he insisted he had
a "choice": "Here for the first and last time I had a choice. . . .
One was Łódz. . . . If there are difficulties in Łódz, these
people must be sent onward to the East. And since I had seen
the preparations, I was determined to do all I could to send these
people to Łódz by any means at my disposal." Counsel for the
defense tried to conclude from this incident that Eichmann had
saved Jews whenever he could—which was patently untrue. The
prosecutor, who cross-examined him later with respect to the
same incident, wished to establish that Eichmann himself had

determined the final destination of all shipments and hence had decided whether or not a particular transport was to be exterminated—which was also untrue. Eichmann's own explanation, that he had not disobeyed an order but only taken advantage of a "choice," finally, was not true either, for there had been difficulties in Lódz, as he knew full well, so that his order read, in so many words: Final destination, Minsk or Riga. Although Eichmann had forgotten all about it, this was clearly the only instance in which he actually had tried to save Jews. Three weeks later, however, there was a meeting in Prague, called by Heydrich, during which Eichmann stated that "the camps used for the detention of [Russian] Communists [a category to be liquidated on the spot by the *Einsatzgruppen*] can also include Jews" and that he had "reached an agreement" to this effect with the local commanders; there was also some discussion about the trouble at Lódz, and it was finally resolved to send fifty thousand Jews from the Reich (that is, including Austria, and Bohemia and Moravia) to the centers of the *Einsatzgruppen* operations at Riga and Minsk. Thus, we are perhaps in a position to answer Judge Landau's question—the question uppermost in the minds of nearly everyone who followed the trial—of whether the accused had a conscience: yes, he had a conscience, and his conscience functioned in the expected way for about four weeks, whereupon it began to function the other way around.

Even during those weeks when his conscience functioned normally, it did its work within rather odd limits. We must remember that weeks and months before he was informed of the Führer's order, Eichmann knew of the murderous activities of the *Einsatzgruppen* in the East; he knew that right behind the front lines all Russian functionaries ("Communists"), all Polish members of the professional classes, and all native Jews were being killed in mass shootings. Moreover, in July of the same year, a few weeks before he was called to Heydrich, he had received a memorandum from an S.S. man stationed in the Warthegau, telling him that "Jews in the coming winter could no longer be fed," and submitting for his consideration a proposal as to "whether it would not be the most humane solution to kill those Jews who were incapable of work through some quicker means. This, at any rate, would be more agreeable than to let them die of starvation." In an accompanying letter, addressed to "Dear Comrade Eichmann," the writer admitted that "these things sound sometimes fantastic, but they are quite feasible." The admission shows that the much more "fantastic" order of the Führer was not yet known to the writer, but the letter also shows to what extent this order was in the air. Eichmann never mentioned this letter and probably had not been in the least shocked by it. For this proposal concerned only *native* Jews, not Jews from the Reich or any of the Western countries. His conscience rebelled not at the idea of murder but at the idea of German Jews being murdered. ("I never denied that I knew that the *Einsatzgruppen* had orders to kill, but I did not know that Jews from the Reich evacuated to the East were subject to the same treatment. That is what I did not know.") It was the same with the conscience of a certain Wilhelm Kube, an old Party member and *Generalkommissar* in Occupied Russia, who was outraged when German Jews with the Iron Cross arrived in Minsk for "special treatment." Since Kube was more articulate than Eichmann, his words may give us an idea of what went on in Eichmann's head during the time he was plagued by his conscience: "I am certainly tough and I am ready to help solve the Jewish question," Kube wrote to his superior in December, 1941, "but people who come from our own cultural milieu are certainly something else than the native animalized hordes." This sort of conscience, which, if it rebelled at all, rebelled at murder of people "from our own cultural milieu," has survived the Hitler regime; among Germans today, there exists a stubborn "misinformation" to the effect that "only" *Ostjuden*, Eastern European Jews, were massacred.

Nor is this way of thinking that distinguishes between the murder of "primitive" and of "cultured" people a monopoly of the German people. Harry Mulisch relates how, in connection with the testimony given by Professor Salo W. Baron about the cultural and spiritual achievements of the Jewish people, the following questions suddenly occurred to him: "Would the death of the Jews have been less of an evil if they were a people without a culture, such as the Gypsies who were also exterminated? Is Eichmann on trial as a destroyer of human beings or as an annihilator of culture? Is a murderer of human beings more guilty when a culture is also destroyed in the process?" And when he put these questions to the Attorney General, it turned out—"He [Hausner] thinks yes, I think no." How ill we can afford to dismiss this matter, bury the troublesome question along with the past, came to light in the recent film *Dr. Strangelove,* where the strange lover of the bomb—characterized, it is true, as a Nazi type—proposes to select in the coming disaster some hundred thousand persons to survive in underground shelters. And who are to be the happy survivors? Those with the highest I.Q.!

This question of conscience, so troublesome in Jerusalem, had by no means been ignored by the Nazi regime. On the contrary, in view of the fact that the participants in the anti-Hitler conspiracy of July, 1944, very rarely mentioned the wholesale massacres in the East in their correspondence or in the statements they prepared for use in the event that the attempt on Hitler's life was successful, one is tempted to conclude that the Nazis greatly overestimated the practical importance of the problem. We may here disregard the early stages of the German opposition to Hitler, when it was still anti-Fascist and entirely a movement of the Left, which as a matter of principle accorded no significance to moral issues and even less to the persecution of the Jews—a mere "diversion" from the class struggle that in the opinion of the Left determined the whole political scene. Moreover, this opposition had all but disappeared during the period in question—destroyed by the horrible terror of the S.A. troops in the concentration camps and Gestapo cellars, unsettled by full employment made possible through rearmament, demoralized by the Communist Party's tactic of joining the ranks of Hitler's party in order to install itself there as a "Trojan horse." What was left of this opposition at the beginning of the war—some trade-union leaders, some intellectuals of the "homeless Left" who did not and could not know if there was anything behind them—gained its importance solely through the conspiracy which finally led to the 20th of July. (It is of course quite inadmissible to measure the strength of the German resistance by the number of those who passed through the concentration camps. Before the outbreak of the war, the inmates belonged in a great number of categories, many of which had nothing whatsoever to do with resistance of any kind: there were the wholly "innocent" ones, such as the Jews; the "asocials," such as confirmed criminals and homosexuals; Nazis who had been found guilty of something or other; etc. During the war the camps were populated by resistance fighters from all over occupied Europe.)

Most of the July conspirators were actually former Nazis or had held high office in the Third Reich. What had sparked their opposition had been not the Jewish question but the fact that Hitler was preparing war, and the endless conflicts and crises of conscience under which they labored hinged almost exclusively on the problem of high treason and the violation of their loyalty oath to Hitler. Moreover, they found themselves on the horns of a dilemma which was indeed insoluble: in the days of Hitler's successes they felt they could do nothing because the people would not understand, and in the years of German defeats they feared nothing more than another "stab-in-the-back" legend. To the last, their greatest concern was how it would be possible to prevent chaos and to ward off the danger of civil war. And the solution was that the Allies must be "reasonable" and grant a "moratorium" until order was restored—and with it, of course, the German Army's ability to offer resistance. They possessed the most precise knowledge of what was going on in the East, but there is hardly any doubt that not one of them would have dared even to think that the best thing that could have happened to Germany under the circumstances would have been open rebellion and civil war. The active resistance in Germany came chiefly from the Right, but in view of the past record of the German Social Democrats, it may be doubted that the situation would have been very different if the Left had played a larger part among the conspirators. The question is academic in any case, for no "organized socialist resistance" existed in Germany during the war years—as the German historian, Gerhard Ritter, has rightly pointed out.

In actual fact, the situation was just as simple as it was hopeless: the overwhelming majority of the German people believed in Hitler—even after the attack on Russia and the feared war on two fronts, even after the United States entered the war, indeed even after Stalingrad, the defection of Italy, and the landings in France. Against this solid majority, there stood an indeterminate number of isolated individuals who were completely aware of the national and of the moral catastrophe; they might occasionally know and trust one another, there were friendships among them and an exchange of opinions, but no plan or intention of revolt. Finally there was the group of those who later became known as the conspirators, but they had never been able to come to an agreement on anything, not even on the question of conspiracy. Their leader was Carl Friedrich Goerdeler, former mayor of Leipzig, who had served three years under the Nazis as price-controller but had resigned rather early —in 1936. He advocated the establishment of a constitutional monarchy, and Wilhelm Leuschner, a representative of the Left, a former trade-union leader and Socialist, assured him of "mass support"; in the Kreisau circle, under the influence of Helmuth von Moltke, there were occasional complaints raised that the rule of law was "now trampled under foot," but the chief concern of this circle was the reconciliation of the two Christian churches and their "sacred mission in the secular state," combined with an outspoken stand in favor of federalism. (On the political bankruptcy of the resistance movement as a whole since 1933 there is a well-documented, impartial study, the doctoral dissertation of George K. Romoser, soon to be published.)

As the war went on and defeat became more certain, political differences should have mattered less and political action become more urgent, but Gerhard Ritter seems right here too: "Without the determination of [Count Klaus von] Stauffenberg, the resistance movement would have bogged down in more or less helpless inactivity." What united these men was that they saw in Hitler a "swindler," a "dilettante," who "sacrificed whole armies against the counsel of his experts," a "madman" and a "demon," "the incarnation of all evil," which in the German context meant something both more and less than when they called him a "criminal and a fool," which they occasionally did. But to hold such opinions about Hitler at this late date "in no way precluded membership in the S.S. or the Party, or the holding of a government post" [Fritz Hesse], hence it did not exclude from the circle of the conspirators quite a number of men who themselves were deeply implicated in the crimes of the regime—as for instance Count Helldorf, then Police Commissioner of Berlin, who would have become Chief of the German Police if the coup d'état had been successful (according to one of Goerdeler's lists of prospective ministers); or Arthur Nebe of the R.S.H.A., former commander of one of the mobile killing units in the East! In the summer of 1943, when the Himmler-directed extermination program had reached its climax, Goerdeler was considering Himmler and Goebbels as potential allies, "since these two men have realized that they are lost with Hitler." (Himmler indeed became a "potential ally"—though Goebbels did not—and was fully informed of their plans; he acted against the conspirators only after their failure.) I am quoting from the draft of a letter by Goerdeler to Field Marshal von Kluge; but these strange alliances cannot be explained away by "tactical considerations" necessary vis-à-vis the Army commanders, for it was, on the contrary, Kluge and Rommel who had given "special orders that those two monsters [Himmler and Göring] should be liquidated" [Ritter]—quite apart from the fact that Goerdeler's biographer, Ritter, insists that the above-quoted letter "represents the most passionate expression of his hatred against the Hitler regime."

No doubt these men who opposed Hitler, however belatedly, paid with their lives and suffered a most terrible death; the courage of many of them was admirable, but it was not inspired by moral indignation or by what they knew other people had been made to suffer; they were motivated almost exclusively by their conviction of the coming defeat and ruin of Germany. This is not to deny that some of them, such as Count York von Wartenburg, may have been roused to political opposition initially by "the revolting agitation against the Jews in November, 1938" [Ritter]. But that was the month when the synagogues went up in flames and the whole population seemed in the grip of some fear: houses of God had been set on fire, and believers as well as the superstitious feared the vengeance of God. To be sure, the higher officer corps was disturbed when Hitler's so-called "commissar order" was issued in May, 1941, and they learned that in the coming campaign against Russia

all Soviet functionaries and naturally all Jews were simply to
be massacred. In these circles, there was of course some concern about the fact that, as Goerdeler said, "in the occupied
areas and against the Jews techniques of liquidating human
beings and of religious persecution are practiced . . . which
will always rest as a heavy burden on our history." But it
seems never to have occurred to them that this signified something more, and more dreadful, than that "it will make our
position [negotiating a peace treaty with the Allies] enormously
difficult," that it was a "blot on Germany's good name" and
was undermining the morale of the Army. "What on earth have
they made of the proud army of the Wars of Liberation
[against Napoleon in 1814] and of Wilhelm I [in the Franco-
Prussian War of 1870]," Goerdeler cried when he heard the
report of an S.S. man who "nonchalantly related that it 'wasn't
exactly pretty to spray with machine-gun fire ditches crammed
with thousands of Jews and then to throw earth on the bodies
that were still twitching.' " Nor did it occur to them that these
atrocities might be somehow connected with the Allies'
demand for unconditional surrender, which they felt free to
criticize as both "nationalistic" and "unreasonable," inspired
by blind hatred. In 1943, when the eventual defeat of Germany
was almost a certainty, and indeed even later, they still believed
that they had a right to negotiate with their enemies "as equals"
for a "just peace," although they knew only too well what an
unjust and totally unprovoked war Hitler had started. Even
more startling are their criteria for a "just peace." Goerdeler
stated them again and again in numerous memoranda: "the
re-establishment of the national borders of 1914 [which meant
the annexation of Alsace-Lorraine], with the addition of Austria and the Sudetenland"; furthermore, a "leading position for
Germany on the Continent" and perhaps the regaining of South
Tyrol!

We also know from statements they prepared how they
intended to present their case to the people. There is for instance
a draft proclamation to the Army by General Ludwig Beck,
who was to become chief of state, in which he talks at length
about the "obstinacy," the "incompetence and lack of modera-
tion" of the Hitler regime, its "arrogance and vanity." But the

crucial point, "the most unscrupulous act" of the regime, was that the Nazis wanted to hold "the leaders of the armed forces responsible" for the calamities of the coming defeat; to which Beck added that crimes had been committed "which are a blot on the honor of the German nation and a defilement of the good reputation it had gained in the eyes of the world." And what would be the next step after Hitler had been liquidated? The German Army would go on fighting "until an honorable conclusion of the war has been assured"—which meant the annexation of Alsace-Lorraine, Austria, and the Sudetenland. There is indeed every reason to agree with the bitter judgment on these men by the German novelist Friedrich P. Reck-Malleczewen, who was killed in a concentration camp on the eve of the collapse and did not participate in the anti-Hitler conspiracy. In his almost totally unknown "Diary of a Man in Despair," [*Tagebuch eines Verzweifelten*, 1947], Reck-Malleczewen wrote, after he had heard of the failure of the attempt on Hitler's life, which of course he regretted: "A little late, gentlemen, you who made this archdestroyer of Germany and ran after him, as long as everything seemed to be going well; you who . . . without hesitation swore every oath demanded of you and reduced yourselves to the despicable flunkies of this criminal who is guilty of the murder of hundreds of thousands, burdened with the lamentations and the curse of the whole world; now you have betrayed him. . . . Now, when the bankruptcy can no longer be concealed, they betray the house that went broke, in order to establish a political alibi for themselves—the same men who have betrayed everything that was in the way of their claim to power."

There is no evidence, and no likelihood, that Eichmann ever came into personal contact with the men of July 20, and we know that even in Argentina he still considered them all to have been traitors and scoundrels. Had he ever had the opportunity, though, to become acquainted with Goerdeler's "original" ideas on the Jewish question, he might have discovered some points of agreement. To be sure, Goerdeler proposed "to pay indemnity to German Jews for their losses and mistreatment" —this in 1942, at a time when it was not only a matter of *German* Jews, and when these were not just being mistreated and robbed but *gassed*; but in addition to such technicalities, he had something more constructive in mind, namely, a "permanent solution" that would "save [all European Jews] from their unseemly position as a more or less undesirable 'guest nation' in Europe." (In Eichmann's jargon, this was called giving them "some firm ground under their feet.") For this purpose, Goerdeler claimed an "independent state in a colonial country"—Canada or South America—a sort of Madagascar, of which he certainly had heard. Still, he made some concessions; not all Jews would be expelled. Quite in line with the early stages of the Nazi regime and the privileged categories which were then current, he was prepared "not to deny German citizenship to those Jews who could produce evidence of special military sacrifice for Germany or who belonged to families with long-established traditions." Well, whatever Goerdeler's "permanent solution of the Jewish question" might have meant, it was not exactly "original"—as Professor Ritter, even in 1954 full of admiration for his hero, called it—and Goerdeler would have been able to find plenty of "potential allies" for this part of his program too within the ranks of the Party and even the S.S.

In the letter to Field Marshal von Kluge, quoted above, Goerdeler once appealed to Kluge's "voice of conscience." But all he meant was that even a general must understand that "to continue the war with no chance for victory was an obvious crime." From the accumulated evidence one can only conclude that conscience as such had apparently got lost in Germany, and this to a point where people hardly remembered it and had ceased to realize that the surprising "new set of German values" was not shared by the outside world. This, to be sure, is not the entire truth. For there were individuals in Germany who from the very beginning of the regime and without ever wavering were opposed to Hitler; no one knows how many there were of them—perhaps a hundred thousand, perhaps many more, perhaps many fewer—for their voices were never heard. They could be found everywhere, in all strata of society, among the simple people as well as among the educated, in all parties, perhaps even in the ranks of the N.S.D.A.P. Very few of them were known publicly, as were the aforementioned Reck-Malleczewen or the philosopher Karl Jaspers. Some of them were truly and deeply pious, like an artisan of whom I know, who preferred having his independent existence destroyed and becoming a simple worker in a factory to taking upon himself the "little formality" of entering the Nazi Party. A few still took an oath seriously and preferred, for example, to renounce an academic career rather than swear by Hitler's name. A more numerous group were the workers, especially in Berlin, and Socialist intellectuals who tried to aid the Jews they knew. There were finally, the two peasant boys whose story is related in Günther Weisenborn's *Der lautlose Aufstand* (1953), who were drafted into the S.S. at the end of the war and refused to sign; they were sentenced to death, and on the day of their execution they wrote in their last letter to their families: "We two would rather die than burden our conscience with such terrible things. We know what the S.S. must carry out." The position of these people, who, practically speaking, did nothing, was altogether different from that of the conspirators. Their ability to tell right from wrong had remained intact, and they never suffered a "crisis of conscience." There may also have been such persons among the members of the resistance, but they were hardly more numerous in the ranks of the conspirators than among the people at large. They were neither heroes nor saints, and they remained completely silent. Only on one occasion, in a single desperate gesture, did this wholly isolated and mute element manifest itself publicly: this was when the Scholls, two students at Munich University, brother and sister, under the influence of their teacher Kurt Huber distributed the famous leaflets in which Hitler was finally called what he was—a "mass murderer."

If, however, one examines the documents and prepared statements of the so-called "other Germany" that would have succeeded Hitler had the July 20 conspiracy succeeded, one can only marvel at how great a gulf separated even them from the rest of the world. How else can one explain the illusions of Goerdeler in particular or the fact that Himmler, of all people, but also Ribbentrop, should have started dreaming, during the last months of the war, of a magnificent new role as negotiators with the Allies for a defeated Germany. And if Ribbentrop certainly was simply stupid, Himmler, whatever else he might have been, was no fool.

The member of the Nazi hierarchy most gifted at solving problems of conscience was Himmler. He coined slogans, like the famous watchword of the S.S., taken from a Hitler speech before the S.S. in 1931, "My Honor is my Loyalty"—catch phrases which Eichmann called "winged words" and the judges "empty talk"—and issued them, as Eichmann recalled, "around the turn of the year," presumably along with a Christmas bonus. Eichmann remembered only one of them and kept repeating it: "These are battles which future generations will not have to fight again," alluding to the "battles" against women, children, old people, and other "useless mouths." Other such phrases, taken from speeches Himmler made to the commanders of the *Einsatzgruppen* and the Higher S.S. and Police Leaders, were: "To have stuck it out and, apart from exceptions caused by human weakness, to have remained decent, that is what has made us hard. This is a page of glory in our history which has never been written and is never to be written." Or: "The order to solve the Jewish question, this was the most frightening order an organization could ever receive." Or: We realize that what we are expecting from you is "superhuman," to be "superhumanly inhuman." All one can say is that their expectations were not disappointed. It is noteworthy, however, that Himmler hardly ever attempted to justify in ideological terms, and if he did, it was apparently quickly forgotten. What stuck in the minds of these men who had become murderers was simply the notion of being involved in something historic, grandiose, unique ("a great task that occurs once in two thousand years"), which must therefore be difficult to bear. This was important, because the murderers were not sadists or killers by nature; on the contrary, a systematic effort was made to weed out all those who derived physical pleasure from what they did. The troops of the *Einsatzgruppe*n had been drafted from the Armed S.S., a military unit with hardly more crimes in its record than any ordinary unit of the German Army, and their commanders had been chosen by Heydrich from the

S.S. élite with academic degrees. Hence the problem was how to overcome not so much their conscience as the animal pity by which all normal men are affected in the presence of physical suffering. The trick used by Himmler—who apparently was rather strongly afflicted with these instinctive reactions himself —was very simple and probably very effective; it consisted in turning these instincts around, as it were, in directing them toward the self. So that instead of saying: What horrible things I did to people!, the murderers would be able to say: What horrible things I had to watch in the pursuance of my duties, how heavily the task weighed upon my shoulders!

Eichmann's defective memory where Himmler's ingenious watchwords were concerned may be an indication that there existed other and more effective devices for solving the problem of conscience. Foremost among them was, as Hitler had rightly foreseen, the simple fact of war. Eichmann insisted time and again on the "different personal attitude" toward death when "dead people were seen everywhere," and when everyone looked forward to his own death with indifference: "We did not care if we died today or only tomorrow, and there were times when we cursed the morning that found us still alive." Especially effective in this atmosphere of violent death was the fact that the Final Solution, in its later stages, was not carried out by shooting, hence through violence, but in the gas factories, which, from beginning to end, were closely connected with the "euthanasia program" ordered by Hitler in the first weeks of the war and applied to the mentally sick in Germany up to the invasion of Russia. The extermination program that was started in the autumn of 1941 ran, as it were, on two altogether different tracks. One track led to the gas factories, and the other to the *Einsatzgruppen*, whose operations in the rear of the Army, especially in Russia, were justified by the pretext of partisan warfare, and whose victims were by no means only Jews. In addition to real partisans, they dealt with Russian functionaries, Gypsies, the asocial, the insane, and Jews. Jews were included as "potential enemies," and, unfortunately, it was months before the Russian Jews came to understand this, and then it was too late to scatter. (The older generation remembered the First World War, when the German Army had been greeted as liberators; neither the young nor the old had heard anything about "how Jews were treated in Germany, or, for that matter, in Warsaw"; they were "remarkably ill-informed," as the German Intelligence service reported from White Russia [Hilberg]. More remarkable, occasionally even German Jews arrived in these regions who were under the illusion they had been sent here as "pioneers" for the Third Reich.) These mobile killing units, of which there existed just four, each of battalion size, with a total of no more than three thousand men, needed and got the close cooperation of the Armed Forces; indeed, relations between them were usually "excellent" and in some instances "affectionate" (*herzlich*). The generals showed a "surprisingly good attitude toward the Jews"; not only did they hand their Jews over to the *Einsatzgruppen*, they often lent their own men, ordinary soldiers, to assist in the massacres. The total number of their Jewish victims is estimated by Hilberg to have reached almost a million and a half, but this was not the result of the Führer's order for the physical extermination of the whole Jewish people. It was the result of an earlier order, which Hitler gave to Himmler in March, 1941, to prepare the S.S. and the police "to carry out special duties in Russia."

The Führer's order for the extermination of all, not only Russian and Polish, Jews, though issued later, can be traced much farther back. It originated not in the R.S.H.A. or in any of Heydrich's or Himmler's other offices, but in the Führer's Chancellery, Hitler's personal office. It had nothing to do with the war and never used military necessities as a pretext. It is one of the great merits of Gerald Reitlinger's *The Final Solution* to have proved, with documentary evidence that leaves no doubt, that the extermination program in the Eastern gas factories grew out of Hitler's euthanasia program, and it is deplorable that the Eichmann trial, so concerned with "historical truth," paid no attention to this factual connection. This would have thrown some light on the much debated question of whether Eichmann, of the R.S.H.A., was involved in *Gasgeschichten*. It is unlikely that he was, though one of his men, Rolf Günther, might have become interested of his own accord. Globocnik, for instance, who set up the gassing installations in the Lublin area, and whom Eichmann visited, did not address him-

self to Himmler or any other police or S.S. authority when he
needed more personnel; he wrote to Viktor Brack, of the
Führer's Chancellery, who then passed the request on to
Himmler.

The first gas chambers were constructed in 1939, to implement
a Hitler decree dated September 1 of that year, which said that
"incurably sick persons should be granted a mercy death." (It
was probably this "medical" origin of gassing that inspired Dr.
Servatius's amazing conviction that killing by gas must be
regarded as "a medical matter.") The idea itself was considerably older. As early as 1935, Hitler had told his Reich
Medical Leader Gerhard Wagner that "if war came, he would
take up and carry out this question of euthanasia, because it
was easier to do so in wartime." The decree was immediately
carried out in respect to the mentally sick, and between December, 1939, and August, 1941, about fifty thousand Germans
were killed with carbon-monoxide gas in institutions where the
death rooms were disguised exactly as they later were in
Auschwitz—as shower rooms and bathrooms. The program was
a flop. It was impossible to keep the gassing a secret from the
surrounding German population; there were protests on all sides
from people who presumably had not yet attained the "objective"
insight into the nature of medicine and the task of a physician.
The gassing in the East—or, to use the language of the Nazis,
"the humane way" of killing "by granting people a mercy
death"—began on almost the very day when the gassing in
Germany was stopped. The men who had been employed in
the euthanasia program in Germany were now sent east to
build the new installations for the extermination of whole peoples—and these men came either from Hitler's Chancellery or
from the Reich Health Department and were only now put under
the administrative authority of Himmler.

None of the various "language rules," carefully contrived to
deceive and to camouflage, had a more decisive effect on the
mentality of the killers than this first war decree of Hitler, in
which the word for "murder" was replaced by the phrase "to
grant a mercy death." Eichmann, asked by the police examiner
if the directive to avoid "unnecessary hardships" was not a bit
ironic, in view of the fact that the destination of these people

was certain death anyhow, did not even understand the question, so firmly was it still anchored in his mind that the unforgivable sin was not to kill people but to cause unnecessary pain. During the trial, he showed unmistakable signs of sincere outrage when witnesses told of cruelties and atrocities committed by S.S. men—though the court and much of the audience failed to see these signs, because his single-minded effort to keep his self-control had misled them into believing that he was "unmovable" and indifferent—and it was not the accusation of having sent millions of people to their death that ever caused him real agitation but only the accusation (dismissed by the court) of one witness that he had once beaten a Jewish boy to death. To be sure, he had also sent people into the area of the *Einsatzgruppen*, who did not "grant a mercy death" but killed by shooting, but he was probably relieved when, in the later stages of the operation, this became unnecessary because of the ever-growing capacity of the gas chambers. He must also have thought that the new method indicated a decisive improvement in the Nazi government's attitude toward the Jews, since at the beginning of the gassing program it had been expressly stated that the benefits of euthanasia were to be reserved for true Germans. As the war progressed, with violent and horrible death raging all around—on the front in Russia, in the deserts of Africa, in Italy, on the beaches of France, in the ruins of the German cities—the gassing centers in Auschwitz and Chelmno, in Majdanek and Belzek, in Treblinka and Sobibor, must actually have appeared the "Charitable Foundations for Institutional Care" that the experts in mercy death called them. Moreover, from January, 1942, on, there were euthanasia teams operating in the East to "help the wounded in ice and snow," and though this killing of wounded soldiers was also "top secret," it was known to many, certainly to the executors of the Final Solution.

It has frequently been pointed out that the gassing of the mentally sick had to be stopped in Germany because of protests from the population and from a few courageous dignitaries of the churches, whereas no such protests were voiced when the program switched to the gassing of Jews, though some of the killing centers were located on what was then German territory and were surrounded by German populations. The protests, however, occurred at the beginning of the war; quite apart from the effects of "education in euthanasia," the attitude toward a "painless death through gassing" very likely changed in the course of the war. This sort of thing is difficult to prove; there are no documents to support it, because of the secrecy of the whole enterprise, and none of the war criminals ever mentioned it, not even the defendants in the Doctors' Trial at Nuremberg, who were full of quotations from the international literature on the subject. Perhaps they had forgotten the climate of public opinion in which they killed, perhaps they never cared to know it, since they felt, wrongly, that their "objective and scientific" attitude was far more advanced than the opinions held by ordinary people. However, a few truly priceless stories, to be found in the war diaries of trustworthy men who were fully aware of the fact that their own shocked reaction was no longer shared by their neighbors, have survived the moral debacle of a whole nation.

Reck-Malleczewen, whom I mentioned before, tells of a female "leader" who came to Bavaria to give the peasants a pep talk in the summer of 1944. She seems not to have wasted much time on "miracle weapons" and victory, she faced frankly the prospect of defeat, about which no good German needed to worry because *the Führer "in his great goodness had prepared for the whole German people a mild death through gassing in case the war should have an unhappy end."* And the writer adds: "Oh, no, I'm not imagining things, this lovely lady is not a mirage, I saw her with my own eyes: a yellow-skinned female pushing forty, with insane eyes. . . . And what happened? Did these Bavarian peasants at least put her into the local lake to cool off her enthusiastic readiness for death? They did nothing of the sort. They went home, shaking their heads."

My next story is even more to the point, since it concerns someone who was not a "leader," may not even have been a Party member. It happened in Königsberg, in East Prussia, an altogether different corner of Germany, in January, 1945, a few days before the Russians destroyed the city, occupied its ruins, and annexed the whole province. The story is told by Count Hans von Lehnsdorff, in his *Ostpreussisches Tagebuch*

(1961). He had remained in the city as a physician to take care of wounded soldiers who could not be evacuated; he was called to one of the huge centers for refugees from the country-side, which was already occupied by the Red Army. There he was accosted by a woman who showed him a varicose vein she had had for years but wanted to have treated now, because she had time. "I try to explain that it is more important for her to get away from Königsberg and to leave the treatment for some later time. Where do you want to go? I ask her. She does not know, but she knows that they will all be brought into the Reich. And then she adds, surprisingly: *'The Russians will never get us. The Führer will never permit it. Much sooner he will gas us.'* I look around furtively, but no one seems to find this statement out of the ordinary." The story, one feels, like most true stories, is incomplete. There should have been one more voice, preferably a female one, which, sighing heavily, replied: And now all that good, expensive gas has been wasted on the Jews!

V I I : *The Wannsee Conference, or*
Pontius Pilate

My report on Eichmann's conscience has thus far followed evidence which he himself had forgotten. In his own presentation of the matter, the turning point came not four weeks but four months later, in January, 1942, during the Conference of the *Staatssekretäre* (Undersecretaries of State), as the Nazis used to call it, or the Wannsee Conference, as it now is usually called, because Heydrich had invited the gentlemen to a house in that suburb of Berlin. As the formal name of the conference indicates, the meeting had become necessary because the Final Solution, if it was to be applied to the whole of Europe, clearly required more than tacit acceptance from the Reich's State apparatus; it needed the active cooperation of all Ministries and of the whole Civil Service. The Ministers themselves, nine years after Hitler's rise to power, were all Party members of long standing—those who in the initial stages of the regime had merely "coordinated" themselves, smoothly enough, had been replaced. Yet most of them were not completely trusted, since few among them owed their careers entirely to the Nazis, as did Heydrich or Himmler; and those who did, like Joachim von Ribbentrop, head of the Foreign Office, a former champagne salesman, were likely to be nonentities. The problem was much more acute, however, with respect to the higher career men in the Civil Service, directly under the Ministers, for these men, the backbone of every government administration, were not easily replaceable, and Hitler had tolerated them, just as Adenauer was to tolerate them, unless they were compromised beyond salvation. Hence the undersecretaries and the legal and other experts in the various Ministries were frequently not even Party members, and

Heydrich's apprehensions about whether he would be able to enlist the active help of these people in mass murder were quite comprehensible. As Eichmann put it, Heydrich "expected the greatest difficulties." Well, he could not have been more wrong.

The aim of the conference was to coordinate all efforts toward the implementation of the Final Solution. The discussion turned first on "complicated legal questions," such as the treatment of half- and quarter-Jews—should they be killed or only sterilized? This was followed by a frank discussion of the "various types of possible solutions to the problem," which meant the various methods of killing, and here, too, there was more than "happy agreement on the part of the participants"; the Final Solution was greeted with "extraordinary enthusiasm" by all present, and particularly by Dr. Wilhelm Stuckart, Undersecretary in the Ministry of the Interior, who was known to be rather reticent and hesitant in the face of "radical" Party measures, and was, according to Dr. Hans Globke's testimony at Nuremberg, a staunch supporter of the Law. There were certain difficulties, however. Undersecretary Josef Bühler, second in command in the General Government in Poland, was dismayed at the prospect that Jews would be evacuated from the West to the East, because this meant more Jews in Poland, and he proposed that these evacuations be postponed and that "the Final Solution be started in the General Government, where no problems of transport existed." The gentlemen from the Foreign Office appeared with their own carefully elaborated memorandum, expressing "the desires and ideas of the Foreign Office with respect to the total solution of the Jewish question in Europe," to which nobody paid much attention. The main point, as Eichmann rightly noted, was that the members of the various branches of the Civil Service did not merely express opinions but made concrete propositions. The meeting lasted no more than an hour or an hour and a half, after which drinks were served and everybody had lunch—"a cozy little social gathering," designed to strengthen the necessary personal contacts. It was a very important occasion for Eichmann, who had never before mingled socially with so many "high personages"; he was by far the lowest in rank and social position of those present. He had sent out the invitations and had prepared some statistical material (full of incredible errors) for Heydrich's introductory speech—eleven million Jews had to be killed, an undertaking of some magnitude—and later he was to prepare the minutes. In short, he acted as secretary of the meeting. This was why he was permitted, after the dignitaries had left, to sit down near the fireplace with his chief Müller and Heydrich, "and that was the first time I saw Heydrich smoke and drink." They did not "talk shop, but enjoyed some rest after long hours of work," being greatly satisfied and, especially Heydrich, in very high spirits.

There was another reason that made the day of this conference unforgettable for Eichmann. Although he had been doing his best right along to help with the Final Solution, he had still harbored some doubts about "such a bloody solution through violence," and these doubts had now been dispelled. "Here now, during this conference, the most prominent people had spoken, the Popes of the Third Reich." Now he could see with his own eyes and hear with his own ears that not only Hitler, not only Heydrich or the "sphinx" Müller, not just the S.S. or the Party, but the élite of the good old Civil Service were vying and fighting with each other for the honor of taking the lead in these "bloody" matters. "At that moment, I sensed a kind of Pontius Pilate feeling, for I felt free of all guilt." *Who was he to judge?* Who was he "to have [his] own thoughts in this matter"? Well, he was neither the first nor the last to be ruined by modesty.

What followed, as Eichmann recalled it, went more or less smoothly and soon became routine. He quickly became an expert in "forced evacuation," as he had been an expert in "forced emigration." In country after country, the Jews had to register, were forced to wear the yellow badge for easy identification, were assembled and deported, the various shipments being directed to one or another of the extermination centers in the East, depending on their relative capacity at the moment; when a trainload of Jews arrived at a center, the strong among them were selected for work, often operating the extermination machinery, all others were immediately killed. There were hitches, but they were minor. The Foreign Office was in contact with the authorities in those foreign countries that were either occupied or allied with the Nazis, to put pressure on them to deport their Jews, or, as the case might be, to prevent them from evacuating them to the East helter-skelter, out of sequence, without proper regard for the absorptive capacity of the death centers. (This was how Eichmann remembered it; it was in fact not quite so simple.) The legal experts drew up the necessary legislation for making the victims stateless, which was important on two counts: it made it impossible for any country to inquire into their fate, and it enabled the state in which they were resident to confiscate their property. The Ministry of Finance and the Reichsbank prepared facilities to receive the huge loot from all over Europe, down to watches and gold teeth, all of which was sorted out in the Reichsbank and then sent to the Prussian State Mint. The Ministry of Transport provided the necessary railroad cars, usually freight cars, even in times of great scarcity of rolling stock, and they saw to it that the schedule of the deportation trains did not conflict with other timetables. The Jewish Councils of Elders were informed by Eichmann or his men of how many Jews were needed to fill each train, and they made out the list of deportees. The Jews registered, filled out innumerable forms, answered pages and pages of questionnaires regarding their property so that it could be seized the more easily; they then assembled at the collection points and boarded the trains. The few who tried to hide or to escape were rounded up by a special Jewish police force. As far as Eichmann could see, no one protested, no one refused to cooperate. *"Immerzu fahren hier die Leute zu ihrem eigenen Begräbnis"* (Day in day out the people here leave for their own funeral), as a Jewish observer put it in Berlin in 1943.

Mere compliance would never have been enough either to smooth out all the enormous difficulties of an operation that was soon to cover the whole of Nazi-occupied and Nazi-allied Europe or to soothe the consciences of the operators, who, after all, had been brought up on the commandment "Thou shalt not kill," and who knew the verse from the Bible, "Thou hast murdered and thou hast inherited," that the judgment of the District Court of Jerusalem quoted so appropriately. What Eichmann called the "death whirl" that descended upon Germany after the immense losses at Stalingrad—the saturation bombing of German cities, his stock excuse for killing civilians and still the stock excuse offered in Germany for the massacres—making an everyday experience of sights different from the atrocities reported at Jerusalem but no less horrible, might have contributed to the easing, or, rather, to the extinguishing, of conscience, had any conscience been left when it occurred, but according to the evidence such was not the case. The extermination machinery had been planned and perfected in all its details long before the horror of war struck Germany herself, and its intricate bureaucracy functioned with the same unwavering precision in the years of easy victory as in those last years of predictable defeat. Defections from the ranks of the ruling élite and notably from among the Higher S.S. officers hardly occurred at the beginning, when people might still have had a conscience; they made themselves felt only when it had become obvious that Germany was going to lose the war. Moreover, such defections were never serious enough to throw the machinery out of gear; they consisted of individual acts not of mercy but of corruption, and they were inspired not by conscience but by the desire to salt some money or some connections away for the dark days to come. Himmler's order in the fall of 1944 to halt the extermination and to dismantle the installations at the death factories sprang from his absurd but sincere conviction that the Allied powers would know how to appreciate this obliging gesture; he told a rather incredulous Eichmann that on the strength of it he would be able to negotiate a *Hubertusburger-Frieden* —an allusion to the Peace Treaty of Hubertusburg that concluded the Seven Years' War of Frederick II of Prussia in 1763 and enabled Prussia to retain Silesia, although she had lost the war.

As Eichmann told it, the most potent factor in the soothing of his own conscience was the simple fact that he could see no one, no one at all, who actually was against the Final Solution. He did encounter one exception, however, which he mentioned several times, and which must have made a deep impression on him. This happened in Hungary when he was negotiating with Dr. Kastner over Himmler's offer to release one million Jews in exchange for ten thousand trucks. Kastner, apparently emboldened by the new turn of affairs, had asked Eichmann to stop "the death mills at Auschwitz," and Eichmann had answered that he would do it "with the greatest pleasure" (*herzlich gern*) but that, alas, it was outside his competence and outside the competence of his superiors—as indeed it was. Of course, he did not expect the Jews to share the general enthusiasm over their destruction, but he did expect more than compliance, he expected—and received, to a truly extraordinary degree—their cooperation. This was "of course the very cornerstone" of everything he did, as it had been the very cornerstone of his activities in Vienna. Without Jewish help in administrative and police work—the final rounding up of Jews in Berlin was, as I have mentioned, done entirely by Jewish police—there would have been either complete chaos or an impossibly severe drain on German manpower. ("There can be no doubt that, without the cooperation of the victims, it would hardly have been possible for a few thousand people, most of whom, moreover, worked in offices, to liquidate many hundreds of thousands of other people. . . . Over the whole way to their deaths the Polish Jews got to see hardly more than a handful of Germans." Thus R. Pendorf in the publication mentioned above. To an even greater extent this applies to those Jews who were transported to Poland to find their deaths there.) Hence, the establishing of Quisling governments in occupied territories was always accompanied by the organization of a central Jewish office, and, as we shall see later, where the Nazis did not succeed in setting up a puppet government, they also failed to enlist the cooperation of the Jews. But whereas the members of the Quisling governments were usually taken from the opposition parties, the members of the Jewish Councils were as a rule the locally recognized Jewish leaders, to whom the Nazis gave enormous powers—until they, too, were deported, to Theresienstadt or Bergen-Belsen, if they happened to be from Central or Western Europe, to Auschwitz if they were from an Eastern European community.

To a Jew this role of the Jewish leaders in the destruction of their own people is undoubtedly the darkest chapter of the whole dark story. It had been known about before, but it has now been exposed for the first time in all its pathetic and sordid detail by Raul Hilberg, whose standard work *The Destruction of the European Jews* I mentioned before. In the matter of cooperation, there was no distinction between the highly assimilated Jewish communities of Central and Western Europe and the Yiddish-speaking masses of the East. In Amsterdam as in Warsaw, in Berlin as in Budapest, Jewish officials could be trusted to compile the lists of persons and of their property, to secure money from the deportees to defray the expenses of their deportation and extermination, to keep track of vacated apartments, to supply police forces to help seize Jews and get them on trains, until, as a last gesture, they handed over the assets of the Jewish community in good order for final confiscation. They distributed the Yellow Star badges, and sometimes, as in Warsaw, "the sale of the armbands became a regular business; there were ordinary armbands of cloth and fancy plastic armbands which were washable." In the Nazi-inspired, but not Nazi-dictated, manifestoes they issued, we still can sense how they enjoyed their new power—"The Central Jewish Council has been granted the right of absolute disposal over all Jewish spiritual and material wealth and over all Jewish manpower," as the first announcement of the Budapest Council phrased it. We know how the Jewish officials felt when they became instruments of murder—like captains "whose ships were about to sink and who succeeded in bringing them safe to port by casting overboard a great part of their precious cargo"; like saviors who "with a hundred victims save a thousand people, with a thousand ten thousand." The truth was even more gruesome. Dr. Kastner, in Hungary, for instance, saved exactly 1,684 people with approximately 476,000 victims. In order not to leave the selection to "blind fate," "truly holy principles" were needed "as the guiding force of the weak human hand which puts down on paper the name of the unknown person and with this decides his life or death." And whom did these "holy principles" single out for salvation? Those "who had worked all their lives for the *zibur* [community]"—i.e., the functionaries—and the "most prominent Jews," as Kastner says in his report.

No one bothered to swear the Jewish officials to secrecy; they were voluntary "bearers of secrets," either in order to assure quiet and prevent panic, as in Dr. Kastner's case, or out of "humane" considerations, such as that "living in the expectation of death by gassing would only be the harder," as in the case of Dr. Leo Baeck, former Chief Rabbi of Berlin. During the Eichmann trial, one witness pointed out the unfortunate consequences of this kind of "humanity"—people volunteered for deportation from Theresienstadt to Auschwitz and denounced those who tried to tell them the truth as being "not sane." We know the physiognomies of the Jewish leaders during the Nazi period very well; they ranged all the way from Chaim Rumkowski, Eldest of the Jews in Lódz, called Chaim I, who issued currency notes bearing his signature and postage stamps engraved with his portrait, and who rode around in a broken-down horse-drawn carriage; through Leo Baeck, scholarly, mild-mannered, highly educated, who believed Jewish policemen would be "more gentle and helpful" and would "make the ordeal easier" (whereas in fact they were, of course, more brutal and less corruptible, since so much more was at stake for them); to, finally, a few who committed suicide—like Adam Czerniakow, chairman of the Warsaw Jewish Council, who was not a rabbi but an unbeliever, a Polish-speaking Jewish engineer, but who must still have remembered the rabbinical saying: "Let them kill you, but don't cross the line."

That the prosecution in Jerusalem, so careful not to embarrass the Adenauer administration, should have avoided, with even greater and more obvious justification, bringing this chapter of the story into the open was almost a matter of course. (These issues, however, are discussed quite openly and with astonishing frankness in Israeli schoolbooks—as may conveniently be gathered from the article "Young Israelis and Jews Abroad—A Study of Selected History Textbooks" by Mark M. Krug, in *Comparative Education Review*, October, 1963.) The chapter must be included here, however, because it accounts for certain otherwise inexplicable lacunae in the documentation of a generally over-documented case. The judges mentioned one such instance, the absence of H. G. Adler's book *Theresienstadt 1941-1945* (1955), which the prosecution, in some embarrassment, admitted to be "authentic, based on irrefutable sources." The reason for the omission was clear. The book describes in

detail how the feared "transport lists" were put together by the
Jewish Council of Theresienstadt after the S.S. had given some
general directives, stipulating how many should be sent away,
and of what age, sex, profession, and country of origin. The
prosecution's case would have been weakened if it had been
forced to admit that the naming of individuals who were sent
to their doom had been, with few exceptions, the job of the
Jewish administration. And the Deputy State Attorney, Mr.
Ya'akov Baror, who handled the intervention from the bench,
in a way indicated this when he said: "I am trying to bring
out those things which somehow refer to the accused without
damaging the picture in its entirety." The picture would indeed
have been greatly damaged by the inclusion of Adler's book,
since it would have contradicted testimony given by the chief
witness on Theresienstadt, who claimed that Eichmann himself
had made these individual selections. Even more important, the
prosecution's general picture of a clear-cut division between
persecutors and victims would have suffered greatly. To make
available evidence that does not support the case for the prosecution is usually the job of the defense, and the question why
Dr. Servatius, who perceived some minor inconsistencies in the
testimony, did not avail himself of such easily obtainable and
widely known documentation is difficult to answer. He could
have pointed to the fact that Eichmann, immediately upon being
transformed from an expert in emigration into an expert in
"evacuation," appointed his old Jewish associates in the
emigration business—Dr. Paul Eppstein, who had been in
charge of emigration in Berlin, and Rabbi Benjamin Murmelstein, who had held the same job in Vienna—as "Jewish Elders"
in Theresienstadt. This would have done more to demonstrate
the atmosphere in which Eichmann worked than all the
unpleasant and often downright offensive talk about oaths,
loyalty, and the virtues of unquestioning obedience.

The testimony of Mrs. Charlotte Salzberger on Theresienstadt,
from which I quoted above, permitted us to cast at least a
glance into this neglected corner of what the prosecution kept
calling the "general picture." The presiding judge did not like
the term and he did not like the picture. He told the Attorney
General several times that "we are not drawing pictures here,"

that there is "an indictment and this indictment is the framework for our trial," that the court "has its own view about this
trial, according to the indictment," and that "the prosecution
must adjust to what the court lays down"—admirable admoni-
tions for criminal proceedings, none of which was heeded. The
prosecution did worse than not heed them, it simply refused
to guide its witnesses—or, if the court became too insistent, it asked a few haphazard questions, very casually—with
the result that the witnesses behaved as though they were
speakers at a meeting chaired by the Attorney General, who
introduced them to the audience before they took the floor.
They could talk almost as long as they wished, and it was a
rare occasion when they were asked a specific question.

This atmosphere, not of a show trial but of a mass meeting,
at which speaker after speaker does his best to arouse the
audience, was especially noticeable when the prosecution called
witness after witness to testify to the rising in the Warsaw ghetto
and to the similar attempts in Vilna and Kovno—matters that
had no connection whatever with the crimes of the accused.
The testimony of these people would have contributed something to the trial if they had told of the activities of the
Jewish Councils, which had played such a great and disastrous
role in their own heroic efforts. Of course, there was some
mention of this—witnesses speaking of "S.S. men and their
helpers" pointed out that they counted among the latter the
"ghetto police which was also an instrument in the hands of
the Nazi murderers" as well as "the *Judenrat*"—but they were
only too glad not to "elaborate" on this side of their story,
and they shifted the discussion to the role of real traitors, of
whom there were few, and who were "nameless people,
unknown to the Jewish public," such as "all undergrounds
which fought against the Nazis suffered from." (The audience
while these witnesses testified had changed again; it consisted
now of *Kibbuzniks*, members of the Israeli communal settlements to which the speakers belonged.) The purest and clearest
account came from Zivia Lubetkin Zuckerman, today a woman
of perhaps forty, still very beautiful, completely free of sentimentality or self-indulgence, her facts well organized, and
always quite sure of the point she wished to make. Legally,

the testimony of these witnesses was immaterial—Mr. Hausner did not mention one of them in his last *plaidoyer*—except insofar as it constituted proof of close contacts between Jewish partisans and the Polish and Russian underground fighters, which, apart from contradicting other testimony ("We had the whole population against us"), could have been useful to the defense, since it offered much better justification for the wholesale slaughter of civilians than Eichmann's repeated claim that "Weizmann had declared war on Germany in 1939." (This was sheer nonsense. All that Chaim Weizmann had said, at the close of the last prewar Zionist Congress, was that the war of the Western democracies "is our war, their struggle is our struggle." The tragedy, as Hausner rightly pointed out, was precisely that the Jews were not recognized by the Nazis as belligerents, for if they had been they would have survived, in prisoner-of-war or civilian internment camps.) Had Dr. Servatius made this point, the prosecution would have been forced to admit how pitifully small these resistance groups had been, how incredibly weak and essentially harmless—and, moreover, how little they had represented the Jewish population, who at one point even took arms against them.

While the legal irrelevance of all this very time-consuming testimony remained pitifully clear, the political intention of the Israeli government in introducing it was also not difficult to guess. Mr. Hausner (or Mr. Ben-Gurion) probably wanted to demonstrate that whatever resistance there had been had come from Zionists, as though, of all Jews, only the Zionists knew that if you could not save your life it might still be worth while to save your honor, as Mr. Zuckerman put it; that the worst that could happen to the human person under such circumstances was to be and to remain "innocent," as became clear from the tenor and drift of Mrs. Zuckerman's testimony. However, these "political" intentions misfired, for the witnesses were truthful and told the court that all Jewish organizations and parties had played their role in the resistance, so the true distinction was not between Zionists and non-Zionists but between organized and unorganized people, and, even more important, between the young and the middle-aged. To be sure, those who resisted were a minority, a tiny minority, but under the circumstances "the miracle was," as one of them pointed out, "that this minority existed."

Legal considerations aside, the appearance in the witness box of the former Jewish resistance fighters was welcome enough. It dissipated the haunting specter of universal cooperation, the stifling, poisoned atmosphere which had surrounded the Final Solution. The well-known fact that the actual work of killing in the extermination centers was usually in the hands of Jewish commandos had been fairly and squarely established by witnesses for the prosecution—how they had worked in the gas chambers and the crematories, how they had pulled the gold teeth and cut the hair of the corpses, how they had dug the graves and, later, dug them up again to extinguish the traces of mass murder; how Jewish technicians had built gas chambers in Theresienstadt, where the Jewish "autonomy" had been carried so far that even the hangman was a Jew. But this was only horrible, it was no moral problem. The selection and classification of workers in the camps was made by the S.S., who had a marked predilection for the criminal elements; and, anyhow, it could only have been the selection of the worst. (This was especially true in Poland, where the Nazis had exterminated a large proportion of the Jewish intelligentsia at the same time that they killed Polish intellectuals and members of the professions—in marked contrast, incidentally, to their policy in Western Europe, where they tended to save prominent Jews in order to exchange them for German civilian internees or prisoners of war; Bergen-Belsen was originally a camp for "exchange Jews.") The moral problem lay in the amount of truth there was in Eichmann's description of Jewish cooperation, even under the conditions of the Final Solution: "The formation of the Jewish Council [at Theresienstadt] and the distribution of business was left to the discretion of the Council, except for the appointment of the president, who the president was to be, which depended upon us, of course. However, this appointment was not in the form of a dictatorial decision. The functionaries with whom we were in constant contact—well, they had to be treated with kid gloves. They were not ordered around, for the simple reason that if the chief officials had been told what to do in the form of: you must, you have to, that would not have helped matters any. If the person in question does not like what he is doing, the whole works will suffer. . . . We did our best to make everything somehow palatable." No doubt they did; the problem is how it was possible for them to succeed.

Thus, the gravest omission from the "general picture" was that of a witness to testify to the cooperation between the Nazi rulers and the Jewish authorities, and hence of an opportunity to raise the question: "Why did you cooperate in the destruction of your own people and, eventually, in your own ruin?" The only witness who had been a prominent member of a *Judenrat* was Pinchas Freudiger, the former Baron Philip von Freudiger, of Budapest, and during his testimony the only serious incidents in the audience took place; people screamed at the witness in Hungarian and in Yiddish, and the court had to interrupt the session. Freudiger, an Orthodox Jew of considerable dignity, was shaken: "There are people here who say they were not told to escape. But fifty per cent of the people who escaped were captured and killed"—as compared with ninety-nine per cent, for those who did not escape. "Where could they have gone to? Where could they have fled?"—but he himself fled, to Rumania, because he was rich and Wisliceny helped him. "What could we have done? What could we have done?" And the only response to this came from the presiding judge: "I do not think this is an answer to the question"—a question raised by the gallery but not by the court.

The matter of cooperation was twice mentioned by the judges; Judge Yitzak Raveh elicited from one of the resistance witnesses an admission that the "ghetto police" were an "instrument in the hands of murderers" and an acknowledgment of "the *Judenrat's* policy of cooperating with the Nazis"; and Judge Halevi found out from Eichmann in cross-examination that the Nazis had regarded this cooperation as the very cornerstone of their Jewish policy. But the question the prosecutor regularly addressed to each witness except the resistance fighters which sounded so very natural to those who knew nothing of the factual background of the trial, the question "Why did you not rebel?," actually served as a smoke screen for the question that was not asked. And thus it came to pass that all answers to the unanswerable question Mr. Hausner put to his witnesses were considerably less than "the truth, the whole truth, and nothing but the truth." True it was that the Jewish people as a whole had not been organized, that they had possessed no territory, no government, and no army, that, in the hour of their greatest need, they had no government-in-exile to represent them among the Allies (the Jewish Agency for Palestine, under Dr. Weizmann's presidency, was at best a miserable substitute), no caches of weapons, no youth with military training. But the whole truth was that there existed Jewish community organizations and Jewish party and welfare organizations on both the local and the international level. Wherever Jews lived, there were recognized Jewish leaders, and this leadership, almost without exception, cooperated in one way or another, for one reason or another, with the Nazis. The whole truth was that if the Jewish people had really been unorganized and leaderless, there would have been chaos and plenty of misery but the total number of victims would hardly have been between four and a half and six million people. (According to Freudiger's calculations about half of them could have saved themselves if they had not followed the instructions of the Jewish Councils. This is of course a mere estimate, which, however, oddly jibes with the rather reliable figures we have from Holland and which I owe to Dr. L. de Jong, the head of the Netherlands State Institute for War Documentation. In Holland, where the *Joodsche Raad* like all the Dutch authorities very quickly became an "instrument of the Nazis," 103,000 Jews were deported to the death camps and some five thousand to Theresienstadt in the usual way, i.e., with the cooperation of the Jewish Council. Only five hundred and nineteen Jews returned from the death camps. In contrast to this figure, ten thousand of those twenty to twenty-five thousand Jews who escaped the Nazis—and that meant also the Jewish Council—and went underground survived; again forty to fifty per cent. Most of the Jews sent to Theresienstadt returned to Holland.)

I have dwelt on this chapter of the story, which the Jerusalem trial failed to put before the eyes of the world in its true dimensions, because it offers the most striking insight into the totality of the moral collapse the Nazis caused in respectable European society—not only in Germany but in almost all countries, not only among the persecutors but also among the victims. Eichmann, in contrast to other elements in the Nazi movement, had always been overawed by "good society," and the politeness he often showed to German-speaking Jewish functionaries was to a large extent the result of his recognition that he was dealing with people who were socially his superiors. He was not at all, as one witness called him, a *"Landsknecht-natur,"* a mercenary, who wanted to escape to regions where there aren't no Ten Commandments an' a man can raise a thirst. What he fervently believed in up to the end was success, the chief standard of "good society" as he knew it. Typical was his last word on the subject of Hitler—whom he and his comrade Sassen had agreed to "shirr out" of their story; Hitler, he said, "may have been wrong all down the line, but one thing is beyond dispute: the man was able to work his way up from lance corporal in the German Army to Führer of a people of almost eighty million. . . . His success alone proved to me that I should subordinate myself to this man." His conscience was indeed set at rest when he saw the zeal and eagerness with which "good society" everywhere reacted as he did. He did not need to "close his ears to the voice of conscience," as the judgment has it, not because he had none, but because his conscience spoke with a "respectable voice," with the voice of respectable society around him.

That there were no voices from the outside to arouse his conscience was one of Eichmann's points, and it was the task of the prosecution to prove that this was not so, that there were voices he could have listened to, and that, anyhow, he had done his work with a zeal far beyond the call of duty. Which turned out to be true enough, except that, strange as it may appear, his murderous zeal was not altogether unconnected with the ambiguity in the voices of those who at one time or another tried to restrain him. We need mention here only in passing the so-called "inner emigration" in Germany—those people who frequently had held positions, even high ones, in the Third Reich and who, after the end of the war, told themselves and the world at large that they had always been "inwardly opposed" to the regime. The question here is not whether or not they are telling the truth; the point is, rather, that no secret in the secret-ridden atmosphere of the Hitler regime was better kept than such "inward opposition." This was almost a matter of course under the conditions of Nazi terror; as a rather well-known "inner emigrant," who certainly believed in his own sincerity, once told me, they had to appear "outwardly" even more like Nazis than ordinary Nazis did, in order to keep their secret. (This, incidentally, may explain why the few known protests against the extermination program came not from the Army commanders but from old Party members.) Hence, the only possible way to live in the Third Reich and not act as a Nazi was not to appear at all: "Withdrawal from significant participation in public life" was indeed the only criterion by which one might have measured individual guilt, as Otto Kirchheimer recently remarked in his *Political Justice* (1961). If the term was to make any sense, the "inner emigrant" could only be one who lived "as though outcast among his own people amidst blindly believing masses," as Professor Hermann Jahrreiss pointed out in his "Statement for All Defense Attorneys" before the Nuremberg Tribunal. For opposition was indeed "utterly pointless" in the absence of all organization. It is true that there were Germans who lived for twelve years in this "outer cold," but their number was insignificant, even among the members of the resistance. In recent years, the slogan of the "inner emigration" (the term itself has a definitely equivocal flavor, as it can mean either an emigration into the inward regions of one's soul or a way of conducting oneself as though he were an emigrant) has become a sort of a joke. The sinister Dr. Otto Bradfisch, former member of one of the *Einsatzgruppen,* who presided over the killing of at least fifteen thousand people, told a German court that he had always been "inwardly opposed" to what he was doing. Perhaps the death of fifteen thousand people was necessary to provide him with an alibi in the eyes of "true Nazis." (The same argument was advanced, though with considerably less success, in a Polish court by former Gauleiter Arthur Greiser of the Warthegau: only his "official soul" had carried out the crimes for which he was hanged in 1946, his "private soul" had always been against them.)

While Eichmann may never have encountered an "inner emigrant," he must have been well acquainted with many of those numerous civil servants who today assert that they stayed in their jobs for no other reason than to "mitigate" matters and to prevent "real Nazis" from taking over their posts. We mentioned the famous case of Dr. Hans Globke, Undersecretary of State and from 1953 to 1963 chief of the personnel division in the West German Chancellery. Since he was the only civil servant in this category to be mentioned during the trial, it may be worth while to look into his mitigating activities. Dr. Globke had been employed in the Prussian Ministry of the Interior before Hitler's rise to power, and had shown there a rather premature interest in the Jewish question. He formulated the first of the directives in which "proof of Aryan descent" was demanded, in this case of persons who applied for permission to change their names. This circular letter of December, 1932—issued at a time when Hitler's rise to power was not yet a certainty, but a strong probability—oddly anticipated the "top secret decrees," that is, the typically totalitarian rule by means of laws that are not brought to the attention of the public, which the Hitler regime introduced much later, in notifying the recipients that "these directives are not for publication." Dr. Globke, as I have mentioned, kept his interest in names, and since it is true that his Commentary on the Nuremberg Laws of 1935 was considerably harsher than the earlier interpretation of *Rassenschande* by the Ministry of the Interior's expert on Jewish affairs, Dr. Bernhard Lösener, an old member of the Party, one could even accuse him of having made things worse than they were under "real Nazis." But even if we were to grant him all his good intentions, it is hard indeed to see what he could have done under the circumstances to make things better than they would otherwise have been. Recently, however, a German newspaper, after much searching, came up with an answer to this puzzling question. They found a document, duly signed by Dr. Globke, which decreed that Czech brides of German soldiers had to furnish photographs of themselves in bathing suits in order to obtain a marriage license. And Dr. Globke explained: "With this confidential ordinance a three-year-old scandal was somewhat *mitigated*"; for until his intervention, Czech brides had to furnish snapshots that showed them stark naked.

Dr. Globke, as he explained at Nuremberg, was fortunate in that he worked under the orders of another "mitigator," Staatssekretär (Undersecretary of State) Wilhelm Stuckart, whom we met as one of the eager members of the Wannsee Conference. Stuckart's attenuation activities concerned half-Jews, whom he proposed to sterilize. (The Nuremberg court, in possession of the minutes of the Wannsee Conference, may not have believed that he had known nothing of the extermination program, but it sentenced him to time served on account of ill health. A German denazification court fined him five hundred marks and declared him a "nominal member of the Party"—a *Mitläufer*—although they must have known at least that Stuckart belonged to the "old guard" of the Party and had joined the S.S. early, as an honorary member.) Clearly, the story of the "mitigators" in Hitler's offices belongs among the postwar fairy tales, and we can dismiss them, too, as voices that might possibly have reached Eichmann's conscience.

The question of these voices became serious, in Jerusalem, with the appearance in court of Propst Heinrich Grüber, a Protestant minister, who had come to the trial as the only German (and, incidentally, except for Judge Michael Musmanno from the United States, the only non-Jewish) witness for the prosecution. (German witnesses for the defense were excluded from the outset, since they would have exposed themselves to arrest and prosecution in Israel under the same law as that under which Eichmann was tried.) Propst Grüber had belonged to the numerically small and politically irrelevant group of persons who were opposed to Hitler on principle, and not out of nationalist considerations, and whose stand on the Jewish question had been without equivocation. He promised to be a splendid witness, since Eichmann had negotiated with him several times, and his mere appearance in the courtroom created a kind of sensation. Unfortunately, his testimony was vague; he did not remember, after so many years, when he had spoken with Eichmann, or, and this was more serious, on what subjects. All he recalled clearly was that he had once asked for unleavened bread to be shipped to Hungary for Passover, and that he had traveled to Switzerland during the war to tell his Christian friends how dangerous the situation was and to urge

that more opportunities for emigration be provided. (The negotiations must have taken place prior to the implementing of the
Final Solution, which coincided with Himmler's decree forbid-
ding all emigration; they probably occurred before the invasion
of Russia.) He got his unleavened bread, and he got safely to
Switzerland and back again. His troubles started later, when the
deportations had begun. Propst Grüber and his group of Protestant clergymen first intervened merely "on behalf of people
who had been wounded in the course of the First World War
and of those who had been awarded high military decorations;
on behalf of the old and on behalf of the widows of those
killed in World War I." These categories corresponded to those
that had originally been exempted by the Nazis themselves.
Now Grüber was told that what he was doing "ran counter to the
policy of the government," but nothing serious happened to him.
But shortly after this, Propst Grüber did something really extraordinary: he tried to reach the concentration camp of Gurs,
in southern France, where Vichy France had interned, together
with German Jewish refugees, some seventy-five hundred Jews
from Baden and the Saarpfalz whom Eichmann had smuggled
across the German-French border in the fall of 1940, and who,
according to Propst Grüber's information, were even worse off
than the Jews deported to Poland. The result of this attempt
was that he was arrested and put in a concentration camp—
first in Sachsenhausen and then in Dachau. (A similar fate befell
the Catholic priest Dompropst Bernard Lichtenberg, of St. Hed-
wig's Cathedral in Berlin; he not only had dared to pray publicly
for all Jews, baptized or not—which was considerably more
dangerous than to intervene for "special cases"—but he had also
demanded that he be allowed to join the Jews on their journey to
the East. He died on his way to a concentration camp.)

Apart from testifying to the existence of "another Germany,"
Propst Grüber did not contribute much to either the legal or
the historical significance of the trial. He was full of pat judgments about Eichmann—he was like "a block of ice," like
"marble," a "*Landsknechtsnatur*," a "bicycle rider" (a current
German idiom for someone who kowtows to his superiors and
kicks his subordinates)—none of which showed him as a particularly good psychologist, quite apart from the fact that the

"bicycle rider" charge was contradicted by evidence which showed Eichmann to have been rather decent toward his subordinates. Anyway, these were interpretations and conclusions that would normally have been stricken from any court record—though in Jerusalem they even found their way into the judgment. Without them Propst Grüber's testimony could have strengthened the case for the defense, for Eichmann had never given Grüber a direct answer, he had always told him to come back, as he had to ask for further instructions. More important, Dr. Servatius for once took the initiative and asked the witness a highly pertinent question: "Did you try to influence him? Did you, as a clergyman, try to appeal to his feelings, preach to him, and tell him that his conduct was contrary to morality?" Of course, the very courageous Propst had done nothing of the sort, and his answers now were highly embarrassing. He said that "deeds are more effective than words," and that "words would have been useless"; he spoke in clichés that had nothing to do with the reality of the situation, where "mere words" would have been deeds, and where it had perhaps been the duty of a clergyman to test the "uselessness of words."

Even more pertinent than Dr. Servatius' question was what Eichmann said about this episode in his last statement: "Nobody," he repeated, "came to me and reproached me for anything in the performance of my duties. Not even Pastor Grüber claims to have done so." He then added: "He came to me and sought alleviation of suffering, but did not actually object to the very performance of my duties as such." From Propst Grüber's own testimony, it appeared that he sought not so much "alleviation of suffering" as exemptions from it, in accordance with well-established categories recognized earlier by the Nazis. The categories had been accepted without protest by German Jewry from the very beginning. And the acceptance of privileged categories—German Jews as against Polish Jews, war veterans and decorated Jews as against ordinary Jews, families whose ancestors were German-born as against recently naturalized citizens, etc.—had been the beginning of the moral collapse of respectable Jewish society. (In view of the fact that today such matters are often treated as though there existed a law of human nature compelling everybody to lose his dignity in the face of disaster, we may recall the attitude of the French Jewish war veterans who were offered the same privileges by their government, and replied: "We solemnly declare that we renounce any exceptional benefits we may derive from our status as ex-servicemen" [*American Jewish Yearbook,* 1945].) Needless to say, the Nazis themselves never took these distinctions seriously, for them a Jew was a Jew, but the categories played a certain role up to the very end, since they helped put to rest a certain uneasiness among the German population: only Polish Jews were deported, only people who had shirked military service, and so on. For those who did not want to close their eyes it must have been clear from the beginning that it "was a general practice to allow certain exceptions in order to be able to maintain the general rule all the more easily" (in the words of Louis de Jong in an illuminating article on "Jews and Non-Jews in Nazi-Occupied Holland").

What was morally so disastrous in the acceptance of these privileged categories was that everyone who demanded to have an "exception" made in his case implicitly recognized the rule, but this point, apparently, was never grasped by these "good men," Jewish and Gentile, who busied themselves about all those "special cases" for which preferential treatment could be asked. The extent to which even the Jewish victims had accepted the standards of the Final Solution is perhaps nowhere more glaringly evident than in the so-called Kastner Report (available in German, *Der Kastner-Bericht über Eichmanns Menschenhandel in Ungarn,* 1961). Even after the end of the war, Kastner was proud of his success in saving "prominent Jews," a category officially introduced by the Nazis in 1942, as though in his view, too, it went without saying that a famous Jew had more right to stay alive than an ordinary one; to take upon himself such "responsibilities"—to help the Nazis in their efforts to pick out "famous" people from the anonymous mass, for this is what it amounted to—"required more courage than to face death." But if the Jewish and Gentile pleaders of "special cases" were unaware of their involuntary complicity, this implicit recognition of the rule, which spelled death for all non-special cases, must have been very obvious to those who were engaged in the business of murder. They must have felt, at least, that by being asked to make exceptions, and by occasionally granting them, and thus earning gratitude, they had convinced their opponents of the lawfulness of what they were doing.

Moreover, Propst Grüber and the Jerusalem court were quite mistaken in assuming that requests for exemptions originated only with opponents of the regime. On the contrary, as Heydrich explicitly stated during the Wannsee Conference, the establishment of Theresienstadt as a ghetto for privileged categories was prompted by the great number of such interventions from all sides. Theresienstadt later became a showplace for visitors from abroad and served to deceive the outside world, but this was not its original *raison d'être*. The horrible thinning-out process that regularly occurred in this "paradise"—"distinguished from other camps as day is from night," as Eichmann rightly remarked—was necessary because there was never enough room to provide for all who were privileged, and we know from a directive issued by Ernst Kaltenbrunner, head of the R.S.H.A., that "special care was taken not to deport Jews with connections and important acquaintances in the outside world." In other words, the less "prominent" Jews were constantly sacrificed to those whose disappearance in the East would create unpleasant inquiries. The "acquaintances in the outside world" did not necessarily live outside Germany; according to Himmler, there were "eighty million good Germans, each of whom has his decent Jew. It is clear, the others are pigs, but this particular Jew is first-rate" (Hilberg). Hitler himself is said to have known three hundred and forty "first-rate Jews," whom he had either altogether assimilated to the status of Germans or granted the privileges of half-Jews. Thousands of half-Jews had been exempted from all restrictions, which might explain Heydrich's role in the S.S. and Generalfeldmarschall Erhard Milch's role in Göring's Air Force, for it was generally known that Heydrich and Milch were half-Jews. (Among the major war criminals, only two repented in the face of death: Heydrich, during the nine days it took him to die from the wounds inflicted by Czech patriots, and Hans Frank in his death cell at Nuremberg. It is an uncomfortable fact, for it is difficult not to suspect that what Heydrich at least repented of was not murder but that he had betrayed his own people.) If interventions on behalf of "prominent" Jews came from "prominent" people, they often were quite successful. Thus Sven Hedin, one of Hitler's most ardent admirers, intervened for a well-known geographer, a Professor Philippsohn of Bonn, who was "living under undignified conditions at Theresienstadt"; in a letter to Hitler, Hedin threatened that "his attitude to Germany would be dependent upon Philippsohn's fate," whereupon (according to H. G. Adler's book on Theresienstadt) Mr. Philippsohn was promptly provided with better quarters.

In Germany today, this notion of "prominent" Jews has not yet been forgotten. While the veterans and other privileged groups are no longer mentioned, the fate of "famous" Jews is still deplored at the expense of all others. There are more than a few people, especially among the cultural élite, who still publicly regret the fact that Germany sent Einstein packing, without realizing that it was a much greater crime to kill little Hans Cohn from around the corner, even though he was no genius.

VIII : *Duties of a Law-Abiding Citizen*

So Eichmann's opportunities for feeling like Pontius Pilate were many, and as the months and the years went by, he lost the need to feel anything at all. This was the way things were, this was the new law of the land, based on the Führer's order; whatever he did he did, as far as he could see, as a law-abiding citizen. He did his *duty*, as he told the police and the court over and over again; he not only obeyed *orders,* he also obeyed the *law.* Eichmann had a muddled inkling that this could be an important distinction, but neither the defense nor the judges ever took him up on it. The well-worn coins of "superior orders" versus "acts of state" were handed back and forth; they had governed the whole discussion of these matters during the Nuremberg Trials, for no other reason than that they gave the illusion that the altogether unprecedented could be judged according to precedents and the standards that went with them. Eichmann, with his rather modest mental gifts, was certainly the last man in the courtroom to be expected to challenge these notions and to strike out on his own. Since, in addition to performing what he conceived to be the duties of a law-abiding citizen, he had also acted upon orders—always so careful to be "covered"—he became completely muddled, and ended by stressing alternately the virtues and the vices of blind obedience, or the "obedience of corpses," *Kadavergehorsam,* as he himself called it.

The first indication of Eichmann's vague notion that there was more involved in this whole business than the question of the soldier's carrying out orders that are clearly criminal in nature and intent appeared during the police examination, when he suddenly declared with great emphasis that he had lived his whole life according to Kant's moral precepts, and especially according to a Kantian definition of duty. This was outrageous, on the face of it, and also incomprehensible, since Kant's moral philosophy is so closely bound up with man's faculty of judgment, which rules out blind obedience. The examining officer did not press the point, but Judge Raveh, either out of curiosity or out of indignation at Eichmann's having dared to invoke Kant's name in connection with his crimes, decided to question the accused. And, to the surprise of everybody, Eichmann came up with an approximately correct definition of the categorical imperative: "I meant by my remark about Kant that the principle of my will must always be such that it can become the principle of general laws" (which is not the case with theft or murder, for instance, because the thief or the murderer cannot conceivably wish to live under a legal system that would give others the right to rob or murder him). Upon further questioning, he added that he had read Kant's *Critique of Practical Reason*. He then proceeded to explain that from the moment he was charged with carrying out the Final Solution he had ceased to live according to Kantian principles, that he had known it, and that he had consoled himself with the thought that he no longer "was master of his own deeds," that he was unable "to change anything." What he failed to point out in court was that in this "period of crimes legalized by the state," as he himself now called it, he had not simply dismissed the Kantian formula as no longer applicable, he had distorted it to read: Act as if the principle of your actions were the same as that of the legislator or of the law of the land—or, in Hans Frank's formulation of "the categorical imperative in the Third Reich," which Eichmann might have known: "Act in such a way that the Führer, if he knew your action, would approve it" (*Die Technik des Staates*, 1942, pp. 15-16). Kant, to be sure, had never intended to say anything of the sort; on the contrary, to him every man was a legislator the moment he started to act: by using his "practical reason" man found the principles that could and should be the principles of law. But it is true that Eichmann's unconscious distortion agrees with what he himself called the version of Kant "for the household use of the little man." In this household use, all that is left of Kant's spirit is the demand that a man do more than obey the law, that he go beyond the mere call of obedience and identify his own will with the principle behind the law—the source from which the law sprang. In Kant's philosophy, that source was practical reason; in Eichmann's household use of him, it was the will of the Führer. Much of the horribly painstaking thoroughness in the execution of the Final Solution—a thoroughness that usually strikes the observer as typically German, or else as characteristic of the perfect bureaucrat—can be traced to the odd notion, indeed very common in Germany, that to be law-abiding means not merely to obey the laws but to act as though one were the legislator of the laws that one obeys. Hence the conviction that nothing less than going beyond the call of duty will do.

Whatever Kant's role in the formation of "the little man's" mentality in Germany may have been, there is not the slightest doubt that in one respect Eichmann did indeed follow Kant's precepts: a law was a law, there could be no exceptions. In Jerusalem, he admitted only two such exceptions during the time when "eighty million Germans" had each had "his decent Jew": he had helped a half-Jewish cousin, and a Jewish couple in Vienna for whom his uncle had intervened. This inconsistency still made him feel somewhat uncomfortable, and when he was questioned about it during cross-examination, he became openly apologetic: he had "confessed his sins" to his superiors. This uncompromising attitude toward the performance of his murderous duties damned him in the eyes of the judges more than anything else, which was comprehensible, but in his own eyes it was precisely what justified him, as it had once silenced whatever conscience he might have had left. No exceptions—this was the proof that he had always acted against his "inclinations," whether they were sentimental or inspired by interest, that he had always done his "duty."

Doing his "duty" finally brought him into open conflict with orders from his superiors. During the last year of the war, more than two years after the Wannsee Conference, he experienced his last crisis of conscience. As the defeat approached, he was confronted by men from his own ranks who fought more and more insistently for exceptions and, eventually, for the cessation of the Final Solution. That was the moment when his caution broke down and he began, once more, taking initiatives—for instance, he organized the foot marches of Jews from Budapest to the Austrian border after Allied bombing had knocked out the transportation system. It now was the fall of 1944, and Eichmann knew that Himmler had ordered the dismantling of the extermination facilities in Auschwitz and that the game was up. Around this time, Eichmann had one of his very few personal interviews with Himmler, in the course of which the latter allegedly shouted at him, "If up to now you have been busy liquidating Jews, you will from now on, since I order it, take good care of Jews, act as their nursemaid. I remind you that it was I—and neither Gruppenführer Müller nor you—who founded the R.S.H.A. in 1933; I am the one who gives orders here!" Sole witness to substantiate these words was the very dubious Mr. Kurt Becher; Eichmann denied that Himmler had shouted at him, but he did not deny that such an interview had taken place. Himmler cannot have spoken in precisely these words, he surely knew that the R.S.H.A. was founded in 1939, not in 1933, and not simply by himself but by Heydrich, with his endorsement. Still, something of the sort must have occurred. Himmler was then giving orders right and left that the Jews be treated well—they were his "soundest investment"—and it must have been a shattering experience for Eichmann.

Eichmann's last crisis of conscience began with his missions to Hungary in March, 1944, when the Red Army was moving through the Carpathian Mountains toward the Hungarian border. Hungary had joined the war on Hitler's side in 1941, for no other reason than to receive some additional territory from her neighbors, Slovakia, Rumania, and Yugoslavia. The Hungarian government had been outspokenly anti-Semitic even before that, and now it began to deport all stateless Jews from the newly acquired territories. (In nearly all countries, anti-Jewish action started with stateless persons.) This was quite outside the Final Solution, and, as a matter of fact, didn't fit in with the elaborate plans then in preparation under which Europe would be "combed from West to East," so that Hungary had a rather low priority in the order of operations. The stateless Jews had been shoved by the Hungarian police into the nearest part of Russia, and the German occupation authorities on the spot had protested their arrival; the Hungarians had taken back some thousands of able-bodied men and had let the others be shot by Hungarian troops under the guidance of German police units. Admiral Horthy, the country's Fascist ruler, had not wanted to go any further, however—probably due to the restraining influence of Mussolini and Italian Fascism—and in the intervening years Hungary, not unlike Italy, had become a haven for Jews, to which even refugees from Poland and Slovakia could sometimes still escape. The annexation of territory and the trickle of incoming refugees had increased the number of Jews in Hungary from about five hundred thousand before the war to approximately eight hundred thousand in 1944, when Eichmann moved in.

As we know today, the safety of these three hundred thousand Jews newly acquired by Hungary was due to the Germans' reluctance to start a separate action for a limited number, rather than to the Hungarians' eagerness to offer asylum. In 1942, under pressure from the German Foreign Office (which never failed to make it clear to Germany's allies that the touchstone of their trustworthiness was their helpfulness not in winning the war but in "solving the Jewish question"), Hungary had offered to hand over all Jewish refugees. The Foreign Office had been willing to accept this as a step in the right direction, but Eichmann had objected: for technical reasons, he thought it "preferable to defer this action until Hungary is ready to include the Hungarian Jews"; it would be too costly "to set in motion the whole machinery of evacuation" for only one category, and hence "without making any progress in the solution of the Jewish problem in Hungary." Now, in 1944, Hungary was "ready," because on the nineteenth of March two divisions of the German Army had occupied the country. With them had arrived the new Reich Plenipotentiary, S.S. Standartenführer Dr. Edmund Veesenmayer, Himmler's agent in the Foreign Office, and S.S. Obergruppenführer Otto Winkelmann, a member of the Higher S.S. and Police Leader Corps and therefore under the direct command of Himmler. The third S.S. official to arrive in the country was Eichmann, the expert on Jewish evacuation and deportation, who was under the command of Müller and Kaltenbrunner of the R.S.H.A. Hitler himself had left no doubt what the arrival of the three gentlemen meant; in a famous interview, prior to the occupation of the country, he had told Horthy that "Hungary had not yet introduced the steps necessary to settle the Jewish question," and had charged him with "not having permitted the Jews to be massacred" (Hilberg).

Eichmann's assignment was clear. His whole office was moved to Budapest (in terms of his career, this was a "gliding down"), to enable him to see to it that all "necessary steps" were taken. He had no foreboding of what was to happen; his worst fear concerned possible resistance on the part of the Hungarians, which he would have been unable to cope with, because he lacked manpower and also lacked knowledge of local conditions. These fears proved quite unfounded. The Hungarian *gendarmerie* was more than eager to do all that was necessary, and the new State Secretary in Charge of Political (Jewish) Affairs in the Hungarian Ministry of the Interior, Lászlo Endre, was a man "well versed in the Jewish problem," and became an intimate friend, with whom Eichmann could spend a good deal of his free time. Everything went "like a dream," as he repeated whenever he recalled this episode; there were no difficulties whatsoever. Unless, of course, one calls difficulties a few minor differences between his orders and the wishes of his new friends; for instance, probably because of the approach of the Red Army from the East, his orders stipulated that the country was to be "combed from East to West," which meant that Budapest Jews would not be evacuated during the first weeks or months—a matter for great grief among the Hungarians, who wanted their capital to take the lead in becoming *judenrein*. (Eichmann's "dream" was an incredible nightmare for the Jews: nowhere else were so many people deported and exterminated in such a brief span of time. In less than two months, 147 trains, carrying 434,351 people in sealed freight cars, a hundred persons to a car, left the country, and the gas chambers of Auschwitz were hardly able to cope with this multitude.)

The difficulties arose from another quarter. Not one man but three had orders specifying that they were to help in "the solution of the Jewish problem"; each of them belonged to a different outfit and stood in a different chain of command. Technically, Winkelmann was Eichmann's superior, but the Higher S.S. and Police Leaders were not under the command of the R.S.H.A., to which Eichmann belonged. And Veesenmayer, of the Foreign Office, was independent of both. At any rate, Eichmann refused to take orders from either of the others, and resented their presence. But the worst trouble came from a fourth man, whom Himmler had charged with a "special mission" in the only country in Europe that still harbored not only a sizable number of Jews but Jews who were still in an important economic position. (Of a total of a hundred and ten thousand commercial stores and industrial enterprises in Hungary, forty thousand were reported to be in Jewish hands.) This man was Obersturmbannführer, later Standartenführer, Kurt Becher.

Becher, an old enemy of Eichmann who is today a prosperous merchant in Bremen, was called, strangely enough, as a witness for the defense. He could not come to Jerusalem, for obvious reasons, and he was examined in his German home town. His testimony had to be dismissed, since he had been shown, well ahead of time, the questions he was later called on to answer under oath. It was a great pity that Eichmann and Becher could not have been confronted with each other, and this not merely for juridical reasons. Such a confrontation would have revealed another part of the "general picture," which, even legally, was far from irrelevant. According to his own account, the reason Becher joined the S.S. was that "from 1932 to the present day he had been actively engaged in horseback riding." Thirty years ago, this was a sport engaged in only by Europe's upper classes. In 1934, his instructor had persuaded him to enter the S.S. cavalry regiment, which at that moment was the very thing for a man to do if he wished to join the "movement" and at the same time maintain a proper regard for his social standing. (A possible reason Becher in his testimony stressed horseback riding was never mentioned: the Nuremberg Tribunal had excluded the *Reiter-S.S.* from its list of criminal organizations.) The war saw Becher on active duty at the front, as a member not of the Army but of the Armed S.S., in which he was a liaison officer with the Army commanders. He soon left the front to become the principal buyer of horses for the

S.S. personnel department, a job that earned him nearly all the decorations that were then available.

Becher claimed that he had been sent to Hungary only in order to buy twenty thousand horses for the S.S.; this is unlikely, since immediately upon his arrival he began a series of very successful negotiations with the heads of big Jewish business concerns. His relations with Himmler were excellent, he could see him whenever he wished. His "special mission" was clear enough. He was to obtain control of major Jewish business concerns behind the backs of the Hungarian government, and, in return, to give the owners free passage out of the country, plus a sizable amount of money in foreign currency. His most important transaction was with the Manfred Weiss steel combine, a mammoth enterprise, with thirty thousand workers, which produced everything from airplanes, trucks, and bicycles to tinned goods, pins, and needles. The result was that forty-five members of the Weiss family emigrated to Portugal while Mr. Becher became head of their business. When Eichmann heard of this *Schweinerei*, he was outraged; the deal threatened to compromise his good relations with the Hungarians, who naturally expected to take possession of Jewish property confiscated on their own soil. He had some reason for his indignation, since these deals were contrary to the regular Nazi policy, which had been quite generous. For their help in solving the Jewish question in any country, the Germans had demanded no part of the Jews' property, only the costs of their deportation and extermination, and these costs had varied widely from country to country—the Slovaks had been supposed to pay between three hundred and five hundred Reichsmarks per Jew, the Croats only thirty, the French seven hundred, and the Belgians two hundred and fifty. (It seems that no one ever paid except the Croats.) In Hungary, at this late stage of the war, the Germans were demanding payment in goods—shipments of food to the Reich, in quantities determined by the amount of food the deported Jews would have consumed.

The Weiss affair was only the beginning, and things were to get considerably worse, from Eichmann's point of view. Becher was a born businessman, and where Eichmann saw only enormous tasks of organization and administration, he saw almost unlimited possibilities for making money. The one thing that stood in his way was the narrow-mindedness of subordinate creatures like Eichmann, who took their jobs seriously. Obersturmbannführer Becher's projects soon led him to cooperate closely in the rescue efforts of Dr. Rudolf Kastner. (It was to Kastner's testimony on his behalf that Becher later, at Nuremberg, owed his freedom. Being an old Zionist, Kastner had moved to Israel after the war, where he held a high position until a journalist published a story about his collaboration with the S.S.—whereupon Kastner sued him for libel. His testimony at Nuremberg weighed heavily against him, and when the case came before the Jerusalem District Court, Judge Halevi, one of the three judges in the Eichmann trial, told Kastner that he "had sold his soul to the devil." In March, 1957, shortly before his case was to be appealed before the Israeli Supreme Court, Kastner was murdered; none of the murderers, it seems, came from Hungary. In the hearing that followed the verdict of the lower court was repealed and Kastner was fully rehabilitated.) The deals Becher made through Kastner were much simpler than the complicated negotiations with the business magnates; they consisted in fixing a price for the life of each Jew to be rescued. There was considerable haggling over prices, and at one point, it seems, Eichmann also got involved in some of the preliminary discussions. Characteristically, his price was the lowest, a mere two hundred dollars per Jew—not, of course, because he wished to save more Jews but simply because he was not used to thinking big. The price finally arrived at was a thousand dollars, and one group, consisting of 1,684 Jews, and including Dr. Kastner's family, actually left Hungary for the exchange camp at Bergen-Belsen, from which they eventually reached Switzerland. A similar deal, through which Becher and Himmler hoped to obtain twenty million Swiss francs from the American Joint Distribution Committee, for the purchase of merchandise of all sorts, kept everybody busy until the Russians liberated Hungary, but nothing came of it.

There is no doubt that Becher's activities had the full approval of Himmler and stood in the sharpest possible opposition to the old "radical" orders, which still reached Eichmann through Müller and Kaltenbrunner, his immediatee superiors in the

R.S.H.A. In Eichmann's view, people like Becher were corrupt, but corruption could not very well have caused his crisis of conscience, for although he was apparently not susceptible to this kind of temptation, he must by this time have been surrounded by corruption for many years. It is difficult to imagine that he did not know that his friend and subordinate Hauptsturmführer Dieter Wisliceny had, as early as 1942, accepted fifty thousand dollars from the Jewish Relief Committee in Bratislava for delaying the deportations from Slovakia, though it is not altogether impossible; but he cannot have been ignorant of the fact that Himmler, in the fall of 1942, had tried to sell exit permits to the Slovakian Jews in exchange for enough foreign currency to pay for the recruitment of a new S.S. division. Now, however, in 1944, in Hungary, it was different, not because Himmler was involved in "business," but because business had now become official policy; it was no longer mere corruption.

At the beginning, Eichmann tried to enter the game and play it according to the new rules; that was when he got involved in the fantastic "blood-for-wares" negotiations—one million Jews for ten thousand trucks for the crumbling German Army— which certainly were not initiated by him. The way he explained his role in this matter, in Jerusalem, showed clearly how he had once justified it to himself: as a military necessity that would bring him the additional benefit of an important new role in the emigration business. What he probably never admitted to himself was that the mounting difficulties on all sides made it every day more likely that he would soon be without a job (indeed, this happened, a few months later) unless he succeeded in finding some foothold amid the new jockeying for power that was going on all around him. When the exchange project met with its predictable failure, it was already common knowledge that Himmler, despite his constant vacillations, chiefly due to his justified physical fear of Hitler, had decided to put an end to the whole Final Solution—regardless of business, regardless of military necessity, and without anything to show for it except the illusions he had concocted about his future role as the bringer of peace to Germany. It was at this time that a "moderate wing" of the S.S. came into existence, consisting of those who were stupid enough to believe that a murderer who could prove he had not killed as many people as he could have killed would have a marvelous alibi, and those who were clever enough to foresee a return to "normal conditions," when money and good connections would again be of paramount importance.

Eichmann never joined this "moderate wing," and it is questionable whether he would have been admitted if he had tried to. Not only was he too deeply compromised and, because of his constant contact with Jewish functionaries, too well known; he was too primitive for these well-educated upper-middle-class "gentlemen," against whom he harbored the most violent resentment up to the very end. He was quite capable of sending millions of people to their death, but he was not capable of talking about it in the appropriate manner without being given his "language rule." In Jerusalem, without any rules, he spoke freely of "killing" and of "murder," of "crimes legalized by the state"; he called a spade a spade, in contrast to counsel for the defense, whose feeling of social superiority to Eichmann was more than once in evidence. (Servatius' assistant Dr. Dieter Wechtenbruch—a disciple of Carl Schmitt who attended the first few weeks of the trial, then was sent to Germany to question witnesses for the defense, and reappeared for the last week in August—was readily available to reporters out of court; he seemed to be shocked less by Eichmann's crimes than by his lack of taste and education. "Small fry," he said; "we must see how we get him over the hurdles"—*wie wir das Würstchen über die Runden bringen*. Servatius himself had declared, even prior to the trial, that his client's personality was that of "a common mailman.")

When Himmler became "moderate," Eichmann sabotaged his orders as much as he dared, to the extent at least that he felt he was "covered" by his immediate superiors. "How does Eichmann dare to sabotage Himmler's orders?"—in this case, to stop the foot marches, in the fall of 1944—Kastner once asked Wisliceny. And the answer was: "He can probably show some telegram. Müller and Kaltenbrunner must have covered him." It is quite possible that Eichmann had some confused plan for liquidating Theresienstadt before the arrival of the Red Army, although we know this only through the dubious testimony of Dieter Wisliceny (who months, and perhaps years, before the end began carefully preparing an alibi for himself at the expense of Eichmann, to which he then treated the court at Nuremberg, where he was a witness for the prosecution; it did him no good, for he was extradited to Czechoslovakia, prosecuted and executed in Prague, where he had no connections and where money was of no help to him). Other witnesses claimed that it was Rolf Günther, one of Eichmann's men, who planned this, and that there existed, on the contrary, a written order from Eichmann that the ghetto be left intact. In any event, there is no doubt that even in April, 1945, when practically everybody had become quite "moderate," Eichmann took advantage of a visit that M. Paul Dunand, of the Swiss Red Cross, paid to Theresienstadt to put it on record that he himself did not approve of Himmler's new line in regard to the Jews.

That Eichmann had at all times done his best to make the Final Solution final was therefore not in dispute. The question was only whether this was indeed proof of his fanaticism, his boundless hatred of Jews, and whether he had lied to the police and committed perjury in court when he claimed he had always obeyed orders. No other explanation ever occurred to the judges, who tried so hard to understand the accused, and treated him with a consideration and an authentic, shining humanity such as he had probably never encountered before in his whole life. (Dr. Wechtenbruch told reporters that Eichmann had "great confidence in Judge Landau," as though Landau would be able to sort things out, and ascribed this confidence to Eichmann's need for authority. Whatever its basis, the confidence was apparent throughout the trial, and it may have been the reason the judgment caused Eichmann such great "disappointment"; he had mistaken humanity for softness.) That they never did come to understand him may be proof of the "goodness" of the three men, of their untroubled and slightly old-fashioned faith in the moral foundations of their profession. For the sad and very uncomfortable truth of the matter probably was that it was not his fanaticism but his very conscience that prompted Eichmann to adopt his uncompromising attitude during the last year of the war, as it had prompted him to move in the opposite direction for a short time three years before. Eichmann knew that Himmler's orders ran directly counter to the Führer's order. For this, he needed to know no factual details, though such details would have backed him up: as the prosecution underlined in the proceedings before the Supreme Court, when Hitler heard, through Kaltenbrunner, of negotiations to exchange Jews for trucks, "Himmler's position in Hitler's eyes was completely undermined." And only a few weeks before Himmler stopped the extermination at Auschwitz, Hitler, obviously unaware of Himmler's newest moves, had sent an ultimatum to Horthy, telling him he "expected that the measures against Jews in Budapest would now be taken without any further delay by the Hungarian government." When Himmler's order to stop the evacuation of Hungarian Jews arrived in Budapest, Eichmann threatened, according to a telegram from Veesenmayer, "to seek a new decision from the Führer," and this telegram the judgment found "more damning than a hundred witnesses could be."

Eichmann lost his fight against the "moderate wing," headed by the Reichsführer S.S. and Chief of the German Police. The first indication of his defeat came in January, 1945, when Obersturmbannführer Kurt Becher was promoted to *Standartenführer*, the very rank Eichmann had been dreaming about all during the war. (His story, that no higher rank was open to him in his outfit, was a half-truth; he could have been made chief of Department IV-B, instead of occupying the desk of IV-B-4, and would then have been automatically promoted. The truth probably was that people like Eichmann, who had risen from the ranks, were never permitted to advance beyond a lieutenant colonelcy except at the front.) That same month Hungary was liberated, and Eichmann was called back to Berlin. There, Himmler had appointed his enemy Becher *Reichssonderkommissar* in charge of all concentration camps, and Eichmann was transferred from the desk concerned with "Jewish Affairs" to the utterly insignificant one concerned with the "Fight Against the Churches," of which, moreover, he knew nothing. The rapidity of his decline during the last months of the war is a most telling sign of the extent to which Hitler was right when he declared, in his Berlin bunker, in April, 1945, that the S.S. were no longer reliable.

In Jerusalem, confronted with documentary proof of his extraordinary loyalty to Hitler and the Führer's order, Eichmann tried a number of times to explain that during the Third Reich "the Führer's words had the force of law" (*Führerworte haben Gesetzeskraft*), which meant, among other things, that if the order came directly from Hitler it did not have to be in writing. He tried to explain that this was why he had never asked for a written order from Hitler (no such document relating to the Final Solution has ever been found; probably it never existed), but had demanded to see a written order from Himmler. To be sure, this was a fantastic state of affairs, and whole libraries of very "learned" juridical comment have been written, all demonstrating that the Führer's *words*, his oral pronouncements, were the basic law of the land. Within this "legal" framework, every order contrary in letter or spirit to a word spoken by Hitler was, by definition, unlawful. Eichmann's position, therefore, showed a most unpleasant resemblance to that of the often-cited soldier who, acting in a normal legal framework, refuses to carry out orders that run counter to his ordinary experience of lawfulness and hence can be recognized by him as criminal. The extensive literature on the subject usually supports its case with the common equivocal meaning of the word "law," which in this context means sometimes the law of the land—that is, posited, positive law—and sometimes the law that supposedly speaks in all men's hearts with an identical voice. Practically speaking, however, orders to be disobeyed must be "manifestly unlawful" and unlawfulness must "fly like a black flag above [them] as a warning reading: 'Prohibited!' "—as the judgment pointed out. And in a criminal regime this "black flag" with its "warning sign" flies as "manifestly" above what normally is a lawful order—for instance, not to kill innocent people just because they happen to be Jews—as it flies above a criminal order under normal circumstances. To fall back on an unequivocal voice of conscience—or, in the even vaguer language of the jurists, on a "general sentiment of humanity" (Oppenheim-Lauterpacht in *International Law*, 1952)—not only begs the question, it signifies a deliberate refusal to take notice of the central moral, legal, and political phenomena of our century.

To be sure, it was not merely Eichmann's conviction that

Himmler was now giving "criminal" orders that determined his actions. But the personal element undoubtedly involved was not fanaticism, it was his genuine, "boundless and immoderate admiration for Hitler" (as one of the defense witnesses called it)—for the man who had made it "from lance corporal to Chancellor of the Reich." It would be idle to try to figure out which was stronger in him, his admiration for Hitler or his determination to remain a law-abiding citizen of the Third Reich when Germany was already in ruins. Both motives came into play once more during the last days of the war, when he was in Berlin and saw with violent indignation how everybody around him was sensibly enough getting himself fixed up with forged papers before the arrival of the Russians or the Americans. A few weeks later, Eichmann, too, began to travel under an assumed name, but by then Hitler was dead, and the "law of the land" was no longer in existence, and he, as he pointed out, was no longer bound by his oath. For the oath taken by the members of the S.S. differed from the military oath sworn by the soldiers in that it bound them only to Hitler, not to Germany.

The case of the conscience of Adolf Eichmann, which is admittedly complicated but is by no means unique, is scarcely comparable to the case of the German generals, one of whom, when asked at Nuremberg, "How was it possible that all you honorable generals could continue to serve a murderer with such unquestioning loyalty?," replied that it was "not the task of a soldier to act as judge over his supreme commander. Let history do that or God in heaven." (Thus General Alfred Jodl, hanged at Nuremberg.) Eichmann, much less intelligent and without any education to speak of, at least dimly realized that it was not an order but a law which had turned them all into criminals. The distinction between an order and the Führer's word was that the latter's validity was not limited in time and space, which is the outstanding characteristic of the former. This is also the true reason why the Führer's order for the Final Solution was followed by a huge shower of regulations and directives, all drafted by expert lawyers and legal advisers, not by mere administrators; this order, in contrast to ordinary orders, was treated as a law. Needless to add, the resulting legal paraphernalia, far from being a mere symptom of German pedantry or thoroughness, served most effectively to give the whole business its outward appearance of legality.

And just as the law in civilized countries assumes that the voice of conscience tells everybody "Thou shalt not kill," even though man's natural desires and inclinations may at times be murderous, so the law of Hitler's land demanded that the voice of conscience tell everybody: "Thou shalt kill," although the organizers of the massacres knew full well that murder is against the normal desires and inclinations of most people. Evil in the Third Reich had lost the quality by which most people recognize it—the quality of temptation. Many Germans and many Nazis, probably an overwhelming majority of them, must have been tempted *not* to murder, *not* to rob, *not* to let their neighbors go off to their doom (for that the Jews were transported to their doom they knew, of course, even though many of them may not have known the gruesome details), and not to become accomplices in all these crimes by benefiting from them. But, God knows, they had learned how to resist temptation.

Between the Wannsee Conference in January, 1942, when
Eichmann felt like Pontius Pilate and washed his hands in innocence, and Himmler's orders in the summer and fall of 1944,
when behind Hitler's back the Final Solution was abandoned as though the massacres had been nothing but a regretta-
ble mistake, Eichmann was troubled by no questions of conscience. His thoughts were entirely taken up with the staggering
job of organization and administration in the midst not only of a
world war but, more important for him, of innumerable intrigues
and fights over spheres of authority among the various State
and Party offices that were busy "solving the Jewish question."
His chief competitors were the Higher S.S. and Police Leaders,
who were under the direct command of Himmler, had easy
access to him, and always outranked Eichmann. There was also
the Foreign Office, which, under its new Undersecretary of
State, Dr. Martin Luther, a protégé of Ribbentrop, had become
very active in Jewish affairs. (Luther tried to oust Ribbentrop, in
an elaborate intrigue in 1943, failed, and was put into a concentration camp; under his successor, Legationsrat Eberhard von
Thadden, a witness for the defense at the trial in Jerusalem,
became *Referent* in Jewish affairs.) It occasionally issued deportation orders to be carried out by its representatives abroad,
who for reasons of prestige preferred to work through the
Higher S.S. and Police Leaders. There were, furthermore, the
Army commanders in the Eastern occupied territories, who liked
to solve problems "on the spot," which meant shooting; the
military men in Western countries were, on the other hand, always reluctant to cooperate and to lend their troops for the

rounding up and seizure of Jews. Finally, there were the Gauleiters, the regional leaders, each of whom wanted to be the first to declare his territory *judenrein,* and who occasionally started deportation procedures on their own.

Eichmann had to coordinate all these "efforts," to bring some order out of what he described as "complete chaos," in which "everyone issued his own orders" and "did as he pleased." And indeed he succeeded, though never completely, in acquiring a key position in the whole process, because his office organized the means of transportation. According to Dr. Rudolf Mildner, Gestapo head in Upper Silesia (where Auschwitz was located) and later chief of the Security Police in Denmark, who testified for the prosecution at Nuremberg, orders for deportations were given by Himmler in writing to Kaltenbrunner, head of the R.S.H.A., who notified Müller, head of the Gestapo, or Section IV of R.S.H.A., who in turn transmitted the orders orally to his referent in IV-B-4—that is, to Eichmann. Himmler also issued orders to the local Higher S.S. and Police Leaders and informed Kaltenbrunner accordingly. Questions of what should be done with the Jewish deportees, how many should be exterminated and how many spared for hard labor, were also decided by Himmler, and his orders concerning these matters went to Pohl's W.V.H.A., which communicated them to Richard Glücks, inspector of the concentration and extermination camps, who in turn passed them along to the commanders of the camps. The prosecution ignored these documents from the Nuremberg Trials, since they contradicted its theory of the extraordinary power held by Eichmann; the defense mentioned Mildner's affidavits, but not to much purpose. Eichmann himself, after "consulting Poliakoff and Reitlinger," produced seventeen multicolored charts, which contributed little to a better understanding of the intricate bureaucratic machinery of the Third Reich, although his general description—"everything was always in a state of continuous flux, a steady stream"—sounded plausible to the student of totalitarianism, who knows that the monolithic quality of this form of government is a myth. He still remembered vaguely how his men, his advisers on Jewish matters in all occupied and semi-independent countries, had reported back to him "what action was at all practicable," how he had then prepared "reports which were later either approved or rejected," and how Müller then had issued his directives; "in practice this could mean that a proposal that came in from Paris or The Hague went out a fortnight later to Paris or The Hague in the form of a directive approved by the R.S.H.A." Eichmann's position was that of the most important conveyor belt in the whole operation, because it was always up to him and his men how many Jews could or should be transported from any given area, and it was through his office that the ultimate destination of the shipment was cleared, though that destination was not determined by him. But the difficulty in synchronizing departures and arrivals, the endless worry over wrangling enough rolling stock from the railroad authorities and the Ministry of Transport, over fixing timetables and directing trains to centers with sufficient "absorptive capacity," over having enough Jews on hand at the proper time so that no trains would be "wasted," over enlisting the help of the authorities in occupied or allied countries to carry out arrests, over following the rules and directives with respect to the various categories of Jews, which were laid down separately for each country and constantly changing—all this became a routine whose details he had forgotten long before he was brought to Jerusalem.

What for Hitler, the sole, lonely plotter of the Final Solution (never had a conspiracy, if such it was, needed fewer conspirators and more executors), was among the war's main objectives, with its implementation given top priority, regardless of economic and military considerations, and what for Eichmann was a job, with its daily routine, its ups and downs, was for the Jews quite literally the end of the world. For hundreds of years, they had been used to understanding their own history, rightly or wrongly, as a long story of suffering, much as the prosecutor described it in his opening speech at the trial; but behind this attitude there had been, for a long time, the triumphant conviction of *"Am Yisrael Chai,"* the *people* of Israel shall live; individual Jews, whole Jewish families might die in pogroms, whole communities might be wiped out, but the people would survive. They had never been confronted with genocide. Moreover, the old consolation no longer worked anyhow, at least not in Western Europe. Since Roman antiquity, that is, since the inception of European history, the Jews had belonged, for better or worse, in misery or in splendor, to the European comity of nations; but during the past hundred and fifty years it had been chiefly for better, and the occasions of splendor had become so numerous that in Central and Western Europe they were felt to be the rule. Hence, the confidence that the people would eventually survive no longer held great significance for large sections of the Jewish communities; they could no more imagine Jewish life outside the framework of European civilization than they could have pictured to themselves a Europe that was *judenrein*.

The end of the world, though carried through with remarkable monotony, took almost as many different shapes and appearances as there existed countries in Europe. This will come as no surprise to the historian familiar with the development of European nations and with the rise of the nation-state system, but it came as a great surprise to the Nazis, who were genuinely convinced that anti-Semitism could become the common denominator that would unite all Europe. This was a huge and costly error. It quickly turned out that in practice, though perhaps not in theory, there existed great differences among anti-Semites in the various countries. What was even more annoying, though it might easily have been predicted, was that the German "radical" variety was fully appreciated only by those peoples in the East—the Ukrainians, the Estonians, the Latvians, the Lithuanians, and, to some extent, the Rumanians—whom the Nazis had decided to regard as "subhuman" barbarian hordes. Notably deficient in proper hostility toward the Jews were the Scandinavian nations (Knut Hamsun and Sven Hedin were exceptions), which, according to the Nazis, were Germany's blood brethren.

The end of the world began, of course, in the German Reich, which at the time embraced not only Germany but Austria, Moravia and Bohemia, the Czech Protectorate, and the annexed Polish Western Regions. In the last of these, the so-called Warthegau, Jews, together with Poles, had been deported eastward after the beginning of the war, in the first huge resettlement project in the East—"an organized wandering of nations," as the judgment of the District Court in Jerusalem called it—

while Poles of German origin (*Volksdeutsche*) were shipped westward "back into the Reich." Himmler, in his capacity as Reich Commissioner for the Strengthening of German Folkdom, had entrusted Heydrich with this "emigration and evacuation," and in January, 1940, Eichmann's first official department in the R.S.H.A., Bureau IV-D-4, was set up. Though this position proved administratively to be the stepping-stone to his later job in Bureau IV-B-4, Eichmann's work here was no more than a kind of apprenticeship, the transition between his old job of making people emigrate and his future task of deporting them. His first deportation jobs did not belong to the Final Solution; they occurred before the official Hitler order. In view of what happened later, they can be regarded as test cases, as an experiment in catastrophe. The first was the deportation of thirteen hundred Jews from Stettin, which was carried out in a single night, on February 13, 1940. This was the first deportation of German Jews, and Heydrich had ordered it under the pretext that "their apartments were urgently required for reasons connected with the war economy." They were taken, under unusually atrocious conditions, to the Lublin area of Poland. The second deportation took place in the fall of the same year: all the Jews in Baden and the Saarpfalz—about seventy-five hundred men, women, and children—were shipped, as I mentioned earlier, to Unoccupied France, which was at that moment quite a trick, since nothing in the Franco-German Armistice agreement stipulated that Vichy France could become a dumping ground for Jews. Eichmann had to accompany the train himself in order to convince the French stationmaster at the border that this was a German "military transport."

These two operations entirely lacked the later elaborate "legal" preparations. No laws had yet been passed depriving Jews of their nationality the moment they were deported from the Reich, and instead of the many forms Jews eventually had to fill out in arranging for the confiscation of their property, the Stettin Jews simply signed a general waiver, covering everything they owned. Clearly, it was not the administrative apparatus that these first operations were supposed to test. The objective seems to have been a test of general political conditions—whether Jews could be made to walk to their doom on their own feet, carrying their own little valises, in the middle of the night, without any previous notification; what the reaction of their neighbors would be when they discovered the empty apartments in the morning; and, last but not least, in the case of the Jews from Baden, how a foreign government would react to being suddenly presented with thousands of Jewish "refugees." As far as the Nazis could see, everything turned out very satisfactorily. In Germany, there were a number of interventions for "special cases"—for the poet Alfred Mombert, for instance, a member of the Stefan George circle, who was permitted to depart to Switzerland—but the population at large obviously could not have cared less. (It was probably at this moment that Heydrich realized how important it would be to separate Jews with connections from the anonymous masses, and decided, with Hitler's agreement, to establish Theresienstadt and Bergen-Belsen.) In France, something even better happened: the Vichy government put all seventy-five hundred Jews from Baden in the notorious concentration camp at Gurs, at the foot of the Pyrenees, which had originally been built for the Spanish Republican Army and had been used since May of 1940 for the so-called *"réfugiés provenant d'Allemagne,"* the large majority of whom were, of course, Jewish. (When the Final Solution was put into effect in France, the inmates of the Gurs camp were all shipped to Auschwitz.) The Nazis, always eager to generalize, thought they had demonstrated that Jews were "undesirables" everywhere and that every non-Jew was an actual or potential anti-Semite. Why, then, should anybody be bothered if they tackled this problem "radically"? Still under the spell of these generalizations, Eichmann complained over and over in Jerusalem that no country had been ready to accept Jews, that this, and only this, had caused the great catastrophe. (As though those tightly organized European nation-states would have reacted any differently if any other group of foreigners had suddenly descended upon them in hordes—penniless, passportless, unable to speak the language of the country!) However, to the never-ending surprise of the Nazi officials, even the convinced anti-Semites in foreign lands were not willing to be "consistent," and showed a deplorable tendency to shy away from "radical" measures. Few of them put it as bluntly as a member of the Spanish Embassy in Berlin—"If only one could be sure they wouldn't be liquidated," he said of some six hundred Jews of Spanish descent who had been given Spanish passports, though they had never been in Spain, and whom the Franco Government wished very much to transfer to German jurisdiction—but most of them thought precisely along these lines.

After these first experiments, there followed a lull in deportations, and we have seen how Eichmann used his enforced inactivity to play around with Madagascar. But in March, 1941, during the preparation for the war against Russia, Eichmann was suddenly put in charge of a new subsection, or rather, the name of his subsection was changed from Emigration and Evacuation to Jewish Affairs, Evacuation. From then on, though he was not yet informed of the Final Solution, he should have been aware not only that emigration had definitely come to an end, but that deportation was to take its place. But Eichmann was not a man to take hints, and since no one had yet told him differently, he continued to think in terms of emigration. Thus at a meeting with representatives of the Foreign Office in October, 1940, during which it had been proposed that the citizenship of all German Jews abroad be canceled, Eichmann protested vigorously that "such a step might influence other countries which to date were still ready to open their gates to Jewish immigrants and to grant entry permits." He always thought within the narrow limits of whatever laws and decrees were valid at a given moment, and the shower of new anti-Jewish legislation descended upon the Reich's Jews only after Hitler's order for the Final Solution had been officially handed down to those who were to implement it. At the same time, it had been decided that the Reich was to be given top priority, its territories made *judenrein* with all speed; it is surprising that it still took almost two years to do the job. The preparatory regulations, which were soon to serve as models for all other countries, consisted, first, of the introduction of the yellow badge (September 1, 1941); second, of a change in the nationality law, providing that a Jew could not be considered a German national if he lived outside the borders of the Reich (whence, of course, he was to be deported); third, of a decree that all property of German Jews who had lost their nationality was to be confiscated by the Reich (November 25, 1941). The preparations culminated in an agreement between Otto Thierack, the Minister

of Justice, and Himmler whereby the former relinquished jurisdiction over "Poles, Russians, Jews, and Gypsies" in favor of
the S.S., since "the Ministry of Justice can make only a small
contribution to the extermination [*sic*] of these peoples." (This
open language, in a letter dated October, 1942, from the Minister
of Justice to Martin Bormann, head of the Party Chancellery, is
noteworthy.) Slightly different directives had to be issued to cover
those who were deported to Theresienstadt because, Theresienstadt being on Reich territory, the Jews deported there did not
automatically become stateless. In the case of these "privileged
categories," an old law of 1933 permitted the government to confiscate property that had been used for activities "hostile to the
nation and the State." This kind of confiscation had been customary in the case of political prisoners in the concentration
camps, and though Jews did not belong in this category—all
concentration camps in Germany and Austria had become *judenrein* by the fall of 1942—it took only one more regulation, issued
in March, 1942, to establish that all deported Jews were "hostile
to the nation and the State." The Nazis took their own legislation
quite seriously, and though they talked among themselves of
"the Theresienstadt ghetto" or "the ghetto for old people,"
Theresienstadt was officially classified as a concentration camp,
and the only people who did not know this—one did not want
to hurt their feelings, since this "place of residence" was reserved
for "special cases"—were the inmates. And to make sure that the
Jews sent there would not become suspicious, the Jewish Association in Berlin (the *Reichsvereinigung*) was directed to draw up
an agreement with each deportee for "the acquisition of residence" in Theresienstadt. The candidate transferred all his property to the Jewish Association, in consideration whereof the
Association guaranteed him housing, food, clothing, and medical
care for life. When, finally, the last officials of the *Reichsvereinigung* were themselves sent to Theresienstadt, the Reich simply
confiscated the considerable amount of money then in the Association's treasury.

All deportations from West to East were organized and coordinated by Eichmann and his associates in Section IV-B-4 of
the R.S.H.A.—a fact that was never disputed during the trial.
But to put the Jews on the trains he needed the help of ordinary

police units; in Germany the Order Police guarded the trains and posted escorts, and in the East the Security Police (not to be confused with Himmler's Security Service, or S.D.) stood ready at the places of destination to receive the trains and hand their inmates over to the authorities in the killing centers. The Jerusalem court followed the definitions of "criminal organizations" established at Nuremberg; this meant that neither the Order Police nor the Security Police were ever mentioned, although their active involvement in the implementation of the Final Solution had by this time been amply substantiated. But even if all the police units had been added to the four organizations recognized as "criminal"—the leadership corps of the Nazi Party, the Gestapo, the S.D., and the S.S.—the Nuremberg distinctions would have remained inadequate and inapplicable to the reality of the Third Reich. For the truth of the matter is that there existed not a single organization or public institution in Germany, at least during the war years, that did not become involved in criminal actions and transactions.

After the troublesome issue of personal interventions had been resolved through the establishment of Theresienstadt, two things still stood in the way of a "radical" and "final" solution. One was the problem of half-Jews, whom the "radicals" wanted to deport along with the full Jews and whom the "moderates" wished to sterilize—because if you permitted the half-Jews to be killed, it meant that you abandoned "that half of their blood which is German," as Stuckart of the Ministry of the Interior phrased it at the Wannsee Conference. (Actually, nothing was ever done about the *Mischlinge*, or about Jews who had made mixed marriages; "a forest of difficulties," in Eichmann's words, surrounded and protected them—their non-Jewish relatives, for one, and, for another, the disappointing fact that the Nazi physicians, despite all their promises, never discovered a quick means of mass sterilization.) The second problem was the presence in Germany of a few thousand foreign Jews, whom Germany could not deprive of their nationality through deportation. A few hundred American and English Jews were interned and held for exchange purposes, but the methods devised for dealing with nationals of neutral countries or those allied with Germany are interesting enough to be recorded, especially since they played a certain role in the trial. It was in reference to these people that Eichmann was accused of having shown inordinate zeal lest a single Jew escape him. This zeal he shared, as Reitlinger says, with the "professional bureaucrats of the Foreign Office, [to whom] the flight of a few Jews from torture and slow death was a matter of the gravest concern," and whom he had to consult on all such cases. As far as Eichmann was concerned, the simplest and most logical solution was to deport all Jews regardless of their nationality. According to the directives of the Wannsee Conference, which was held in the heyday of Hitler's victories, the Final Solution was to be applied to all European Jews, whose number was estimated at eleven million, and such things as nationality or the rights of allied or neutral countries with respect to their citizens were not even mentioned. But since Germany, even in the brightest days of the war, depended upon local good will and cooperation everywhere, these little formalities could not be sneezed at. It was the task of the experienced diplomats of the Foreign Service to find ways out of this particular "forest of difficulties," and the most ingenious of these consisted in the use of foreign Jews in German territory to test the general atmosphere in their home countries. The method by which this was done, though simple, was somewhat subtle, and was certainly quite beyond Eichmann's mental grasp and political apprehension. (This was borne out by the documentary evidence; letters that his department addressed to the Foreign Office in these matters were signed by Kaltenbrunner or Müller.) The Foreign Office wrote to the authorities in other countries, saying that the German Reich was in the process of becoming *judenrein* and that it was therefore imperative that foreign Jews be called home if they were not to be included in the anti-Jewish measures. There was more in this ultimatum than meets the eye. These foreign Jews, as a rule, either were naturalized citizens of their respective countries, or, worse, were in fact stateless but had obtained passports by some highly dubious method that worked well enough as long as their bearers stayed abroad. This was especially true of Latin American countries, whose consuls abroad sold passports to Jews quite openly; the fortunate holders of such passports had every right, including some consular protection, except the right ever to enter their "homeland." Hence, the ultimatum of the Foreign Office was aimed at getting foreign governments to agree to the application of the Final Solution at least to those Jews who were only nominally their nationals. Was it not logical to believe that a government that had shown itself unwilling to offer asylum to a few hundred or a few thousand Jews, who in any case were in no position to establish permanent residence there, would be unlikely to raise many objections on the day when its whole Jewish population was to be expelled and exterminated? Perhaps it was logical, but it was not reasonable, as we shall see shortly.

On June 30, 1943, considerably later than Hitler had hoped, the Reich—Germany, Austria, and the Protektorat—was declared *judenrein*. There are no definite figures as to how many Jews were actually deported from this area, but we know that of the two hundred and sixty-five thousand people who, according to German statistics, were either deported or were eligible for deportation by January, 1942, very few escaped; perhaps a few hundred, at the most a few thousand, succeeded in hiding and surviving the war. How easy it was to set the conscience of the Jews' neighbors at rest is best illustrated by the official explanation of the deportations given in a circular issued by the Party Chancellery in the fall of 1942: "It is the nature of things that these, in some respects, very difficult problems can be solved in the interests of the permanent security of our people only with *ruthless toughness"* —*rücksichtsloser Härte* (my italics).

X : *Deportations from Western Europe—France, Belgium, Holland, Denmark, Italy*

"Ruthless toughness," a quality held in the highest esteem by the rulers of the Third Reich, is frequently characterized in postwar Germany, which has developed a veritable genius for understatement with respect to her Nazi past, as being *ungut—* lacking goodness—as though nothing had been wrong with those endowed with this quality but a deplorable failure to act according to the exacting standards of Christian charity. In any case, men sent by Eichmann's office to other countries as "advisers on Jewish affairs"—to be attached to the regular diplomatic missions, or to the military staff, or to the local command of the Security Police—were all chosen because they possessed this virtue to the highest degree. In the beginning, during the fall and winter of 1941-42, their main job seems to have been to establish satisfactory relations with the other German officials in the countries concerned, especially with the German embassies in nominally independent countries and with the Reich commissioners in occupied territories; in either case, there was perpetual conflict over jurisdiction in Jewish matters.

In June, 1942, Eichmann recalled his advisers in France, Belgium, and Holland in order to lay plans for deportations from these countries. Himmler had ordered that FRANCE be given top priority in "combing Europe from West to East," partly because of the inherent importance of the *nation par excellence*, and partly because the Vichy government had shown a truly amazing "understanding" of the Jewish problem and had introduced, on its own initiative, a great deal of anti-Jewish legislation; it had even established a special Department for Jewish Affairs, headed first by Xavier Vallant and somewhat later by Darquier de Pellepoix, both well-known anti-Semites. As a concession to the French brand of anti-Semitism, which was intimately connected with a strong, generally chauvinistic xenophobia in all strata of the population, the operation was to start with foreign Jews, and since in 1942 more than half of France's foreign Jews were stateless—refugees and émigrés from Russia, Germany, Austria, Poland, Rumania, Hungary—that is, from areas that either were under German domination or had passed anti-Jewish legislation before the outbreak of war—it was decided to begin by deporting an estimated hundred thousand stateless Jews. (The total Jewish population of the country was now well over three hundred thousand; in 1939, before the influx of refugees from Belgium and Holland in the spring of 1940, there had been about two hundred and seventy thousand Jews, of whom at least a hundred and seventy thousand were foreign or foreign-born.) Fifty thousand each were to be evacuated from the Occupied Zone and from Vichy France with all speed. This was a considerable undertaking, which needed not only the agreement of the Vichy government but the active help of the French police, who were to do the work done in Germany by the Order Police. At first, there were no difficulties whatever, since, as Pierre Laval, Premier under Marshal Pétain, pointed out, "these foreign Jews had always been a problem in France," so that the "French government was glad that a change in the German attitude toward them gave France an opportunity to get rid of them." It must be added that Laval and Pétain thought in terms of these Jews' being resettled in the East; they did not yet know what "resettlement" meant.

Two incidents, in particular, attracted the attention of the Jerusalem court, both of which occurred in the summer of 1942, a few weeks after the operation had started. The first concerned a train due to leave Bordeaux on July 15, which had to be canceled because only a hundred and fifty stateless Jews could be found in Bordeaux—not enough to fill the train, which Eichmann had obtained with great difficulty. Whether or not Eichmann recognized this as the first indication that things might not be quite as easy as everybody felt entitled to believe, he became very excited, telling his subordinates that this was "a matter of prestige"—not in the eyes of the French but in those of the Ministry of Transport, which might get wrong ideas about the efficiency of his apparatus—and that he would "have to consider whether France should not be dropped altogether as far as evacuation was concerned" if such an incident was repeated. In Jerusalem, this threat was taken very seriously, as proof of Eichmann's power; if he wished, he could "drop France." Actually, it was one of Eichmann's ridiculous boasts, proof of his "driving power" but hardly "evidence of . . . his status in the eyes of his subordinates," except insofar as he had plainly threatened them with losing their very cozy war jobs. But if the Bordeaux incident was a farce, the second was the basis for one of the most horrible of the many hair-raising stories told at Jerusalem. This was the story of four thousand children, separated from their parents who were already on their way to Auschwitz. The children had been left behind at the French collection point, the concentration camp at Drancy, and on July 10 Eichmann's French representative, Hauptsturm-führer Theodor Dannecker, phoned him to ask what was to be done with them. Eichmann took ten days to decide; then he called Dannecker back to tell him that "as soon as transports could again be dispatched to the General Government area [of Poland], transports of children could roll." Dr. Servatius pointed out that the whole incident actually demonstrated that the "persons affected were determined neither by the accused nor by any members of his office." But what, unfortunately, no one mentioned was that Dannecker had informed Eichmann that Laval himself had proposed that children under sixteen be included in the deportations; this meant that the whole grue-some episode was not even the result of "superior orders" but the outcome of an agreement between France and Germany, negotiated at the highest level.

During the summer and fall of 1942, twenty-seven thousand stateless Jews—eighteen thousand from Paris and nine thousand from Vichy France—were deported to Auschwitz. Then, when there were about seventy thousand stateless Jews left in all of France, the Germans made their first mistake. Confident that the French had by now become so accustomed to deporting Jews that they wouldn't mind, they asked for permission to include French Jews also—simply to facilitate administrative matters. This caused a complete turnabout; the French were adamant in their refusal to hand over their own Jews to the Germans. And Himmler, upon being informed of the situation —not by Eichmann or his men, incidentally, but by one of the Higher S.S. and Police Leaders—immediately gave in and promised to spare French Jews. But now it was too late. The first rumors about "resettlement" had reached France, and while French anti-Semites, and non-anti-Semites too, would have liked to see foreign Jews settle somewhere else, not even the anti-Semites wished to become accomplices in mass murder. Hence, the French now refused to take a step they had eagerly contemplated only a short time before, that is, to revoke naturalizations granted to Jews after 1927 (or after 1933), which would have made about fifty thousand more Jews eligible for deportation. They also started making such endless difficulties with regard to the deportation of stateless and other foreign Jews that all the ambitious plans for the evacuation of Jews from France did indeed have to be "dropped." Tens of thousands of stateless persons went into hiding, while thousands more fled to the Italian-occupied French zone, the Côte d'Azur, where Jews were safe, whatever their origin or nationality. In the summer of 1943, when Germany was declared *judenrein* and the Allies had just landed in Sicily, no more than fifty-two thousand Jews, certainly less than twenty per cent of the total, had been deported, and of these no more than six thousand possessed French nationality. Not even Jewish prisoners of war in the German internment camps for the French Army were singled out for "special treatment." In April, 1944, two months before the Allies landed in France, there were still two hundred and fifty thousand Jews in the country, and they all survived the war. The Nazis, it turned out, possessed neither the manpower nor the will power to remain "tough" when they met determined opposition. The truth of the matter was, as we shall see, that even the members of the Gestapo and the S.S. combined ruthlessness with softness.

At the June, 1942, meeting in Berlin, the figures set for immediate deportations from Belgium and the Netherlands had been rather low, probably because of the high figure set for

France. No more than ten thousand Jews from Belgium and fifteen thousand from Holland were to be seized and deported in the immediate future. In both cases the figures were later significantly enlarged, probably because of the difficulties encountered in the French operation. The situation of BELGIUM was peculiar in some respects. The country was ruled exclusively by German military authorities, and the police, as a Belgian government report submitted to the court pointed out, "did not have the same influence upon the other German administration services that they enjoyed in other places." (Belgium's governor, General Alexander von Falkenhausen, was later implicated in the July, 1944, conspiracy against Hitler.) Native collaborators were of importance only in Flanders; the Fascist movement among the French-speaking Walloons, headed by Degrelle, had little influence. The Belgian police did not cooperate with the Germans, and the Belgian railway men could not even be trusted to leave deportation trains alone. They contrived to leave doors unlocked or to arrange ambushes, so that Jews could escape. Most peculiar was the composition of the Jewish population. Before the outbreak of war, there were ninety thousand Jews, of whom about thirty thousand were German Jewish refugees, while another fifty thousand came from other European countries. By the end of 1940, nearly forty thousand Jews had fled the country, and among the fifty thousand who remained there were at the most five thousand native-born Belgian citizens. Moreover among those who had fled were all the more important Jewish leaders, most of whom had been foreigners anyway, so that the Jewish Council did not command any authority among native Jews. With this "lack of understanding" on all sides, it is not surprising that very few Belgian Jews were deported. But recently naturalized and stateless Jews—of Czech, Polish, Russian, and German origin, many of whom had only recently arrived—were easily recognizable and most difficult to hide in the small, completely industrialized country. By the end of 1942, fifteen thousand had been shipped to Auschwitz, and by the fall of 1944, when the Allies liberated the country, a total of twenty-five thousand had been killed. Eichmann had his usual "adviser" in Belgium, but the adviser seems not to have been very active in these operations. They were carried out, finally, by the military administration, under increased pressure from the Foreign Office.

As in practically all other countries, the deportations from HOLLAND started with stateless Jews, who in this instance consisted almost entirely of refugees from Germany, whom the prewar Dutch government had officially declared to be "undesirable." There were about thirty-five thousand foreign Jews altogether in a total Jewish population of a hundred and forty thousand. Unlike Belgium, Holland was placed under a civil administration, and, unlike France, the country had no government of its own, since the cabinet, together with the royal family, had fled to London. The small nation was utterly at the mercy of the Germans and of the S.S. Eichmann's "adviser" in Holland was a certain Willi Zöpf (recently arrested in Germany, while the much more efficient adviser in France, Mr. Dannecker, is still at large) but he apparently had very little to say and could hardly do more than keep the Berlin office posted. Deportations and everything connected with them were handled by the lawyer Erich Rajakowitsch, Eichmann's former legal adviser in Vienna and Prague, who was admitted to the S.S. upon Eichmann's recommendation. He had been sent to Holland by Heydrich in April, 1941, and was directly responsible not to the R.S.H.A. in Berlin but to the local head of the Security Service in The Hague, Dr. Wilhelm Harsten, who in turn was under the command of the Higher S.S. and Police Leader Obergruppenführer Hans Rauter and his assistant in Jewish affairs, Ferdinand aus der Fünten. (Rauter and Fünten were condemned to death by a Dutch court; Rauter was executed and Fünten's sentence, allegedly after special intervention from Adenauer, was commuted to life imprisonment. Harsten, too, was brought to trial in Holland, sentenced to twelve years' imprisonment, and released in 1957, whereupon he entered the civil service of the Bavarian state government. The Dutch authorities are considering proceedings against Rajakowitsch, who seems to live in either Switzerland or Italy. All these details have become known in the last year through the publication of Dutch documents and the report by E. Jacob, Dutch correspondent for the *Basler Nationalzeitung*, a Swiss newspaper.) The prose-

cution in Jerusalem, partly because it wanted to build up Eichmann at all costs and partly because it got genuinely lost in
the intricacies of German bureaucracy, claimed that all these
officers had carried out Eichmann's orders. But the Higher S.S.
and Police Leaders took orders only directly from Himmler,
and that Rajakowitsch was still taking orders from Eichmann
at this time is highly unlikely, especially in view of what was
then going to happen in Holland. The judgment, without engag-
ing in polemics, quietly corrected a great number of errors made
by the prosecution—though probably not all—and showed the
constant jockeying for position that went on between the
R.S.H.A. and the Higher S.S. and Police Leaders and other offices—the "tenacious, eternal, everlasting negotiations," as
Eichmann called them.

Eichmann had been especially upset by the arrangements in
Holland, because it was clearly Himmler himself who was
cutting him down to size, quite apart from the fact that the zeal
of the gentlemen in residence created great difficulties for him
in the timing of his own transports and generally made a mock-
ery of the importance of the "coordinating center" in Berlin.
Thus, right at the beginning, twenty thousand instead of fifteen
thousand Jews were deported, and Eichmann's Mr. Zöpf, who
was far inferior in rank as well as in position to all others
present, was almost forced to speed up deportations in 1943.
Conflicts of jurisdiction in these matters were to plague Eichmann at all times, and it was in vain that he explained to
anybody who would listen that "it would be contradictory to
the order of the Reichsführer S.S. [i.e., Himmler] and illogical
if at this stage other authorities again were to handle the Jewish
problem." The last clash in Holland came in 1944, and this
time even Kaltenbrunner tried to intervene, for the sake of
uniformity. In Holland, Sephardic Jews, of Spanish origin, had
been exempted, although Jews of that origin had been sent to
Auschwitz from Salonika. The judgment was in error when it
ventured that the R.S.H.A. "had the upper hand in this dispute"
—for God knows what reasons, some three hundred and seventy
Sephardic Jews remained unmolested in Amsterdam.

The reason Himmler preferred to work in Holland through his
Higher S.S. and Police Leaders was simple. These men knew

their way around the country, and the problem posed by the
Dutch population was by no means an easy one. Holland had
been the only country in all Europe where students went on
strike when Jewish professors were dismissed and where a wave
of strikes broke out in response to the first deportation of
Jews to German concentration camps—and that deportation, in
contrast to those to extermination camps, was merely a punitive
measure, taken long before the Final Solution had reached Holland. (The Germans, as de Jong points out, were taught a
lesson. From now on, "the persecution was carried out not with
the cudgels of the Nazi storm troops . . . , but by decrees published in *Verordeningenblad* . . . , which the *Joodsche Weekblad*
was forced to carry." Police raids in the streets no longer
occurred and there were no strikes on the part of the population.)
However, the widespread hostility in Holland toward anti-
Jewish measures and the relative immunity of the Dutch people
to anti-Semitism were held in check by two factors, which
eventually proved fatal to the Jews. First, there existed a very
strong Nazi movement in Holland, which could be trusted to
carry out such police measures as seizing Jews, ferreting out
their hiding places, and so on; second, there existed an inordinately strong tendency among the native Jews to draw a line
between themselves and the new arrivals, which was probably
the result of the very unfriendly attitude of the Dutch government toward refugees from Germany, and probably also because
anti-Semitism in Holland, just as in France, focused on foreign
Jews. This made it relatively easy for the Nazis to form their
Jewish Council, the *Joodsche Raad,* which remained for a long
time under the impression that only German and other foreign
Jews would be victims of the deportations, and it also enabled
the S.S. to enlist, in addition to Dutch police units, the help
of a Jewish police force. The result was a catastrophe unparalleled in any Western country; it can be compared only with
the extinction, under vastly different and, from the beginning,
completely desperate conditions, of Polish Jewry. Although, in
contrast with Poland, the attitude of the Dutch people permitted
a large number of Jews to go into hiding—twenty to twenty-
five thousand, a very high figure for such a small country—yet
an unusually large number of Jews living underground, at least

half of them, were eventually found, no doubt through the efforts of professional and occasional informers. By July, 1944, a hundred and thirteen thousand Jews had been deported, most of them to Sobibor, a camp in the Lublin area of Poland, by the river Bug, where no selections of able-bodied workers ever took place. Three-fourths of all Jews living in Holland were killed, about two-thirds of these native-born Dutch Jews. The last shipments left in the fall of 1944, when Allied patrols were at the Dutch borders. Of the ten thousand Jews who survived in hiding, about seventy-five per cent were foreigners—a percentage that testifies to the unwillingness of Dutch Jews to face reality.

At the Wannsee Conference, Martin Luther, of the Foreign Office, warned of great difficulties in the Scandinavian countries, notably in Norway and Denmark. (Sweden was never occupied, and Finland, though in the war on the side of the Axis, was the one country the Nazis hardly ever even approached on the Jewish question. This surprising exception of Finland, with some two thousand Jews, may have been due to Hitler's great esteem for the Finns, whom perhaps he did not want to subject to threats and humiliating blackmail.) Luther proposed postponing evacuations from Scandinavia for the time being, and as far as Denmark was concerned, this really went without saying, since the country retained its independent government, and was respected as a neutral state, until the fall of 1943, although it, along with Norway, had been invaded by the German Army in April, 1940. There existed no Fascist or Nazi movement in Denmark worth mentioning, and therefore no collaborators. In NORWAY, however, the Germans had been able to find enthusiastic supporters; indeed, Vidkun Quisling, leader of the pro-Nazi and anti-Semitic Norwegian party, gave his name to what later became known as a "quisling government." The bulk of Norway's seventeen hundred Jews were stateless, refugees from Germany; they were seized and interned in a few lightning operations in October and November, 1942. When Eichmann's office ordered their deportation to Auschwitz, some of Quisling's own men resigned their government posts. This may not have come as a surprise to Mr. Luther and the Foreign Office, but what was much more serious, and certainly totally unexpected, was that Sweden immediately offered asylum, and sometimes even Swedish nationality, to all who were persecuted. Ernst von Weizsäcker, Undersecretary of State of the Foreign Office, who received the proposal, refused to discuss it, but the offer helped nevertheless. It is always relatively easy to get out of a country illegally, whereas it is nearly impossible to enter the place of refuge without permission and to dodge the immigration authorities. Hence, about nine hundred people, slightly more than half of the small Norwegian community, could be smuggled into Sweden.

It was in DENMARK, however, that the Germans found out how fully justified the Foreign Office's apprehensions had been. The story of the Danish Jews is *sui generis*, and the behavior of the Danish people and their government was unique among all the countries of Europe—whether occupied, or a partner of the Axis, or neutral and truly independent. One is tempted to recommend the story as required reading in political science for all students who wish to learn something about the enormous power potential inherent in non-violent action and in resistance to an opponent possessing vastly superior means of violence. To be sure, a few other countries in Europe lacked proper "understanding of the Jewish question," and actually a majority of them were opposed to "radical" and "final" solutions. Like Denmark, Sweden, Italy, and Bulgaria proved to be nearly immune to anti-Semitism, but of the three that were in the German sphere of influence, only the Danes dared speak out on the subject to their German masters. Italy and Bulgaria sabotaged German orders and indulged in a complicated game of double-dealing and double-crossing, saving their Jews by a tour de force of sheer ingenuity, but they never contested the policy as such. That was totally different from what the Danes did. When the Germans approached them rather cautiously about introducing the yellow badge, they were simply told that the King would be the first to wear it, and the Danish government officials were careful to point out that anti-Jewish measures of any sort would cause their own immediate resignation. It was decisive in this whole matter that the Germans did not even succeed in introducing the vitally important distinction between native Danes of Jewish origin, of whom there were about sixty-four hundred, and the fourteen hundred German Jewish refugees who had found asylum in the country prior to the war and who now had been declared stateless by the German government. This refusal must have surprised the Germans no end, since it appeared so "illogical" for a government to protect people to whom it had categorically denied naturalization and even permission to work. (Legally, the prewar situation of refugees in Denmark was not unlike that in France, except that the general corruption in the Third Republic's civil services enabled a few of them to obtain naturalization papers, through bribes or "connections," and most refugees in France could work illegally, without a permit. But Denmark, like Switzerland, was no country *pour se débrouiller*.) The Danes, however, explained to the German officials that because the stateless refugees were no longer German citizens, the Nazis could not claim them without Danish assent. This was one of the few cases in which statelessness turned out to be an asset, although it was of course not statelessness per se that saved the Jews but, on the contrary, the fact that the Danish government had decided to protect them. Thus, none of the preparatory moves, so important for the bureaucracy of murder, could be carried out, and operations were postponed until the fall of 1943.

What happened then was truly amazing; compared with what took place in other European countries, everything went topsy-turvy. In August, 1943—after the German offensive in Russia had failed, the Afrika Korps had surrendered in Tunisia, and the Allies had invaded Italy—the Swedish government canceled its 1940 agreement with Germany which had permitted German troops the right to pass through the country. Thereupon, the Danish workers decided that they could help a bit in hurrying things up; riots broke out in Danish shipyards, where the dock workers refused to repair German ships and then went on strike. The German military commander proclaimed a state of emergency and imposed martial law, and Himmler thought this was the right moment to tackle the Jewish question, whose "solution" was long overdue. What he did not reckon with was that—quite apart from Danish resistance—the German officials who had been living in the country for years were no longer the same. Not only did General von Hannecken, the military commander, refuse to put troops at the disposal of the Reich plenipotentiary, Dr. Werner Best; the special S.S. units (*Einsatzkommandos*) employed in Denmark very frequently objected to "the measures they were ordered to carry out by the central agencies"—according to Best's testimony at Nuremberg. And Best himself, an old Gestapo man and former legal adviser to Heydrich, author of a then famous book on the police, who had worked for the military government in Paris to the entire satisfaction of his superiors, could no longer be trusted, although it is doubtful that Berlin ever learned the extent of his unreliability. Still, it was clear from the beginning that things were not going well, and Eichmann's office sent one of its best men to Denmark—Rolf Günther, whom no one had ever accused of not possessing the required "ruthless toughness." Günther made no impression on his colleagues in Copenhagen, and now von Hannecken refused even to issue a decree requiring all Jews to report for work.

Best went to Berlin and obtained a promise that all Jews from Denmark would be sent to Theresienstadt regardless of their category—a very important concession, from the Nazis' point of view. The night of October 1 was set for their seizure and immediate departure—ships were ready in the harbor— and since neither the Danes nor the Jews nor the German troops stationed in Denmark could be relied on to help, police units arrived from Germany for a door-to-door search. At the last moment, Best told them that they were not permitted to break into apartments, because the Danish police might then interfere, and they were not supposed to fight it out with the Danes. Hence they could seize only those Jews who voluntarily opened their doors. They found exactly 477 people, out of a total of more than 7,800, at home and willing to let them in. A few days before the date of doom, a German shipping agent, Georg F. Duckwitz, having probably been tipped off by Best himself, had revealed the whole plan to Danish government officials, who, in turn, had hurriedly informed the heads of the Jewish community. They, in marked contrast to Jewish leaders in other countries, had then communicated the news openly in the synagogues on the occasion of the New Year services. The Jews had just time enough to leave their apartments and go into hiding, which was very easy in Denmark, because, in the words of the judgment, "all sections of the Danish people, from the King down to simple citizens," stood ready to receive them.

They might have remained in hiding until the end of the war if the Danes had not been blessed with Sweden as a neighbor. It seemed reasonable to ship the Jews to Sweden, and this was done with the help of the Danish fishing fleet. The cost of transportation for people without means—about a hundred dollars per person—was paid largely by wealthy Danish citizens, and that was perhaps the most astounding feat of all, since this was a time when Jews were paying for their own deportation, when the rich among them were paying fortunes for exit permits (in Holland, Slovakia, and, later, in Hungary) either by bribing the local authorities or by negotiating "legally" with the S.S., who accepted only hard currency and sold exit permits, in Holland, to the tune of five or ten thousand dollars per person. Even in places where Jews met with genuine sympathy and a sincere willingness to help, they had to pay for it, and the chances poor people had of escaping were nil.

It took the better part of October to ferry all the Jews across the five to fifteen miles of water that separates Denmark from Sweden. The Swedes received 5,919 refugees, of whom at least 1,000 were of German origin, 1,310 were half-Jews, and 686 were non-Jews married to Jews. (Almost half the Danish Jews seem to have remained in the country and survived the war in hiding.) The non-Danish Jews were better off than ever before, they all received permission to work. The few hundred Jews whom the German police had been able to arrest were shipped to Theresienstadt. They were old or poor people, who either had not received the news in time or had not been able to comprehend its meaning. In the ghetto, they enjoyed greater privileges than any other group because of the never-ending "fuss" made about them by Danish institutions and private persons. Forty-eight persons died, a figure that was not particularly high, in view of the average age of the group. When everything was over, it was the considered opinion of Eichmann that "for various reasons the action against the Jews in Denmark has been a failure," whereas the curious Dr. Best declared that "the objective of the operation was not to seize a great number of Jews but to clean Denmark of Jews, and this objective has now been achieved."

Politically and psychologically, the most interesting aspect of this incident is perhaps the role played by the German authorities in Denmark, their obvious sabotage of orders from Berlin. It is the only case we know of in which the Nazis met with *open* native resistance, and the result seems to have been that those exposed to it changed their minds. They themselves apparently no longer looked upon the extermination of a whole people as a matter of course. They had met resistance based on principle, and their "toughness" had melted like butter in the sun, they had even been able to show a few timid beginnings of genuine courage. That the ideal of "toughness," except, perhaps, for a few half-demented brutes, was nothing but a myth of self-deception, concealing a ruthless desire for conformity at any price, was clearly revealed at the Nuremberg Trials, where the defendants accused and betrayed each other and asssured the world that they "had always been against it" or claimed, as Eichmann was to do, that their best qualities had been "abused" by their superiors. (In Jerusalem, he accused "those in power" of having abused his "obedience." "The subject of a good government is lucky, the subject of a bad government is unlucky. I had no luck.") The atmosphere had changed, and although most of them must have known that they were doomed, not a single one of them had the guts to defend the Nazi ideology. Werner Best claimed at Nuremberg that he had played a complicated double role and that it was thanks to him that the Danish officials had been warned of the impending catastrophe; documentary evidence showed, on the contrary, that he himself had proposed the Danish operation in Berlin, but he explained that this was all part of the game. He was extradited to Denmark and there condemned to death, but he appealed the sentence, with surprising results; because of "new evidence," his sentence was commuted to five years in prison, from which he was released soon afterward. He must have been able to prove to the satisfaction of the Danish court that he really had done his best.

ITALY was Germany's only real ally in Europe, treated as an equal and respected as a sovereign independent state. The alliance presumably rested on the very highest kind of common interest, binding together two similar, if not identical, new forms of government, and it is true that Mussolini had once been greatly admired in German Nazi circles. But by the time war broke out and Italy, after some hesitation, joined in the German enterprise, this was a thing of the past. The Nazis knew well enough that they had more in common with Stalin's version of Communism than with Italian Fascism, and Mussolini on his part had neither much confidence in Germany nor much admiration for Hitler. All this, however, belonged among the secrets of the higher-ups, especially in Germany, and the deep, decisive differences between the totalitarian and the Fascist forms of government were never entirely understood by the world at large. Nowhere did they come more conspicuously into the open than in the treatment of the Jewish question.

Prior to the Badoglio *coup d'état* in the summer of 1943, and the German occupation of Rome and northern Italy, Eichmann and his men were not permitted to be active in the country. They were, however, confronted with the Italian way of *not* solving anything in the Italian-occupied areas of France, Greece, and Yugoslavia, because the persecuted Jews kept escaping into these zones, where they could be sure of temporary asylum. On levels much higher than Eichmann's, Italy's sabotage of the Final Solution had assumed serious proportions, chiefly because of Mussolini's influence on other Fascist governments in Europe —on Pétain's in France, on Horthy's in Hungary, on Antonescu's in Rumania, and even on Franco's in Spain. If Italy could get away with not murdering her Jews, German satellite countries might try to do the same. Thus, Dome Sztojai, the Hungarian Prime Minister whom the Germans had forced upon Horthy, always wanted to know, when it came to anti-Jewish measures, if the same regulations applied to Italy. Eichmann's chief, Gruppenführer Müller, wrote a long letter on the subject to the Foreign Office pointing all this out, but the gentlemen of the Foreign Office could not do much about it, because they always met the same subtly veiled resistance, the same promises and the same failures to fulfill them. The sabotage was all the more infuriating as it was carried out openly, in an almost mocking manner. The promises were given by Mussolini himself or other high-ranking officials, and if the generals simply failed to fulfill them, Mussolini would make excuses for them on the ground of their "different intellectual formation." Only occasionally would the Nazis be met with a flat refusal, as when General Roatta declared that it was "incompatible with the honor of the Italian Army" to deliver the Jews from Italian-occupied territory in Yugoslavia to the appropriate German authorities.

It could be considerably worse when Italians seemed to be fulfilling their promises. One instance of this took place after the Allied landing in French North Africa, when all of France was occupied by the Germans except the Italian Zone in the south, where about fifty thousand Jews had found safety. Under considerable German pressure, an Italian "Commissariat for Jewish Affairs" was established, whose sole function was to register all Jews in this region and expel them from the Mediterranean coast. Twenty-two thousand Jews were indeed seized and removed to the interior of the Italian Zone, with the result, according to Reitlinger, that "a thousand Jews of the poorest class were living in the best hotels of Isère and Savoie." Eichmann thereupon sent Alois Brunner, one of his toughest men, down to Nice and Marseilles, but by the time he arrived, the French police had destroyed all the lists of the registered Jews. In the fall of 1943, when Italy declared war on Germany, the German army could finally move into Nice, and Eichmann himself hastened to the Côte d'Azur. There he was told—and believed—that between ten and fifteen thousand Jews were living in hiding in Monaco (that tiny principality, with some twenty-five thousand residents altogether, whose territory, the *New York Times Magazine* noted, "could fit comfortably inside Central Park"), which caused the R.S.H.A. to start a kind of research program. It sounds like a typically Italian joke. The Jews, in any event, were no longer there; they had fled to Italy proper, and those who were still hiding in the surrounding mountains found their way to Switzerland or to Spain. The same thing happened when the Italians had to abandon their zone in Yugoslavia; the Jews left with the Italian Army and found refuge in Fiume.

An element of farce had never been lacking even in Italy's most serious efforts to adjust to its powerful friend and ally. When Mussolini, under German pressure, introduced anti-Jewish legislation in the late thirties he stipulated the usual exemptions—war veterans, Jews with high decorations, and the like—but he added one more category, namely, former members of the Fascist Party, together with their parents and grandparents, their wives and children and grandchildren. I know of no statistics relating to this matter, but the result must have been that the great majority of Italian Jews were exempted. There can hardly have been a Jewish family without at least one member in the Fascist Party, for this happened at a time when Jews, like other Italians, had been flocking for almost twenty years into the Fascist movement, since positions in the Civil Service were open only to members. And the few Jews who had objected to Fascism on principle, Socialists and Communists chiefly, were no longer in the country. Even convinced Italian anti-Semites seemed unable to take the thing seriously, and Roberto Farinacci, head of the Italian anti-Semitic movement, had a Jewish secretary in his employ. To be sure, such things had happened in Germany too; Eichmann mentioned, and there is no reason not to believe him, that there were Jews even among ordinary S.S. men, but the Jewish origin of people like Heydrich, Milch, and others was a highly confidential matter, known only to a handful of people, whereas in Italy these things were done openly and, as it were, innocently. The key to the riddle was, of course, that Italy actually was one of the few countries in Europe where all anti-Jewish measures were decidedly unpopular, since, in the words of Ciano, they "raised a problem which fortunately did not exist."

Assimilation, that much abused word, was a sober fact in Italy, which had a community of not more than fifty thousand native Jews, whose history reached back into the centuries of the Roman Empire. It was not an ideology, something one was supposed to believe in, as in all German-speaking countries, or a myth and an obvious self-deception, as notably in France. Italian Fascism, not to be outdone in "ruthless toughness," had tried to rid the country of foreign and stateless Jews prior to the outbreak of the war. This had never been much of a success, because of the general unwillingness of the minor Italian officials to get "tough," and when things had become a matter of life and death, they refused, under the pretext of maintaining their sovereignty, to abandon this part of their Jewish population; they put them instead into Italian camps, where they were quite safe until the Germans occupied the country. This conduct can hardly be explained by objective conditions alone—the absence of a "Jewish question"—for these foreigners naturally created a problem in Italy, as they did in every European nation-state based upon the ethnic and cultural homogeneity of its population. What in Denmark was the result of an authentically political sense, an inbred comprehension of the requirements and responsibilities of citizenship and independence—"for the Danes . . . the Jewish question was a political and not a humanitarian question" (Leni Yahil)—was in Italy the outcome of the almost automatic general humanity of an old and civilized people.

Italian humanity, moreover, withstood the test of the terror that descended upon the people during the last year and a half of the war. In December, 1943, the German Foreign Office addressed a formal request for help to Eichmann's boss, Müller: "In view of the lack of zeal shown over the last months by Italian officials in the implementation of anti-Jewish measures recommended by the Duce, we of the Foreign Office deem it urgent and necessary that the implementation . . . be supervised by German officials." Whereupon famous Jew-killers from Poland, such as Odilo Globocnik from the death camps in the Lublin area, were dispatched to Italy; even the head of the military administration was not an Army man but a former governor of Polish Galicia, Gruppenführer Otto Wächter. This put an end to practical jokes. Eichmann's office sent out a circular advising its branches that "Jews of Italian nationality" would at once become subject to "the necessary measures," and the first blow was to fall upon eight thousand Jews in Rome, who were to be arrested by German police regiments, since the Italian police were not reliable. They were warned in time, frequently by old Fascists, and seven thousand escaped. The

Germans, yielding, as usual, when they met resistance, now agreed that Italian Jews, even if they did not belong to exempted categories, should not be subject to deportation but should merely be concentrated in Italian camps; this "solution" should be "final" enough for Italy. Approximately thirty-five thousand Jews in northern Italy were caught and put into concentration camps near the Austrian border. In the spring of 1944, when the Red Army had occupied Rumania and the Allies were about to enter Rome, the Germans broke their promise and began shipping Jews from Italy to Auschwitz—about seventy-five hundred people, of whom no more than six hundred returned. Still, this came to considerably less than ten per cent of all Jews then living in Italy.

To those who followed the case for the prosecution and read the judgment, which reorganized its confused and confusing "general picture," it came as a surprise that the line sharply distinguishing the Nazi-controlled territories to the east and southeast from the system of nation-states in Central and Western Europe was never mentioned. The belt of mixed population that stretches from the Baltic Sea in the north to the Adriatic in the south, the whole area most of which today lies behind the Iron Curtain, then consisted of the so-called Successor States, established by the victorious powers after the First World War. A new political order was granted to the numerous ethnic groups that had lived for centuries under the domination of empires—the Russian Empire in the north, the Austro-Hungarian Empire in the south, and the Turkish Empire in the southeast. Of the nation-states that resulted, none possessed anything even approaching the ethnic homogeneity of the old European nations that had served as models for their political constitutions. The result was that each of these countries contained large ethnic groups that were violently hostile to the ruling government because their own national aspirations had been frustrated in favor of their only slightly more numerous neighbors. If any proof of the political instability of these recently founded states had been needed, the case of Czechoslovakia amply provided it. When Hitler marched into Prague, in March, 1939, he was enthusiastically welcomed not only by the *Sudetendeutschen*, the German minority, but also by the Slovaks, whom he "liberated" by offering them an "independent" state. Exactly the same thing happened later in Yugoslavia, where the Serbian majority, the former rulers of the country, was treated as the enemy, and the Croatian minority was given its own national government. Moreoever, because the populations in these regions fluctuated, there existed no natural or historical boundaries, and those that had been established by the Treaties of Trianon and St. Germain were quite arbitrary. Hence, Hungary, Rumania, and Bulgaria could be won as Axis partners by generous enlargements of their territories, and the Jews in these newly annexed areas were always denied the status of nationals; they automatically became stateless and therefore suffered the same fate as the refugees in Western Europe—they were invariably the first to be deported and liquidated.

What also came crashing down during these years was the elaborate system of minority treaties whereby the Allies had vainly hoped to solve a problem that, within the political framework of the nation-state, is insoluble. The Jews were an officially recognized minority in all Successor States, and this status had not been forced upon them but had been the outcome of claims entered and negotiations conducted by their own delegates to the Versailles Peace Conference. This had marked an important turning point in Jewish history, because it was the first time that Western, or assimilated, Jews had not been recognized as the spokesmen for the whole Jewish people. To the surprise, and also sometimes to the dismay, of the Western-educated Jewish "notables" it had turned out that the large majority of the people desired some sort of social and cultural, though not political, autonomy. Legally, the status of the Eastern European Jews was just like that of any other minority, but politically—and this was to be decisive—they were the only ethnic group in the region without a "homeland," that is, without a territory in which they formed the majority of the population. Still, they did not live in the same kind of dispersion as their brethren in Western and Central Europe, and whereas there, prior to Hitler, it had been a sign of anti-Semitism to call a Jew a Jew, Eastern European Jews were recognized by friend and foe alike as a distinct people. This was of great consequence for the status of those Jews in the East who *were* assimilated, making it utterly different from that in the West, where assimilation in one form or another had been the rule. The great body of middle-class Jews, so characteristic of Western and Central Europe, did not exist in the East; in its stead we find a thin layer of upper-middle-class families who actually belonged to the ruling classes and the degree of whose assimilation—through money, through baptism, through inter-marriage—to Gentile society was infinitely greater than that of most Jews in the West.

Among the first countries in which the executors of the Final Solution were confronted with these conditions was the puppet state of CROATIA, in Yugoslavia, whose capital was Zagreb. The Croat government, headed by Dr. Ante Pavelic, very obligingly introduced anti-Jewish legislation three weeks after its establishment, and when asked what was to be done with the few dozen Croat Jews in Germany, it sent word that they "would appreciate deportation to the East." The Reich Minister of the Interior demanded that the country be *judenrein* by February, 1942, and Eichmann sent Hauptsturmführer Franz Abromeit to work with the German police attaché in Zagreb. The deportations were carried out by the Croats themselves, notably by members of the strong Fascist movement, the Ustashe, and the Croats paid the Nazis thirty marks for each Jew deported. In exchange, they received all the property of the deportees. This was in accordance with the Germans' official "territorial principle," applicable to all European countries, whereby the state inherited the property of every murdered Jew who had resided within its boundaries, regardless of his nationality. (The Nazis did not by any means always respect the "territorial principle"; there were many ways to get around it if it seemed worth the trouble. German businessmen could buy directly from the Jews before they were deported, and the *Einsatzstab* Rosenberg, initially empowered to confiscate all Hebraica and Judaica for German anti-Semitic research centers, soon enlarged its activities to include valuable furnishings and art works.) The original deadline of February, 1942, could not be met, because Jews were able to escape from Croatia to Italian-occupied territory, but after the Badoglio coup Hermann Krumey, another of Eichmann's men, arrived in Zagreb, and by the fall of 1943 thirty thousand Jews had been deported to the killing centers.

Only then did the Germans realize that the country was still not *judenrein*. In the initial anti-Jewish legislation, they had noted a curious paragraph that transformed into "honorary

Aryans" all Jews who made contributions to "the Croat cause."
The number of these Jews had of course greatly increased during
the intervening years. The very rich, in other words, who parted
voluntarily with their property were exempted. Even more interesting was the fact that the S.S. Intelligence service (under
Sturmbannführer Wilhelm Höttl, who was first called as a defense
witness in Jerusalem, but whose affidavit was then used by the
prosecution) had discovered that nearly all members of the ruling
clique in Croatia, from the head of the government to the leader
of the Ustashe, were married to Jewish women. The fifteen
hundred survivors among the Jews in this area—five per cent,
according to a Yugoslav government report—were clearly all
members of this highly assimilated, and extraordinarily rich,
Jewish group. And since the percentage of assimilated Jews
among the masses in the East has often been estimated at about
five per cent, it is tempting to conclude that assimilation in the
East, when it was at all possible, offered a much better chance
for survival than it did in the rest of Europe.

Matters were very different in the adjoining territory of SERBIA,
where the German occupation army, almost from its first day
there, had to contend with a kind of partisan warfare that
can be compared only with what went on in Russia behind
the front. I mentioned earlier the single incident that connected
Eichmann with the liquidation of Jews in Serbia. The judgment
admitted that "the ordinary lines of command in dealing with
the Jews of Serbia did not become quite clear to us," and the
explanation is that Eichmann's office was not involved at all in
that area because no Jews were deported. The "problem" was
all taken care of on the spot. On the pretext of executing
hostages taken in partisan warfare, the Army killed the male
Jewish population by shooting; women and children were handed
over to the commander of the Security Police, a certain Dr.
Emanuel Schäfer, a special protégé of Heydrich, who killed them
in gas vans. In August, 1942, Staatsrat Harald Turner, head of
the civilian branch of the military government, reported proudly
that Serbia was "the only country in which the problems of both
Jews and Gypsies were solved," and returned the gas vans to

Berlin. An estimated five thousand Jews joined the partisans, and this was the only avenue of escape.

Schäfer had to stand trial in a German criminal court after the war. For the gassing of 6,280 women and children, he was sentenced to six years and six months in prison. The military governor of the region, General Franz Böhme, committed suicide, but Staatsrat Turner was handed over to the Yugoslav government and condemned to death. It is the same story repeated over and over again: those who escaped the Nuremberg Trials and were not extradited to the countries where they had committed their crimes either were never brought to justice, or found in the German courts the greatest possible "understanding." One is unhappily reminded of the Weimar Republic, whose specialty it was to condone political murder if the killer belonged to one of the violently anti-republican groups of the Right.

BULGARIA had more cause than any other of the Balkan countries to be grateful to Nazi Germany, because of the considerable territorial aggrandizement she received at the expense of Rumania, Yugoslavia, and Greece. And yet Bulgaria was not grateful, neither her government nor her people were soft enough to make a policy of "ruthless toughness" workable. This showed not only on the Jewish question. The Bulgarian monarchy had no reason to be worried about the native Fascist movement, the Ratnizi, because it was numerically small and politically without influence, and the Parliament remained a highly respected body, which worked smoothly with the King. Hence, they dared refuse to declare war on Russia and never even sent a token expeditionary force of "volunteers" to the Eastern front. But most surprising of all, in the belt of mixed populations where anti-Semitism was rampant among all ethnic groups and had become official governmental policy long before Hitler's arrival, the Bulgarians had no "understanding of the Jewish problem" whatever. It is true that the Bulgarian Army had agreed to have all the Jews—they numbered about fifteen thousand—deported from the newly annexed territories, which were under military government and whose population was anti-Semitic; but it is doubtful that they knew what "resettlement in the East" actually signified. Somewhat earlier, in

January, 1941, the government had also agreed to introduce some anti-Jewish legislation, but that, from the Nazi viewpoint, was simply ridiculous: some six thousand able-bodied men were mobilized for work; all baptized Jews, regardless of the date of their conversion, were exempted, with the result that an epidemic of conversions broke out; five thousand more Jews—out of a total of approximately fifty thousand—received special privileges; and for Jewish physicians and businessmen a *numerus clausus* was introduced that was rather high, since it was based on the percentage of Jews in the cities, rather than in the country at large. When these measures had been put into effect, Bulgarian government officials declared publicly that things were now stabilized to everybody's satisfaction. Clearly, the Nazis would not only have to enlighten them about the requirements for a "solution of the Jewish problem," but also to teach them that legal stability and a totalitarian movement could not be reconciled.

The German authorities must have had some suspicion of the difficulties that lay ahead. In January, 1942, Eichmann wrote a letter to the Foreign Office in which he declared that "sufficient possibilities exist for the reception of Jews from Bulgaria"; he proposed that the Bulgarian government be approached, and assured the Foreign Office that the police attaché in Sofia would "take care of the technical implementation of the deportation." (This police attaché seems not to have been very enthusiastic about his work either, for shortly thereafter Eichmann sent one of his own men, Theodor Dannecker, from Paris to Sofia as "adviser.") It is quite interesting to note that this letter ran directly contrary to the notification Eichmann had sent to Serbia only a few months earlier, stating that no facilities for the reception of Jews were yet available and that even Jews from the Reich could not be deported. The high priority given to the task of making Bulgaria *judenrein* can be explained only by Berlin's having received accurate information that great speed was necessary then in order to achieve anything at all. Well, the Bulgarians were approached by the German embassy, but not until about six months later did they take the first step in the direction of "radical" measures—the introduction of the Jewish badge. For the Nazis, even this turned out to be a great disappointment. In the first place, as they dutifully reported, the badge was only a "very little star"; second, most Jews simply did not wear it; and, third, those who did wear it received "so many manifestations of sympathy from the misled population that they actually are proud of their sign"—as Walter Schellenberg, Chief of Counterintelligence in the R.S.H.A., wrote in an S.D. report transmitted to the Foreign Office in November, 1942. Whereupon the Bulgarian government revoked the decree. Under great German pressure, the Bulgarian government finally decided to expel all Jews from Sofia to rural areas, but this measure was definitely not what the Germans demanded, since it dispersed the Jews instead of concentrating them.

This expulsion actually marked an important turning point in the whole situation, because the population of Sofia tried to stop Jews from going to the railroad station and subsequently demonstrated before the King's palace. The Germans were under the illusion that King Boris was primarily responsible for keeping Bulgaria's Jews safe, and it is reasonably certain that German Intelligence agents murdered him. But neither the death of the monarch nor the arrival of Dannecker, early in 1943, changed the situation in the slightest, because both Parliament and the population remained clearly on the side of the Jews. Dannecker succeeded in arriving at an agreement with the Bulgarian Commissar for Jewish Affairs to deport six thousand "leading Jews" to Treblinka, but none of these Jews ever left the country. The agreement itself is noteworthy because it shows that the Nazis had no hope of enlisting the Jewish leadership for their own purposes. The Chief Rabbi of Sofia was unavailable, having been hidden by Metropolitan Stephan of Sofia, who had declared publicly that "God had determined the Jewish fate, and men had no right to torture Jews, and to persecute them" (Hilberg)—which was considerably more than the Vatican had ever done. Finally, the same thing happened in Bulgaria as was to happen in Denmark a few months later—the local German officials became unsure of themselves and were no longer reliable. This was true of both the police attaché, a member of the S.S., who was supposed to round up and arrest the Jews, and the German Ambassador in Sofia, Adolf Beckerle, who in June, 1943, had advised the Foreign Office that the situation was hopeless, because "the Bulgarians had lived for too long with peoples like Armenians, Greeks, and

Gypsies to appreciate the Jewish problem"—which, of course, was sheer nonsense, since the same could be said *mutatis mutandis* for all countries of Eastern and Southeastern Europe. It was Beckerle too who informed the R.S.H.A., in a clearly irritated tone, that nothing more could be done. And the result was that not a single Bulgarian Jew had been deported or had died an unnatural death when, in August, 1944, with the approach of the Red Army, the anti-Jewish laws were revoked

I know of no attempt to explain the conduct of the Bulgarian people, which is unique in the belt of mixed populations. But one is reminded of Georgi Dimitrov, a Bulgarian Communist who happened to be in Germany when the Nazis came to power, and whom they chose to accuse of the *Reichstagsbrand*, the mysterious fire in the Berlin Parliament of February 27, 1933. He was tried by the German Supreme Court and confronted with Göring, whom he questioned as though he were in charge of the proceedings; and it was thanks to him that all those accused, except van der Lubbe, had to be acquitted. His conduct was such that it won him the admiration of the whole world, Germany not excluded. "There is one man left in Germany," people used to say, "and he is a Bulgarian."

GREECE, being occupied in the north by the Germans and in the south by the Italians, offered no special problems and could therefore be left waiting her turn to become *judenrein*. In February, 1943, two of Eichmann's specialists, Hauptsturmführers Dieter Wisliceny and Alois Brunner, arrived to prepare everything for the deportation of the Jews from Salonika, where two-thirds of Greek Jewry, approximately fifty-five thousand people, were concentrated. This was according to plan "within the framework of the Final Solution of the Jewish problem in Europe," as their letter of appointment from IV-B-4 had it. Working closely with a certain Kriegsverwaltungsrat Dr. Max Merten, who represented the military government of the region, they immediately set up the usual Jewish Council, with Chief Rabbi Koretz at its head. Wisliceny, who headed the *Sonderkommando für Judenangelegenheiten* in Salonika, introduced the yellow badge, and promptly made it known that no exemptions would be tolerated. Dr. Merten moved the whole Jewish population into a ghetto, from which they could easily be removed, since it was near the railroad station. The only privileged categories were Jews with foreign passports and, as usual, the personnel of the *Judenrat*—not more than a few hundred persons all told, who were eventually shipped to the exchange camp of Bergen-Belsen. There was no avenue of escape except flight to the south, where the Italians, as elsewhere, refused to hand Jews over to the Germans, and the safety in the Italian Zone was short-lived. The Greek population was indifferent at best, and even some of the partisan groups looked upon the operations "with approval." Within two months, the whole community had been deported, trains for Auschwitz leaving almost daily, carrying from two thousand to twenty-five hundred Jews each, in freight cars. In the fall of the same year, when the Italian Army had collapsed, evacuation of some thirteen thousand Jews from the southern part of Greece, including Athens and the Greek islands, was swiftly completed.

In Auschwitz, many Greek Jews were employed in the so-called death commandos, which operated the gas chambers and the crematoria, and they were still alive in 1944, when the Hungarian Jews were exterminated and the Lódz ghetto was liquidated. At the end of that summer, when rumor had it that the gassing would soon be terminated and the installations dismantled, one of the very few revolts in any of the camps broke out; the death commandos were certain that now they, too, would be killed. The revolt was a complete disaster—only one survivor remained to tell the story.

It would seem that the indifference of the Greeks to the fate of their Jews has somehow survived their liberation. Dr. Merten, a witness for the defense in Eichmann's trial, today, somewhat inconsistently, claims both to have known nothing and to have saved the Jews from the fate of which he was ignorant. He quietly returned to Greece after the war as a representative of a travel agency; he was arrested, but was soon released and allowed to return to Germany. His case is perhaps unique, since trials for war crimes in countries other than Germany have always resulted in severe punishment. And his testimony for the defense, which he gave in Berlin in the presence of representatives of both the defense and the prosecution, was certainly unique. He claimed that Eichmann had been very helpful in an attempt to save some twenty thousand women and children in Salonika, and that all the evil had come from Wisliceny. However, he eventually stated that before testifying he had been approached by Eichmann's brother, a lawyer in Linz, and by a German organization of former members of the S.S. Eichmann himself denied everything—he had never been in Salonika, and he had never seen the helpful Dr. Merten.

Eichmann claimed more than once that his organizational gifts, the coordination of evacuations and deportations achieved by his office, had in fact helped his victims; it had made their fate easier. If this thing had to be done at all, he argued, it was better that it be done in good order. During the trial no one, not even counsel for the defense, paid any attention to this claim, which was obviously in the same category as his foolish and stubborn contention that he had saved the lives of hundreds of thousands of Jews through "forced emigration." And yet, in the light of what took place in RUMANIA, one begins to wonder. Here, too, everything was topsy-turvy, but not as in Denmark, where even the men of the Gestapo began sabotaging orders from Berlin; in Rumania even the S.S. were taken aback, and occasionally frightened, by the horrors of old-fashioned, spontaneous pogroms on a gigantic scale; they often intervened to save Jews from sheer butchery, so that the killing could be done in what, according to them, was a civilized way.

It is hardly an exaggeration to say that Rumania was the most anti-Semitic country in prewar Europe. Even in the nineteenth century, Rumanian anti-Semitism was a well-established fact; in 1878, the great powers had tried to intervene, through the Treaty of Berlin, and to get the Rumanian government to recognize its Jewish inhabitants as Rumanian nationals—though they would have remained second-class citizens. They did not succeed, and at the end of the First World War all Rumanian Jews—with the exception of a few hundred Sephardic families and some Jews of German origin—were still resident aliens. It took the whole might of the Allies, during the peace-treaty negotiations, to "persuade" the Rumanian government to accept a minority treaty and to grant the Jewish minority citizenship. This concession to world opinion was withdrawn in 1937 and 1938, when, trusting in the power of Hitler Germany, the Rumanians felt they could risk denouncing the minority treaties as an imposition upon their "sovereignty," and could deprive several hundred thousand Jews, roughly a quarter of the total Jewish population, of their citizenship. Two years later, in August, 1940, some months prior to Rumania's entry into the war on the side of Hitler Germany, Marshal Ion Antonescu, head of the new Iron Guard dictatorship, declared all Rumanian Jews to be stateless, with the exception of the few hundred families who had been Rumanian citizens before the peace treaties. That same month, he also instituted anti-Jewish legislation that was the severest in Europe, Germany not excluded. The privileged categories, war veterans and Jews who had been Rumanians prior to 1918, comprised no more than ten thousand people, hardly more than one per cent of the whole group. Hitler himself was aware that Germany was in danger of being outdone by Rumania, and he complained to Goebbels in August, 1941, a few weeks after he had given the order for the Final Solution, that "a man like Antonescu proceeds in these matters in a far more radical fashion than we have done up to the present."

Rumania entered the war in February, 1941, and the Rumanian Legion became a military force to be reckoned with in the coming invasion of Russia. In Odessa alone, Rumanian soldiers were responsible for the massacre of sixty thousand people. In contrast to the governments of other Balkan countries, the Rumanian government had very exact information from the very beginning about the massacres of Jews in the East, and Rumanian soldiers, even after the Iron Guard had been ousted from the government, in the summer of 1941, embarked upon a program of massacres and deportations that even "dwarfed the Bucharest outburst of the Iron Guard" in January of the same year—a program that for sheer horror is unparalleled in the whole atrocity-stricken record (Hilberg). Deportation Rumanian style consisted in herding five thousand people into freight cars and letting them die there of suffocation while the train traveled through the countryside without plan or aim for days on end; a favorite follow-up to these killing operations was to expose the corpses in Jewish butcher shops. Also, the horrors of Rumanian concentration camps, which were established and run by the Ru-

manians themselves because deportation to the East was not
feasible, were more elaborate and more atrocious than anything
we know of in Germany. When Eichmann sent the customary
adviser on Jewish affairs, Hauptsturmführer Gustav Richter, to
Bucharest, Richter reported that Antonescu now wished to ship
a hundred and ten thousand Jews into "two forests across the
river Bug," that is, into German-held Russian territory, for liquidation. The Germans were horrified, and everybody intervened:
the Army commanders, Rosenberg's Ministry for Occupied Eastern Territories, the Foreign Office in Berlin, the Minister to
Bucharest, Freiherr Manfred von Killinger—the last, a former
high S.A. officer, a personal friend of Röhm's and therefore suspect in the eyes of the S.S., was probably spied upon by Richter,
who "advised" him on Jewish affairs. On this matter, however,
they were all in agreement. Eichmann himself implored the Foreign Office, in a letter dated April, 1942, to stop these unorganized
and premature Rumanian efforts "to get rid of the Jews" at this
stage; the Rumanians must be made to understand that "the
evacuation of German Jews, which is already in full swing," had
priority, and he concluded by threatening to "bring the Security
Police into action."

However reluctant the Germans were to give Rumania a higher
priority in the Final Solution that had originally been planned
for any Balkan country, they had to come around if they did not
want the situation to deteriorate into bloody chaos, and, much as
Eichmann may have enjoyed his threat to use the Security Police,
the saving of Jews was not exactly what they had been trained
for. Hence, in the middle of August—by which time the
Rumanians had killed close to three hundred thousand of their
Jews mostly without any German help—the Foreign Office concluded an agreement with Antonescu "for the evacuation of Jews
from Rumania, to be carried out by German units," and Eichmann
began negotiations with the German railroads for enough cars
to transport two hundred thousand Jews to the Lublin death
camps. But now, when everything was ready and these great
concessions had been granted, the Rumanians suddenly did an
about-face. Like a bolt from the blue, a letter arrived in Berlin
from the trusted Mr. Richter—Marshal Antonescu had changed
his mind; as Ambassador Killinger reported, the Marshal now

wanted to get rid of Jews "in a comfortable manner." What the Germans had not taken into account was that this was not only a country with an inordinately high percentage of plain murderers, but that Rumania was also the most corrupt country in the Balkans. Side by side with the massacres, there had sprung up a flourishing business in exemption sales, in which every branch of the bureaucracy, national or municipal, had happily engaged. The government's own specialty was huge taxes, which were levied haphazardly upon certain groups or whole communities of Jews. Now it had discovered that one could sell Jews abroad for hard currency, so the Rumanians became the most fervent adherents of Jewish emigration—at thirteen hundred dollars a head. This is how Rumania came to be one of the few outlets for Jewish emigration to Palestine during the war. And as the Red Army drew nearer, Antonescu became even more "moderate," he now was willing to let Jews go without any compensation.

It is a curious fact that Antonescu, from beginning to end, was not more "radical" than the Nazis (as Hitler thought), but simply always a step ahead of German developments. He had been the first to deprive all Jews of nationality, and he had started large-scale massacres openly and unashamedly at a time when the Nazis were still busy trying out their first experiments. He had hit upon the sales idea more than a year before Himmler offered "blood for trucks," and he ended, as Himmler finally did, by calling the whole thing off as though it had been a joke. In August, 1944, Rumania surrendered to the Red Army, and Eichmann, specialist in evacuation, was sent pell-mell to the area in order to save some "ethnic Germans," without success. About half of Rumania's eight hundred and fifty thousand Jews survived, a great number of whom—several hundred thousand—found their way to Israel. Nobody knows how many Jews are left in the country today. The Rumanian murderers were all duly executed, and Killinger committed suicide before the Russians could lay their hands on him; only Hauptsturmführer a.D. Richter, who, it is true, had never had a chance to get into the act, lived peacefully in Germany until 1961, when he became a belated victim of the Eichmann trial.

XII : *Deportations from Central Europe—*
Hungary and Slovakia

HUNGARY, mentioned earlier in connection with the troublesome question of Eichmann's conscience, was constitutionally a kingdom without a king. The country, though without access to the sea and possessing neither navy nor merchant fleet, was ruled— or, rather, held in trust for the nonexistent king—by an admiral, Regent or *Reichsverweser* Nikolaus von Horthy. The only visible sign of royalty was an abundance of *Hofräte,* councilors to the nonexistent court. Once upon a time, the Holy Roman Emperor had been King of Hungary, and more recently, after 1806, the *kaiserlichkönigliche Monarchie* on the Danube had been precariously held together by the Hapsburgs, who were emperors (*Kaiser*) of Austria and kings of Hungary. In 1918, the Hapsburg Empire had been dissolved into Successor States, and Austria was now a republic, hoping for *Anschluss,* for union with Germany. Otto von Hapsburg was in exile, and he would never have been accepted as King of Hungary by the fiercely nationalistic Magyars; an authentically Hungarian royalty, on the other hand, did not even exist as a historical memory. So what Hungary was, in terms of recognized forms of government, only Admiral Horthy knew.

Behind the delusions of royal grandeur was an inherited feudal structure, with greater misery among the landless peasants and greater luxury among the few aristocratic families who literally owned the country than anywhere else in these poverty-stricken territories, the homeland of Europe's stepchildren. It was this background of unsolved social questions and general backwardness that gave Budapest society its specific flavor, as though Hungarians were a group of illusionists who had fed so long on self-deception that they had lost any sense of incongruity. Early in the thirties, under the influence of Italian Fascism, they had produced a strong Fascist movement, the so-called Arrow Cross men, and in 1938 they followed Italy by passing their first anti-Jewish legislation; despite the strong influence of the Catholic Church in the country, the rulings applied to baptized Jews who had been converted after 1919, and even those converted before that date were included three years later. And yet, when an all-inclusive anti-Semitism, based on race, had become official government policy, eleven Jews continued to sit in the upper chamber of the Parliament, and Hungary was the only Axis country to send Jewish troops—a hundred and thirty thousand of them, in auxiliary service, but in Hungarian uniform—to the Eastern front. The explanation of these inconsistencies is that the Hungarians, their official policy notwithstanding, were even more emphatic than other countries in distinguishing between native Jews and *Ostjuden*, between the "Magyarized" Jews of "Trianon Hungary" (established, like the other Successor States, by the Treaty of Trianon) and those of recently annexed territories. Hungary's sovereignty was respected by the Nazi government until March, 1944, with the result that for Jews the country became an island of safety in "an ocean of destruction." While it is understandable enough that—with the Red Army approaching through the Carpathian Mountains and the Hungarian government desperately trying to follow the example of Italy and conclude a separate armistice—the German government should have decided to occupy the country, it is almost incredible that at this stage of the game it should still have been "the order of the day to come to grips with the Jewish problem," the "liquidation" of which was "a prerequisite for involving Hungary in the war," as Veesenmayer put it in a report to the Foreign Office in December, 1943. For the "liquidation" of this "problem" involved the evacuation of eight hundred thousand Jews, plus an estimated hundred or hundred and fifty thousand converted Jews.

Be that as it may, as I have said earlier, because of the greatness and the urgency of the task Eichmann arrived in Budapest in March, 1944, with his whole staff, which he could easily assemble, since the job had been finished everywhere else. He called Wisliceny and Brunner from Slovakia and Greece,

Abromeit from Yugoslavia, Dannecker from Paris and Bulgaria, Siegfried Seidl from his post as Commander of Theresienstadt, and, from Vienna, Hermann Krumey, who became his deputy in Hungary. From Berlin, he brought all the more important members of his office staff: Rolf Günther, who had been his chief deputy; Franz Novak, his deportation officer; and Otto Hunsche, his legal expert. Thus, the *Sondereinsatzkommando* Eichmann (Eichmann Special Operation Unit) consisted of about ten men, plus some clerical assistants, when it set up its headquarters in Budapest. On the very evening of their arrival, Eichmann and his men invited the Jewish leaders to a conference, to persuade them to form a Jewish Council, through which they could issue their orders and to which they would give, in return, absolute jurisdiction over all Jews in Hungary. This was no easy trick at this moment and in that place. It was a time when, in the words of the Papal Nuncio, "the whole world knew what deportation meant in practice"; in Budapest, moreover, the Jews had "had a unique opportunity to follow the fate of European Jewry. We knew very well about the work of the *Einsatzgruppen*. We knew more than was necessary about Auschwitz," as Dr. Kastner was to testify at Nuremberg. Clearly, more than Eichmann's allegedly "hypnotic powers" was needed to convince anyone that the Nazis would recognize the sacred distinction between "Magyarized" and Eastern Jews; self-deception had to have been developed to a high art to allow Hungarian Jewish leaders to believe at this moment that "it can't happen here"—"How can they send the Jews of Hungary outside Hungary?"—and to keep believing it even when the realities contradicted this belief every day of the week. How this was achieved came to light in one of the most remarkable non sequiturs uttered on the witness stand: the future members of the Central Jewish Committee (as the Jewish Council was called in Hungary) had heard from neighboring Slovakia that Wisliceny, who was now negotiating with them, accepted money readily, and they also knew that despite all bribes he "had deported all the Jews in Slovakia. . . ." From which Mr. Freudiger concluded: "I understood that it was necessary to find ways and means to establish relationships with Wisliceny."

Eichmann's cleverest trick in these difficult negotiations was to see to it that he and his men acted as though they were corrupt.

The president of the Jewish community, Hofrat Samuel Stern, a member of Horthy's Privy Council, was treated with exquisite courtesy and agreed to be head of the Jewish Council. He and the other members of the Council felt reassured when they were asked to supply typewriters and mirrors, women's lingerie and eau de cologne, original Watteaus and eight pianos—even though seven of these were gracefully returned by Hauptsturm-führer Novak, who remarked, "But, gentlemen, I don't want to open a piano store. I only want to play the piano." Eichmann himself visited the Jewish Library and the Jewish Museum, and assured everybody that all measures would be temporary. And corruption, first simulated as a trick, soon turned out to be real enough, though it did not take the form the Jews had hoped. Nowhere else did Jews spend so much money without any results whatever. In the words of the strange Mr. Kastner, "A Jew who trembles for his life and that of his family loses all sense of money." *(Sic!)* This was confirmed during the trial through testimony given by Philip von Freudiger, mentioned above, as well as through the testimony of Joel Brand, who had represented a rival Jewish body in Hungary, the Zionist Relief and Rescue Committee. Krumey received no less than two hundred and fifty thousand dollars from Freudiger in April, 1944, and the Rescue Committee paid twenty thousand dollars merely for the privilege of meeting with Wisliceny and some men of the S.S. Counterintelligence service. At this meeting, each of those present received an additional tip of a thousand dollars, and Wisliceny brought up again the so-called Europe Plan, which he had proposed in vain in 1942 and according to which Himmler supposedly would be prepared to spare all Jews except those in Poland for a ransom of two or three million dollars. On the strength of this proposal, which had been shelved long before, the Jews now started paying installments to Wisliceny. Even Eichmann's "idealism" broke down in this land of unheard-of abundance. The prosecution, though it could not prove that Eichmann had profited financially while on the job, stressed rightly his high standard of living in Budapest, where he could afford to stay at one of the best hotels, was driven around by a chauffeur in an amphibious car, an unforgettable gift from his later enemy Kurt Becher, went hunting and horseback riding, and enjoyed all sorts of previously unknown luxuries under the tutelage of his new friends in the Hungarian government.

There existed, however, a sizable group of Jews in the country whose leaders, at least, indulged less in self-deception. The Zionist movement had always been particularly strong in Hungary, and it now had its own representation in the recently formed Relief and Rescue Committee (the *Vaadat Ezra va Hazalah*), which, maintaining close contact with the Palestine Office, had helped refugees from Poland and Slovakia, from Yugoslavia and Rumania; the committee was in constant communication with the American Joint Distribution Committee, which financed their work, and they had also been able to get a few Jews into Palestine, legally or illegally. Now that catastrophe had come to their own country, they turned to forging "Christian papers," certificates of baptism, whose bearers found it easier to go underground. Whatever else they might have been, the Zionist leaders knew they were outlaws, and they acted accordingly. Joel Brand, the unlucky emissary who was to present to the Allies, in the midst of the war, Himmler's proposal to give them a million Jewish lives in exchange for ten thousand trucks, was one of the leading officials of the Relief and Rescue Committee, and he came to Jerusalem to testify about his dealings with Eichmann, as did his former rival in Hungary, Philip von Freudiger. While Freudiger, whom Eichmann, incidentally, did not remember at all, recalled the rudeness with which he had been treated at these interviews, Brand's testimony actually substantiated much of Eichmann's own account of how he had negotiated with the Zionists. Brand had been told that "an idealistic German" was now talking to him, "an idealistic Jew"—two honorable enemies meeting as equals during a lull in the battle. Eichmann had said to him: "Tomorrow perhaps we shall again be on the battlefield." It was, of course, a horrible comedy, but it did go to show that Eichmann's weakness for uplifting phrases with no real meaning was not a pose fabricated expressly for the Jerusalem trial. What is more interesting, one cannot fail to note that in meeting with the Zionists neither Eichmann nor any other member of the *Sondereinsatzkommando* employed the tactics of sheer lying that they had used for the benefit of the gentlemen of the Jewish Council. Even "language rules" were suspended, and most of the time a spade was called a spade. Moreoever, when it was a question of serious negotiations— over the amount of money that might buy an exit permit, over the Europe Plan, over the exchange of lives for trucks—not only Eichmann but everybody concerned: Wisliceny, Becher, the gentlemen of the Counterintelligence service whom Joel Brand used to meet every morning in a coffee house, turned to the Zionists as a matter of course. The reason for this was that the Relief and Rescue Committee possessed the required international connections and could more easily produce foreign currency, whereas the members of the Jewish Council had nothing behind them but the more than dubious protection of Regent Horthy. It also became clear that the Zionist functionaries in Hungary had received greater privileges than the usual temporary immunity to arrest and deportation granted the members of the Jewish Council. The Zionists were free to come and go practically as they pleased, they were exempt from wearing the yellow star, they received permits to visit concentration camps in Hungary, and, somewhat later, Dr. Kastner, the original founder of the Relief and Rescue Committee, could even travel about Nazi Germany without any identification papers showing he was a Jew.

The organization of a Jewish Council was for Eichmann, with all his experience in Vienna, Prague, and Berlin, a routine matter that took no more than two weeks. The question now was whether he himself would be able to enlist the help of Hungarian officials for an operation of this magnitude. For him this was something new. In the ordinary course of events, it would have been handled for him by the Foreign Office and its representatives, in this instance, by the newly appointed Reich plenipotentiary, Dr. Edmund Veesenmayer, to whom Eichmann would have sent a "Jewish adviser." Eichmann himself clearly had no inclination for playing the role of adviser, a post that had nowhere carried a rank higher than *Hauptsturmführer,* or captain, whereas he was an *Obersturmbannführer*, or lieutenant colonel, two ranks higher. His greatest triumph in Hungary was that he could establish his own contacts. Three men were primarily concerned—László Endre, who because of an anti-Semitism that even Horthy had called "insane" had recently been appointed

State Secretary in Charge of Political (Jewish) Affairs in the
Ministry of the Interior; László Baky, also an undersecretary in
the Ministry of the Interior, who was in charge of the *Gendarmerie*, the Hungarian police; and the police officer Lieutenant
Colonel Ferenczy, who was directly in charge of deportations.
With their help, Eichmann could be sure that everything, the is-
suance of the necessary decrees and the concentration of the Jews
in the provinces, would proceed with "lightning speed." In
Vienna, a special conference was held with the German State
Railroad officials, since this matter involved the transportation
of nearly half a million people. Höss, at Auschwitz, was informed
of the plans through his own superior, General Richard Glücks
of the W.V.H.A., and ordered a new branch line of the railway
built, to bring the cars within a few yards of the crematoria; the
number of death commandos manning the gas chambers was
increased from 224 to 860, so that everything was ready for
killing between six thousand and twelve thousand people a day.
When the trains began arriving, in May, 1944, very few "able-
bodied men" were selected for labor, and these few worked in
Krupp's fuse factory at Auschwitz. (Krupp's newly built factory
near Breslau, in Germany, the Berthawerk, collected Jewish
manpower wherever it could find it and kept those men in conditions that were unsurpassed even among the labor gangs in the
death camps.)

The whole operation in Hungary lasted less than two months
and came to a sudden stop at the beginning of July. Thanks
chiefly to the Zionists, it had been better publicized than any other
phase of the Jewish catastrophe, and Horthy had been deluged
with protests from neutral countries and from the Vatican. The
Papal Nuncio, though, deemed it appropriate to explain that the
Vatican's protest did not spring "from a false sense of compassion"—a phrase that is likely to be a lasting monument to what
the continued dealings with, and the desire to compromise with,
the men who preached the gospel of "ruthless toughness" had
done to the mentality of the highest dignitaries of the Church.
Sweden once more led the way with regard to practical measures,
by distributing entry permits, and Switzerland, Spain, and Portugal followed her example, so that finally about thirty-three thousand Jews were living in special houses in Budapest under the

protection of neutral countries. The Allies had received and made public a list of seventy men whom they knew to be the chief culprits, and Roosevelt had sent an ultimatum threatening that "Hungary's fate will not be like any other civilized nation . . . unless the deportations are stopped." The point was driven home by an unusually heavy air raid on Budapest on July 2. Thus pressed from all sides, Horthy gave the order to stop the deportations, and one of the most damning pieces of evidence against Eichmann was the rather obvious fact that he had not obeyed "the old fool's" order but, in mid-July, deported another fifteen hundred Jews who were at hand in a concentration camp near Budapest. To prevent the Jewish officials from informing Horthy, he assembled the members of the two representative bodies in his office, where Dr. Hunsche detained them, on various pretexts, until he learned that the train had left Hungarian territory. Eichmann remembered nothing of this episode, in Jerusalem, and although the judges were "convinced that the accused remembers his victory over Horthy very well," this is doubtful, since to Eichmann Horthy was not such a great personage.

This seems to have been the last train that left Hungary for Auschwitz. In August, 1944, the Red Army was in Rumania, and Eichmann was sent there on his wild-goose chase. When he came back, the Horthy regime had gathered sufficient courage to demand the withdrawal of the Eichmann commando, and Eichmann himself asked Berlin to let him and his men return, since they "had become superfluous." But Berlin did nothing of the sort, and was proved right, for in mid-October the situation once more changed abruptly. With the Russians no more than a hundred miles from Budapest, the Nazis succeeded in overthrowing the Horthy government and in appointing the leader of the Arrow Cross men, Ferenc Szalasi, head of state. No more transports could be sent to Auschwitz, since the extermination facilities were about to be dismantled, while at the same time the German shortage of labor had grown even more desperate. Now it was Veesenmayer, the Reich plenipotentiary, who negotiated with the Hungarian Ministry of the Interior for permission to ship fifty thousand Jews—men between sixteen and sixty, and women under forty—to the Reich; he added in his report that

Eichmann hoped to send fifty thousand more. Since railroad facilities no longer existed, this led to the foot marches of November, 1944, which were stopped only by an order from Himmler. The Jews who were sent on the marches had been arrested at random by the Hungarian police, regardless of exemptions, to which by now many were entitled, regardless also of the age limits specified in the original directives. The marchers were escorted by Arrow Cross men, who robbed them and treated them with the utmost brutality. And that was the end. Of an original Jewish population of eight hundred thousand, some hundred and sixty thousand must still have remained in the Budapest ghetto—the countryside was *judenrein*—and of these tens of thousands became victims of spontaneous pogroms. On February 13, 1945, the country surrendered to the Red Army.

The chief Hungarian culprits in the massacre were all put on trial, condemned to death, and executed. None of the German initiators, except Eichmann, paid with more than a few years in prison.

SLOVAKIA, like Croatia, was an invention of the German Foreign Office. The Slovaks had come to Berlin to negotiate their "independence" even before the Germans occupied Czechoslovakia, in March, 1939, and at that time they had promised Göring that they would follow Germany faithfully in their handling of the Jewish question. But this had been in the winter of 1938-39, when no one had yet heard of such a thing as the Final Solution. The tiny country, with a poor peasant population of about two and a half million and with ninety thousand Jews, was primitive, backward, and deeply Catholic. It was ruled at the time by a Catholic priest, Father Josef Tiso. Even its Fascist movement, the Hlinka Guard, was Catholic in outlook, and the vehement anti-Semitism of these clerical Fascists or Fascist clerics differed in both style and content from the ultramodern racism of their German masters. There was only one modern anti-Semite in the Slovak government, and that was Eichmann's good friend Sano Mach, Minister of the Interior. All the others were Christians, or thought they were, whereas the Nazis were in principle, of course, as anti-Christian as they were anti-Jewish. The Slovaks' being Christians meant not only that they felt obliged to emphasize what the Nazis considered an "obsolete" distinction between baptized and nonbaptized Jews, but also that they thought of the whole issue in medieval terms. For them a "solution" consisted in expelling the Jews and inheriting their property but not in systematic "exterminating," although they did not mind occasional killing. The greatest "sin" of the Jews was not that they belonged to an alien "race" but that they were rich. The Jews in Slovakia were not very rich by Western standards, but when fifty-two thousand of them had to declare their possessions because they owned more than two hundred dollars' worth, and it turned out that their total property amounted to a hundred million dollars, every single one of them must have looked to the Slovaks like an incarnation of Croesus.

During their first year and a half of "independence," the Slovaks were busy trying to solve the Jewish question according to their own lights. They transferred the larger Jewish enterprises to non-Jews, enacted some anti-Jewish legislation, which, according to the Germans, had the "basic defect" of exempting baptized Jews who had been converted prior to 1918, planned to set up ghettos "following the example of the General Government," and mobilized Jews for forced labor. Very early, in September, 1940, they had been given a Jewish adviser; Hauptsturmführer Dieter Wisliceny, once Eichmann's greatly admired superior and friend in the Security Service (his eldest son was named Dieter) and now his equal in rank, was attached to the German legation in Bratislava. Wisliceny did not marry and, therefore, could not be promoted further, so a year later he was outranked by Eichmann and became his subordinate. Eichmann thought that this must have rankled with him, and that it helped explain why he had given such damning evidence against him as witness in the Nuremberg Trials, and had even offered to find out his hiding place. But this is doubtful. Wisliceny probably was interested only in saving his own skin, he was utterly unlike Eichmann. He belonged to the educated stratum of the S.S., lived among books and records, had himself addressed as "Baron" by the Jews in Hungary, and, generally, was much more concerned with money than worried about his career; consequently, he was one of the very first in the S.S. to develop "moderate" tendencies.

Nothing much happened in Slovakia during these early years, until March, 1942, when Eichmann appeared in Bratislava to negotiate the evacuation of twenty thousand "young and strong labor Jews." Four weeks later, Heydrich himself came to see the Prime Minister, Vojtek Tuka, and persuaded him to let all Jews be resettled in the East, including the converted Jews who had thus far been exempted. The government, with a priest at its head, did not at all mind correcting the "basic defect" of distinguishing between Christians and Jews on the grounds of religion when it learned that "no claim was put forward by the Germans in regard to the property of these Jews except the payment of five hundred Reichsmarks in exchange for each Jew received"; on the contrary, the government demanded an additional guaranty from the German Foreign Office that "Jews removed from Slovakia and received by [the Germans] would stay in the Eastern areas forever, and would not be given an opportunity of returning to Slovakia." To follow up these negotiations on the highest level, Eichmann paid a second visit to Bratislava, the one that coincided with Heydrich's assassination, and by June, 1942, fifty-two thousand Jews had been deported by the Slovak police to the killing centers in Poland.

There were still some thirty-five thousand Jews left in the country, and they all belonged to the originally exempted categories—converted Jews and their parents, members of certain professions, young men in forced labor battalions, a few businessmen. It was at this moment, when most of the Jews had already been "resettled," that the Bratislava Jewish Relief and Rescue Committee, a sister body of the Hungarian Zionist group, succeeded in bribing Wisliceny, who promised to help to slow down the pace of the deportations, and who also proposed the so-called Europe Plan, which he was to bring up again later in Budapest. It is very unlikely that Wisliceny ever did anything except read books and listen to music, and, of course, accept whatever he could get. But it was just at this moment that the Vatican informed the Catholic clergy of the true meaning of the word "resettlement." From then on, as the German Ambassador, Hans Elard Ludin, reported to the Foreign Office in Berlin, the deportations became very unpopular, and the Slovak government began pressing the Germans for permission to visit the "resettlement" centers—which, of course, neither Wisliceny nor Eichmann could grant, since the "resettled" Jews were no longer among the living. In December, 1943, Dr. Edmund Veesenmayer came to Bratislava to see Father Tiso himself; he had been sent by Hitler and his orders specified that he should tell Tiso "to come down to earth" *(Fraktur mit ihm reden)*. Tiso promised to put between sixteen and eighteen thousand unconverted Jews in concentration camps and to establish a special camp for about ten thousand baptized Jews, but he did not agree to deportations. In June, 1944, Veesenmayer, now Reich plenipotentiary in Hungary, appeared again, and demanded that the remaining Jews in the country be included in the Hungarian operations. Tiso refused again.

In August, 1944, as the Red Army drew near, a full-fledged revolt broke out in Slovakia, and the Germans occupied the country. By this time, Wisliceny was in Hungary, and he probably was no longer trusted anyway. The R.S.H.A. sent Alois Brunner to Bratislava to arrest and deport the remaining Jews. Brunner first arrested and deported the officials of the Relief and Rescue Committee, and then, this time with the help of German S.S. units, deported another twelve or fourteen thousand people. On April 4, 1945, when the Russians arrived in Bratislava, there were perhaps twenty thousand Jews left who had survived the catastrophe.

XIII : *The Killing Centers in the East*

When the Nazis spoke of the East, they meant a huge area that embraced Poland, the Baltic States, and occupied Russian territory. It was divided into four administrative units: the Warthegau, consisting of the Polish Western Regions annexed to the Reich, under Gauleiter Artur Greiser; the Ostland, including Lithuania, Latvia, and Estonia, and the rather indefinite area of White Russia, with Riga as the seat of the occupation authorities; the General Government of central Poland, under Hans Frank; and the Ukraine, under Alfred Rosenberg's Ministry for the Occupied Eastern Territories. These were the first countries on which testimony was presented in the case for the prosecution, and they were the last to be dealt with in the judgment.

No doubt both the prosecution and the judges had excellent reasons for their opposite decisions. The East was the central scene of Jewish suffering, the gruesome terminal of all deportations, the place from which there was hardly ever any escape and where the number of survivors rarely reached more than five per cent. The East, moreover, had been the center of the prewar Jewish population in Europe; more than three million Jews had lived in Poland, two hundred and sixty thousand in the Baltic states, and more than half of the estimated three million Russian Jews in White Russia, the Ukraine, and the Crimea. Since the prosecution was interested primarily in the suffering of the Jewish people and "the dimensions of the genocide" attempted upon it, it was logical to start here, and then see how much specific responsibility for this unmitigated hell could be blamed upon the accused. The trouble was that the evidence relating Eichmann to the East was "scanty," and this was blamed on the fact that the Gestapo files, and particularly the files of Eichmann's section, had been destroyed by the Nazis. This scarcity of documentary evidence gave the prosecution a probably welcome pretext for calling an endless procession of witnesses to testify to events in the East, though this was hardly its only reason for doing so. The prosecution—as had been hinted during the trial but was fully described later (in the special *Bulletin* issued in April, 1962, by Yad Vashem, the Israeli archive on the Nazi period) —had been under considerable pressure from Israeli survivors, who constitute about twenty per cent of the present population of the country. They had flocked spontaneously to the trial authorities and also to Yad Vashem, which had been officially commissioned to prepare some of the documentary evidence, to offer themselves as witnesses. The worst cases of "strong imagination," people who had "seen Eichmann at various places where he had never been," were weeded out, but fifty-six "sufferings-of-the-Jewish-people witnesses," as the trial authorities called them, were finally put on the stand, instead of some fifteen or twenty "background witnesses," as originally planned; twenty-three sessions, out of a total of a hundred and twenty-one, were entirely devoted to "background," which meant they had no apparent bearing upon the case. Though the witnesses for the prosecution were hardly ever cross-examined by either the defense or the judges, the judgment did not accept evidence that had bearing on Eichmann unless it was given some other corroboration. (Thus, the judges refused to charge Eichmann with the murder of the Jewish boy in Hungary; or with having instigated the *Kristallnacht* in Germany and Austria, of which he certainly knew nothing at the time and, even in Jerusalem, knew considerably less than the least well-informed student of the period; or with the murder of ninety-three children of Lidice, who, after Heydrich's assassination, were deported to Lódz, since "it has not been proved beyond reasonable doubt, according to the evidence before us, that they were murdered"; or with responsibility for the hideous operations of Unit 1005, "amongst the most horrifying parts of all the evidence submitted by the prosecution," which had had the task of opening the mass graves in the East and disposing of the corpses in order to efface all traces of slaughter, and was commanded by Standartenführer Paul Blobel, who, according to his own testimony at Nuremberg, took orders from Müller, the head of Section IV of the R.S.H.A.; or with the dreadful conditions under which Jews left alive in the extermination camps were evacuated to German concentration camps, especially to Bergen-Belsen, during the last months of the war.) The gist of the background witnesses' testimony about conditions in the Polish ghettos, about procedures in the various death camps, about forced labor and, generally, the attempt to exterminate through labor, was never in dispute; on the contrary, there was hardly anything in what they told that had not been known before. If Eichmann's name was mentioned at all, it obviously was hearsay evidence, "rumors testified to," hence without legal validity. The testimony of all witnesses who had "seen him with their own eyes" collapsed the moment a question was addressed to them, and the judgment found "that the center of gravity of his activities was within the Reich itself, the Protectorate, and in the countries of Europe to the west, north, south, southeast and Central Europe"—that is, everywhere except in the East. Why, then, did the court not waive these hearings, which lasted for weeks and months on end? In discussing this question, the judgment was somewhat apologetic, and finally gave an explanation that was curiously inconsistent: "Since the accused denied all the counts in the indictment," the judges could not dismiss "evidence on the factual background." The accused, however, had never denied these facts in the indictment, he had only denied that he was responsible for them "in the sense of the indictment."

Actually, the judges were faced with a highly unpleasant dilemma. At the very beginning of the trial, Dr. Servatius had impugned the impartiality of the judges; no Jew, in his opinion, was qualified to sit in judgment on the implementers of the Final Solution, and the presiding judge had replied: "We are professional judges, used and accustomed to weighing evidence brought before us and to doing our work in the public eye and subject to public criticism. . . . When a court sits in judgment, the judges who compose it are human beings, are flesh and blood, with feelings and senses, but they are obliged by the law to restrain those feelings and senses. Otherwise, no judge could ever be found to try a criminal case where his abhorrence might be aroused. . . . It cannot be denied that the memory of the Nazi holocaust stirs every Jew, but while this case is being tried before us it will be our duty to restrain these feelings, and this duty we shall honor." Which was good and fair enough, unless Dr. Servatius meant to imply that Jews might lack a proper understanding of the problem their presence caused in the midst of the nations of the world, and hence would fail to appreciate a "final solution" of it. But the irony of the situation was that in case he had felt inclined to make this argument, he could have been answered that the accused, according to his own, emphatically repeated testimony, had learned all he knew about the Jewish question from Jewish-Zionist authors, from the "basic books" of Theodor Herzl and Adolf Böhm. Who, then, could be better qualified to try him than these three men, who had all been Zionists since their early youth?

It was not with respect to the accused, then, but with respect to the background witnesses that the fact of the Jewishness of the judges, of their living in a country where every fifth person was a survivor, became acute and troublesome. Mr. Hausner had gathered together a "tragic multitude" of sufferers, each of them eager not to miss this unique opportunity, each of them convinced of his right to his day in court. The judges might, and did, quarrel with the prosecutor about the wisdom and even the appropriateness of using the occasion for "painting general pictures," but once a witness had taken the stand, it was difficult indeed to interrupt him, to cut short such testimony, "because of the honor of the witness and because of the matters about which he speaks," as Judge Landau put it. Who were they, humanly speaking, to deny any of these people their day in court? And who would have dared, humanly speaking, to question their veracity as to detail when they "poured out their hearts as they stood in the witness box," even though what they had to tell could only "be regarded as by-products of the trial"?

There was an additional difficulty. In Israel, as in most other countries, a person appearing in court is deemed innocent until proved guilty. But in the case of Eichmann this was an obvious fiction. If he had not been found guilty before he appeared in Jerusalem, guilty beyond any reasonable doubt, the Israelis would never have dared, or wanted, to kidnap him; Prime Minister Ben-Gurion, explaining to the President of Argentina, in a letter dated June 3, 1960, why Israel had committed a "formal violation of Argentine law," wrote that "it was Eichmann who organized the mass murder [of six million of our people], on a gigantic and unprecedented scale, throughout Europe." In contrast to normal arrests in ordinary criminal cases, where suspicion of guilt must be proved to be substantial and reasonable but not beyond reasonable doubt—that is the task of the ensuing trial—Eichmann's illegal arrest could be justified, and was justified in the eyes of the world, only by the fact that the outcome of the trial could be safely anticipated. His role in the Final Solution, it now turned out, had been wildly exaggerated —partly because of his own boasting, partly because the defendants at Nuremberg and in other postwar trials had tried to exculpate themselves at his expense, and chiefly because he had been in close contact with Jewish functionaries, since he was the one German official who was an "expert in Jewish affairs" and in nothing else. The prosecution, basing its case upon sufferings that were not a bit exaggerated, had exaggerated the exaggeration beyond rhyme or reason—or so one thought until the judgment of the Court of Appeal was handed down, in which one could read: "It was a fact that the appellant had received no 'superior orders' at all. He was his own superior, and he gave all orders in matters that concerned Jewish affairs." That had been precisely the argument of the prosecution, which the judges in the District Court had not accepted, but, dangerous nonsense though it was, the Court of Appeal fully endorsed it. (It was supported chiefly by the testimony of Justice Michael A. Musmanno, author of *Ten Days to Die* [1950], and a former judge at Nuremberg, who had come from America to testify for the prosecution. Mr. Musmanno had sat on the trials of the administrators of the concentration camps, and of the members of the mobile killing units in the East; and while Eichmann's name had come up in the proceedings, he had mentioned it only once in his judgments. He had, however, interviewed the Nuremberg defendants in their prison. And there Ribbentrop had told him that Hitler would have been all right if he had not fallen under Eichmann's influence. Well, Mr. Musmanno did not believe all he was told, but he did believe that Eichmann had been given his commission by Hitler himself and that his power "came by speaking through Himmler and through Heydrich." A few sessions later, Mr. Gustave M. Gilbert, professor of psychology at Long Island University and author of *Nuremberg Diary* [1947], appeared as a witness for the prosecution. He was more cautious than Justice Musmanno, whom he had introduced to the defendants at Nuremberg. Gilbert testified that "Eichmann . . . wasn't thought of very much by the major Nazi war criminals . . . at that time," and also that Eichmann, whom they both assumed dead, had not been mentioned in discussions of the war crimes between Gilbert and Musmanno.) The District Court judges, then, because they saw through the exaggerations of the prosecution and had no wish to make Eichmann the superior of Himmler and the inspirer of Hitler, were put in the position of having to defend the accused. The task, apart from its unpleasantness, was of no consequence for either judgment or sentence, as "the legal and moral responsibility of him who delivers the victim to his death is, in our opinion, no smaller and may even be greater than the liability of him who does the victim to death."

The judges' way out of all these difficulties was through compromise. The judgment falls into two parts, and the by far larger part consists of a rewriting of the prosecution's case. The judges indicated their fundamentally different approach by starting with Germany and ending with the East, for this meant that they intended to concentrate on what had been done instead of on what the Jews had suffered. In an obvious rebuff to the prosecution, they said explicitly that sufferings on so gigantic a scale were "beyond human understanding," a matter for "great authors and poets," and did not belong in a courtroom, whereas the deeds and motives that had caused them were neither beyond understanding nor beyond judgment. They even went so far as to state that they would base their findings upon their own presentation, and, indeed, they would have been lost if they had not gone to the enormous amount of work that this implied. They got a firm grasp on the intricate bureaucratic setup of the Nazi machinery of destruction, so that the position of the accused could be understood. In contrast to the introductory speech of Mr. Hausner, which has already been published as a book, the judgment can be studied with profit by those with a historical interest in this period. But the judgment, so pleasantly devoid of cheap oratory, would have destroyed the case for the prosecution altogether if the judges had not found reason to charge Eichmann with some responsibility for crimes in the East, in addition to the main crime, to which he had confessed, namely, that he had shipped people to their death in full awareness of what he was doing.

Four points were chiefly in dispute. There was, first, the question of Eichmann's participation in the mass slaughter carried out in the East by the *Einsatzgruppen*, which had been set up by Heydrich at a meeting, held in March, 1941, at which Eichmann was present. However, since the commanders of the *Einsatzgruppen* were members of the intellectual élite of the S.S., while their troops were either criminals or ordinary soldiers drafted for punitive duty—nobody could volunteer—Eichmann was connected with this important phase of the Final Solution only in that he received the reports of the killers, which he then had to summarize for his superiors. These reports, though "top secret," were mimeographed and went to between fifty and seventy other offices in the Reich, in each of which there sat, of course, some *Oberregierungsrat* who summarized them for the higher-ups. There was, in addition to this, the testimony of Justice Musmanno, who claimed that Walter Schellenberg, who had drawn up the draft agreement between Heydrich and General Walter von Brauchitsch, of the military command, specifying that the *Einsatzgruppen* were to enjoy full freedom in "the execution of their plans as regards the civil population," that is, in the killing of civilians, had told him in a conversation at Nuremberg that Eichmann had "controlled these operations" and had even "personally supervised" them. The judges "for reasons of caution" were unwilling to rely on an uncorroborated statement of Schellenberg's, and threw out this evidence. Schellenberg must have had a remarkably low opinion of the Nuremberg judges and their ability to find their way through the labyrinthine administrative structure of the Third Reich. Hence, all that was left was evidence that Eichmann was well informed of what was going on in the East, which had never been in dispute, and the judgment, surprisingly, concluded that this evidence was sufficient to constitute proof of actual participation.

The second point, dealing with the deportation of Jews from Polish ghettos to the nearby killing centers, had more to recommend it. It was indeed "logical" to assume that the transportation expert would have been active in the territory under the General Government. However, we know from many other sources that the Higher S.S. and Police Leaders were in charge of transportation for this whole area—to the great grief of Governor General Hans Frank, who in his diary complained endlessly about interference in this matter without ever mentioning Eichmann's name. Franz Novak, Eichmann's transportation officer, testifying for the defense, corroborated Eichmann's version: occasionally, of course, they had had to negotiate with the manager of the Ostbahn, the Eastern Railways, because shipments from the western parts of Europe had to be coordinated with local operations. (Of these transactions, Wisliceny had given a good account at Nuremberg. Novak used to contact the Ministry of Transport, which, in turn, had to obtain clearance from the Army if the trains entered a theater of war. The Army could veto transports. What Wisliceny did not tell, and what is perhaps more interesting, is that the Army used its right of veto only in the initial years, when German troops were on the offensive; in 1944, when the deportations from Hungary clogged the lines of retreat for whole German armies in desperate flight, no vetoes were forthcoming.) But when, for instance, the Warsaw ghetto was evacuated in 1942, at the rate of five thousand people a day, Himmler himself conducted the negotiations with the railway authorities, and Eichmann and his outfit had nothing whatever to do with them. The judgment finally fell back on testimony given by a witness at the Höss trial that some Jews from the General Government area had arrived in Auschwitz together with Jews from Bialystok, a Polish city that had been incorporated into the German province of East Prussia, and hence fell within Eichmann's jurisdiction. Yet even in the Warthegau, which was Reich territory, it was not the R.S.H.A. but Gauleiter Greiser who was in charge of extermination and deportation. And although in January, 1944, Eichmann visited the Lódz ghetto— the largest in the East and the last to be liquidated—again it was Himmler himself who, a month later, came to see Greiser and ordered the liquidation of Lódz. Unless one accepted the prosecution's preposterous claim that Eichmann had been able to inspire Himmler's orders, the mere fact that Eichmann shipped Jews to Auschwitz could not possibly prove that all Jews who arrived there had been shipped by him. In view of Eichmann's strenuous denials and the utter lack of corroborative evidence, the conclusions of the judgment on this point appeared, unhappily, to constitute a case of *in dubio contra reum*.

The third point to be considered was Eichmann's liability for what went on in the extermination camps, in which, according to the prosecution, he had enjoyed great authority. It spoke for the high degree of independence and fairness of the judges that they threw out all the accumulated testimony of the witnesses on these matters. Their argument here was foolproof and showed their true understanding of the whole situation. They started by explaining that there had existed two categories of Jews in the camps, the so-called "transport Jews" (*Transportjuden*), who made up the bulk of the population and who had never committed an offense, even in the eyes of the Nazis, and the Jews "in protective custody" (*Schutzhaftjuden*), who had been sent to German concentration camps for some transgression and who, under the totalitarian principle of directing the full terror of the regime against the "innocents," were considerably better off than the others, even when they were shipped to the East in order to make the concentration camps in the Reich *judenrein*. (In the words of Mrs. Raja Kagan, an excellent witness on Auschwitz, it was "the great paradox of Auschwitz. Those caught committing a criminal offense were treated better than the others." They were not subject to the selection and, as a rule, they survived.) Eichmann had nothing to do with *Schutzhaftjuden*; but *Transportjuden*, his speciality, were, by definition, condemned to death, except for the twenty-five per cent of especially strong individuals, who might be selected for labor in some camps. In the version presented by the judgment, however, that question was no longer at issue. Eichmann knew, of course, that the overwhelming majority of his victims were condemned to death; but since the selection for labor was made by the S.S. physicians on the spot, and since the lists of deportees were usually made up by the Jewish Councils in the home countries or by the Order Police, but never by Eichmann or his men, the truth was that he had no authority to say who would die and who would live; he could not even know. The question was whether Eichmann had lied when he said: "I never killed a Jew or, for that matter, I never killed a non-Jew. . . . I never gave an order to kill a Jew nor an order to kill a non-Jew." The prosecution, unable to understand a mass murderer who had never killed (and who in this particular instance probably did not even have the guts to kill), was constantly trying to prove individual murder.

This brings us to the fourth, and last, question concerning Eichmann's general authority in the Eastern territories—the question of his responsibility for living conditions in the ghettos, for the unspeakable misery endured in them, and for their final liquidation, which had been the subject of testimony by most witnesses. Again, Eichmann had been fully informed, but none of this had anything to do with his job. The prosecution made a laborious effort to prove that it had, on the ground that Eichmann had freely admitted that every once in a while he had to decide, according to ever-changing directives on this matter, what to do with the Jews of foreign nationality who were trapped in Poland. This, he said, was a question of "national importance," involving the Foreign Office, and was "beyond the horizon" of the local authorities. With respect to such Jews, there existed two different trends in all German offices, the "radical" trend, which would have ignored all distinctions—a Jew was a Jew, period—and the "moderate" trend, which thought it better to put these Jews "on ice" for exchange purposes. (The notion of exchange Jews seems to have been Himmler's idea. After America's entry into the war, he wrote to Müller, in December, 1942, that "all Jews with influential relatives in the United States should be put into a special camp . . . and stay alive," adding, "Such Jews are for us precious hostages. I have a figure of ten thousand in mind.") Needless to say, Eichmann belonged to the "radicals," he was against making exceptions, for administrative as well as "idealistic" reasons. But when in April, 1942, he wrote to the Foreign Office that "in the future foreign nationals would be included in the measures taken by the Security Police within the Warsaw Ghetto," where Jews with foreign passports had previously been carefully weeded out, he was hardly acting as "a decision-maker on behalf of the R.S.H.A." in the East, and he certainly did not possess "executive powers" there. Still less could such powers or authority be derived from his having been used occasionally by Heydrich or Himmler to transmit certain orders to local commanders.

In a sense, the truth of the matter was even worse than the court in Jerusalem assumed. Heydrich, the judgment argued, had been given central authority over the implementation of the Final Solution, without any territorial limitations, hence Eichmann, his chief deputy in this field, was everywhere equally responsible. This was quite true for the framework of the Final Solution, but although Heydrich, for purposes of coordination, had called a representative of Hans Frank's General Government, Undersecretary of State Dr. Josef Bühler, to the Wannsee Conference, the Final Solution did not really apply to the Eastern occupied territories, for the simple reason that the fate of the Jews there had never been in the balance. The massacre of Polish Jewry had been decided on by Hitler not in May or June, 1941, the date of the order for the Final Solution, but in September, 1939, as the judges knew from testimony given at Nuremberg by Erwin Lahousen of the German Counterintelligence: "As early as September, 1939, Hitler had decided the murder of Polish Jews." (Hence, the Jewish star was introduced into the General Government immediately after the occupation of the territory, in November, 1939, while it was introduced into the German Reich only in 1941, at the time of the Final Solution.) The judges had before them also the minutes of two conferences at the beginning of the war, one of which Heydrich had called on September 21, 1939, as a meeting of "department heads and commanders of the mobile killing units" at which Eichmann, then still a mere *Hauptsturmführer*, had represented the Berlin Center for Jewish Emigration; the other took place on January 30, 1940, and dealt with "questions of evacuation and resettlement." At both meetings, the fate of the entire native population in the occupied territories was discussed—that is, the "solution" of the Polish as well as the "Jewish question."

Even at this early date, the "solution of the Polish problem" was well advanced: of the "political leadership," it was reported, no more than three per cent was left; in order to "render this three per cent harmless," they would have "to be sent into concentration camps." The middle strata of the Polish intelligentsia were to be registered and arrested—"teachers, clergy, nobility, legionaries, returning officers, etc."—while the "primitive Poles" were to be added to German manpower as "migratory laborers" and to be "evacuated" from their homes. "The goal is: The Pole has to become the eternal seasonal and migratory laborer, his permanent residence should be in the region of Cracow." The Jews were to be gathered into urban centers and "assembled in ghettos where they can be easily controlled and conveniently evacuated later on." Those Eastern territories that had been incorporated into the Reich—the so-called Warthegau, West Prussia, Danzig, the province of Poznan, and Upper Silesia—had to be immediately cleared of all Jews; together with 30,000 Gypsies they were sent in freight trains into the General Government. Himmler finally, in his capacity as "Reich Commissioner for the Strengthening of German Folkdom," gave orders for the evacuation of large portions of the Polish population from these territories recently annexed to the Reich. The implementation of this "organized migration of peoples," as the judgment called it, was assigned to Eichmann as chief of Subsection IV-D-4 in the R.S.H.A., whose task consisted in "emigration, evacuation." (It is important to remember that this "negative demographic policy" was by no means improvised as a result of German victories in the East. It had been outlined, as early as November, 1937, in the secret speech addressed by Hitler to members of the German High Command—see the so-called Hössbach Protocol. Hitler had pointed out that he rejected all notions of conquering foreign nations, that what he demanded was an "empty space" [*volkloser Raum*] in the East for the settlement of Germans. His audience—Blomberg, Fritsch, and Räder, among others—knew quite well that no such "empty space" existed, hence they must have known that a German victory in the East would automatically result in the "evacuation" of the entire native population. The measures against Eastern Jews were not only the result of anti-Semitism, they were part and parcel of an all-embracing demographic policy, in the course of which, had the Germans won the war, the Poles would have suffered the same fate as the Jews—genocide. This is no mere conjecture: the Poles in Germany were already being forced to wear a distinguishing badge in which the

"P" replaced the Jewish star, and this, as we have seen, was always the first measure to be taken by the police in instituting the process of destruction.)

An express letter, sent to the commanders of the mobile killing units after the September meeting, was among the documents submitted at the trial and was of special interest. It refers only to "the Jewish question in occupied territories" and distinguishes between the "final goal," which must be kept secret, and "preliminary measures" for reaching it. Among the latter, the document mentions expressly the concentration of Jews in the vicinity of railroad tracks. It is characteristic that the phrase "Final Solution of the Jewish question" does not occur; the "final goal" probably was the destruction of Polish Jews, clearly nothing new to those present at the meeting; what was new was only that those Jews who lived in newly annexed provinces of the Reich should be evacuated to Poland, for this was indeed a first step toward making Germany *judenrein*, hence toward the Final Solution.

As far as Eichmann was concerned the documents clearly showed that even at this stage he had next to nothing to do with what happened in the East. Here, too, his role was that of an expert for "transportation" and "emigration"; in the East, no "Jewish expert" was needed, no special "directives" were required, and there existed no privileged categories. Even the members of the Jewish Councils were invariably exterminated when the ghettos were finally liquidated. There were no exceptions, for the fate accorded the slave laborers was only a different, slower kind of death. Hence the Jewish bureaucracy, whose role in these administrative massacres was felt to be so essential that the institution of "Jewish Councils of Elders" was immediately established, played no part in the seizure and the concentration of the Jews. The whole episode signals the end of the initial wild mass shootings in the rear of the armies. It seems that the Army commanders had protested against the massacres of civilians, and that Heydrich had come to an agreement with the German High Command establishing the principle of a complete "cleanup once and for all" of Jews, the Polish intelligentsia, the Catholic clergy, and the nobility, but determining that, because of the magnitude of an operation in which two million Jews would have to be "cleaned up," the Jews should first be concentrated in ghettos.

If the judges had cleared Eichmann completely on these counts connected with the hair-raising stories told over and over by witnesses at the trial, they would not have arrived at a different judgment of guilt, and Eichmann would not have escaped capital punishment. The result would have been the same. But they would have destroyed utterly, and without compromise, the case as the prosecution presented it.

XIV : *Evidence and Witnesses*

During the last weeks of the war, the S.S. bureaucracy was occupied chiefly with forging identity papers and with destroying the paper mountains that testified to six years of systematic murder. Eichmann's department, more successful than others, had burned its files, which, of course, did not achieve much, since all its correspondence had been addressed to other State and Party offices, whose files fell into the hands of the Allies. There were more than enough documents left to tell the story of the Final Solution, most of them known already from the Nuremberg Trials and the successor trials. The story was confirmed by sworn and unsworn statements, usually given by witnesses and defendants in previous trials and frequently by persons who were no longer alive. (All this, as well as a certain amount of hearsay testimony, was admitted as evidence according to Section 15 of the law under which Eichmann was tried, which stipulates that the court "may deviate from the rules of evidence" provided it "places on record the reasons which prompted" such deviation.) The documentary evidence was supplemented by testimony taken abroad, in German, Austrian, and Italian courts, from sixteen witnesses who could not come to Jerusalem, because the Attorney General had announced that he "intended to put them on trial for crimes against the Jewish people." Although during the first session he had declared, "And if the defense has people who are ready to come and be witnesses, I shall not block the way. I shall not put any obstacles," he later refused to grant such people immunity. (Such immunity was entirely dependent upon the good will of the government; prosecution under the Nazis and Nazi Collaborators [Punishment] Law is not mandatory.) Since it was highly unlikely that any of the sixteen gentlemen would have come to Israel under any circumstances—

seven of them were in prison—this was a technical point, but it was of considerable importance. It served to refute Israel's claim that an Israeli court was, at least technically, the "most suitable for a trial against the implementers of the Final Solution," because documents and witnesses were "more abundant than in any other country"; and the claim with respect to documents was doubtful in any event, since the Israeli archive Yad Vashem was founded at a comparatively late date and is in no way superior to other archives. It quickly turned out that Israel was the only country in the world where defense witnesses could not be heard, and where certain witnesses for the prosecution, those who had given affidavits in previous trials, could not be cross-examined by the defense. And this was all the more serious as the accused and his lawyer were indeed not "in a position to obtain their own defense documents." (Dr. Servatius had submitted a hundred and ten documents, as against fifteen hundred submitted by the prosecution, but of the former only about a dozen originated with the defense, and they consisted mostly of excerpts from books by Poliakov or Reitlinger; all the rest, with the exception of the seventeen charts drawn by Eichmann, had been picked out of the wealth of material gathered by the prosecution and the Israeli police. Obviously, the defense had received the crumbs from the rich man's table.) In fact, it had neither "the means nor the time" to conduct the affair properly, it did not have at its disposal "the archives of the world and the instruments of government." The same reproach had been leveled against the Nuremberg Trials, where the inequality of status between prosecution and defense was even more glaring. The chief handicap of the defense, at Nuremberg as at Jerusalem, was that it lacked the staff of trained research assistants needed to go through the mass of documents and find whatever might be useful in the case. Even today, eighteen years after the war, our knowledge of the immense archival material of the Nazi regime rests to a large extent on the selection made for purposes of prosecution.

No one could have been more aware of this decisive disadvantage for the defense than Dr. Servatius, who was one of the defense counsels at Nuremberg. Which, obviously, makes the question of why he offered his services to begin with even more intriguing. His answer to this question was that for him this was "a mere business matter" and that he wished "to make money," but he must have known, from his Nuremberg experience, that the sum paid him by the Israeli government—twenty thousand dollars, as he himself had stipulated—was ridiculously inadequate, even though Eichmann's family in Linz had given him another fifteen thousand marks. He began complaining about being underpaid almost the first day of the trial, and soon thereafter he openly voiced the hope that he would be able to sell whatever "memoirs" Eichmann would write in prison "for future generations." Leaving aside the question of whether such a business deal would have been proper, his hopes were disappointed because the Israeli government confiscated all papers written by Eichmann while in jail. (They have now been deposited in the National Archives.) Eichmann had written a "book" in the time between the adjournment of the court in August and the pronouncement of judgment in December, and the defense offered it as "new factual evidence" in the revision proceedings before the Court of Appeal—which of course the newly written book was not.

As to the position of the defendant, the court could rely upon the detailed statement he had made to the Israeli police examiner, supplemented by many handwritten notes he had handed in during the eleven months needed for the preparation of the trial. No doubt was ever raised that these were voluntary statements; most of them had not even been elicited by questions. Eichmann had been confronted with sixteen hundred documents, some of which, it turned out, he must have seen before, because they had been shown to him in Argentina during his interview with Sassen, which Mr. Hausner with some justification called a "dress rehearsal." But he had started working on them seriously only in Jerusalem, and when he was put on the stand, it soon became apparent that he had not wasted his time: now he knew how to read documents, something he had not known during the police examination, and he could do it better than his lawyer. Eichmann's testimony in court turned out to be the most important evidence in the case. His counsel put him on the stand on June 20, during the seventy-fifth session, and interrogated him almost uninterruptedly for fourteen sessions, until July 7.

That same day, during the eighty-eighth session, the cross-examination by the prosecution began, and it lasted for another seventeen sessions, up to the twentieth of July. There were a few incidents: Eichmann once threatened to "confess everything" Moscow style, and he once complained that he had been "grilled until the steak was done," but he was usually quite calm and he was not serious when he threatened that he would refuse to answer any more questions. He told Judge Halevi how "pleased [he was] at this opportunity to sift the truth from the untruths that had been unloaded upon [him] for fifteen years," and how proud of being the subject of a cross-examination that lasted longer than any known before. After a short re-examination by his lawyer, which took less than a session, he was examined by the three judges, and they got more out of him in two and a half short sessions than the prosecution had been able to elicit in seventeen.

Eichmann was on the stand from June 20 to July 24, or a total of thirty-three and a half sessions. Almost twice as many sessions, sixty-two out of a total of a hundred and twenty-one, were spent on a hundred prosecution witnesses who, country after country, told their tales of horrors. Their testimony lasted from April 24 to June 12, the entire intervening time being taken up with the submission of documents, most of which the Attorney General read into the record of the court's proceedings, which was handed out to the press each day. All but a mere handful of the witnesses were Israeli citizens, and they had been picked from hundreds and hundreds of applicants. (Ninety of them were survivors in the strict sense of the word, they had survived the war in one form or another of Nazi captivity.) How much wiser it would have been to resist these pressures altogether (it was done up to a point, for none of the potential witnesses mentioned in *Minister of Death*, written by Quentin Reynolds on the basis of material provided by two Israeli journalists, and published in 1960, was ever called to the stand) and to seek out those who had not volunteered! As though to prove the point, the prosecution called upon a writer, well known on both sides of the Atlantic under the name of K-Zetnik—a slang word for a concentration-camp inmate—as the author of several books on Auschwitz that dealt with brothels, homosexuals, and other "human interest stories." He started off, as he had done at many of his public appearances, with an explanation of his adopted name. It was not a "pen-name," he said. "I must carry this name as long as the world will not awaken after the crucifying of the nation . . . as humanity has risen after the crucifixion of one man." He continued with a little excursion into astrology: the star "influencing our fate in the same way as the star of ashes at Auschwitz is there facing our planet, radiating toward our planet." And when he had arrived at "the unnatural power above Nature" which had sustained him thus far, and now, for the first time, paused to catch his breath, even Mr. Hausner felt that something had to be done about this "testimony," and, very timidly, very politely, interrupted: "Could I perhaps put a few questions to you if you will consent?" Whereupon the presiding judge saw his chance as well: "Mr. Dinoor, *please, please,* listen to Mr. Hausner and to me." In response, the disappointed witness, probably deeply wounded, fainted and answered no more questions.

This, to be sure, was an exception, but if it was an exception that proved the rule of normality, it did not prove the rule of simplicity or of ability to tell a story, let alone of the rare capacity for distinguishing between things that had happened to the storyteller more than sixteen, and sometimes twenty, years ago, and what he had read and heard and imagined in the meantime. These difficulties could not be helped, but they were not improved by the predilection of the prosecution for witnesses of some prominence, many of whom had published books about their experiences, and who now told what they had previously written, or what they had told and retold many times. The procession started, in a futile attempt to proceed according to chronological order, with eight witnesses from Germany, all of them sober enough, but they were not "survivors"; they had been high-ranking Jewish officials in Germany and were now prominent in Israeli public life, and they had all left Germany prior to the outbreak of war. They were followed by five witnesses from Prague and then by just one witness from Austria, on which country the prosecution had submitted the valuable reports of the late Dr. Löwenherz, written during and shortly after the end of the war. There appeared one witness each from France,

Holland, Denmark, Norway, Luxembourg, Italy, Greece, and Soviet Russia; two from Yugoslavia; three each from Rumania and Slovakia; and thirteen from Hungary. But the bulk of the witnesses, fifty-three, came from Poland and Lithuania, where Eichmann's competence and authority had been almost nil. (Belgium and Bulgaria were the only countries not covered by witnesses.) These were all "background witnesses," and so were the sixteen men and women who told the court about Auschwitz (ten) and Treblinka (four), about Chelmno and Majdanek. It was different with those who testified on Theresienstadt, the old-age ghetto on Reich territory, the only camp in which Eichmann's power had indeed been considerable; there were four witnesses for Theresienstadt and one for the exchange camp at Bergen-Belsen.

At the end of this procession, "the right of the witnesses to be irrelevant," as Yad Vashem, summing up the testimony in its *Bulletin*, phrased it, was so firmly established that it was a mere formality when Mr. Hausner, during the seventy-third session, asked permission of the court "to complete his picture," and Judge Landau, who some fifty sessions before had protested so strenuously against this "picture painting," agreed immediately to the appearance of a former member of the Jewish Brigade, the fighting force of Palestine Jews that had been attached to the British Eighth Army during the war. This last witness for the prosecution, Mr. Aharon Hoter-Yishai, now an Israeli lawyer, had been assigned the task of coordinating all efforts to search for Jewish survivors in Europe, under the auspices of Aliyah Beth, the organization responsible for arranging for illegal immigration into Palestine. The surviving Jews were dispersed among some eight million displaced persons from all over Europe, a floating mass of humanity that the Allies wanted to repatriate as quickly as possible. The danger was that the Jews, too, would be returned to their former homes. Mr. Hoter-Yishai told how he and his comrades were greeted when they presented themselves as members of "the Jewish fighting nation," and how it "was sufficient to draw a Star of David on a sheet in ink and pin it to a broomstick" to shake these people out of the dangerous apathy of near-starvation. He also told how some of them "had wandered home from the D.P. camps," only to come back to another camp, for "home" was, for instance, a small Polish town where of six thousand former Jewish inhabitants fifteen had survived, and where four of these survivors had been murdered upon their return by the Poles. He described finally how he and the others had tried to forestall the repatriation attempts of the Allies and how they frequently arrived too late: "In Theresienstadt, there were thirty-two thousand survivors. After a few weeks we found only four thousand. About twenty-eight thousand had returned, or been returned. Those four thousand whom we found there—of them, of course, not one person returned to his place of origin, because in the meantime the road was pointed out to them"—that is, the road to what was then Palestine and was soon to become Israel. This testimony perhaps smacked more strongly of propaganda than anything heard previously, and the presentation of the facts was indeed misleading. In November, 1944, after the last shipment had left Theresienstadt for Auschwitz, there were only about ten thousand of the original inmates left. In February, 1945, there arrived another six to eight thousand people, the Jewish partners of mixed marriages, whom the Nazis shipped to Theresienstadt at a moment when the whole German transportation system was already in a state of collapse. All the others—roughly fifteen thousand—had poured in in open freight cars or on foot in April, 1945, after the camp had been taken over by the Red Cross. These were survivors of Auschwitz, members of the labor gangs, and they were chiefly from Poland and Hungary. When the Russians liberated the camp—on May 9, 1945—many Czech Jews, who had been in Theresienstadt since the beginning, left the camp immediately and started home; they were in their own country. When the quarantine ordered by the Russians because of the epidemics was lifted, the majority left on its own initiative. So that the remnant found by the Palestine emissaries probably consisted of people who could not return or be returned for various reasons—the ill, the aged, single lonely survivors of families who did not know where to turn. And yet Mr. Hoter-Yishai told the simple truth: those who had survived the ghettos and the camps, who had come out alive from the nightmare of absolute helplessness and abandonment—as though the whole world was a jungle and they its prey—had only one wish, to go where they would never see a non-Jew again. They needed the emissaries of the Jewish people in Palestine in order to learn that they could come, legally or illegally, by hook or by crook, and that they would be welcome; they did not need them in order to be convinced.

Thus, every once in a long while one was glad that Judge Landau had lost his battle, and the first such moment occurred even before the battle had started. For Mr. Hausner's first background witness did not look as though he had volunteered. He was an old man, wearing the traditional Jewish skullcap, small, very frail, with sparse white hair and beard, holding himself quite erect; in a sense, his name was "famous," and one understood why the prosecution wanted to begin its picture with him. He was Zindel Grynszpan, father of Herschel Grynszpan, who, on November 7, 1938, at the age of seventeen, had walked up to the German embassy in Paris and shot to death its third secretary, the young Legationsrat Ernst vom Rath. The assassination had triggered the pogroms in Germany and Austria, the so-called *Kristallnacht* of November 9, which was indeed a prelude to the Final Solution, but with whose preparation Eichmann had nothing to do. The motives for Grynszpan's act have never been cleared up, and his brother, whom the prosecution also put on the stand, was remarkably reluctant to talk about it. The court took it for granted that it was an act of vengeance for the expulsion of some seventeen thousand Polish Jews, the Grynszpan family among them, from German territory during the last days of October, 1938, but it is generally known that this explanation is unlikely. Herschel Grynszpan was a psychopath, unable to finish school, who for years had knocked about Paris and Brussels, being expelled from both places. His lawyer in the French court that tried him introduced a confused story of homosexual relations, and the Germans, who later had him extradited, never put him on trial. (There are rumors that he survived the war—as though to substantiate the "paradox of Auschwitz" that those Jews who had committed a criminal offense were spared.) Vom Rath was a singularly inadequate victim, he had been shadowed by the Gestapo because of his openly anti-Nazi views and his sympathy for Jews; the story of his homosexuality was probably fabricated by the Gestapo. Grynszpan might have acted as an unwitting tool of Gestapo agents in Paris, who could have wanted to kill two birds with one stone—create a pretext for pogroms in Germany and get rid of an opponent to the Nazi regime—without realizing that they could not have it both ways, that is, could not slander vom Rath as a homosexual having illicit relations with Jewish boys and also make of him a martyr and a victim of "world Jewry."

However that may have been, it is a fact that the Polish government in the fall of 1938 decreed that all Polish Jews residing in Germany would lose their nationality by October 29; it probably was in possession of information that the German government intended to expel these Jews to Poland and wanted to prevent this. It is more than doubtful that people like Mr. Zindel Grynszpan even knew that such a decree existed. He had come to Germany in 1911, a young man of twenty-five, to open a grocery store in Hanover, where, in due time, eight children were born to him. In 1938, when catastrophe overcame him, he had been living in Germany for twenty-seven years, and, like many such people, he had never bothered to change his papers and to ask for naturalization. Now he had come to tell his story, carefully answering questions put to him by the prosecutor; he spoke clearly and firmly, without embroidery, using a minimum of words.

"On the twenty-seventh of October, 1938, it was a Thursday night, at eight o'clock, a policeman came and told us to come to Region [police station] Eleven. He said: 'You are going to come back immediately; don't take anything with you, only your passports.'" Grynszpan went, with his family, a son, a daughter, and his wife. When they arrived at the police station he saw "a large number of people, some sitting, some standing, people were crying. They [the police] were shouting, 'Sign, sign, sign.' . . . I had to sign, all of them did. One of us did not, his name was, I believe, Gershon Silber, and he had to stand in the corner for twenty-four hours. They took us to the concert hall, and . . . there were people from all over town, about six hundred people. There we stayed until Friday night, about twenty-four hours, yes, until Friday night. . . . Then they took us in police trucks, in prisoners' lorries, about twenty men in each truck, and they took us to the railroad station. The streets were black with people shouting: '*Juden raus* to Palestine!' . . . They took us by train to Neubenschen, on the German-Polish border. It was Shabbat morning when we arrived there, six o'clock in the morning. There came trains from all sorts of places, from Leipzig, Cologne, Düsseldorf, Essen, Biederfeld, Bremen. Together we were about twelve thousand people. . . . It was the Shabbat, the twenty-ninth of October. . . . When we reached the border we were searched to see if anybody had any money, and anybody who had more than ten marks—the balance was taken away. This was the German law, no more than ten marks could be taken out of Germany. The Germans said, 'You didn't bring any more with you when you came, you can't take out any more.'" They had to walk a little over a mile to the Polish border, since the Germans intended to smuggle them into Polish territory. "The S.S. men were whipping us, those who lingered they hit, and blood was flowing on the road. They tore away our suitcases from us, they treated us in a most brutal way, this was the first time that I'd seen the wild brutality of the Germans. They shouted at us, 'Run! Run!' I was hit and fell into the ditch. My son helped me, and he said: 'Run, Father, run, or you'll die!' When we got to the open border . . . the women went in first. The Poles knew nothing. They called a Polish general and some officers who examined our papers, and they saw that we were Polish citizens, that we had special passports. It was decided to let us enter. They took us to a village of about six thousand people, and we were twelve thousand. The rain was driving hard, people were fainting—on all sides one saw old men and women. Our suffering was great. There was no food, since Thursday we had not eaten. . . ." They were taken to a military camp and put into "stables, as there was no room elsewhere. . . . I think it was our second day [in Poland]. On the first day, a lorry with bread came from Poznan, that was on Sunday. And then I wrote a letter to France . . . to my son: 'Don't write any more letters to Germany. We are now in Zbaszyn.'"

This story took no more than perhaps ten minutes to tell, and when it was over—the senseless, needless destruction of twenty-seven years in less than twenty-four hours—one thought foolishly: Everyone, everyone should have his day in court. Only to find out, in the endless sessions that followed, how difficult it was to tell the story, that—at least outside the transforming realm of poetry—it needed a purity of soul, an unmirrored, unreflected innocence of heart and mind that only the righteous possess. No one either before or after was to equal the shining honesty of Zindel Grynszpan.

No one could claim that Grynszpan's testimony created anything remotely resembling a "dramatic moment." But such a moment came a few weeks later, and it came unexpectedly, just when Judge Landau was making an almost desperate attempt to bring the proceedings back under the control of normal criminal-court procedures. On the stand was Abba Kovner, "a poet and an author," who had not so much testified as addressed an audience with the ease of someone who is used to speaking in public and resents interruptions from the floor. He had been asked by the presiding judge to be brief, which he obviously disliked, and Mr. Hausner, who had defended his witness, had been told that he could not "complain about a lack of patience on the part of the court," which of course he did not like either. At this slightly tense moment, the witness happened to mention the name of Anton Schmidt, a *Feldwebel*, or sergeant, in the German Army—a name that was not entirely unknown to this audience, for Yad Vashem had published Schmidt's story some years before in its Hebrew *Bulletin*, and a number of Yiddish papers in America had picked it up. Anton Schmidt was in charge of a patrol in Poland that collected stray German soldiers who were cut off from their units. In the course of doing this, he had run into members of the Jewish underground, including Mr. Kovner, a prominent member, and he had helped the Jewish partisans by supplying them with forged papers and military trucks. Most important of all: "He did not do it for money." This had gone on for five months, from October, 1941, to March, 1942, when Anton Schmidt was arrested and executed. (The prosecution had elicited the story because Kovner declared that he had first heard the name of Eichmann from Schmidt, who had told him about rumors in the Army that it was Eichmann who "arranges everything.")

This was by no means the first time that help from the outside, non-Jewish world had been mentioned. Judge Halevi had been asking the witnesses: "Did the Jews get any help?" with the same regularity as that with which the prosecution had asked: "Why did you not rebel?" The answers had been various and inconclusive—"We had the whole population against us," Jews hidden by Christian families could "be counted on the fingers of one hand," perhaps five or six out of a total of thirteen thousand—but on the whole the situation had, surprisingly, been better in Poland than in any other Eastern European country. (There was, I have said, no testimony on Bulgaria.) A Jew, now married to a Polish woman and living in Israel, testified how his wife had hidden him and twelve other Jews throughout the war; another had a Christian friend from before the war to whom he had escaped from a camp and who had helped him, and who was later executed because of the help he had given to Jews. One witness claimed that the Polish underground had supplied many Jews with weapons and had saved thousands of Jewish children by placing them with Polish families. The risks were prohibitive; there was the story of an entire Polish family who had been executed in the most brutal manner because they had adopted a six-year-old Jewish girl. But this mention of Schmidt was the first and the last time that any such story was told of a German, for the only other incident involving a German was mentioned only in a document: an Army officer had helped indirectly by sabotaging certain police orders; nothing happened to him, but the matter had been thought sufficiently serious to be mentioned in correspondence between Himmler and Bormann.

During the few minutes it took Kovner to tell of the help that had come from a German sergeant, a hush settled over the courtroom; it was as though the crowd had spontaneously decided to observe the usual two minutes of silence in honor of the man named Anton Schmidt. And in those two minutes, which were like a sudden burst of light in the midst of impenetrable, unfathomable darkness, a single thought stood out clearly, irrefutably, beyond question—how utterly different everything would be today in this courtroom, in Israel, in Germany, in all of Europe, and perhaps in all countries of the world, if only more such stories could have been told.

There are, of course, explanations of this devastating shortage, and they have been repeated many times. I shall give the gist of them in the words of one of the few subjectively sincere memoirs of the war published in Germany. Peter Bamm, a German Army physician who served at the Russian front, tells in *Die*

Unsichtbare Flagge (1952) of the killing of Jews in Sevastopol. They were collected by "the others," as he calls the S.S. mobile killing units, to distinguish them from ordinary soldiers, whose decency the book extols, and were put into a sealed-off part of the former G.P.U. prison that abutted on the officer's lodgings, where Bamm's own unit was quartered. They were then made to board a mobile gas van, in which they died after a few minutes, whereupon the driver transported the corpses outside the city and unloaded them into tank ditches. "We knew this. We did nothing. Anyone who had seriously protested or done anything against the killing unit would have been arrested within twenty-four hours and would have disappeared. It belongs among the refinements of totalitarian governments in our century that they don't permit their opponents to die a great, dramatic martyr's death for their convictions. A good many of us might have accepted such a death. The totalitarian state lets its opponents disappear in silent anonymity. It is certain that anyone who had dared to suffer death rather than silently tolerate the crime would have sacrificed his life in vain. This is not to say that such a sacrifice would have been morally meaningless. It would only have been practically useless. None of us had a conviction so deeply rooted that we could have taken upon ourselves a practically useless sacrifice for the sake of a higher moral meaning." Needless to add, the writer remains unaware of the emptiness of his much emphasized "decency" in the absence of what he calls a "higher moral meaning."

But the hollowness of respectability—for decency under such circumstances is no more than respectability—was not what became apparent in the example afforded by Sergeant Anton Schmidt. Rather it was the fatal flaw in the argument itself, which at first sounds so hopelessly plausible. It is true that totalitarian domination tried to establish these holes of oblivion into which all deeds, good and evil, would disappear, but just as the Nazis' feverish attempts, from June, 1942, on, to erase all traces of the massacres—through cremation, through burning in open pits, through the use of explosives and flame-throwers and bone-crushing machinery—were doomed to failure, so all efforts to let their opponents "disappear in silent anonymity" were in vain. The holes of oblivion do not exist. Nothing human is that perfect, and there are simply too many people in the world to make oblivion possible. One man will always be left alive to tell the story. Hence, nothing can ever be "practically useless," at least, not in the long run. It would be of great practical usefulness for Germany today, not merely for her prestige abroad but for her sadly confused inner condition, if there were more such stories to be told. For the lesson of such stories is simple and within everybody's grasp. Politically speaking, it is that under conditions of terror most people will comply but *some people will not*, just as the lesson of the countries to which the Final Solution was proposed is that "it could happen" in most places but *it did not happen everywhere*. Humanly speaking, no more is required, and no more can reasonably be asked, for this planet to remain a place fit for human habitation.

XV : *Judgment, Appeal, and Execution*

Eichmann spent the last months of the war cooling his heels in Berlin, with nothing to do, cut by the other department heads in the R.S.H.A., who had lunch together every day in the building where he had his office but did not once ask him to join them. He kept himself busy with his defense installations, so as to be ready for "the last battle" for Berlin, and, as his only official duty, paid occasional visits to Theresienstadt, where he showed Red Cross delegates around. To them, of all people, he unburdened his soul about Himmler's new "humane line" in regard to the Jews, which included an avowed determination to have, "next time," concentration camps after "the English model." In April, 1945, Eichmann had the last of his rare interviews with Himmler, who ordered him to select "a hundred to two hundred prominent Jews in Theresienstadt," transport them to Austria, and install them in hotels, so that Himmler could use them as "hostages" in his forthcoming negotiations with Eisenhower. The absurdity of this commission seems not to have dawned upon Eichmann; he went, "with grief in my heart, as I had to desert my defense installations," but he never reached Theresienstadt, because all the roads were blocked by the approaching Russian armies. Instead, he ended up at Alt-Aussee, in Austria, where Kaltenbrunner had taken refuge. Kaltenbrunner had no interest in Himmler's "prominent Jews," and told Eichmann to organize a commando for partisan warfare in the Austrian mountains. Eichmann responded with the greatest enthusiasm: "This was again something worth doing, a task I enjoyed." But just as he had collected some hundred more or less unfit men, most of whom had never seen a rifle, and had taken possession of an arsenal of abandoned weapons of all sorts, he received the latest Himmler order: "No fire is to be opened on English and Americans." This was the end. He sent his men home and gave a small strongbox containing paper money and gold coins to his trusted legal adviser, Regierungsrat Hunsche: "Because, I said to myself, he is a man from the higher civil services, he will be correct in the management of funds, he will put down his expenses . . . for I still believed that accounts would be demanded some day."

With these words Eichmann had to conclude the autobiography he had spontaneously given the police examiner. It had taken only a few days, and filled no more than 315 of the 3,564 pages copied off the tape-recorder. He would like to have gone on, and he obviously did tell the rest of the story to the police, but the trial authorities, for various reasons, had decided not to admit any testimony covering the time after the close of the war. However, from affidavits given at Nuremberg, and, more important, from a much discussed indiscretion on the part of a former Israeli civil servant, Moshe Pearlman, whose book *The Capture of Adolf Eichmann* appeared in London four weeks before the trial opened, it is possible to complete the story; Mr. Pearlman's account was obviously based upon material from Bureau 06, the police office that was in charge of the preparations for the trial. (Mr. Pearlman's own version was that since he had retired from government service three weeks before Eichmann was kidnaped, he had written the book as a "private individual," which is not very convincing, because the Israeli police must have known of the impending capture several months before his retirement.) The book caused some embarrassment in Israel, not only because Mr. Pearlman had been able to divulge information about important prosecution documents prematurely and had stated that the trial authorities had already made up their minds about the untrustworthiness of Eichmann's testimony, but because a reliable account of how Eichmann was captured in Buenos Aires was of course the last thing they wanted to have published.

The story told by Mr. Pearlman was considerably less exciting than the various rumors upon which previous tales had been based. Eichmann had never been in the Near East or the Middle East, he had no connection with any Arab country, he had never returned to Germany from Argentina, he had never been to any other Latin American country, he had played no role in postwar Nazi activities or organizations. At the end of the war, he had tried to speak once more with Kaltenbrunner, who was still in Alt-Aussee, playing solitaire, but his former chief was in no mood to receive him, since "for this man he saw no chances any more." (Kaltenbrunner's own chances were not so very good either, he was hanged at Nuremberg.) Almost immediately thereafter, Eichmann was caught by American soldiers and put in a camp for S.S. men, where numerous interrogations failed to uncover his identity, although it was known to some of his fellow-prisoners. He was cautious and did not write to his family, but let them believe he was dead; his wife tried to obtain a death certificate, but failed when it was discovered that the only "eyewitness" to her husband's death was her brother-in-law. She had been left penniless, but Eichmann's family in Linz supported her and the three children.

In November, 1945, the trials of the major war criminals opened in Nuremberg, and Eichmann's name began to appear with uncomfortable regularity. In January, 1946, Wisliceny appeared as a witness for the prosecution and gave his damning evidence, whereupon Eichmann decided that he had better disappear. He escaped from the camp, with the help of the inmates, and went to the Lüneburger Heide, a heath about fifty miles south of Hamburg, where the brother of one of his fellow-prisoners provided him with work as a lumberjack. He stayed there, under the name of Otto Heninger, for four years, and he was probably bored to death. Early in 1950, he succeeded in establishing contact with ODESSA, a clandestine organization of S.S. veterans, and in May of that year he was passed through Austria to Italy, where a Franciscan priest, fully informed of his identity, equipped him with a refugee passport in the name of Richard Klement and sent him on to Buenos Aires. He arrived in mid-July and, without any difficulty, obtained identification papers and a work permit as Ricardo Klement, Catholic, a bachelor, stateless, aged thirty-seven—seven years less than his real age.

He was still cautious, but he now wrote to his wife in his own handwriting and told her that "her children's uncle" was alive. He worked at a number of odd jobs—sales representative, laundry man, worker on a rabbit farm—all poorly paid, but in the summer of 1952 he had his wife and children join him. (Mrs. Eichmann obtained a German passport in Zurich, Switzerland, though she was a resident of Austria at the time, and under her real name, as a "divorcée" from a certain Eichmann. How this came about has remained a mystery, and the file containing her application has disappeared from the German consulate in Zurich.) Upon her arrival in Argentina, Eichmann got his first steady job, in the Mercedes-Benz factory in Suarez, a suburb of Buenos Aires, first as a mechanic and later as a foreman, and when a fourth son was born to him, he remarried his wife, supposedly under the name of Klement. This is not likely, however, for the infant was registered as Ricardo Francisco (presumably as a tribute to the Italian priest) Klement *Eichmann*, and this was only one of many hints that Eichmann dropped in regard to his identity as the years went by. It does seem to be true, however, that he told his children he was Adolf Eichmann's brother, though the children, being well acquainted with their grandparents and uncles in Linz, must have been rather dull to believe it; the oldest son, at least, who had been nine years old when he last saw his father, should have been able to recognize him seven years later in Argentina. Mrs. Eichmann's Argentine identity card, moreover, was never changed (it read "Veronika Liebl de Eichmann"), and in 1959, when Eichmann's stepmother died, and a year later, when his father died, the newspaper announcements in Linz carried Mrs. Eichmann's name among the survivors, contradicting all stories of divorce and remarriage. Early in 1960, a few months before his capture, Eichmann and his elder sons finished building a primitive brick house in one of the poor suburbs of Buenos Aires—no electricity, no running water—where the family settled down. They must have been very poor, and Eichmann must have led a dreary life, for which not even the children could compensate, for they showed "absolutely no interest in being educated and did not even try to develop their so-called talents."

Eichmann's only compensation consisted in talking endlessly with members of the large Nazi colony, to whom he readily admitted his identity. In 1955, this finally led to the interview with the Dutch journalist Willem S. Sassen, a former member of the Armed S.S. who had exchanged his Dutch nationality for a German passport during the war and had later been condemned to death *in absentia* in Belgium as a war criminal. Eichmann made copious notes for the interview, which was tape-recorded and then rewritten by Sassen, with considerable embellishments; the notes in Eichmann's own handwriting were discovered and they were admitted as evidence at his trial, though the statement as a whole was not. Sassen's version appeared in abbreviated form first in the German illustrated magazine *Der Stern*, in July, 1960, and then, in November and December, as a series of articles in *Life*. But Sassen, obviously with Eichmann's consent, had offered the story four years before to a *Time-Life* correspondent in Buenos Aires, and even if it is true that Eichmann's name was withheld, the content of the material could have left no doubt about the original source of the information. The truth of the matter is that Eichmann had made many efforts to break out of his anonymity, and it is rather strange that it took the Israeli Secret Services several years—until August, 1959—to learn that Adolf Eichmann was living in Argentina under the name of Ricardo Klement. Israel has never divulged the source of her information, and today at least half a dozen persons claim they found Eichmann, while "well-informed circles" in Europe insist that it was the Russian Intelligence service that spilled the news. However that may have been, the puzzle is not how it was possible to discover Eichmann's hideout but, rather, how it was possible not to discover it earlier—provided, of course, that the Israelis had indeed pursued this search through the years. Which, in view of the facts, seems doubtful.

No doubt, however, exists about the identity of the captors. All talk of private "avengers" was contradicted at the outset by Ben-Gurion himself, who on May 23, 1960, announced to Israel's wildly cheering Knesset that Eichmann had been "found by the Israeli Secret Service." Dr. Servatius, who tried strenuously and unsuccessfully both before the District Court and before the Court of Appeal to call Zvi Tohar, chief pilot of the El-Al plane that flew Eichmann out of the country, and Yad Shimoni, an official of the air line in Argentina, as witnesses, mentioned Ben-Gurion's statement; the Attorney General countered by saying that the Prime Minister had "admitted no more than that Eichmann was *found out* by the Secret Service," not that he also had been kidnaped by government agents. Well, in actual fact, it seems that it was the other way round: Secret Service men had not "found" him but only picked him up, after making a few preliminary tests to assure themselves that the information they had received was true. And even this was not done very expertly, for Eichmann had been well aware that he was being shadowed: "I told you that months ago, I believe, when I was asked if I had known that I was found out, and I could give you then precise reasons [that is, in the part of the police examination that was not released to the press]. . . . I learned that people in my neighborhood had made inquiries about real-estate purchases and so on and so forth for the establishment of a factory for sewing machines—a thing that was quite impossible, since there existed neither electricity nor water in that area. Furthermore, I was informed that these people were Jews from North America. I could easily have disappeared, but I did not do it, I just went on as usual, and let things catch up with me. I could have found employment without any difficulty, with my papers and references. But I did not want that."

There was more proof than was revealed in Jerusalem of his willingness to go to Israel and stand trial. Counsel for the defense, of course, had to stress the fact that, after all, the accused had been kidnaped and "brought to Israel in conflict with international law," because this enabled the defense to challenge the right of the court to prosecute him, and though neither the prosecution nor the judges ever admitted that the kidnaping had been an "act of state," they did not deny it either. They argued that the breach of international law concerned only the states of Argentina and Israel, not the rights of the defendant, and that this breach was "cured" through the joint declaration of the two governments, on August 3, 1960, that they "resolved to view as settled the incident which was caused in the wake of the action of citizens of Israel which violated the basic rights of the State of Argentina." The court decided that it did not matter whether these Israelis were government agents or private citizens. What neither the defense nor the court mentioned was that Argentina would not have waived her rights so obligingly had Eichmann been an Argentine citizen. He had lived there under an assumed name, thereby denying himself the right to government protection, at least as Ricardo Klement (born on May 23, 1913, at Bolzano—in Southern Tyrol—as his Argentine identity card stated), although he had declared himself of "German nationality." And he had never invoked the dubious right of asylum, which would not have helped him anyhow, since Argentina, although she has in fact offered asylum to many known Nazi criminals, had signed an International Convention declaring that the perpetrators of crimes against humanity "will not be deemed to be political criminals." All this did not make Eichmann stateless, it did not legally deprive him of his German nationality, but it gave the West German republic a welcome pretext for withholding the customary protection due its citizens abroad. In other words, and despite pages and pages of legal argument, based on so many precedents that one finally got the impression that kidnaping was among the most frequent modes of arrest, it was Eichmann's de facto statelessness, and nothing else, that enabled the Jerusalem court to sit in judgment on him. Eichmann, though no legal expert, should have been able to appreciate that, for he knew from his own career that one could do as one pleased only with stateless people; the Jews had had to lose their nationality before they could be exterminated. But he was in no mood to ponder such niceties, for if it was a fiction that he had come voluntarily to Israel to stand trial, it was true that he had made fewer difficulties than anybody had expected. In fact, he had made none.

On May 11, 1960, at six-thirty in the evening, when Eichmann alighted, as usual, from the bus that brought him home from his place of work, he was seized by three men and, in less than a minute, bundled into a waiting car, which took him to a previously rented house in a remote suburb of Buenos Aires. No drugs, no ropes, no handcuffs were used, and Eichmann immediately recognized that this was professional work, as no unnecessary violence had been applied; he was not hurt. Asked who he was, he instantly said: "*Ich bin Adolf Eichmann,*" and, surprisingly, added: "I know I am in the hands of Israelis." (He later explained that he had read in some newspaper of Ben-Gurion's order that he be found and caught.) For eight days, while the Israelis were waiting for the El-Al plane that was to carry them and their prisoner to Israel, Eichmann was tied to a bed, which was the only aspect of the whole affair that he complained about, and on the second day of his captivity he was asked to state in writing that he had no objection to being tried by an Israeli court. The statement was, of course, already prepared, and all he was supposed to do was to copy it. To everybody's surprise, however, he insisted on writing his own text, for which, as can be seen from the following lines, he probably used the first sentences of the prepared statement: "I, the undersigned, Adolf Eichmann, hereby declare out of my own free will that since now my true identity has been revealed, I see clearly that it is useless to try and escape judgment any longer. I hereby express my readiness to travel to Israel to face a court of judgment, an authorized court of law. It is clear and understood that I shall be given legal advice [thus far, he probably copied], and I shall try to write down the facts of my last years of public activities in Germany, without any embellishments, in order that future generations will have a true picture. This declaration I declare out of my own free will, not for promises given and not because of threats. I wish to be at peace with myself at last. Since I cannot remember all the details, and since I seem to mix up facts, I request assistance by putting at my disposal documents and affidavits to help me in my effort to seek the truth." Signed: "Adolf Eichmann, Buenos Aires, May 1960." (This document, though doubtless genuine, has one peculiarity: its date omits the day it was signed. The omission gives rise to the suspicion that the letter was written not in Argentina but in Jerusalem, where Eichmann arrived on May 22. The letter was needed less for the trial, during which the prosecution did submit it as evidence, but without attaching much importance to it, than for Israel's first explanatory official note to the Argentine government, to which it was duly attached. Servatius, who asked Eichmann about the letter in court, did not mention the peculiarity of the date, and Eichmann could not very well mention it himself since, upon being asked a leading question by his lawyer, he confirmed, though somewhat reluctantly, that he had given the statement under duress, while tied to the bed in the Buenos Aires suburb. The prosecutor, who may have known better, did not cross-examine him on this point; clearly, the less said about this matter the better.) Mrs. Eichmann had notified the Argentine police of her husband's disappearance, but without revealing his identity, so no check of railway stations, highways, and airfields was made. The Israelis were lucky, they would never have been able to spirit Eichmann out of the country ten days after his capture if the police had been properly alerted.

Eichmann provided two reasons for his astounding cooperation with the trial authorities. (Even the judges who insisted that Eichmann was simply a liar had to admit that they knew no answer to the question: "Why did the accused confess before Superintendent Less to a number of incriminating details of which, on the face of it, there could be no proof but for his confession, in particular to his journeys to the East, where he saw the atrocities with his own eyes?") In Argentina, years before his capture, he had written how tired he was of his anonymity, and the more he read about himself, the more tired he must have become. His second explanation, given in Israel, was more dramatic: "About a year and a half ago [i.e., in the spring of 1959], I heard from an acquaintance who had just returned from a trip to Germany that a certain feeling of guilt had seized some sections of German youth . . . and the fact of this guilt complex was for me as much of a landmark as, let us say, the landing of the first man-bearing rocket on the moon. It became an essential point of my inner life, around which many thoughts crystallized. This was why I did not escape . . . when I knew the search commando was closing in on me. . . . After these conversations about the guilt feeling among young people in Germany, which made such a deep impression on me, I felt I no longer had the right to disappear. This is also why I offered, in a written statement, at the beginning of this examination . . . to hang myself in public. I wanted to do my part in lifting the burden of guilt from German youth, for these young people are, after all, innocent of the events, and of the acts of their fathers, during the last war"—which, incidentally, he was still calling, in another context, a "war forced upon the German Reich." Of course, all this was empty talk. What prevented him from returning to Germany of his own free will to give himself up? He was asked this question, and he replied that in his opinion German courts still lacked the "objectivity" needed for dealing with people like him. But if he did prefer to be tried by an Israeli court—as he somehow implied, and which was just barely possible—he could have spared the Israeli government much time and trouble. We have seen before that this kind of talk gave him feelings of elation, and indeed it kept him in something approaching good spirits throughout his stay in the Israeli prison. It even enabled him to look upon death with remarkable equanimity—"I know that the death sentence is in store for me," he declared at the beginning of the police examination.

There was some truth behind the empty talk, and the truth emerged quite clearly when the question of his defense was put to him. For obvious reasons, the Israeli government had decided to admit a foreign counselor, and on July 14, 1960, six weeks after the police examination had started, with Eichmann's explicit consent, he was informed that there were three possible counselors among whom he might choose, in arranging his defense—Dr. Robert Servatius, who was recommended by his family (Servatius had offered his services in a long-distance call to Eichmann's stepbrother in Linz), another German lawyer now residing in Chile, and an American law firm in New York, which had contacted the trial authorities. (Only Dr. Servatius' name was divulged.) There might, of course, be other possibilities, which Eichmann was entitled to explore, and he was told repeatedly that he could take his time. He did nothing of the sort, but said on the spur of the moment that he would like to retain Dr. Servatius, since he seemed to be an acquaintance of his stepbrother and, also, had defended other war criminals, and he insisted on signing the necessary papers immediately. Half an hour later, it occurred to him that the trial could assume "global dimensions," that it might become a "monster process," that there were several attorneys for the prosecution, and that Servatius alone would hardly be able "to digest all the material." He was reminded that Servatius, in a letter asking for power of attorney, had said that he "would lead a group of attorneys" (he never did), and the police officer added, "It must be assumed that Dr. Servatius won't appear alone. That would be a physical impossibility." But Dr. Servatius, as it turned out, appeared quite alone most of the time. The result of all this was that Eichmann became the chief assistant to his own defense counsel, and, quite apart from writing books "for future generations," worked very hard throughout the trial.

On June 29, 1961, ten weeks after the opening of the trial on April 11, the prosecution rested its case, and Dr. Servatius opened the case for the defense; on August 14, after a hundred and fourteen sessions, the main proceedings came to an end. The court then adjourned for four months, and reassembled on December 11 to pronounce judgment. For two days, divided into five sessions, the three judges read the two hundred and forty-four sections of the judgment. Dropping the prosecution's charge of "conspiracy," which would have made him a "chief war criminal," automatically responsible for everything which had to do with the Final Solution, they convicted Eichmann on all fifteen counts of the indictment, although he was acquitted on some particulars. "Together with others," he had committed crimes "against the Jewish people," that is, crimes against Jews *with intent to destroy the people,* on four counts: (1) by "causing the killing of millions of Jews"; (2) by placing "millions of Jews under conditions which were likely to lead to their physical destruction"; (3) by "causing serious bodily and mental harm" to them; and (4) by "directing that births be banned and pregnancies interrupted among Jewish women" in Theresienstadt. But they acquitted him of any such charges bearing on the period prior to August, 1941, when he was informed of the Führer's order; in his earlier activities, in Berlin, Vienna, and Prague, he had no intention "to destroy the Jewish people." These were the first four counts of the indictment. Counts 5 through 12 dealt with "crimes against humanity"—a strange concept in the Israeli law, inasmuch as it included both genocide if practiced against non-Jewish peoples (such as the Gypsies or the Poles) and all other crimes, including murder, committed against either Jews or non-Jews, provided that these crimes were not committed with intent to destroy the people as a whole. Hence, everything Eichmann had done prior to the Führer's order and all his acts against non-Jews were lumped together as crimes against humanity, to which were added, once again, all his later crimes against Jews, since these were ordinary crimes as well. The result was that Count 5 convicted him of the same crimes enumerated in Counts 1 and 2, and that Count 6 convicted him of having "persecuted Jews on racial, religious, and political grounds"; Count 7 dealt with "the plunder of property . . . linked with the murder . . . of these Jews," and Count 8 summed up all these deeds again as "war crimes," since most of them had been committed during the war. Counts 9 through 12 dealt with crimes against non-Jews: Count 9 convicted him of the "expulsion of . . . hundreds of thousands of Poles from their homes," Count 10 of "the expulsion of fourteen thousand Slovenes" from Yugoslavia, Count 11 of the deportation of "scores of thousands of Gypsies" to Auschwitz. But the judgment held that "it has not been proved before us that the accused knew that the Gypsies were being transported to destruction"—which meant that no genocide charge except the "crime against the Jewish people" was brought. This was difficult to understand, for, apart from the fact that the extermination of Gypsies was common knowledge, Eichmann had admitted during the police examination that he knew of it: he had remembered vaguely that this had been an order from Himmler, that no "directives" had existed for Gypsies as they existed for Jews, and that there had been no "research" done on the "Gypsy problem"—"origins, customs, habits, organization . . . folklore . . . economy." His department had been commissioned to undertake the "evacuation" of thirty thousand Gypsies from Reich territory, and he could not remember the details very well, because there had been no intervention from any side; but that Gypsies, like Jews, were shipped off to be exterminated he had never doubted. He was guilty of their extermination in exactly the same way he was guilty of the extermination of the Jews. Count 12 concerned the deportation of ninety-three children from Lidice, the Czech village whose inhabitants had been massacred after the assassination of Heydrich; he was, however, rightly acquitted of the murder of these

children. The last three counts charged him with membership
in three of the four organizations that the Nuremberg Trials
had classified as "criminal"—the S.S.; the Security Service, or
S.D.; and the Secret State Police, or Gestapo. (The fourth such
organization, the leadership corps of the National Socialist Party,
was not mentioned, because Eichmann obviously had not been
one of the Party leaders.) His membership in them prior to May,
1940, fell under the statute of limitations (twenty years) for
minor offenses. (The Law of 1950 under which Eichmann was
tried specifies that there is no statute of limitation for major
offenses, and that the argument *res judicata* shall not avail—a
person can be tried in Israel "even if he has already been tried
abroad, whether before an international tribunal or a tribunal
of a foreign state, for the same offense.") All crimes enumerated
under Counts 1 through 12 carried the death penalty.

— Eichmann, it will be remembered, had steadfastly insisted
that he was guilty only of "aiding and abetting" in the commission of the crimes with which he was charged, that he himself
had never committed an overt act. The judgment, to one's great
relief, in a way recognized that the prosecution had not succeeded in proving him wrong on this point. For it was an
important point; it touched upon the very essence of this crime,
which was no ordinary crime, and the very nature of this
criminal, who was no common criminal; by implication, it also
took cognizance of the weird fact that in the death camps it
was usually the inmates and the victims who had actually
wielded "the fatal instrument with [their] own hands." What the
judgment had to say on this point was more than correct, it was
the truth: "Expressing his activities in terms of Section 23 of
our Criminal Code Ordinance, we should say that they were
mainly those of a person soliciting by giving counsel or advice
to others and of one who enabled or aided others in [the
criminal] act." But "in such an enormous and complicated crime
as the one we are now considering, wherein many people
participated, on various levels and in various modes of activity
—the planners, the organizers, and those executing the deeds,
according to their various ranks—there is not much point in
using the ordinary concepts of counseling and soliciting to commit a crime. For these crimes were committed en masse, not

only in regard to the number of victims, but also in regard to the numbers of those who perpetrated the crime, and the extent to which any one of the many criminals was close to or remote from the actual killer of the victim means nothing, as far as the measure of his responsibility is concerned. On the contrary, in general *the degree of responsibility increases as we draw further away from the man who uses the fatal instrument with his own hands* [my italics]."

What followed the reading of the judgment was routine. Once more, the prosecution rose to make a rather lengthy speech demanding the death penalty, which, in the absence of mitigating circumstances, was mandatory, and Dr. Servatius replied even more briefly than before: the accused had carried out "acts of state," what had happened to him might happen in future to anyone, the whole civilized world faced this problem, Eichmann was "a scapegoat," whom the present German government had abandoned to the court in Jerusalem, contrary to international law, in order to clear itself of responsibility. The competence of the court, never recognized by Dr. Servatius, could be construed only as trying the accused "in a representative capacity, as representing the legal powers vested in [a German court]"—as, indeed, one German state prosecutor had formulated the task of Jerusalem. Dr. Servatius had argued earlier that the court must acquit the defendant because, according to the Argentine statute of limitations, he had ceased to be liable to criminal proceedings against him on May 7, 1960, "a very short time before the abduction"; he now argued, in the same vein, that no death penalty could be pronounced because capital punishment had been abolished unconditionally in Germany.

Then came Eichmann's last statement: His hopes for justice were disappointed; the court had not believed him, though he had always done his best to tell the truth. The court did not understand him: he had never been a Jew-hater, and he had never willed the murder of human beings. His guilt came from his obedience, and obedience is praised as a virtue. His virtue had been abused by the Nazi leaders. But he was not one of the ruling clique, he was a victim, and only the leaders deserved punishment. (He did not go quite as far as many of the other low-ranking war criminals, who complained bitterly that they had been told never to worry about "responsibilities," and that they were now unable to call those responsible to account because these had "escaped and deserted" them—by committing suicide, or by having been hanged.) "I am not the monster I am made out to be," Eichmann said. "I am the victim of a fallacy." He did not use the word "scapegoat," but he confirmed what Servatius had said: it was his "profound conviction that [he] must suffer for the acts of others." After two more days, on Friday, December 15, 1961, at nine o'clock in the morning, the death sentence was pronounced.

Three months later, on March 22, 1962, review proceedings were opened before the Court of Appeal, Israel's Supreme Court, before five judges presided over by Itzhak Olshan. Mr. Hausner appeared again, with four assistants, for the prosecution, and Dr. Servatius, with none, for the defense. Counsel for the defense repeated all the old arguments against the competence of the Israeli court, and since all his efforts to persuade the West German government to start extradition proceedings had been in vain, he now demanded that Israel *offer* extradition. He had brought with him a new list of witnesses, but there was not a single one among them who could conceivably have produced anything resembling "new evidence." He had included in the list Dr. Hans Globke, whom Eichmann had never seen in his life and of whom he had probably heard for the first time in Jerusalem, and, even more startling, Dr. Chaim Weizmann, who had been dead for ten years. The *plaidoyer* was an incredible hodgepodge, full of errors (in one instance, the defense offered as new evidence the French translation of a document that had already been submitted by the prosecution, in two other cases it had simply misread the documents, and so on), its carelessness contrasted vividly with the rather careful introduction of certain remarks that were bound to be offensive to the court: gassing was again a "medical matter"; a Jewish court had no right to sit in judgment over the fate of the children from Lidice, since they were not Jewish; Israeli legal procedure ran counter to Continental procedure—to which Eichmann, because of his national origin, was entitled—in that it required the defendant to provide the evidence for his defense, and this the accused had been unable to do because neither witnesses nor defense documents were available in Israel. In short, the trial had been unfair, the judgment unjust.

The proceedings before the Court of Appeal lasted only a week, after which the court adjourned for two months. On May 29, 1962, the second judgment was read—somewhat less voluminous than the first, but still fifty-one single-spaced legal-sized pages. It ostensibly confirmed the District Court on all points, and to make this confirmation the judges would not have needed two months and fifty-one pages. The judgment of the Court of Appeal was actually a revision of the judgment of the lower court, although it did not say so. In conspicuous contrast to the original judgment, it was now found that "the appellant had received no 'superior orders' at all. He was his own superior, and he gave all orders in matters that concerned Jewish affairs"; he had, moreover, "eclipsed in importance all his superiors, including Müller." And, in reply to the obvious argument of the defense that the Jews would have been no better off had Eichmann never existed, the judges now stated that "the idea of the Final Solution would never have assumed the infernal forms of the flayed skin and tortured flesh of millions of Jews without the fanatical zeal and the unquenchable blood thirst of the appellant and his accomplices." Israel's Supreme Court had not only accepted the arguments of the prosecution, it had adopted its very language.

The same day, May 29, Itzhak Ben-Zvi, President of Israel, received Eichmann's plea for mercy, four handwritten pages, made "upon instructions of my counsel," together with letters from his wife and his family in Linz. The President also received hundreds of letters and telegrams from all over the world, pleading for clemency; outstanding among the senders were the Central Conference of American Rabbis, the representative body of Reform Judaism in this country, and a group of professors from the Hebrew University in Jerusalem, headed by Martin Buber, who had been opposed to the trial from the start, and who now tried to persuade Ben-Gurion to intervene for clemency. Mr. Ben-Zvi rejected all pleas for mercy on May 31, two days after the Supreme Court had delivered its judgment, and a few hours later on that same day—it was a Thursday—shortly before midnight, Eichmann was hanged, his body was cremated, and the ashes were scattered in the Mediterranean outside Israeli waters.

The speed with which the death sentence was carried out was extraordinary, even if one takes into account that Thursday night was the last possible occasion before the following Monday, since Friday, Saturday, and Sunday are all religious holidays for one or another of the three denominations in the country. The execution took place less than two hours after Eichmann was informed of the rejection of his plea for mercy; there had not even been time for a last meal. The explanation may well be found in two last-minute attempts Dr. Servatius made to save his client—an application to a court in West Germany to force the government to demand Eichmann's extradition, even now, and a threat to invoke Article 25 of the Convention for the Protection of Human Rights and Fundamental Freedoms. Neither Dr. Servatius nor his assistant was in Israel when Eichmann's plea was rejected, and the Israeli government probably wanted to close the case, which had been going on for two years, before the defense could even apply for a stay in the date of execution.

The death sentence had been expected, and there was hardly anyone to quarrel with it; but things were altogether different when it was learned that the Israelis had carried it out. The protests were short-lived, but they were widespread and they were voiced by people of influence and prestige. The most common argument was that Eichmann's deeds defied the possibility of human punishment, that it was pointless to impose the death sentence for crimes of such magnitude—which, of course, was true, in a sense, except that it could not conceivably mean that he who had murdered millions should for this very reason escape punishment. On a considerably lower level, the death sentence was called "unimaginative," and very imaginative alternatives were proposed forthwith—Eichmann "should have spent the rest of his life at hard labor in the arid stretches of the Negev, helping with his sweat to reclaim the Jewish homeland," a punishment he would probably not have survived for more than a single day, to say nothing of the fact that in Israel the desert of the south is hardly looked upon as a penal colony; or, in Madison Avenue style, Israel should have reached "divine heights," rising above "the understandable, legal, political, and even human considerations," by calling together "all those who took part in the capture, trial, and sentencing to a public ceremony, with Eichmann there in shackles, and with television cameras and radio to decorate them as the heroes of the century."

Martin Buber called the execution a "mistake of historical dimensions," as it might "serve to expiate the guilt felt by many young persons in Germany"—an argument that oddly echoed Eichmann's own ideas on the matter, though Buber hardly knew that he had wanted to hang himself in public in order to lift the burden of guilt from the shoulders of German youngsters. (It is strange that Buber, a man not only of eminence but of very great intelligence, should not see how spurious these much publicized guilt feelings necessarily are. It is quite gratifying to feel guilty if you haven't done anything wrong: how noble! Whereas it is rather hard and certainly depressing to admit guilt and to repent. The youth of Germany is surrounded, on all sides and in all walks of life, by men in positions of authority and in public office who are very guilty indeed but who *feel* nothing of the sort. The normal reaction to this state of affairs should be indignation, but indignation would be quite risky—not a danger to life and limb but definitely a handicap in a career. Those young German men and women who every once in a while—on the occasion of all the *Diary of Anne Frank* hubbub and of the Eichmann trial—treat us to hysterical outbreaks of guilt feelings are not staggering under the burden of the past, their fathers' guilt; rather, they are trying to escape from the pressure of very present and actual problems into a cheap sentimentality.) Professor Buber went on to say that he felt "no pity at all" for Eichmann, because he could feel pity "only for those whose actions I understand in my heart," and he stressed what he had said many years ago in Germany—that he had "only in a formal sense a common humanity with those who took part" in the acts of the Third Reich. This lofty attitude was, of course, more of a luxury than those who had to try Eichmann could afford, since the law presupposes precisely that we have a common humanity with those whom we accuse and judge and condemn. As far as I know, Buber was the only philosopher to go on public record on the subject of Eichmann's execution (shortly before the trial started, Karl Jaspers had given a radio interview in Basel, later published in *Der Monat,* in which he argued the case for an international tribunal); it was disappointing to find him dodging, on the highest possible level, the very problem Eichmann and his deeds had posed.

Least of all was heard from those who were against the death penalty on principle, unconditionally; their arguments would have remained valid, since they would not have needed to specify them for this particular case. They seem to have felt—rightly, I think—that this was not a very promising case on which to fight.

Adolf Eichmann went to the gallows with great dignity. He had asked for a bottle of red wine and had drunk half of it. He refused the help of the Protestant minister, the Reverend William Hull, who offered to read the Bible with him: he had only two more hours to live, and therefore no "time to waste." He walked the fifty yards from his cell to the execution chamber calm and erect, with his hands bound behind him. When the guards tied his ankles and knees, he asked them to loosen the bonds so that he could stand straight. "I don't need that," he said when the black hood was offered him. He was in complete command of himself, nay, he was more: he was completely himself. Nothing could have demonstrated this more convincingly than the grotesque silliness of his last words. He began by stating emphatically that he was a *Gottgläubiger,* to express in common Nazi fashion that he was no Christian and did not believe in life after death. He then proceeded: "After a short while, gentlemen, *we shall all meet again.* Such is the fate of all men. Long live Germany, long live Argentina, long live Austria. *I shall not forget them.*" In the face of death, he had found the cliché used in funeral oratory. Under the gallows, his memory played him the last trick; he was "elated" and he forgot that this was his own funeral.

It was as though in those last minutes he was summing up the lesson that this long course in human wickedness had taught us—the lesson of the fearsome, word-and-thought-defying *banality of evil.*

The irregularities and abnormalities of the trial in Jerusalem were so many, so varied, and of such legal complexity that they overshadowed during the trial, as they have in the surprisingly small amount of post-trial literature, the central moral, political, and even legal problems that the trial inevitably posed. Israel herself, through the pre-trial statements of Prime Minister Ben-Gurion and through the way the accusation was framed by the prosecutor, confused the issues further by listing a great number of purposes the trial was supposed to achieve, all of which were ulterior purposes with respect to the law and to courtroom procedure. The purpose of a trial is to render justice, and nothing else; even the noblest of ulterior purposes—"the making of a record of the Hitler regime which would withstand the test of history," as Robert G. Storey, executive trial counsel at Nuremberg, formulated the supposed higher aims of the Nuremberg Trials—can only detract from the law's main business: to weigh the charges brought against the accused, to render judgment, and to mete out due punishment.

The judgment in the Eichmann case, whose first two sections were written in reply to the higher-purpose theory as it was expounded both inside and outside the courtroom, could not have been clearer in this respect and more to the point: All attempts to widen the range of the trial had to be resisted, because the court could not "allow itself to be enticed into provinces which are outside its sphere. . . . the judicial process has ways of its own, which are laid down by law, and which do not change, whatever the subject of the trial may be." The court, moreover, could not overstep these limits without ending "in complete failure." Not only does it not have at its disposal "the tools required for the investigation of general questions," it speaks with an authority whose very weight depends upon its limitation. "No one has made us judges" of matters outside the realm of law, and "no greater weight is to be attached to our opinion on them than to that of any person devoting study and thought" to them. Hence, to the question most commonly asked about the Eichmann trial: What good does it do?, there is but one possible answer: It will do justice.

The objections raised against the Eichmann trial were of three kinds. First, there were those objections that had been raised against the Nuremberg Trials and were now repeated: Eichmann was tried under a retroactive law and appeared in the court of the victors. Second, there were those objections that applied only to the Jerusalem court, in that they questioned either its competence as such or its failure to take into account the act of kidnaping. And, finally, and most important, there were objections to the charge itself, that Eichmann had committed crimes "against the Jewish people," instead of "against humanity," and hence to the law under which he was tried; and this objection led to the logical conclusion that the only proper court to try these crimes was an international tribunal.

The court's reply to the first set of objections was simple: the Nuremberg Trials were cited in Jerusalem as valid precedent, and, acting under municipal law, the judges could hardly have done otherwise, since the Nazis and Nazi Collaborators (Punishment) Law of 1950 was itself based on this precedent. "This particular legislation," the judgment pointed out, "is totally different from any other legislation usual in criminal codes," and the reason for its difference lies in the nature of the crimes it deals with. Its retroactivity, one may add, violates only formally, not substantially, the principle *nullum crimen, nulla poena sine lege,* since this applies meaningfully only to acts known to the legislator; if a crime unknown before, such as genocide, suddenly makes its appearance, justice itself demands a judgment according to a new law; in the case of Nuremberg, this new law was the Charter (the London Agreement of 1945), in the case of Israel, it was the Law of 1950. The question is not whether these laws were retroactive, which, of course, they had to be, but whether they were adequate, that is, whether they applied only to crimes previously unknown. This prerequisite for retroactive legislation had been seriously marred in the Charter that provided for the establishment of the International Military Tribunal at Nuremberg, and it may be for this reason that the discussion of these matters has remained somewhat confused.

The Charter accorded jurisdiction over three sorts of crimes: "crimes against peace," which the Tribunal called the "supreme international crime . . . in that it contains within itself the accumulated evil of the whole"; "war crimes"; and "crimes against humanity." Of these, only the last, the crime against humanity, was new and unprecedented. Aggressive warfare is at least as old as recorded history, and while it had been denounced as "criminal" many times before, it had never been recognized as such in any formal sense. (None of the current justifications of the Nuremberg court's jurisdiction over this matter has much to commend it. It is true that Wilhelm II had beeen cited before a tribunal of the Allied powers after the First World War, but the crime the former German Kaiser had been charged with was not war but breach of treaties—and specifically, the violation of Belgium's neutrality. It is also true that the Briand-Kellogg pact of August, 1928, had ruled out war as an instrument of national policy, but the pact contained neither a criterion of aggression nor a mention of sanctions—quite apart from the fact that the security system that the pact was meant to bring about had collapsed prior to the outbreak of war.) Moreover, one of the judging countries, namely, Soviet Russia, was open to the *tu-quoque* argument. Hadn't the Russians attacked Finland and divided Poland in 1939 with complete impunity? "War crimes," on the other hand, surely no more unprecedented than the "crimes against peace," were covered by international law. The Hague and Geneva Conventions had defined these "violations of the laws or customs of war"; they consisted chiefly of ill-treatment of prisoners and of warlike acts against civilian populations. No new law with retroactive force was needed here, and the main difficulty at Nuremberg lay in the indisputable fact that here, again, the *tu-quoque* argument applied: Russia, which had never signed the Hague Convention (Italy, incidentally, had not ratified it either), was more than suspected of mistreatment of prisoners, and, according to recent investigations, the Russians also seem to be responsible for the murder of fifteen thousand Polish officers whose bodies were found at Katyn Forest (in the neighborhood of Smolensk, in Russia). Worse, the saturation bombing of open cities and, above all, the dropping of atomic bombs on Hiroshima and Nagasaki clearly constituted war crimes in the sense of the Hague Convention. And while the bombing of German cities had been provoked by the enemy, by the bombing of London and Coventry and Rotterdam, the same cannot be said of the use of an entirely new and overwhelmingly powerful weapon, whose existence could have been announced and demonstrated in many other ways. To be sure, the most obvious reason that the violations of the Hague Convention committed by the Allies were never even discussed in legal terms was that the International Military Tribunals were international in name only, that they were in fact the courts of the victors, and the authority of their judgment, doubtful in any case, was not enhanced when the coalition that had won the war and then undertaken this joint enterprise broke up, to quote Otto Kirchheimer, "before the ink on the Nuremberg judgments had time to dry." But this most obvious reason is neither the only nor, perhaps, the most potent reason that no Allied war crimes, in the sense of the Hague Convention, were cited and prosecuted, and it is only fair to add, that the Nuremberg Tribunal was at least very cautious about convicting the German defendants on charges that were open to the *tu-quoque* argument. For the truth of the matter was that by the end of the Second World War everybody knew that technical developments in the instruments of violence had made the adoption of "criminal" warfare inevitable. It was precisely the distinction between soldier and civilian, between army and home population, between military targets and open cities, upon which the Hague Convention's definitions of war crimes rested, that had become obsolete. Hence, it was felt that under these new conditions war crimes were only those outside all military necessities, where a deliberate inhuman purpose could be demonstrated.

This factor of gratuitous brutality was a valid criterion for determining what, under the circumstances, constituted a war crime. It was not valid for, but was unfortunately introduced into the fumbling definitions of, the only entirely new crime, the "crime against humanity," which the Charter (in Article 6-c) defined as an "inhuman act"—as though this crime, too, were a matter of criminal excess in the pursuit of war and victory. However, it was by no means this sort of well-known offense that had prompted the Allies to declare, in the words of Churchill, that "punishment of war criminals [was] one of the principal war aims" but, on the contrary, reports of unheard-of atrocities, the blotting out of whole peoples, the "clearance" of whole regions of their native population, that is, not only crimes that "no conception of military necessity could sustain" but crimes that were in fact independent of the war and that announced a policy of systematic murder to be continued in time of peace. This crime was indeed not covered by international or municipal law, and, moreover, it was the only crime to which the *tu-quoque* argument did not apply. And yet there was no other crime in the face of which the Nuremberg judges felt so uncomfortable, and which they left in a more tantalizing state of ambiguity. It is perfectly true that—in the words of the French judge at Nuremberg, Donnedieu de Vabres, to whom we owe one of the best analyses of the trial (*Le Procès de Nuremberg*, 1947)—"the category of crimes against humanity which the Charter had let enter by a very small door evaporated by virtue of the Tribunal's judgment." The judges, however, were as little consistent as the Charter itself, for although they preferred to convict, as Kirchheimer says, "on the war crime charge, which embraced all the traditional common crimes, while underemphasizing as much as possible the charges of crimes against humanity," when it came to pronouncing sentence, they revealed their true sentiment by meting out their most severe punishment, the death penalty, only to those who had been found guilty of those quite uncommon atrocities that actually constituted a "crime against humanity," or, as the French prosecutor François de Menthon called it, with greater accuracy, a "crime against the human status." The notion that aggression is "the supreme international crime" was silently abandoned when a number of men were sentenced to death who had never been convicted of a "conspiracy" against peace.

In justification of the Eichmann trial, it has frequently been maintained that although the greatest crime committed during the last war had been against the Jews, the Jews had been only bystanders in Nuremberg, and the judgment of the Jerusalem court made the point that now, for the first time, the Jewish catastrophe "occupied the central place in the court proceedings, and [that] it was this fact which distinguished this trial from those which preceded it," at Nuremberg and elsewhere. But this is, at best, a half-truth. It was precisely the Jewish catastrophe that prompted the Allies to conceive of a "crime against humanity" in the first place, because, Julius Stone has written, in *Legal Controls of International Conflict* (1954), "the mass murder of the Jews, if they were Germany's own nationals, could only be reached by the humanity count." And what had prevented the Nuremberg Tribunal from doing full justice to this crime was not that its victims were Jews but that the Charter demanded that this crime, which had so little to do with war that its commission actually conflicted with and hindered the war's conduct, was to be tied up with the other crimes. How deeply the Nuremberg judges were aware of the outrage perpetrated against the Jews may perhaps best be gauged by the fact that the only defendant to be condemned to death on a crime-against-humanity charge alone was Julius Streicher, whose specialty had been anti-Semitic obscenities. In this instance, the judges disregarded all other considerations.

What distinguished the trial in Jerusalem from those that preceded it was not that the Jewish people now occupied the central place. In this respect, on the contrary, the trial resembled the postwar trials in Poland and Hungary, in Yugoslavia and Greece, in Soviet Russia and France, in short, in all formerly Nazi-occupied countries. The International Military Tribunal at Nuremberg had been established for war criminals whose crimes could not be localized, all others were delivered to the countries where they had committed their crimes. Only the "major war criminals" had acted without territorial limitations, and Eichmann certainly was not one of them. (This—and not, as was frequently maintained, his disappearance—was the reason he was not accused at Nuremberg; Martin Bormann, for instance, was accused, tried, and condemned to death *in absentia*.) If Eichmann's activities had spread all over occupied Europe, this was so not because he was so important that territorial limits did not apply to him but because it was in the nature of his task, the collection and deportation of all Jews, that he and his men had to roam the continent. It was the territorial dispersion of the Jews that made the crime against them an "international" concern in the limited, legal sense of the Nuremberg Charter. Once the Jews had a territory of their own, the State in Israel, they obviously had as much right to sit in judgment on the crimes committed against their people as the Poles had to judge crimes committed in Poland. All objections raised against the Jerusalem trial on the ground of the principle of territorial jurisdiction were legalistic in the extreme, and although the court spent a number of sessions discussing all these objections, they were actually of no great relevance. There was not the slightest doubt that Jews had been killed *qua* Jews, irrespective of their nationalities at the time, and though it is true that the Nazis killed many Jews who had chosen to deny their ethnic origin, and would perhaps have preferred to be killed as Frenchmen or as Germans, justice could be done even in these cases only if one took the intent and the purpose of the criminals into account.

Equally unfounded, I think, was the even more frequent argument against the possible partiality of Jewish judges—that they, especially if they were citizens of a Jewish State, were judging in their own cause. It is difficult to see how the Jewish judges differed in this respect from their colleagues in any of the other Successor trials, where Polish judges pronounced sentence for crimes against the Polish people, or Czech judges sat in judgment on what had happened in Prague and in Bratislava. (Mr. Hausner, in the last of his articles in the *Saturday Evening Post*, unwittingly added new fuel to this argument: he said that the prosecution realized at once that Eichmann could not be defended by an Israeli lawyer, because there would be a conflict between "professional duties" and "national emotions." Well, this conflict constituted the gist of all the objections to Jewish judges, and Mr. Hausner's argument in their favor, that a judge may hate the crime and yet be fair to the criminal, applies to the defense counsel as well: the lawyer who defends a murderer does not defend murder. The truth of the matter is that pressures outside the courtroom made it inadvisable, to put it mildly, to charge an Israeli citizen with the defense of Eichmann.) Finally, the argument that no Jewish State had existed at the time when the crime was committed is surely so formalistic, so out of tune with reality and with all demands that justice must be done, that we may safely leave it to the learned debates of the experts. In the interest of justice (as distinguished from the concern with certain procedures which, important in its own right, can never be permitted to overrule justice, the law's chief concern), the court, to justify its competence, would have needed to invoke neither the principle of passive personality—that the victims were Jews and that only Israel was entitled to speak in their names—nor the principle of universal jurisdiction, applying to Eichmann because he was *hostis generis humani* the rules that are applicable to piracy. Both theories, discussed at length inside and outside the Jerusalem courtroom, actually blurred the issues and obscured the obvious similarity between the Jerusalem trial and the trials that had preceded it in other countries where special legislation had likewise been enacted to ensure the punishment of the Nazis or their collaborators.

The passive-personality principle, which in Jerusalem was based upon the learned opinion of P. N. Drost, in *Crime of State* (1959), that under certain circumstances "the *forum patriae victimae* may be competent to try the case," unfortunately implies that criminal proceedings are initiated by the government in the name of the victims, who are assumed to have a right to revenge. This was indeed the position of the prosecution, and Mr. Hausner opened his address with the following words: "When I stand before you, judges of Israel, in this court, to accuse Adolf Eichmann, I do not stand alone. Here with me at this moment stand six million prosecutors. But alas, they cannot rise to level the finger of accusation in the direction of the glass dock and cry out *J'accuse* against the man who sits there. . . . Their blood cries to Heaven, but their voice cannot be heard. Thus it falls to me to be their mouthpiece and to deliver the heinous accusation in their name." With such rhetoric the prosecution gave substance to the chief argument against the trial, that it was established not in order to satisfy the demands of justice but to still the victims' desire for and, perhaps, right to vengeance. Criminal proceedings, since they are mandatory and thus initiated even if the victim would prefer to forgive and forget, rest on laws whose "essence"—to quote Telford Taylor, writing in the *New York Times Magazine*— "is that a crime is not committed only against the victim but primarily against the community whose law is violated." The wrongdoer is brought to justice because his act has disturbed and gravely endangered the community as a whole, and not because, as in civil suits, damage has been done to individuals who are entitled to reparation. The reparation effected in criminal cases is of an altogether different nature; it is the body politic itself that stands in need of being "repaired," and it is the general public order that has been thrown out of gear and must be restored, as it were. It is, in other words, the law, not the plaintiff, that must prevail.

Even less justifiable than the prosecution's effort to rest its case on the passive-personality principle was the inclination of the court to claim competence in the name of universal jurisdiction, for it was in flagrant conflict with the conduct of the trial as well as with the law under which Eichmann was tried. The principle of universal jurisdiction, it was said, was applicable because crimes against humanity are similar to the old crime of piracy, and who commits them has become, like the pirate in traditional international law, *hostis humani generis*. Eichmann, however, was accused chiefly of crimes against the Jewish people, and his capture, which the theory of universal jurisdiction was meant to excuse, was certainly not due to his also having committed crimes against humanity but exclusively to his role in the Final Solution of the Jewish problem.

Yet even if Israel had kidnaped Eichmann solely because he was *hostis humani generis* and not because he was *hostis Judaeorum*, it would have been difficult to justify the legality of his arrest. The pirate's exception to the territorial principle— which, in the absence of an international penal code, remains the only valid legal principle—is made not because he is the enemy of all, and hence can be judged by all, but because his crime is committed on the high seas, and the high seas are no man's land. The pirate, moreover, "in defiance of all law, acknowledging obedience to no flag whatsoever" (H. Zeisel,

Britannica Book of the Year, 1962), is, by definition, in business entirely for himself; he is an outlaw because he has chosen to put himself outside all organized communities, and it is for this reason that he has become "the enemy of all alike." Surely, no one will maintain that Eichmann was in business for himself or that he acknowledged obedience to no flag whatsoever. In this respect, the piracy theory served only to dodge one of the fundamental problems posed by crimes of this kind, namely, that they were, and could only be, committed under a criminal *law* and by a criminal *state*.

The analogy between genocide and piracy is not new, and it is therefore of some importance to note that the Genocide Convention, whose resolutions were adopted by the United Nations General Assembly on December 9, 1948, expressly rejected the claim to universal jurisdiction and provided instead that "persons charged with genocide . . . shall be tried by a competent tribunal of the States in the territory of which the act was committed or by such international penal tribunal as may have jurisdiction." In accordance with this Convention, of which Israel was a signatory, the court should have either sought to establish an international tribunal or tried to reformulate the territorial principle in such a way that it applied to Israel. Both alternatives lay definitely within the realm of possibility and within the court's competence. The possibility of establishing an international tribunal was cursorily dismissed by the court for reasons which we shall discuss later, but the reason no meaningful redefinition of the territorial principle was sought— so that the court finally claimed jurisdiction on the ground of all three principles: territorial as well as passive-personality and universal-jurisdiction, as though merely adding together three entirely different legal principles would result in a valid claim— was certainly closely connected with the extreme reluctance of all concerned to break fresh ground and act without precedents. Israel could easily have claimed territorial jurisdiction if she had only explained that "territory," as the law understands it, is a political and a legal concept, and not merely a geographical term. It relates not so much, and not primarily, to a piece of land as to the space between individuals in a group whose members are bound to, and at the same time separated and protected from, each other by all kinds of relationships, based on a common language, religion, a common history, customs, and laws. Such relationships become spatially manifest insofar as they themselves constitute the space wherein the different members of a group relate to and have intercourse with each other. No State of Israel would ever have come into being if the Jewish people had not created and maintained its own specific in-between space throughout the long centuries of dispersion, that is, prior to the seizure of its old territory. The court, however, never rose to the challenge of the unprecedented, not even in regard to the unprecedented nature of the origins of the Israel state, which certainly was closest to its heart and thought. Instead, it buried the proceedings under a flood of precedents—during the sessions of the first week of the trial, to which the first fifty-three sections of the judgment correspond— many of which sounded, at least to the layman's ear, like elaborate sophisms.

The Eichmann trial, then, was in actual fact no more, but also no less, than the last of the numerous Successor trials which followed the Nuremberg Trials. And the indictment quite properly carried in an appendix the official interpretation of the Law of 1950 by Pinhas Rosen, then Minister of Justice, which could not be clearer and less equivocal: "While other peoples passed suitable legislation for the punishment of the Nazis and their collaborators soon after the end of the war, and some even before it was over, the Jewish people . . . had no political authority to bring the Nazi criminals and their collaborators to justice until the establishment of the State." Hence, the Eichmann trial differed from the Successor trials only in one respect—the defendant had not been duly arrested and extradited to Israel; on the contrary, a clear violation of international law had been committed in order to bring him to justice. We mentioned before that only Eichmann's *de facto* statelessness enabled Israel to get away with kidnaping him, and it is understandable that despite the innumerable precedents cited in Jerusalem to justify the act of kidnaping, the only relevant one, the capture of Berthold Jakob, a Leftist German Jewish journalist, in Switzerland by Gestapo agents in 1935, was never mentioned. (None of the other precedents applied, because they invariably concerned a fugitive from justice who was brought back not only to the place of his crimes but to a court that had issued, or could have issued, a valid warrant of arrest—conditions that Israel could not have fulfilled.) In this instance, Israel had indeed violated the territorial principle, whose great significance lies in the fact that the earth is inhabited by many peoples and that these peoples are ruled by many different laws, so that every extension of one territory's law beyond the borders and limitations of its validity will bring it into immediate conflict with the law of another territory.

This, unhappily, was the only almost unprecedented feature in the whole Eichmann trial, and certainly it was the least entitled ever to become a valid precedent. (What are we going to say if tomorrow it occurs to some African state to send its agents into Mississippi and to kidnap one of the leaders of the segregationist movement there? And what are we going to reply if a court in Ghana or the Congo quotes the Eichmann case as a precedent?) Its justification was the unprecedentedness of the crime and the coming into existence of a Jewish State. There were, moreover, important mitigating circumstances in that there hardly existed a true alternative if one indeed wished to bring Eichmann to justice. Argentina had an impressive record for not extraditing Nazi criminals; even if there had been an extradition treaty between Israel and Argentina, an extradition request would almost certainly not have been honored. Nor would it have helped to hand Eichmann over to the Argentine police for extradition to West Germany; for the Bonn government had earlier sought extradition from Argentina of such well-known Nazi criminals as Karl Klingenfuss and Dr. Josef Mengele (the latter implicated in the most horrifying medical experiments at Auschwitz and in charge of the "selection") without any success. In the case of Eichmann, such a request would have been doubly hopeless, since, according to Argentine law, all offenses connected with the last war had fallen under the statute of limitation fifteen years after the end of the war, so that after May 7, 1960, Eichmann could not have been legally extradited anyway. In short, the realm of legality offered no alternative to kidnaping.

Those who are convinced that justice, and nothing else, is the end of law will be inclined to condone the kidnaping act, though not because of precedents but, on the contrary, as a desperate, unprecedented and no-precedent-setting act, necessitated by the unsatisfactory condition of international law. In this perspective, there existed but one real alternative to what Israel had done: instead of capturing Eichmann and flying him to Israel, the Israeli agents could have killed him right then and there, in the streets of Buenos Aires. This course of action was frequently mentioned in the debates on the case and, somewhat oddly, was recommended most fervently by those who were most shocked by the kidnaping. The notion was not without merit, because the facts of the case were beyond dispute, but those who proposed it forgot that he who takes the law into his own hands will render a service to justice only if he is willing to transform the situation in such a way that the law can again operate and his act can, at least posthumously, be validated. Two precedents in the recent past come immediately to mind. There was the case of Shalom Schwartzbard, who in Paris on May 25, 1926, shot and killed Simon Petlyura, former hetman of the Ukrainian armies and responsible for the pogroms during the Russian civil war that claimed about a hundred thousand victims between 1917 and 1920. And there was the case of the Armenian Tehlirian, who, in 1921, in the middle of Berlin, shot to death Talaat Bey, the great killer in the Armenian pogroms of 1915, in which it is estimated that a third (six hundred thousand) of the Armenian population in Turkey was massacred. The point is that neither of these assassins was satisfied with killing "his" criminal, but that both immediately gave themselves up to the police and insisted on being tried. Each used his trial to show the world through court procedure what crimes against his people had been committed and gone unpunished. In the Schwartzbard trial, especially, methods very similar to those in the Eichmann trial were used. There was the same stress on extensive documentation of the crimes, but that time it was prepared for the defense (by the Comité des Délégations Juives, under the chairmanship of the late Dr. Leo Motzkin, which needed a year and a half to collect the material and then published it in *Les Pogromes en Ukraine sous les gouvernements ukrainiens 1917-1920*, 1927), just as that time it was the accused and his lawyer who spoke in the name of the victims, and who, incidentally, even then raised the point about the Jews "who had never defended themselves." (See the *plaidoyer* of Henri Torrès in his book *Le Procès des Pogromes*, 1928). Both men were acquitted, and in both cases it was felt that their gesture "signified that their race had finally decided to defend itself, to leave behind its moral abdication, to overcome its resignation in the face of insults," as Georges Suarez admiringly put it in the case of Shalom Schwartzbard.

The advantages of this solution to the problem of legalities that stand in the way of justice are obvious. The trial, it is true, is again a "show" trial, and even a show, but its "hero," the one in the center of the play, on whom all eyes are fastened, is now the true hero, while at the same time the trial character of the proceedings is safeguarded, because it is not "a spectacle with prearranged results" but contains that element of "irreducible risk" which, according to Kirchheimer, is an indispensable factor in all criminal trials. Also, the *J'accuse*, so indispensable from the viewpoint of the victim, sounds, of course, much more convincing in the mouth of a man who has been forced to take the law into his own hands than in the voice of a government-appointed agent who risks nothing. And yet—quite apart from practical considerations, such as that Buenos Aires in the sixties hardly offers either the same guarantees or the same publicity for the defendant that Paris and Berlin offered in the twenties—it is more than doubtful that this solution would have been justifiable in Eichmann's case, and it is obvious that it would have been altogether unjustifiable if carried out by government agents. The point in favor of Schwartzbard and Tehlirian was that each was a member of an ethnic group that did not possess its own state and legal system, that there was no tribunal in the world to which either group could have brought its victims. Schwartzbard, who died in 1938, more than ten years before the proclamation of the Jewish State, was not a Zionist, and not a nationalist of any sort; but there is no doubt that he would have welcomed the State of Israel enthusiastically, for no other reason than that it would have provided a tribunal for crimes that had so often gone unpunished. His sense of justice would have been satisfied. And when we read the letter he addressed from his prison in Paris to his brothers and sisters in Odessa—*"Faites savoir dans les villes et dans les villages de Balta, Proskouro, Tzcherkass, Ouman, Jitomir . . . , portez-y le message édifiant: la colère juive a tiré sa vengeance! Le sang de l'assassin Petlioura, qui a jailli dans la ville mondiale, à Paris, . . . rappellera le crime féroce . . . commis envers le pauvre et abandonné peuple juif"*—we recognize immediately not, perhaps, the language that Mr. Hausner actually spoke during the trial (Shalom Schwartz-bard's language was infinitely more dignified and more moving) but certainly the sentiments and the state of mind of Jews all over the world to which it was bound to appeal.

I have insisted on the similarities between the Schwartzbard trial in 1927 in Paris and the Eichmann trial in 1961 in Jerusalem because they demonstrate how little Israel, like the Jewish people in general, was prepared to recognize, in the crimes that Eichmann was accused of, an unprecedented crime, and precisely how difficult such a recognition must have been for the Jewish people. In the eyes of the Jews, thinking exclusively in terms of their own history, the catastrophe that had befallen them under Hitler, in which a third of the people perished, appeared not as the most recent of crimes, the unprecedented crime of genocide, but, on the contrary, as the oldest crime they knew and remembered. This misunderstanding, almost inevitable if we consider not only the facts of Jewish history but also, and more important, the current Jewish historical self-understanding, is actually at the root of all the failures and shortcomings of the Jerusalem trial. None of the participants ever arrived at a clear understanding of the actual horror of Auschwitz, which is of a different nature from all the atrocities of the past, because it appeared to prosecution and judges alike as not much more than the most horrible pogrom in Jewish history. They therefore believed that a direct line existed from the early anti-Semitism of the Nazi Party to the Nuremberg Laws and from there to the expulsion of Jews from the Reich and, finally, to the gas chambers. Politically and legally, however, these were "crimes" different not only in degree of seriousness but in essence.

The Nuremberg Laws of 1935 legalized the discrimination practiced before that by the German majority against the Jewish minority. According to international law, it was the privilege of the sovereign German nation to declare to be a national minority whatever part of its population it saw fit, as long as its minority laws conformed to the rights and guarantees established by internationally recognized minority treaties and agreements. International Jewish organizations therefore promptly tried to obtain for this newest minority the same rights and guarantees that minorities in Eastern and Southeastern Europe had been granted at Geneva. But even though this protection was not granted, the Nuremberg Laws were generally recognized by other nations as part of German law, so that it was impossible for a German national to enter into a "mixed marriage" in Holland, for instance. The crime of the Nuremberg Laws was a national crime; it violated national, constitutional rights and liberties, but it was of no concern to the comity of nations. "Enforced emigration," however, or expulsion, which became official policy after 1938, did concern the international community, for the simple reason that those who were expelled appeared at the frontiers of other countries, which were forced either to accept the uninvited guests or to smuggle them into another country, equally unwilling to accept them. Expulsion of nationals, in other words, is already an offense against humanity, if by "humanity" we understand no more than the comity of nations. Neither the national crime of legalized discrimination, which amounted to persecution by law, nor the international crime of expulsion was unprecedented, even in the modern age. Legalized discrimination had been practiced by all Balkan countries, and expulsion on a mass scale had occurred after many revolutions. It was when the Nazi regime declared that the German people not only were unwilling to have any Jews in Germany but wished to make the entire Jewish people disappear from the face of the earth that the new crime, the crime against humanity—in the sense of a crime "against the human status," or against the very nature of mankind—appeared. Expulsion and genocide, though both are international offenses, must remain distinct; the former is an offense against fellow-nations, whereas the latter is an attack upon human diversity as such, that is, upon a characteristic of the "human status" without which the very words "mankind" or "humanity" would be devoid of meaning.

Had the court in Jerusalem understood that there were distinctions between discrimination, expulsion, and genocide, it would immediately have become clear that the supreme crime it was confronted with, the physical extermination of the Jewish people, was a crime against humanity, perpetrated upon the body of the Jewish people, and that only the choice of victims, not the nature of the crime, could be derived from the long history of Jew-hatred and anti-Semitism. Insofar as the victims were Jews, it was right and proper that a Jewish court should sit in judgment; but insofar as the crime was a crime against humanity, it needed an international tribunal to do justice to it. (The failure of the court to draw this distinction was surprising, because it had actually been made before by the former Israeli Minister of Justice, Mr. Rosen, who in 1950 had insisted on "a distinction between this bill [for crimes against the Jewish people] and the Law for the Prevention and Punishment of Genocide," which was discussed but not passed by the Israeli Parliament. Obviously, the court felt it had no right to overstep the limits of municipal law, so that genocide, not being covered by an Israeli law, could not properly enter into its considerations.) Among the numerous and highly qualified voices that raised objections to the court in Jerusalem and were in favor of an international tribunal, only one, that of Karl Jaspers, stated clearly and unequivocally—in a radio interview held before the trial began and later published in *Der Monat*—that "the crime against the Jews was also a crime against mankind," and that "consequently the verdict can be handed down only by a court of justice representing all mankind." Jaspers proposed that the court in Jerusalem, after hearing the factual evidence, "waive" the right to pass sentence, declaring itself "incompetent" to do so, because the legal nature of the crime in question was still open to dispute, as was the subsequent question of who would be competent to pass sentence on a crime which had been committed on government orders. Jaspers stated further that one thing alone was certain: "This crime is both more and less than common murder," and though it was not a "war crime," either, there was no doubt that "mankind would certainly be destroyed if states were permitted to perpetrate such crimes."

Jaspers' proposal, which no one in Israel even bothered to discuss, would, in this form, presumably have been impracticable from a purely technical point of view. The question of a court's jurisdiction must be decided before the trial begins; and once a court has been declared competent, it must also pass judgment. However, these purely formalistic objections could easily have been met if Jaspers had called not upon the court, but rather upon the state of Israel to waive its right to carry out the sentence once it had been handed down, in view of the unprecedented nature of the court's findings. Israel might then have had recourse to the United Nations and demonstrated, with all the evidence at hand, that the need for an international criminal court was imperative, in view of these new crimes committed against mankind as a whole. It would then have been in Israel's power to make trouble, to "create a wholesome disturbance," by asking again and again just what it should do with this man whom it was holding prisoner; constant repetition would have impressed on worldwide public opinion the need for a permanent international criminal court. Only by creating, in this way, an "embarrassing situation" of concern to the representatives of all nations would it be possible to prevent "mankind from setting its mind at ease" and "massacre of the Jews . . . from becoming a model for crimes to come, perhaps the small-scale and quite paltry example of future genocide." The very monstrousness of the events is "minimized" before a tribunal that represents one nation only.

This argument in favor of an international tribunal was unfortunately confused with other proposals based on different and considerably less weighty considerations. Many friends of Israel, both Jews and non-Jews, feared that the trial would harm Israel's prestige and give rise to a reaction against Jews the world over. It was thought that Jews did not have the right to appear as judges in their own case, but could act only as accusers; Israel should therefore hold Eichmann prisoner until a special tribunal could be created by the United Nations to judge him. Quite apart from the fact that Israel, in the proceedings against Eichmann, was doing no more than what all the countries which had been occupied by Germany had long since done, and that justice was at stake here, not the prestige of Israel or of the Jewish people, all these proposals had one flaw in common: they could too easily be countered by Israel. They were indeed quite unrealistic in view of the fact that the U.N. General Assembly had "twice rejected proposals to consider the establishment of a permanent international criminal court" (*A.D.L. Bulletin*). But another, more practical proposition, which usually is not mentioned precisely because it *was* feasible, was made by Dr. Nahum Goldmann, president of the World Jewish Congress. Goldmann called upon Ben-Gurion to set up an international court in Jerusalem, with judges from each of the countries that had suffered under Nazi occupation. This would not have been enough; it would have been only an enlargement of the Successor trials, and the chief impairment of justice, that it was being rendered in the court of the victors, would not have been cured. But it would have been a practical step in the right direction.

Israel, as may be remembered, reacted against all these proposals with great violence. And while it is true, as has been pointed out by Yosal Rogat (in *The Eichmann Trial and the Rule of Law*, published by the Center for the Study of Democratic Institutions, Santa Barbara, California, 1962), that Ben-Gurion always "seemed to misunderstand completely when asked, 'Why should he not be tried before an international court?,' " it is also true that those who asked the question did not understand that for Israel the only unprecedented feature of the trial was that, for the first time (since the year 70, when Jerusalem was destroyed by the Romans), Jews were able to sit in judgment on crimes committed against their own people, that, for the first time, they did not need to appeal to others for protection and justice, or fall back upon the compromised phraseology of the rights of man— rights which, as no one knew better than they, were claimed only by people who were too weak to defend their "rights of Englishmen" and to enforce their own laws. (The very fact that Israel had her own law under which such a trial could be held had been called, long before the Eichmann trial, an expression of "a revolutionary transformation that has taken place in the

272 Eichmann in Jerusalem

political position of the Jewish people"—by Mr. Rosen on the occasion of the First Reading of the Law of 1950 in the Knesset.) It was against the background of these very vivid experiences and aspirations that Ben-Gurion said: "Israel does not need the protection of an International Court."

Moreover, the argument that the crime against the Jewish people was first of all a crime against mankind, upon which the valid proposals for an international tribunal rested, stood in flagrant contradiction to the law under which Eichmann was tried. Hence, those who proposed that Israel give up her prisoner should have gone one step further and declared: The Nazis and Nazi Collaborators (Punishment) Law of 1950 is wrong, it is in contradiction to what actually happened, it does not cover the facts. And this would indeed have been quite true. For just as a murderer is prosecuted because he has violated the law of the community, and not because he has deprived the Smith family of its husband, father, and breadwinner, so these modern, state-employed mass murderers must be prosecuted because they violated the order of mankind, and not because they killed millions of people. Nothing is more pernicious to an understanding of these new crimes, or stands more in the way of the emergence of an international penal code that could take care of them, than the common illusion that the crime of murder and the crime of genocide are essentially the same, and that the latter therefore is "no new crime properly speaking." The point of the latter is that an altogether different order is broken and an altogether different community is violated. And, indeed, it was because Ben-Gurion knew quite well that the whole discussion actually concerned the validity of the Israeli law that he finally reacted nastily, and not just with violence, against the critics of Israeli procedures: Whatever these "so-called experts" had to say, their arguments were "sophisms," inspired either by anti-Semitism, or, in the case of Jews, by inferiority complexes. "Let the world understand: We shall not give up our prisoner."

It is only fair to say that this was by no means the tone in which the trial was conducted in Jerusalem. But I think it is safe to predict that this last of the Successor trials will no more, and perhaps even less than its predecessors, serve as a valid precedent for future trials of such crimes. This might be of little import in view of the fact that its main purpose—to prosecute and to defend, to judge and to punish Adolf Eichmann—was achieved, if it were not for the rather uncomfortable but hardly deniable possibility that similar crimes may be committed in the future. The reasons for this sinister potentiality are general as well as particular. It is in the very nature of things human that every act that has once made its appearance and has been recorded in the history of mankind stays with mankind as a potentiality long after its actuality has become a thing of the past. No punishment has ever possessed enough power of deterrence to prevent the commission of crimes. On the contrary, whatever the punishment, once a specific crime has appeared for the first time, its reappearance is more likely than its initial emergence could ever have been. The particular reasons that speak for the possibility of a repetition of the crimes committed by the Nazis are even more plausible. The frightening coincidence of the modern population explosion with the discovery of technical devices that, through automation, will make large sections of the population "superfluous" even in terms of labor, and that, through nuclear energy, make it possible to deal with this twofold threat by the use of instruments beside which Hitler's gassing installations look like an evil child's fumbling toys, should be enough to make us tremble.

It is essentially for this reason: that the unprecedented, once it has appeared, may become a precedent for the future, that all trials touching upon "crimes against humanity" must be judged according to a standard that is today still an "ideal." If genocide is an actual possibility of the future, then no people on earth—least of all, of course, the Jewish people, in Israel or elsewhere—can feel reasonably sure of its continued existence without the help and the protection of international law. Success or failure in dealing with the hitherto unprecedented can lie only in the extent to which this dealing may serve as a valid precedent on the road to international penal law. And this demand, addressed to the judges in such trials, does not overshoot the mark and ask for more than can reasonably be expected. International law, Justice Jackson pointed out at Nuremberg, "is an outgrowth of treaties and agreements between nations and of accepted customs. Yet every custom has its origin in some single act. . . . Our own day has the right to institute customs and to conclude agreements that will themselves become sources of a newer and strengthened international law." What Justice Jackson failed to point out is that, in consequence of this yet unfinished nature of international law, it has become the task of ordinary trial judges to render justice without the help of, or beyond the limitation set upon them through, positive, posited laws. For the judge, this may be a predicament, and he is only too likely to protest that the "single act" demanded of him is not his to perform but is the business of the legislator.

And, indeed, before we come to any conclusion about the success or failure of the Jerusalem court, we must stress the judges' firm belief that they had no right to become legislators, that they had to conduct their business within the limits of Israeli law, on the one side, and of accepted legal opinion, on the other. It must be admitted furthermore that their failures were neither in kind nor in degree greater than the failures of the Nuremberg Trials or the Successor trials in other European countries. On the contrary, part of the failure of the Jerusalem court was due to its all too eager adherence to the Nuremberg precedent wherever possible.

In sum, the failure of the Jerusalem court consisted in its not coming to grips with three fundamental issues, all of which have been sufficiently well known and widely discussed since the establishment of the Nuremberg Tribunal: the problem of impaired justice in the court of the victors; a valid definition of the "crime against humanity"; and a clear recognition of the new criminal who commits this crime.

As to the first of these, justice was more seriously impaired in Jerusalem than it was at Nuremberg, because the court did not admit witnesses for the defense. In terms of the traditional requirements for fair and due process of law, this was the most serious flaw in the Jerusalem proceedings. Moreover, while judgment in the court of the victors was perhaps inevitable at the close of the war (to Justice Jackson's argument in Nuremberg: "Either the victors must judge the vanquished or we must leave the defeated to judge themselves," should be added the understandable feeling on the part of the Allies that they "who had risked everything could not admit neutrals" [Vabres]), it was not the same sixteen years later, and under circumstances in which the argument against the admission of neutral countries did not make sense.

As to the second issue, the findings of the Jerusalem court were incomparably better than those at Nuremberg. I have mentioned before the Nuremberg Charter's definition of "crimes against humanity" as "inhuman acts," which were translated into German as *Verbrechen gegen die Menschlichkeit*—as though the Nazis had simply been lacking in human kindness, certainly the understatement of the century. To be sure, had the conduct of the Jerusalem trial depended entirely upon the prosecution, the basic misunderstanding would have been even worse than at Nuremberg. But the judgment refused to let the basic character of the crime be swallowed up in a flood of atrocities, and it did not fall into the trap of equating this crime with ordinary war crimes. What had been mentioned at Nuremberg only occasionally and, as it were, marginally—that "the evidence shows that . . . the mass murders and cruelties were not committed solely for the purpose of stamping out opposition" but were "part of a plan to get rid of whole native populations"—was in the center of the Jerusalem proceedings, for the obvious reason that Eichmann stood accused of a crime against the Jewish people, a crime that could not be explained by any utilitarian purpose; Jews had been murdered all over Europe, not only in the East, and their annihilation was not due to any desire to gain territory that "could be used for colonization by Germans." It was the great advantage of a trial centered on the crime against the Jewish people that not only did the difference between war crimes, such as shooting of partisans and killing of hostages, and "inhuman acts," such as "expulsion and annihilation" of native populations to permit colonization by an invader, emerge with sufficient clarity to become part of a future international penal code, but also that the difference between "inhuman acts" (which were undertaken for some known, though criminal, purpose, such as expansion through colonization) and the "crime against humanity," whose intent and purpose were unprecedented, was clarified. At no point, however, either in the proceedings or in the judgment, did the Jerusalem trial ever mention even the possibility that extermination of whole ethnic groups—the Jews, or the Poles, or the

Gypsies—might be more than a crime against the Jewish or the Polish or the Gypsy people, that the international order, and mankind in its entirety, might have been grievously hurt and endangered.

Closely connected with this failure was the conspicuous helplessness the judges experienced when they were confronted with the task they could least escape, the task of understanding the criminal whom they had come to judge. Clearly, it was not enough that they did not follow the prosecution in its obviously mistaken description of the accused as a "perverted sadist," nor would it have been enough if they had gone one step further and shown the inconsistency of the case for the prosecution, in which Mr. Hausner wanted to try the most abnormal monster the world had ever seen and, at the same time, try in him "many like him," even the "whole Nazi movement and anti-Semitism at large." They knew, of course, that it would have been very comforting indeed to believe that Eichmann was a monster, even though if he had been Israel's case against him would have collapsed or, at the very least, lost all interest. Surely, one can hardly call upon the whole world and gather correspondents from the four corners of the earth in order to display Bluebeard in the dock. The trouble with Eichmann was precisely that so many were like him, and that the many were neither perverted nor sadistic, that they were, and still are, terribly and terrifyingly normal. From the viewpoint of our legal institutions and of our moral standards of judgment, this normality was much more terrifying than all the atrocities put together, for it implied—as had been said at Nuremberg over and over again by the defendants and their counsels—that this new type of criminal, who is in actual fact *hostis generis humani*, commits his crimes under circumstances that make it well-nigh impossible for him to know or to feel that he is doing wrong. In this respect, the evidence in the Eichmann case was even more convincing than the evidence presented in the trial of the major war criminals, whose pleas of a clear conscience could be dismissed more easily because they combined with the argument of obedience to "superior orders" various boasts about occasional disobedience. But although the bad faith of the defendants was manifest, the only ground on which guilty conscience could actually be proved was the fact that the Nazis, and especially the criminal organizations to which Eichmann belonged, had been so very busy destroying the evidence of their crimes during the last months of the war. And this ground was rather shaky. It proved no more than recognition that the law of mass murder, because of its novelty, was not yet accepted by other nations; or, in the language of the Nazis, that they had lost their fight to "liberate" mankind from the "rule of subhumans," especially from the domination of the Elders of Zion; or, in ordinary language, it proved no more than the admission of defeat. Would any one of them have suffered from a guilty conscience if they had won?

Foremost among the larger issues at stake in the Eichmann trial was the assumption current in all modern legal systems that intent to do wrong is necessary for the commission of a crime. On nothing, perhaps, has civilized jurisprudence prided itself more than on this taking into account of the subjective factor. Where this intent is absent, where, for whatever reasons, even reasons of moral insanity, the ability to distinguish between right and wrong is impaired, we feel no crime has been committed. We refuse, and consider as barbaric, the propositions "that a great crime offends nature, so that the very earth cries out for vengeance; that evil violates a natural harmony which only retribution can restore; that a wronged collectivity owes a duty to the moral order to punish the criminal" (Yosal Rogat). And yet I think it is undeniable that it was precisely on the ground of these long-forgotten propositions that Eichmann was brought to justice to begin with, and that they were, in fact, the supreme justification for the death penalty. Because he had been implicated and had played a central role in an enterprise whose open purpose was to eliminate forever certain "races" from the surface of the earth, he had to be eliminated. And if it is true that "justice must not only be done but must be seen to be done," then the justice of what was done in Jerusalem would have emerged to be seen by all if the judges had dared to address their defendant in something like the following terms:

"You admitted that the crime committed against the Jewish people during the war was the greatest crime in recorded history,

and you admitted your role in it. But you said you had never acted
from base motives, that you had never had any inclination to
kill anybody, that you had never hated Jews, and still that you
could not have acted otherwise and that you did not feel guilty.
We find this difficult, though not altogether impossible, to believe; there is some, though not very much, evidence against
you in this matter of motivation and conscience that could be
proved beyond reasonable doubt. You also said that your role
in the Final Solution was an accident and that almost anybody
could have taken your place, so that potentially almost all Germans are equally guilty. What you meant to say was that
where all, or almost all, are guilty, nobody is. This is an indeed
quite common conclusion, but one we are not willing to grant
you. And if you don't understand our objection, we would recommend to your attention the story of Sodom and Gomorrah,
two neighboring cities in the Bible, which were destroyed by
fire from Heaven because all the people in them had become
equally guilty. This, incidentally, has nothing to do with the
newfangled notion of 'collective guilt,' according to which
people supposedly are guilty of, or feel guilty about, things done
in their name but not by them—things in which they did not participate and from which they did not profit. In other words, guilt
and innocence before the law are of an objective nature, and even
if eighty million Germans had done as you did, this would not
have been an excuse for you.

"Luckily, we don't have to go that far. You yourself claimed
not the actuality but only the potentiality of equal guilt on the
part of all who lived in a state whose main political purpose had
become the commission of unheard-of crimes. And no matter
through what accidents of exterior or interior circumstances you
were pushed onto the road of becoming a criminal, there is an
abyss between the actuality of what you did and the potentiality
of what others might have done. We are concerned here only
with what you did, and not with the possible noncriminal nature
of your inner life and of your motives or with the criminal
potentialities of those around you. You told your story in terms
of a hard-luck story, and, knowing the circumstances, we are,
up to a point, willing to grant you that under more favorable
circumstances it is highly unlikely that you would ever have

come before us or before any other criminal court. Let us assume, for the sake of argument, that it was nothing more than misfortune that made you a willing instrument in the organization of mass murder; there still remains the fact that you have carried out, and therefore actively supported, a policy of mass murder. For politics is not like the nursery; in politics obedience and support are the same. And just as you supported and carried out a policy of not wanting to share the earth with the Jewish people and the people of a number of other nations—as though you and your superiors had any right to determine who should and who should not inhabit the world—we find that no one, that is, no member of the human race, can be expected to want to share the earth with you. This is the reason, and the only reason, you must hang."

Postscript

This book contains a *trial report*, and its main source is the transcript of the trial proceedings which was distributed to the press in Jerusalem. Save for the opening speech of the prosecution, and the general plea of the defense, the record of the trial has not been published and is not easily accessible. The language of the courtroom was Hebrew; the materials handed to the press were stated to be "an unedited and unrevised transcript of the simultaneous translation" that "should not be regarded as stylistically perfect or devoid of linguistic errors." I have used the English version throughout except in those instances when the proceedings were conducted in German; when the German transcript contained the original wording I felt free to use my own translation.

Except for the prosecutor's introductory speech and for the final verdict, the translations of which were prepared outside the courtroom, independently of the simultaneous translation, none of these records can be regarded as absolutely reliable. The only authoritative version is the official record in Hebrew, which I have not used. Nevertheless, all this material was officially given to the reporters for their use, and, so far as I know, no significant discrepancies between the official Hebrew record and the translation have yet been pointed out. The German simultaneous translation was very poor, but it may be assumed that the English and French translations are trustworthy.

No such doubts about the dependability of the sources arise in connection with the following courtroom materials, which—with one exception—were also given to the press by the Jerusalem authorities:

1) The transcript in German of Eichmann's interrogation by the police, recorded on tape, then typed, and the typescript

presented to Eichmann, who corrected it in his own hand. Along with the transcript of the courtroom proceedings, this is the most important of the documents.

2) The documents submitted by the prosecution, and the "legal material" made available by the prosecution.

3) The sixteen sworn affidavits by witnesses originally called by the defense, although part of their testimony was subsequently used by the prosecution. These witnesses were: Erich von dem Bach-Zelewski, Richard Baer, Kurt Becher, Horst Grell, Dr. Wilhelm Höttl, Walter Huppenkothen, Hans Jüttner, Herbert Kappler, Hermann Krumey, Franz Novak, Alfred Josef Slawik, Dr. Max Merten, Professor Alfred Six, Dr. Eberhard von Thadden, Dr. Edmund Veesenmayer, Otto Winkelmann.

4) Finally, I also had at my disposal a manuscript of seventy typewritten pages written by Eichmann himself. It was submitted as evidence by the prosecution and accepted by the court, but not made available to the press. Its heading reads in translation: "Re: My comments on the matter of 'Jewish questions and measures of the National Socialist Government of the German Reich with regard to solution of this matter during the years 1933 to 1945.' " This manuscript contains notes made by Eichmann in Argentina in preparation for the Sassen interview (see Bibliography).

The Bibliography lists only the material I actually used, not the innumerable books, articles, and newspaper stories I read and collected during the two years between Eichmann's kidnaping and his execution. I regret this incompleteness only in regard to the reports of correspondents in the German, Swiss, French, English, and American press, since these were often on a far higher level than the more pretentious treatments of the subject in books and magazines, but it would have been a disproportionately large task to fill this gap. I have therefore contented myself with adding to the Bibliography of this revised edition a selected number of books and magazine articles which appeared after the publication of my book, if they contained more than a rehashed version of the case for the prosecution. Among them are two accounts of the trial that often come to conclusions astonishingly similar to my own, and a study of the prominent figures in the Third Reich, which I have now added

to my sources for background material. These are Robert
Pendorf's *Mörder und Ermordete. Eichmann und die Judenpolitik des Dritten Reiches,* which also takes into account the
role of the Jewish Councils in the Final Solution; *Strafsache
40/61* by the Dutch correspondent Harry Mulisch (I used the
German translation), who is almost the only writer on the subject
to put the person of the defendant at the center of his report
and whose evaluation of Eichmann coincides with my own on
some essential points; and finally the excellent, recently published portraits of leading Nazis by T. C. Fest in his *Das
Gesicht des Dritten Reiches*; Fest is very knowledgeable and
his judgments are on a remarkably high level.

The problems faced by the writer of a report may best be
compared with those attendant on the writing of a historical
monograph. In either case, the nature of the work requires a
deliberate distinction between the use of primary and secondary
material. Primary sources only may be used in the treatment
of the special subject—in this case the trial itself—while secondary material is drawn upon for everything that constitutes the
historical background. Thus, even the documents I have quoted
were with very few exceptions presented in evidence at the
trial (in which case they constituted my primary sources) or
are drawn from authoritative books dealing with the period in
question. As can be seen from the text, I have used Gerald
Reitlinger's *The Final Solution,* and I have relied even more
on Raul Hilberg's *The Destruction of the European Jews,* which
appeared after the trial and constitutes the most exhaustive and
the most soundly documented account of the Third Reich's Jewish
policies.

Even before its publication, this book became both the center
of a controversy and the object of an organized campaign. It
is only natural that the campaign, conducted with all the well-
known means of image-making and opinion-manipulation, got
much more attention than the controversy, so that the latter was
somehow swallowed up by and drowned in the artificial noise
of the former. This became especially clear when a strange
mixture of the two, in almost identical phraseology—as though
the pieces written against the book (and more frequently against

its author) came "out of a mimeographing machine" (Mary McCarthy)—was carried from America to England and then to Europe, where the book was not yet even available. And this was possible because the clamor centered on the "image" of a book which was never written, and touched upon subjects that often had not only not been mentioned by me but had never occurred to me before.

The debate—if that is what it was—was by no means devoid of interest. Manipulations of opinion, insofar as they are inspired by well-defined interests, have limited goals; their effect, however, if they happen to touch upon an issue of authentic concern, is no longer subject to their control and may easily produce consequences they never foresaw or intended. It now appeared that the era of the Hitler regime, with its gigantic, unprecedented crimes, constituted an "unmastered past" not only for the German people or for the Jews all over the world, but for the rest of the world, which had not forgotten this great catastrophe in the heart of Europe either, and had also been unable to come to terms with it. Moreover—and this was perhaps even less expected—general moral questions, with all their intricacies and modern complexities, which I would never have suspected would haunt men's minds today and weigh heavily on their hearts, stood suddenly in the foreground of public concern.

The controversy began by calling attention to the conduct of the Jewish people during the years of the Final Solution, thus following up the question, first raised by the Israeli prosecutor, of whether the Jews could or should have defended themselves. I had dismissed that question as silly and cruel, since it testified to a fatal ignorance of the conditions at the time. It has now been discussed to exhaustion, and the most amazing conclusions have been drawn. The well-known historico-sociological construct of a "ghetto mentality" (which in Israel has taken its place in history textbooks and in this country has been espoused chiefly by the psychologist Bruno Bettelheim— against the furious protest of official American Judaism) has been repeatedly dragged in to explain behavior which was not at all confined to the Jewish people and which therefore cannot be explained by specifically Jewish factors. The suggestions proliferated until someone who evidently found the whole discussion too dull had the brilliant idea of evoking Freudian theories and attributing to the whole Jewish people a "death wish"—unconscious, of course. This was the unexpected conclusion certain reviewers chose to draw from the "image" of a book, created by certain interest groups, in which I allegedly had claimed that the Jews had murdered themselves. And why had I told such a monstrously implausible lie? Out of "self-hatred," of course.

Since the role of the Jewish leadership had come up at the trial, and since I had reported and commented on it, it was inevitable that it too should be discussed. This, in my opinion, is a serious question, but the debate has contributed little to its clarification. As can be seen from the recent trial in Israel at which a certain Hirsch Birnblat, a former chief of the Jewish police in a Polish town and now a conductor at the Israeli Opera, first was sentenced by a district court to five years' imprisonment, and then was exonerated by the Supreme Court in Jerusalem, whose unanimous opinion indirectly exonerated the Jewish Councils in general, the Jewish Establishment is bitterly divided on this issue. In the debate, however, the most vocal participants were those who either identified the Jewish people with its leadership—in striking contrast to the clear distinction made in almost all the reports of survivors, which may be summed up in the words of a former inmate of Theresienstadt: "The Jewish people as a whole behaved magnificently. Only the leadership failed"—or justified the Jewish functionaries by citing all the commendable services they had rendered before the war, and above all before the era of the Final Solution, as though there were no difference between helping Jews to emigrate and helping the Nazis to deport them.

While these issues had indeed some connection with this book, although they were inflated out of all proportion, there were others which had no relation to it whatsoever. There was, for instance, a hot discussion of the German resistance movement from the beginning of the Hitler regime on, which I naturally did not discuss, since the question of Eichmann's conscience, and that of the situation around him, relates only to the period of the war and the Final Solution. But there were more fantastic items. Quite a number of people began to debate the question of whether the victims of persecution may not always be "uglier" than their murderers; or whether anyone who was not present is entitled "to sit in judgment" over the past; or whether the defendant or the victim holds the center of the stage in a trial. On the latter point, some went so far as to assert not only that I was wrong in being interested in what kind of person Eichmann was, but that he should not have been allowed to speak at all—that is, presumably, that the trial should have been conducted without any defense.

As is frequently the case in discussions that are conducted with a great show of emotion, the down-to-earth interests of certain groups, whose excitement is entirely concerned with factual matters and who therefore try to distort the facts, become quickly and inextricably involved with the untrammeled inspirations of intellectuals who, on the contrary, are not in the least interested in facts but treat them merely as a springboard for "ideas." But even in these sham battles, there could often be detected a certain seriousness, a degree of authentic concern, and this even in the contributions by people who boasted that they had not read the book and promised that they never would read it.

Compared with these debates, which wandered so far afield, the book itself dealt with a sadly limited subject. The report of a trial can discuss only the matters which were treated in the course of the trial, or which in the interests of justice should have been treated. If the general situation of a country in which the trial takes place happens to be important to the conduct of the trial, it too must be taken into account. This book, then, does not deal with the history of the greatest disaster that ever befell the Jewish people, nor is it an account of totalitarianism, or a history of the German people in the time of the Third Reich, nor is it, finally and least of all, a theoretical treatise on the nature of evil. The focus of every trial is upon the person of the defendant, a man of flesh and blood with an individual history, with an always unique set of qualities, peculiarities, behavior patterns, and circumstances. All the things that go beyond that, such as the history of the Jewish people in the dispersion, and of anti-Semitism, or the conduct of the German people and other peoples, or the ideologies of the time and the governmental apparatus of the Third Reich, affect the trial only insofar as they form the background and the conditions under which the defendant committed his acts. All the things that the defendant did not come into contact with, or that did not influence him, must be omitted from the proceedings of the trial and consequently from the report on it.

It may be argued that all the general questions we involuntarily raise as soon as we begin to speak of these matters—why did it have to be the Germans? why did it have to be the Jews? what is the nature of totalitarian rule?—are far more important than the question of the kind of crime for which a man is being tried, and the nature of the defendant upon whom justice must be pronounced; more important, too, than the question of how well our present system of justice is capable of dealing with this special type of crime and criminal it has had repeatedly to cope with since the Second World War. It can be held that the issue is no longer a particular human being, a single distinct individual in the dock, but rather the German people in general, or anti-Semitism in all its forms, or the whole of modern history, or the nature of man and original sin—so that ultimately the entire human race sits invisibly beside the defendant in the dock. All this has often been argued, and especially by those who will not rest until they have discovered an "Eichmann in every one of us." If the defendant is taken as a symbol and the trial as a pretext to bring up matters which are apparently more interesting than the guilt or innocence of one person, then consistency demands that we bow to the assertion made by Eichmann and his lawyer: that he was brought to book because a scapegoat was needed, not only for the German Federal Republic, but also for the events as a whole and for what made them possible—that is, for anti-Semitism and totalitarian government as well as for the human race and original sin.

I need scarcely say that I would never have gone to Jerusalem if I had shared these views. I held and hold the opinion that this trial had to take place in the interests of justice and nothing else. I also think the judges were quite right when they stressed in their verdict that "the State of Israel was established and

recognized as the State of the Jews," and therefore had jurisdiction over a crime committed against the Jewish people; and in
view of the current confusion in legal circles about the meaning
and usefulness of punishment, I was glad that the judgment
quoted Grotius, who, for his part, citing an older author,
explained that punishment is necessary "to defend the honor or
the authority of him who was hurt by the offence so that the
failure to punish may not cause his degradation."

There is of course no doubt that the defendant and the
nature of his acts as well as the trial itself raise problems of a
general nature which go far beyond the matters considered
in Jerusalem. I have attempted to go into some of these problems in the Epilogue, which ceases to be simple reporting. I
would not have been surprised if people had found my treatment inadequate, and I would have welcomed a discussion of
the general significance of the entire body of facts, which could
have been all the more meaningful the more directly it referred
to the concrete events. I also can well imagine that an authentic
controversy might have arisen over the subtitle of the book;
for when I speak of the banality of evil, I do so only on
the strictly factual level, pointing to a phenomenon which
stared one in the face at the trial. Eichmann was not Iago and
not Macbeth, and nothing would have been farther from his
mind than to determine with Richard III "to prove a villain."
Except for an extraordinary diligence in looking out for his
personal advancement, he had no motives at all. And this
diligence in itself was in no way criminal; he certainly would
never have murdered his superior in order to inherit his post.
He *merely*, to put the matter colloquially, *never realized what
he was doing*. It was precisely this lack of imagination which
enabled him to sit for months on end facing a German Jew
who was conducting the police interrogation, pouring out his
heart to the man and explaining again and again how it was that
he reached only the rank of lieutenant colonel in the S.S. and
that it had not been his fault that he was not promoted. In
principle he knew quite well what it was all about, and in his
final statement to the court he spoke of the "revaluation of
values prescribed by the [Nazi] government." He was not
stupid. It was sheer thoughtlessness—something by no means

identical with stupidity—that predisposed him to become one
of the greatest criminals of that period. And if this is "banal"
and even funny, if with the best will in the world one cannot
extract any diabolical or demonic profundity from Eichmann,
that is still far from calling it commonplace. It surely cannot
be so common that a man facing death, and, moreover, standing beneath the gallows, should be able to think of nothing
but what he has heard at funerals all his life, and that these
"lofty words" should completely becloud the reality of his own
death. That such remoteness from reality and such thoughtlessness can wreak more havoc than all the evil instincts taken
together which, perhaps, are inherent in man—that was, in fact,
the lesson one could learn in Jerusalem. But it was a lesson,
neither an explanation of the phenomenon nor a theory about it.

Seemingly more complicated, but in reality far simpler than
examining the strange interdependence of thoughtlessness and
evil, is the question of what kind of crime is actually involved
here—a crime, moreover, which all agree is unprecedented. For
the concept of genocide, introduced explicitly to cover a crime
unknown before, although applicable up to a point is not fully
adequate, for the simple reason that massacres of whole peoples
are not unprecedented. They were the order of the day in antiquity, and the centuries of colonization and imperialism provide
plenty of examples of more or less successful attempts of that sort.
The expression "administrative massacres" seems better to fill
the bill. The term arose in connection with British imperialism;
the English deliberately rejected such procedures as a means
of maintaining their rule over India. The phrase has the virtue
of dispelling the prejudice that such monstrous acts can be
committed only against a foreign nation or a different race. There
is the well-known fact that Hitler began his mass murders by
granting "mercy deaths" to the "incurably ill," and that he
intended to wind up his extermination program by doing away
with "genetically damaged" Germans (heart and lung patients).
But quite aside from that, it is apparent that this sort of killing
can be directed against any given group, that is, that the principle of selection is dependent only upon circumstantial factors.
It is quite conceivable that in the automated economy of a not-

too-distant future men may be tempted to exterminate all those whose intelligence quotient is below a certain level.

In Jerusalem this matter was inadequately discussed because it is actually very difficult to grasp juridically. We heard the protestations of the defense that Eichmann was after all only a "tiny cog" in the machinery of the Final Solution, and of the prosecution, which believed it had discovered in Eichmann the actual motor. I myself attributed no more importance to both theories than did the Jerusalem court, since the whole cog theory is legally pointless and therefore it does not matter at all what order of magnitude is assigned to the "cog" named Eichmann. In its judgment the court naturally conceded that such a crime could be committed only by a giant bureaucracy using the resources of government. But insofar as it remains a crime—and that, of course, is the premise for a trial—all the cogs in the machinery, no matter how insignificant, are in court forthwith transformed back into perpetrators, that is to say, into human beings. If the defendant excuses himself on the ground that he acted not as a man but as a mere functionary whose functions could just as easily have been carried out by anyone else, it is as if a criminal pointed to the statistics on crime—which set forth that so-and-so many crimes per day are committed in such-and-such a place—and declared that he only did what was statistically expected, that it was mere accident that he did it and not somebody else, since after all somebody had to do it.

Of course it is important to the political and social sciences that the essence of totalitarian government, and perhaps the nature of every bureaucracy, is to make functionaries and mere cogs in the administrative machinery out of men, and thus to dehumanize them. And one can debate long and profitably on the rule of Nobody, which is what the political form known as bureau-cracy truly is. Only one must realize clearly that the administration of justice can consider these factors only to the extent that they are circumstances of the crime—just as, in a case of theft, the economic plight of the thief is taken into account without excusing the theft, let alone wiping it off the slate. True, we have become very much accustomed by modern psychology and sociology, not to speak of modern bureaucracy, to explaining away the responsibility of the doer for his deed in terms of this or that kind of determinism. Whether such seemingly deeper explanations of human actions are right or wrong is debatable. But what is not debatable is that no judicial procedure would be possible on the basis of them, and that the administration of justice, measured by such theories, is an extremely unmodern, not to say outmoded, institution. When Hitler said that a day would come in Germany when it would be considered a "disgrace" to be a jurist, he was speaking with utter consistency of his dream of a perfect bureaucracy.

As far as I can see, jurisprudence has at its disposal for treating this whole battery of questions only two categories, both of which, to my mind, are quite inadequate to deal with the matter. These are the concepts of "acts of state" and of acts "on superior orders." At any rate, these are the only categories in terms of which such matters are discussed in this kind of trial, usually on the motion of the defendant. The theory of the act of state is based on the argument that one sovereign state may not sit in judgment upon another, *par in parem non habet jurisdictionem*. Practically speaking, this argument had already been disposed of at Nuremberg; it stood no chance from the start, since, if it were accepted, even Hitler, the only one who was really responsible in the full sense, could not have been brought to account—a state of affairs which would have violated the most elementary sense of justice. However, an argument that stands no chance on the practical plane has not necessarily been demolished on the theoretical one. The usual evasions— that Germany at the time of the Third Reich was dominated by a gang of criminals to whom sovereignty and parity cannot very well be ascribed—were hardly useful. For on the one hand everyone knows that the analogy with a gang of criminals is applicable only to such a limited extent that it is not really applicable at all, and on the other hand these crimes undeniably took place within a "legal" order. That, indeed, was their outstanding characteristic.

Perhaps we can approach somewhat closer to the matter if we realize that back of the concept of act of state stands the theory of *raison d'état*. According to that theory, the actions of the state, which is responsible for the life of the country and thus also for the laws obtaining in it, are not subject to the same rules as the acts of the citizens of the country. Just as the rule of law, although devised to eliminate violence and the war of all against all, always stands in need of the instruments of violence in order to assure its own existence, so a government may find itself compelled to commit actions that are generally regarded as crimes in order to assure its own survival and the survival of lawfulness. Wars are frequently justified on these grounds, but criminal acts of state do not occur only in the field of international relations, and the history of civilized nations knows many examples of them—from Napoleon's assassination of the Duc d'Enghien, to the murder of the Socialist leader Matteotti, for which Mussolini himself was presumably responsible.

Raison d'état appeals—rightly or wrongly, as the case may be—to *necessity*, and the state crimes committed in its name (which are fully criminal in terms of the dominant legal system of the country where they occur) are considered emergency measures, concessions made to the stringencies of *Realpolitik,* in order to preserve power and thus assure the continuance of the existing legal order as a whole. In a normal political and legal system, such crimes occur as an exception to the rule and are not subject to legal penalty (are *gerichtsfrei,* as German legal theory expresses it) because the existence of the state itself is at stake, and no outside political entity has the right to deny a state its existence or prescribe how it is to preserve it. However—as we may have learned from the history of Jewish policy in the Third Reich—in a state founded upon criminal principles, the situation is reversed. Then a non-criminal act (such as, for example, Himmler's order in the late summer of 1944 to halt the deportation of Jews) becomes a concession to necessity imposed by reality, in this case the impending defeat. Here the question arises: what is the nature of the sovereignty of such an entity? Has it not violated the parity (*par in parem non habet jurisdictionem*) which international law accords it? Does the *"par in parem"* signify no more than the paraphernalia of sovereignty? Or does it also imply a substantive equality or likeness? Can we apply the same principle that is applied to a

governmental apparatus in which crime and violence are exceptions and borderline cases to a political order in which crime
is legal and the rule?

Just how inadequate juristic concepts really are to deal with
the criminal facts which were the subject matter of all these
trials appears perhaps even more strikingly in the concept of acts
performed on superior orders. The Jerusalem court countered the
argument advanced by the defense with lengthy quotations from
the penal and military lawbooks of civilized countries, particularly of Germany; for under Hitler the pertinent articles had
by no means been repealed. All of them agree on one point:
manifestly criminal orders must not be obeyed. The court,
moreover, referred to a case that came up in Israel several
years ago: soldiers were brought to trial for having massacred
the civilian inhabitants of an Arab village on the border shortly
before the beginning of the Sinai campaign. The villagers had
been found outside their houses during a military curfew of
which, it appeared, they were unaware. Unfortunately, on closer
examination the comparison appears to be defective on two
accounts. First of all, we must again consider that the relationship of exception and rule, which is of prime importance for
recognizing the criminality of an order executed by a subordinate, was reversed in the case of Eichmann's actions. Thus, on
the basis of this argument one could actually defend Eichmann's failure to obey certain of Himmler's orders, or his obey-
ing them with hesitancy: they were manifest exceptions to the
prevailing rule. The judgment found this to be especially
incriminating to the defendant, which was certainly very understandable but not very consistent. This can easily be seen from
the pertinent findings of Israeli military courts, which were
cited in support by the judges. They ran as follows: the order
to be disobeyed must be "manifestly unlawful"; unlawfulness
"should fly like a black flag above [it], as a warning reading,
'Prohibited.' " In other words, the order, to be recognized by the
soldier as "manifestly unlawful," must violate by its unusualness
the canons of the legal system to which he is accustomed. And
Israeli jurisprudence in these matters coincides completely with
that of other countries. No doubt in formulating these articles
the legislators were thinking of cases in which an officer who

suddenly goes mad, say, commands his subordinates to kill another officer. In any normal trial of such a case, it would at once become clear that the soldier was not being asked to consult the voice of conscience, or a "feeling of lawfulness that lies deep within every human conscience, also of those who are not conversant with books of law . . . provided the eye is not blind and the heart is not stony and corrupt." Rather, the soldier would be expected to be able to distinguish between a rule and a striking exception to the rule. The German military code, at any rate, explicitly states that conscience is not enough. Paragraph 48 reads: "Punishability of an action or omission is not excluded on the ground that the person considered his behavior required by his conscience or the prescripts of his religion." A striking feature of the Israeli court's line of argument is that the concept of a sense of justice grounded in the depths of every man is presented solely as a substitute for familiarity with the law. Its plausibility rests on the assumption that the law expresses only what every man's conscience would tell him anyhow.

If we are to apply this whole reasoning to the Eichmann case in a meaningful way, we are forced to conclude that Eichmann acted fully within the framework of the kind of judgment required of him: he acted in accordance with the rule, examined the order issued to him for its "manifest" legality, namely regularity; he did not have to fall back upon his "conscience," since he was not one of those who were unfamiliar with the laws of his country. The exact opposite was the case.

The second account on which the argument based on comparison proved to be defective concerns the practice of the courts of admitting the plea of "superior orders" as important extenuating circumstances, and this practice was mentioned explicitly by the judgment. The judgment cited the case I have mentioned above, that of the massacre of the Arab inhabitants at Kfar Kassem, as proof that Israeli jurisdiction does not clear a defendant of responsibility for the "superior orders" he received. And it is true, the Israeli soldiers were indicted for murder, but "superior orders" constituted so weighty an argument for mitigating circumstances that they were sentenced to relatively short prison terms. To be sure, this case concerned an isolated act, not—as in Eichmann's case—an activity extending over years, in which crime followed crime. Still, it was undeniable that he had always acted upon "superior orders," and if the provisions of ordinary Israeli law had been applied to him, it would have been difficult indeed to impose the maximum penalty upon him. The truth of the matter is that Israeli law, in theory and practice, like the jurisdiction of other countries cannot but admit that the fact of "superior orders," even when their unlawfulness is "manifest," can severely disturb the normal working of a man's conscience.

This is only one example among many to demonstrate the inadequacy of the prevailing legal system and of current juridical concepts to deal with the facts of administrative massacres organized by the state apparatus. If we look more closely into the matter we will observe without much difficulty that the judges in all these trials really passed judgment solely on the basis of the monstrous deeds. In other words, they judged freely, as it were, and did not really lean on the standards and legal precedents with which they more or less convincingly sought to justify their decisions. That was already evident in Nuremberg, where the judges on the one hand declared that the "crime against peace" was the gravest of all the crimes they had to deal with, since it included all the other crimes, but on the other hand actually imposed the death penalty only on those defendants who had participated in the new crime of administrative massacre—supposedly a less grave offense than conspiracy against peace. It would indeed be tempting to pursue these and similar inconsistencies in a field so obsessed with consistency as jurisprudence. But of course that cannot be done here.

There remains, however, one fundamental problem, which was implicitly present in all these postwar trials and which must be mentioned here because it touches upon one of the central moral questions of all time, namely upon the nature and function of human judgment. What we have demanded in these trials, where the defendants had committed "legal" crimes, is that human beings be capable of telling right from wrong even when all they have to guide them is their own judgment, which, moreover, happens to be completely at odds with what they must regard as the unanimous opinion of all those around them. And this question is all the more serious as we know that the few who were "arrogant" enough to trust only their own judgment were by no means identical with those persons who continued to abide by old values, or who were guided by a religious belief. Since the whole of respectable society had in one way or another succumbed to Hitler, the moral maxims which determine social behavior and the religious commandments—"Thou shalt not kill!"—which guide conscience had virtually vanished. Those few who were still able to tell right from wrong went really only by their own judgments, and they did so freely; there were no rules to be abided by, under which the particular cases with which they were confronted could be subsumed. They had to decide each instance as it arose, because no rules existed for the unprecedented.

How troubled men of our time are by this question of judgment (or, as is often said, by people who dare "sit in judgment") has emerged in the controversy over the present book, as well as the in many respects similar controversy over Hochhuth's *The Deputy*. What has come to light is neither nihilism nor cynicism, as one might have expected, but a quite extraordinary confusion over elementary questions of morality—as if an instinct in such matters were truly the last thing to be taken for granted in our time. The many curious notes that have been struck in the course of these disputes seem particularly revealing. Thus, some American literati have professed their naïve belief that temptation and coercion are really the same thing, that no one can be asked to resist temptation. (If someone puts a pistol to your heart and orders you to shoot your best friend, then you simply *must* shoot him. Or, as it was argued—some years ago in connection with the quiz program scandal in which a university teacher had hoaxed the public—when so much money is at stake, who could possibly resist?) The argument that we cannot judge if we were not present and involved ourselves seems to convince everyone everywhere, although it seems obvious that if it were true, neither the administration of justice nor the writing of history would ever be possible. In contrast to these confusions, the reproach of self-righteousness raised against those who do judge is age-old; but that does not make it any the more valid. Even the judge who condemns a murderer can still say when he goes home: "And there, but for the grace of God, go I." All German Jews unanimously have condemned the wave of coordination which passed over the German people in 1933 and from one day to the next turned the Jews into pariahs. Is it conceivable that none of them ever asked himself how many of his own group would have done just the same if only they had been allowed to? But is their condemnation today any the less correct for that reason?

The reflection that you yourself might have done wrong under the same circumstances may kindle a spirit of forgiveness, but those who today refer to Christian charity seem strangely confused on this issue too. Thus we can read in the postwar statement of the *Evangelische Kirche in Deutschland,* the Protestant church, as follows: "We aver that before the God of Mercy we share in the guilt for the outrage committed against the Jews by our own people through omission and silence."* It seems to me that a Christian is guilty before the God of *Mercy* if he repays evil with evil, hence that the churches would have sinned against mercy if millions of Jews had been killed as punishment for some evil they committed. But if the churches shared in the guilt for an outrage pure and simple, as they themselves attest, then the matter must still be considered to fall within the purview of the God of *Justice.*

This slip of the tongue, as it were, is no accident. Justice, but not mercy, is a matter of judgment, and about nothing does public opinion everywhere seem to be in happier agreement than that no one has the right to judge somebody else. What public opinion permits us to judge and even to condemn are trends, or whole groups of people—the larger the better—in short, something so general that distinctions can no longer be made, names no longer be named. Needless to add, this taboo applies doubly when the deeds or words of famous

---

* Quoted from the minister Aurel v. Jüchen in an anthology of critical reviews of Hochhuth's play—*Summa Iniuria,* Rowohl Verlag, p. 195.

people or men in high position are being questioned. This is currently expressed in high-flown assertions that it is "superficial" to insist on details and to mention individuals, whereas it is the sign of sophistication to speak in generalities according to which all cats are gray and we are all equally guilty. Thus the charge Hochhuth has raised against a single Pope—one man, easily identifiable, with a name of his own—was immediately countered with an indictment of all Christianity. The charge against Christianity in general, with its two thousand years of history, cannot be proved, and if it could be proved, it would be horrible. No one seems to mind this so long as no *person* is involved, and it is quite safe to go one step further and to maintain: "Undoubtedly there is reason for grave accusations, but the defendant is *mankind* as a whole." (Thus Robert Weltsch in *Summa Iniuria*, quoted above, italics added.)

Another such escape from the area of ascertainable facts and personal responsibility are the countless theories, based on non-specific, abstract, hypothetical assumptions—from the *Zeitgeist* down to the Oedipus complex—which are so general that they explain and justify every event and every deed: no alternative to what actually happened is even considered and no person could have acted differently from the way he did act. Among the constructs that "explain" everything by obscuring all details, we find such notions as a "ghetto mentality" among European Jews; or the collective guilt of the German people, derived from an *ad hoc* interpretation of their history; or the equally absurd assertion of a kind of collective innocence of the Jewish people. All these clichés have in common that they make judgment superfluous and that to utter them is devoid of all risk. And although we can understand the reluctance of those immediately affected by the disaster—Germans and Jews —to examine too closely the conduct of groups and persons that seemed to be or should have been unimpaired by the totality of the moral collapse—that is, the conduct of the Christian churches, the Jewish leadership, the men of the anti-Hitler conspiracy of July 20, 1944—this understandable disinclination is insufficient to explain the reluctance evident everywhere to make judgments in terms of individual moral responsibility.

Many people today would agree that there is no such thing

as collective guilt or, for that matter, collective innocence, and that if there were, no one person could ever be guilty or innocent. This, of course, is not to deny that there is such a thing as *political* responsibility which, however, exists quite apart from what the individual member of the group has done and therefore can neither be judged in moral terms nor be brought before a criminal court. Every government assumes political responsibility for the deeds and misdeeds of its predecessor and every nation for the deeds and misdeeds of the past. When Napoleon, seizing power in France after the Revolution, said: I shall assume the responsibility for everything France ever did from Saint Louis to the Committee of Public Safety, he was only stating somewhat emphatically one of the basic facts of all political life. It means hardly more, generally speaking, than that every generation, by virtue of being born into a historical continuum, is burdened by the sins of the fathers as it is blessed with the deeds of the ancestors. But this kind of responsibility is not what we are talking about here; it is not personal, and only in a metaphorical sense can one say he *feels* guilty for what not he but his father or his people have done. (Morally speaking, it is hardly less wrong to feel guilty without having done something specific than it is to feel free of all guilt if one is actually guilty of something.) It is quite conceivable that certain political responsibilities among nations might some day be adjudicated in an international court; what is inconceivable is that such a court would be a criminal tribunal which pronounces on the guilt or innocence of individuals.

And the question of individual guilt or innocence, the act of meting out justice to both the defendant and the victim, are the only things at stake in a criminal court. The Eichmann trial was no exception, even though the court here was confronted with a crime it could not find in the lawbooks and with a criminal whose like was unknown in any court, at least prior to the Nuremberg Trials. The present report deals with nothing but the extent to which the court in Jerusalem succeeded in fulfilling the demands of justice.

Bibliography

Adler, H. G., *Theresienstadt 1941-1945*, Tübingen, 1955
————, *Die verheimlichte Wahrheit. Theresienstädter Dokumente*, Tübingen, 1958
American Jewish Committee, *The Eichmann Case in the American Press*, New York, n.d.
Anti-Defamation League, *Bulletin*, March, 1961
Baade, Hans W., "Some Legal Aspects of the Eichmann Trial" in *Duke Law Journal*, 1961
Bamm, Peter, *Die unsichtbare Flagge*, Munich, 1952
Barkai, Meyer, *The Fighting Ghettos*, New York, 1962
Baumann, Jürgen, "Gedanken zum Eichmann-Urteil" in *Juristenzeitung*, 1963, Nr. 4.
Benton, Wilbourn E., and Grimm, Georg, eds., *Nuremberg: German Views of the War Trials*, Dallas, 1955
Bertelsen, Aage, *October '43*, New York, 1954. (About Denmark)
Bondy, François, "Karl Jaspers zum Eichmann-Prozess," *Der Monat*, May, 1961
Buchheim, Hans, "Die SS in der Verfassung des Dritten Reichs," *Vierteljahrshefte für Zeitgeschichte*, April, 1955
Centre de Documentation Juive Contemporaine, *Le Dossier Eichmann*, Paris, 1960
de Jong, Louis, "Jews and Non-Jews in Nazi-occupied Holland" in *On the Track of Tyranny*, ed. M. Beloff, Wiener Library, London
Dicey, Albert Venn, *Introduction to the Study of the Law of the Constitution*, 9th edition, New York, 1939
Drost, Peiter N., *The Crime of State*, 2 vols., Leyden, 1959
"Eichmann Tells His Own Damning Story," *Life*, November 28 and December 5, 1960

Einstein, Siegfried, *Eichmann, Chefbuchhalter des Todes*, Frankfurt, 1961

Fest, T. C., *Das Gesicht des Dritten Reiches*, Munich, 1963

Finch, George A., "The Nuremberg Trials and International Law," *American Journal for International Law*, vol. XLI, 1947

Flender, Harold, *Rescue in Denmark*, New York, 1963

Frank, Hans, *Die Technik des Staates*, Munich, 1942

Globke, Hans, *Kommentare zur deutschen Rassegesetzgebung*, Munich-Berlin, 1936

Green, L. C., "The Eichmann Case," *Modern Law Review*, vol. XXIII, London, 1960

Hausner, Gideon, "Eichmann and His Trial," *Saturday Evening Post*, November 3, 10, and 17, 1962

Heiber, Helmut, "Der Fall Grünspan," *Vierteljahrshefte für Zeitgeschichte*, April, 1957

Henk, Emil, *Die Tragödie des 20. Juli 1944*, 1946

Hesse, Fritz, *Das Spiel um Deutschland*, Munich, 1953

Hilberg, Raul, *The Destruction of the European Jews*, Chicago, 1961

Höss, Rudolf, *Commandant of Auschwitz*, New York, 1960

Hofer, Walther, *Der Nationalsozialismus. Dokumente 1933-1945*, Frankfurt, 1957

Holborn, Louise, ed., *War and Peace Aims of the United Nations*, 2 vols., Boston, 1943, 1948

Jäger, Herbert, "Betrachtungen zum Eichmann-Prozess" in *Kriminologie und Strafrechtsreform*, Heft 3/4, 1962

Jaspers, Karl, "Beispiel für das Verhängnis des Vorrangs nationalpolitischen Denkens" in *Lebensfragen der deutschen Politik*, 1963

Kaltenbrunner, Ernst, *Spiegelbild einer Verschwörung*, Stuttgart, 1961

Kastner, Rudolf, *Der Kastner Bericht*, Munich, 1961

Kempner, Robert M. W., *Eichmann und Komplizen*, Zurich, 1961. (Contains the complete minutes of the Wannsee Conference)

Kimche, Jon and David, *The Secret Roads. The "Illegal" Migration of a People, 1938-48*, London, 1954

Kirchheimer, Otto, *Political Justice*, Princeton, 1961

Kirchhoff, Hans, "What Saved the Danish Jews?" in *Peace News,* London, November 8, 1963

Klein, Bernard, "The Judenrat" in *Jewish Social Studies,* vol. 22, January, 1960

Knierim, August von, *The Nuremberg Trials,* Chicago, 1959

Krug, Mark M., "Young Israelis and Jews Abroad—A Study of Selected History Textbooks" in *Comparative Education Review,* October, 1963

Lamm, Hans, *Über die Entwicklung des deutschen Judentums im Dritten Reich,* mimeographed dissertation, Erlangen, 1951

———, *Der Eichmannprozess in der deutschen öffentlichen Meinung,* Frankfurt, 1961

Lankin, Doris, *The Legal System,* "Israel Today" series, No. 19, Jerusalem, 1961

Lederer, Zdenek, *Ghetto Theresienstadt,* London, 1953

Lehnsdorff, Hans Graf von, *Ostpreussisches Tagebuch,* Munich, 1961

Lévai, Eugene, *Black Book on the Martyrdom of Hungarian Jews,* Zurich, 1948

Lösener, Bernhard, *Die Nürnberger Gesetze,* Sammlung Vahlen, vol. XXIII, Berlin, 1936

Maschmann, Melitta, *Fazit,* Stuttgart, 1963

Maunz, Theodor, *Gestalt und Recht der Polizei,* Hamburg, 1943

Monneray, Henri, *La Persécution des Juifs en France,* Paris, 1947

Motzkin, Leo, ed., *Les Pogromes en Ukraine sous les gouvernements ukrainiens 1917-1920,* Comité des Délégations Juives, Paris, 1927

Mulisch, Harry, *Strafsache 40/61,* Köln, 1963

Nazi Conspiracy and Aggression, 11 vols., Washington, 1946-1948

Oppenheim, L., and Lauterpacht, Sir Hersch, *International Law,* 7th ed., 1952

Paechter, Henry, "The Legend of the 20th of July, 1944" in *Social Research,* Spring, 1962.

Pearlman, Moshe, *The Capture of Adolf Eichmann,* London, 1961

Pendorf, Robert, *Mörder und Ermordete. Eichmann und die Judenpolitik des Dritten Reiches*, Hamburg, 1961

Poliakov, Léon, *Auschwitz*, Paris, 1964

Poliakov, Léon, and Wulf, Josef, *Das Dritte Reich und die Juden*, Berlin, 1955

Reck-Malleczewen, Friedrich P., *Tagebuch eines Verzweifelten*, Stuttgart, 1947

Reitlinger, Gerald, *The Final Solution*, New York, 1953; Perpetua ed., 1961

Reynolds, Quentin; Katz, Ephraim; and Aldouby, Zwy, *Minister of Death*, New York, 1960

Ritter, Gerhard, *The German Resistance: Carl Goerdeler's Struggle against Tyranny*, New York, 1958

Robinson, Jacob, "Eichmann and the Question of Jurisdiction," *Commentary*, July, 1960

Robinson, Jacob, and Friedman, Philip, *Guide to Jewish History under Nazi Impact*, a bibliography published jointly by YIVO Institute for Jewish Research and Yad Vashem, New York and Jerusalem, 1960

Rogat, Yosal, *The Eichmann Trial and the Rule of Law*, published by the Center for the Study of Democratic Institutions, Santa Barbara, California, 1961

Romoser, George K., *The Crisis of Political Direction in the German Resistance to Nazism*, University of Chicago dissertation, 1958

————, "The Politics of Uncertainty: The German Resistance Movement" in *Social Research*, Spring, 1964

Rothfels, Hans, *German Opposition to Hitler*, Chicago, 1948

Rotkirchen, Livia, *The Destruction of Slovak Jewry*, Jerusalem, 1961

Rousset, David, *Les Jours de notre mort*, Paris, 1947

Schneider, Hans, *Gerichtsfreie Hoheitsakte*, Tübingen, 1950

Schramm, Percy Ernst, "Adolf Hitler—Anatomie eines Diktators" in *Hitlers Tischgespräche*, 1964

Servatius, Robert, *Verteidigung Adolf Eichmann, Plädoyer*, Bad Kreuznach, 1961

Silving, Helen, "In Re Eichmann: A Dilemma of Law and Morality," *American Journal of International Law*, vol. LV, 1961

Stone, Julius, *Legal Controls of International Conflict,* New York, 1954

Strauss, Walter, "Das Reichsministerium des Innern und die Judengesetzgebung. Aufzeichnungen von Bernhard Lösener," *Vierteljahrshefte für Zeitgeschichte,* July, 1961

Strecker, Reinhard, ed., *Dr. Hans Globke,* Hamburg, n.d.

Taylor, Telford, "Large Questions in the Eichmann Case," *New York Times Magazine,* January 22, 1961

Torrès, Henri, *Le Procès des Pogromes,* Paris, 1928

Trial of the Major War Criminals, The, 42 vols., Nuremberg, 1947-1948

Trials of War Criminals before the Nuremberg Military Tribunals, 15 vols., Washington, 1949-1953

Vabres, Donnedieu de, *Le Procès de Nuremberg,* Paris, 1947

Wade, E. C. S., "Act of State in English Law," *British Year Book of International Law,* 1934

Wechsler, Herbert, "The Issues of the Nuremberg Trials," *Principles, Politics, and Fundamental Law,* New York, 1961

Weisenborn, Günther, *Der lautlose Aufstand,* Hamburg, 1953

Wighton, Charles, *Eichmann, His Career and His Crimes,* London, 1961

Woetzel, Robert K., *The Nuremberg Trials in International Law,* New York, 1960

Wucher, Albert, *Eichmanns gab es Viele,* Munich-Zurich, 1961

Wulf, Josef, *Lodz. Das letzte Ghetto auf polnischem Boden,* Schriftenreihe der Bundeszentrale für Heimatdienst, vol. LIX, Bonn, 1962

————, *Vom Leben, Kampf und Tod im Ghetto Warschau,* op. cit., vol. XXXII, Bonn, 1960

Yad Vashem, *Bulletin,* Jerusalem, April, 1961 and April-May, 1962

Zaborowski, Jan, *Dr. Hans Globke, the Good Clerk,* Poznan, 1962

Zeisel, Hans, "Eichmann, Adolf," *Britannica Book of the Year,* 1962

Index

Abromeit, Franz, 183, 196
Adenauer, Konrad, 13, 16, 17-18, 19, 112, 119, 167
Adler, H. G., 119, 120, 134
Albania, 66
Aliyah Beth, 62, 225
Alsace-Lorraine, 101, 102
Alt-Aussee, 234, 236
Amsterdam, 12, 14, 118, 168
Anschluss, 37, 42, 194
Antonescu, Ion, 176, 191, 192-93
Arabs, 9, 10, 12-13, 235, 292
Argentina, 22, 34, 47, 49, 52, 54, 78, 84, 102, 209-10, 222, 235, 237, 238, 239-40, 241-42, 247, 252, 264, 281
Armenian pogroms of 1915, 265
Arrow Cross men, 195, 201, 202
Assimilationists, 40, 41, 58, 59
Aufbau, Der, 27
Aurel v. Jüchen, 296
Auschwitz, 12, 14, 42, 51, 64, 71, 79, 80, 81, 86, 89, 90, 92, 108, 109, 112, 119, 138, 140, 147, 152, 156, 164, 166, 168, 170, 180, 189, 196, 200, 201, 213, 214, 223-24, 225, 226, 227, 264, 267
Austria, 12, 14, 28, 32, 34, 37, 42, 43-48, 61, 75, 88, 95, 101, 102, 138, 154, 161, 163, 194, 207, 220, 224, 227, 234, 236, 252
"Austrian Legion in exile" (in Bavaria), 34
Austro-Hungarian Empire, 181

Bach-Zelewski, Erich von dem, 15-16, 91, 281
Baden, 130, 155, 156
Badoglio, Pietro, 176, 183
Baeck, Leo, 119
Baer, Richard, 14, 281
Baky, László, 200
Bamm, Peter, 231-32
Baron, Salo W., 19, 96
Baror, Ya'akov, 120
Basler Nationalzeitung, 167
Bauer, Fritz, 17

Becher, Kurt, 138, 141-44, 147, 197, 199, 281
Beck, Ludwig, 101-02
Beckerle, Adolf, 187-88
Beckmann, Heinz, 58
Belgium, 142, 162, 163, 165-67, 225, 238, 255
Belzek, 109
Ben-Gurion, David, 4-5, 9, 10, 11, 12, 13, 14, 19, 20, 122, 209-10, 238-39, 241, 255, 271, 272
Ben-Zvi, Itzhak, 249
Bergen-Belsen, 86, 117, 123, 143, 156, 189, 208, 225
Berlin, 33, 39, 40, 44, 45, 62, 64, 65, 67, 72, 73, 89, 100, 104, 112, 115, 117, 118, 119, 120, 130, 147, 156, 165, 173, 185, 196, 199, 202, 216, 234, 244, 265, 266
Berlin, Treaty of, 190
Berthawerk, 200
Best, Werner, 173, 174-75
Beth Ha'am, *see* House of the People
Beth Hamishpath, *see* House of Justice
Bettelheim, Bruno, 283
Bialystok, 213
Birnblat, Hirsch, 284
Blobel, Paul, 207-08
Blomberg, Werner von, 217
Bohemia, 66, 79, 80, 82, 95, 154
Böhm, Adolf, 41, 209
Böhme, Franz, 23, 185
Bonnet, Georges, 76
Bordeaux, 163-64
Boris III, King of Bulgaria, 185, 187
Bormann, Martin, 158, 231, 258
Boycott Day (April 1, 1933), 59
Brack, Viktor, 84, 108
Bradfisch, Otto, 15, 127
Brand, Joel, 197, 198, 199
Brandt, Karl, 70
Brandt, Willy, 58
Bratislava, 81, 82, 144, 203, 204, 205, 259
Brauchitsch, Walter von, 212

Breslau, 200
Briand-Kellogg pact, 255
Brunner, Alois, 177, 188, 195, 205
Buber, Martin, 249, 251-52
Bucharest, 191, 192
Buchenwald, 11, 12
Budapest, 25, 26-30, 118, 124, 138, 140, 147, 194, 195, 196, 197-98, 200-01, 202, 204
Buenos Aires, 21, 235, 236, 238, 240, 241, 242, 265, 266
Bühler, Joseph, 113, 216
Bulgaria, 171, 182, 185-88, 196, 225, 230
Bureau IV, R.S.H.A., 31, 70, 73, 147, 207-08
Bureau O6, *see* Israeli police

Cairo, 13, 62
Canada, 103
Carmel, Mount, 62
Catholic Academy in Bavaria, 22
Center for Emigration of Austrian Jews (in Vienna), 44-48
Central Agency for the Investigation of Nazi Crimes (West German), 14
Central Association of German Citizens of Jewish Faith, 59
Central Conference of American Rabbis, 249
Central Jewish Council (of Budapest), 118, 196, 197, 198, 199
Chaim I, *see* Rumkowski, Chaim
Chelmno, 15, 87, 109, 225
Christian X, King of Denmark, 171, 174
Churchill, Winston, 257
Ciano, Galeazzo, 178
Cohn, Benno, 39
Communists, 38, 70, 95, 97, 177
Convention for the Protection of Human Rights and Fundamental Freedoms, 250
Côte d'Azur, 165, 177
Court of Appeal, Israeli, *see* Supreme Court of Israel
Cracow, 217
Crimea, 206
Croatia, 142, 182, 183-84, 205
Czechoslovakia, 29, 66, 75, 79-82, 128, 145, 154, 181, 202, 226, 259
Czerniakow, Adam, 119

Dachau, 34, 130
Daluege, Kurt, 68
Dannecker, Theodor, 164, 167, 186, 187, 196
Danzig, 217

Davar, 9
de: *for names combining this element, see that part of the name following "de"*
Denmark, 152, 170, 171-75, 179, 187, 190, 225
Deputy, The, 295
Diary of Anne Frank, The, 251
Diaspora, 7, 8, 10, 80
Dicey, Albert Venn, 93
Dimitrov, Georgi, 188
Dinoor, Mr., 223-24
District Court of Jerusalem, 3, 10, 19, 21, 65, 115, 143, 154, 210, 211-19, 238, 244-48, 249
Dr. Strangelove, 97
Dostoevski, 52
Drancy, 164
Dreyfus Affair, 10
Drost, P. N., 260
Duckwitz, George F., 173
Dunand, Paul, 146

East, the, *see* Estonia; Latvia; Lithuania; Poland, Nazi; Ukraine; Warthegau; *and* White Russia
East Germany, 13, 166
Ebner (Gestapo officer), 51
Egypt, Eichmann in, 62
Egyptian National Assembly, 20
Eichmann Commando, 14, 196, 198, 201
Eichmann, Dieter (eldest son of [Otto] Adolf), 203
Eichmann family, members of, 25-26, 29, 137, 190, 221, 237, 243, 249
Eichmann, Karl Adolf ([Otto] Adolf's father), 5, 21, 28, 29, 30, 114, 237
Eichmann, Maria, *née* Schefferling ([Otto] Adolf's mother), 21, 29, 30, 237
Eichmann, Ricardo Francisco Klement (fourth son of [Otto] Adolf), 237
Eichmann, Veronika (or Vera) Liebl ([Otto] Adolf's wife), 29, 236, 237, 242, 249
Einsatzgruppen (mobile killing units of the S.S.), the, 15, 16, 50, 67, 70, 71, 74, 77, 83, 85, 90, 94, 95, 96, 100, 105, 106, 107, 109, 127, 196, 210, 212, 216, 218, 232
Einsatzstab Rosenberg, 183
Einstein, Albert, 134
Eisenhower, Dwight D., 234
El Al Israel Airlines, 238, 241
Endre, Vitez Láslo, 26, 140, 199-200

Eppstein, Paul, 64, 120
Estonia, 154, 206
Europe Plan, 197, 198, 204
Evian Conference, 66
Ezekiel, 19

Falkenhausen, Alexander von, 166
Farben, I. G., 79
Farinacci, Roberto, 178
Fellenz, Martin, 16
Ferenczy, Lieutenant Colonel, 200
Fest, T. C., 282
Finland, 170, 255
Fiume, 178
Flanders, 166
France, Italian-occupied, 165, 176, 177
France, Nazi-occupied, 99, 132, 142, 163-65, 173, 177, 224
France, pre–World War II, 76, 172
France, World War II, *see* France, Italian-occupied; France, Nazi-occupied; *and* Vichy France
Franco, Francisco, 176
Franco-Prussian War, 101
Frank, Hans, 9, 73, 75, 133-34, 136, 206, 213, 216
Frank, Karl Hermann, 80
Fränkel, Wolfgang Immerwahr, 16
Frankfurter Rundschau, 18
Franz Joseph, Emperor of Austria, 88
Freemasonry, 32, 37, 70
Freudiger, Philip von, *see* Freudiger, Pinchas
Freudiger, Pinchas, 124, 125, 196, 197, 198
Fritsch, Werner von, 217
Fünten, Ferdinand aus der, 167

General Government of Poland, *see* Poland, Nazi
Geneva Convention, 255, 268
Genocide Convention (U.N.), 262
George, Stefan, 156
German Army and High Command, 18, 23-24, 83, 84, 97, 98, 100, 101-03, 105, 107, 127, 170, 172, 213, 217, 218, 230
German Civil Service, 38, 43, 112, 113, 114, 178
German Federal Republic, *see* West Germany
German Foreign Office, 13, 22, 23, 24, 47, 72, 85, 112, 113, 114, 139, 141, 151, 157, 160-61, 167, 170, 171, 176, 179, 186, 187, 192, 195, 199, 202, 204, 215

German Intelligence Service, 107, 187
German Ministry for Occupied Eastern Territories, 192, 206
German Ministry of Finance, 46, 115
German Ministry of the Interior, 72, 113, 128, 159, 183
German Ministry of Justice, 158
German Ministry of Transport, 115, 153, 164, 213
Germany (the Third Reich), *see* Germany, Nazi
Germany, East, *see* East Germany
Germany, Nazi, *see under the names of the various arms and functionaries of the German government and organizations and leaders of the Nazi Party* (German Army; German Foreign Office; Gestapo; Hitler, Adolf; Himmler, Heinrich; Nazi Party; S.S.; *etc.*)
Germany, post-Nazi, *see* East Germany *and* West Germany
Germany, pre-Nazi, *see* Weimar Republic
Germany, West, *see* West Germany *and* Adenauer, Konrad
Gestapo, 36, 60, 66, 68, 70, 97, 152, 159, 165, 173, 190, 206, 227-28, 246, 263
Gilbert, Gustave M., 211
Gillon, Philip, 7
Glickman Corporation, 5
Globke, Hans, 19, 72, 113, 128-29, 248
Globocnik, Odilo, 84, 86-87, 89, 107-08, 179
Glücks, Richard, 86, 152, 200
Goebbels, Joseph Paul, 22, 52, 180, 191
Goerdeler, Carl Friedrich, 99, 100, 101, 102-03, 104
Goldmann, Nahum, 271
Göring, Hermann Wilhelm, 44, 65, 83, 93, 133, 188, 202
Grand Mufti of Jerusalem, the ex-, 13, 19
Great Britain, 61, 288
Greece, 176, 185, 188, 190, 195, 225, 258
Greiser, Artur, 127, 206, 213
Grell, Horst, 47, 281
Grotius, 287
Gruber, Heinrich, 129, 131, 133
Grynszpan, Herschel, 227-28
Grynszpan, Zindel, 227, 228-30

Günther, Rolf, 69, 107, 146, 173, 196
Gurs, 130, 156
Gypsies, 23, 94, 96, 106, 158, 184, 188, 217, 244, 245, 276

Ha'avarah, 60
Haganah, 62
Hagen, Herbert, 62
Hague, The, 153, 167
Hague Convention, 255, 256
Haifa, 62
Halevi, Benjamin, 42, 69, 124, 143, 223, 230; *see also* District Court of Jerusalem
Haman, 19
Hamsun, Knut, 154
Hannecken, General von, 172-73
Hapsburg, Otto von, 194
Harsten, Wilhelm, 167
Hausner, Gideon, 3, 4, 5, 7, 8, 18, 19, 20, 26, 57, 94-95, 97, 120, 121, 122, 124-25, 153, 209, 211, 220, 222, 223, 224, 225, 227, 230, 239, 248, 259, 260-61, 267, 276, 283
Head Office for Reich Security (of the S.S.), *see* R.S.H.A.
Hebrew University in Jerusalem, 249
Hedin, Sven, 134, 154
Hegel, 20
Helldorf, Count, 100
"Heninger, Otto," (pseud. of [Otto] Adolf Eichmann), 236
Herzl, Theodor, 40, 41, 57, 76, 209
Hesse, Fritz, 99
Heydrich, Reinhardt, 36, 44, 45, 47, 58, 65-66, 68, 69, 70, 72, 74-75, 77, 79-80, 81, 82, 83-84, 94, 95, 105-06, 107, 112, 113, 114, 133-34, 138, 155, 156, 167, 173, 178, 184, 204, 207, 210, 212, 216, 218
Higher S.S. and Police Leader Corps, 15, 16, 68, 70, 71, 84, 105, 139, 141, 151, 165, 167, 168, 213
Hilberg, Raul, 23, 71, 79, 107, 118, 133, 140, 187, 191, 282
Himmler, Heinrich, 13, 15, 25, 35, 36, 50, 51, 53, 57, 58, 68, 69, 70, 71, 74, 76, 79, 84, 86, 93, 94, 100, 104-05, 106, 107, 108, 112, 114, 115, 116, 130, 133, 138, 139, 141, 142, 143, 144, 145, 146, 147, 148, 149, 151, 155-58, 159, 165, 168, 172, 193, 197, 198, 202, 210, 211, 213-14, 215, 216, 217, 231, 234-35, 291, 292
Hiroshima, 256

Hitler, Adolf, 13, 17, 20, 24, 37, 52, 57, 63, 67, 70, 72, 78, 83, 84, 93-94, 95, 96, 97, 98, 99, 100, 101-02, 103, 104, 105, 106, 107, 108, 112, 114, 126, 127, 128, 129, 133, 134, 136, 137, 139-40, 144, 147, 148, 149, 151, 153, 155, 156, 157, 160, 161, 176, 182, 191, 193, 210, 211, 216, 217, 244, 245, 253, 267, 273, 283, 284, 288, 290, 292, 295; conspiracy against, *see* July Conspiracy
Hlinka Guard, 202
Hochhuth, Rolf, 295, 297
Holland, *see* Netherlands, the
Horthy, Nikolaus von, 139, 140, 147, 176, 194, 197, 199, 200, 201
Höss, Rudolf, 14, 50-51, 71, 86, 89, 92, 200, 213
Hössbach protocol, 217
Hoter-Yishai, Aharon, 225-26
Höttl, Wilhelm, 184, 281
House of Justice, 3
House of the People, 4
Hubertusburg, Treaty of, 116
Hull, William, 252
Hungary, 15, 22, 26, 42, 47, 116, 118, 124, 129, 138-44, 147, 163, 174, 182, 189, 194-202, 205, 207, 213, 225, 226, 258
Hunsche, Otto, 14, 15, 196, 201, 235
Huppenkothen, Walter, 281
Husseini, Haj Amin el, *see* Grand Mufti of Jerusalem, the ex-

India, 288
International Red Cross, *see* Red Cross, International
Iron Guard, 191
Isère, 177
Israel, 3, 4, 5, 7, 8, 10, 13, 17, 20, 21, 193, 221, 222, 238, 239, 241-42, 250, 259-60, 261, 265, 266, 272, 286-87, 292; *see also* Ben Gurion, David; Hausner, Gideon; *various headings under* Israeli; Palestine, District Court of Jerusalem; *and* Supreme Court of Israel
Israeli Army, 62
Israeli Court of Appeal, *see* Supreme Court of Israel
Israeli law, 7, 8, 244-45, 248-49; *see also* Nazis and Nazi Collaborators (Punishment) Law of 1950
Israeli National Archive, *see* Yad Vashem
Israeli Opera, 284
Israeli Parliament, *see* Knesset, the

Israeli police, 75, 235; *see also* Less, Avner
Israeli Secret Service, 238, 239
Israeli Supreme Court, *see* Supreme Court of Israel
Italy, Fascist, 99, 139, 171, 176-80, 195, 225

Jackson, Robert H., 273-74
Jacob, E., 167
Jäger, Herbert, 33
Jahrreiss, Herman, 127
Jakob, Berthold, 263
Jansen, J. J., 17
Jaspers, Karl, 104, 252, 269-70
Jerusalem District Court, *see* District Court of Jerusalem
Jewish Agency for Palestine, 60, 125
Jewish Association in Berlin, 60, 64, 158
Jewish Brigade, 225
Jewish Councils, 74, 91, 115, 117, 118, 121, 123, 125, 166, 169, 188, 196, 214, 218, 282, 284
Jewish Frontier, 7
Jewish Relief Committee, *see* Relief and Rescue Committee, Jewish
Jodl, Alfred, 149
Joint Distribution Committee, American Jewish, 143, 198
Jong, Louis de, 125, 132, 169
Jüdische Rundschau, Die, 59
July Conspiracy, 97-105, 166, 297
Jungfrontkämpfeverband, the, 32
Jüttner, Hans, 281

Kadow, Walter, 92
Kagan, Mrs. Raja, 214
Kaiser, the, *see* Wilhelm II of Germany
Kaltenbrunner, Ernst, 31, 32, 33, 34, 37, 68, 70, 72, 133, 139, 143-44, 145, 147, 160, 168, 234, 236
Kant, Immanuel, 135-37
Kappler, Herbert, 281
Kastner, Rudolf, 30, 42, 116-17, 118, 119, 132, 142, 145, 196, 197, 199
Katyn Forest, 256
Kennedy, John F., 6
Kersten, Felix, 57
Kfar Kassem, 292, 293-94
Kibbuzniks, 121
Killinger, Manfred von, 192-93
Kimche, Jon and David, 61
Kirchheimer, Otto, 127, 256, 257, 266
"Klement, Richard (*or* Ricardo),"

(pseud. of [Otto] Adolf Eichmann), 236, 237, 238, 240
Klingenfuss, Karl, 264
Kluge, Gunther von, 100, 103
Knesset, the, 13, 238, 269, 272
Königsberg, 110
Koppe, Wilhelm, 15
Koretz, Chief Rabbi (of Salonika), 188
Kovner, Abba, 230, 231
Kovno, 121
Kreisau, 99
Kristallnacht, 39, 44, 65, 207, 227
Krug, Mark M., 119
Krüger, Friedrich-Wilhelm, 15
Krumey, Hermann, 14, 183, 196, 197, 281
Krupp Werke, 79, 200
Kube, Wilhelm, 96
Kulm, *see* Chelmno
"K-Zetnik," *see* Dinoor, Mr.

Lahousen, Erwin, 216
Lamm, Hans, 40, 58
Landau, Moshe, 4, 6, 9, 48, 53, 56, 91, 95, 120, 124, 146, 208-09, 225, 227, 230, *see also* District Court of Jerusalem
Lankin, Doris, 8
Latvia, 154, 206
Lauterpacht, Hersch, 148
Laval, Pierre, 163, 164
Law for the Prevention and Punishment of Genocide, 269
League of Nations, 38
Lechfeld, 34
Lechthaler, Joseph, 15
Lehnsdorf, Hans von, 110-17
Leipzig, 99, 229
Lemberg, *see* Lwów
Less, Avner, 28, 29, 49-50, 81-82, 242
Leuschner, Wilhelm, 99
Ley, Robert, 52
Lichtenberg, Bernard, 130
Lidice, 207, 245-46, 248
Life, 22, 238
Linz, 28, 30, 31, 32, 68, 190, 236, 237, 243, 249
Lithuania, 154, 206, 225
Lódz, 87, 94, 119, 189, 207, 213
Lolita, 49
London Agreement of 1945, *see* Nuremberg Charter
Lösener, Bernhard, 128
Löwenherz, Josef, 30, 47, 63, 66, 224
Lubbe, Marinus van der, 188

Lublin, 79, 84, 86, 87, 89, 107, 155, 170, 179, 192
Ludin, Hans Elard, 204
Lunenburger Heide, 236
Luther, Martin, 23, 76, 151, 170
Luxembourg, 225
Lwów, 88-89

McCarthy, Mary, 283
Mach, Sano, 81, 202
Madagascar project, 33, 47, 76-78, 79, 103, 157
Magyars, 194
Majdanek, 109, 225
Mapai Party, 9
Marseilles, 177
Matteotti, Giacomo, 291
Maunz, Theodor, 24
Mauthausen, 12
Mein Kampf, 33
Mengele, Josef, 264
Menthon, François de, 257
Mercedes-Benz factory (in Argentina), 237
Merten, Max, 188-90, 281
Meyer, Franz, 64
Milch, Erhard, 133, 178
Mildenstein, von (S.S. officer), 40
Mildner, Rudolf, 152
Minsk, 12, 15, 88, 89, 94, 95, 96
Mogilev, 15
Moltke, Helmuth von, 99
Mombert, Alfred, 156
Monaco, 177
Monat, Der, 252, 269
Moravia, 66, 79, 80, 82, 95, 154
Motzkin, Leo, 265-66
Mulisch, Harry, 27, 28, 96, 282
Muller, Heinrich, 31, 57, 58, 65-66, 67, 70, 72, 87-88, 89, 114, 138, 139, 143-44, 145, 153, 160, 176, 179, 207-08, 215, 249
Münchener Illustrierten Zeitung, 36
Munich University, 104
Murmelstein, Benjamin, 120
Musmanno, Michael A., 129, 179, 210, 211, 212
Mussolini, Benito, 139, 176, 177, 178, 291

Nagasaki, 256
Napoleon, 101, 291, 298
National Archive of Israel, *see* Yad Vashem
National Archives (United States), 75
National Socialist Party, *see* Nazi Party

Nationalsozialistische Deutsche Arbeiterpartei, or N.S.D.A.P., *see* Nazi Party
Nazi Party, 18, 29, 30, 31, 32, 33, 34, 36, 43, 58, 65, 69, 84, 99, 103, 112, 113, 114, 128, 129, 154, 159, 220, 246, 267, 277, 281
Nazis and Nazi Collaborators (Punishment) Law of 1950 (Israel), 21, 91-93, 220, 246, 254, 263, 272
Nebe, Arthur, 100
Negev, the, 250
Netherlands, the, 12, 45, 75, 125, 162, 163, 165-66, 167-70, 225, 268
Netherlands State Institute for War Documentation, 44, 125
Neubenschen, 228-29
Nice, 177
Nisko project, 33, 73, 75
Norway, 58, 170, 171, 225
Novak, Franz, 14, 196, 197, 213, 281
N.S.D.A.P., *see* Nazi Party
Nuremberg Charter, 254-59, 275
Nuremberg Laws of 1935, 7, 19, 30, 39, 40, 128, 267, 268, 294
Nuremberg Trials, 6-7, 9, 15, 16, 21, 22, 53, 70, 72, 84, 91, 93, 104, 110, 113, 127, 129, 133, 135, 141, 143, 146, 149, 152, 159, 173, 175, 185, 196, 203, 207-08, 210, 211, 212, 213, 216, 220, 221, 235, 236, 246, 253, 254-59, 273, 274-75, 276, 290, 298

Oberösterreichischen Elektrobau Company, 29
Odessa, 191, 267
ODESSA (organization of former S.S. men), 236
Olshan, Itzhak, 248
Oppenheim-Lauterpacht, 148
Organisation Todt, 40

Palestine, 28, 41, 47, 59, 60, 61, 62, 63, 65, 125, 193, 198, 225, 226
Paris, 153, 164, 173, 186, 196, 227, 265, 266, 267
Passau, 34
Pavelic, Ante, 183
Pearlman, Moshe, 235
Pellepoix, Darquier de, 163
Pendorf, Robert, 86, 117, 282
Pétain, Henri Philippe, 163, 176
Petlyura, Simon, 265, 267
Philippsohn, Professor, 134
Pohl, Oswald, 68, 79, 86, 152
Poland, Nazi, 9, 15, 16, 67, 73, 74, 75, 93, 95, 113, 117, 122, 123, 130, 132, 139, 169, 198, 204, 206,

208, 212-13, 215, 216-19, 225, 226, 231, 244, 245
Poland, pre–World War II, 37, 43, 66, 76, 155
Poliakov, Léon, 152, 221
Portugal, 142, 200
Poznan, 217, 229
Prague, 44, 66, 67, 73, 79, 81, 95, 146, 167, 181, 199, 224, 244, 259

Quisling, Vidkun, 117, 170

Rademacher, Franz, 22-23, 24
Räder, Erich, 217
Radom District (of Poland), 74
Rajakowitsch, Erich, 44-45, 75, 167, 168
Rath, Ernst vom, 227-28
Ratnizi, the, 185
Rauter, Hans, 167
Raveh, Yitzhak, 124, 136; *see also* District Court of Jerusalem
Reck-Malleczewen, Friedrich P., 102, 103-04, 110
Red Cross, International, 82, 85, 146, 226
Reich Center for Jewish Emigration (in Berlin), 65, 67, 74
Reich Health Department, 108
Reichsbank, 115
Reichssicherheitshauptamt (Head Office for Reich Security of the S.S.), *see* R.S.H.A.
Reichstag Fire, 188
Reichsvereinigung, see Jewish Association in Berlin
Reichsvertretung, 39-40, 60, 64
Reitlinger, Gerald, 36, 83, 107, 152, 160, 177, 221, 282
Relief and Rescue Committee, Jewish, in Bratislava, 144, 204, 205; in Hungary, 197, 198, 199
Reynolds, Quentin, 223
Rheinischer Merkur, 17, 22, 58
Rhineland, 37, 92, 94
Ribbentrop, Joachim von, 76, 104-05, 112, 151, 210
Richter, Gustav, 14, 192-93
Riga, 12, 94, 95, 206
Ritter, Gerhard, 98, 99, 100, 103
Roatta, General, 177
Rogat, Yosal, 271, 277
Röhm, Ernst, 15, 40, 192
Roman Empire, 153-54, 178, 271
Rome, 176, 179, 180
Rommel, Erwin, 100
Romoser, George K., 99
Roosevelt, Franklin D., 201
Rosen, Pinhas, 263, 269, 272

Rosenberg, Alfred, 183, 193, 206
Rothschild Palais, 64
Rousset, David, 11
R.S.H.A. (Head Office for Reich Security of the S.S.), 24, 31, 36, 68, 70, 72, 74, 76, 79, 84, 100, 107, 133, 138, 139, 141, 144, 153, 155, 158, 167, 168, 177, 187, 188, 205, 208, 213, 215, 217; *see also* Bureau IV, R.S.H.A.; *and* Subsection IV-B-4, R.S.H.A.
Rumania, 14, 66, 124, 138, 154, 163, 176, 180, 182, 185, 190-93, 198, 201, 225
Rumanian Legion, 191
Rumkowski, Chaim, 119
Russia *and* Russian, *see under* Soviet
Russian Empire, 181
Russia, White, *see* White Russia

S.A. (*Sturm Abteilung*), 38, 40, 97, 192
Saarpfalz, the, 130, 155
Sabri, Hussain Zulficar, 20
Sachsenhausen, 130
St. Germain, Treaty of, 182
Salonika, 168, 188, 190
Salzberger, Charlotte, 120
Salzburg, 31
Sassen, Willem S., 22, 48, 54, 57, 126, 222, 238, 281
Saturday Evening Post, 26, 259
Saukel, Fritz, 93
Savoie, 177
Schäfer, Emanuel, 184, 185
Schellenberg, Walter, 187, 212
Schlageter, Leo, 92
Schlaraffia, 32-33, 37
Schmidt, Anton, 230, 231, 232
Schmitt, Carl, 145
Schüle, Erwin, 14
Schutzstaffeln, see S.S.
Schwartzbard, Shalom, 265-67
S.D. (*Sicherheitsdienst, or* Security Service of the Reichsführer S.S.), the, 35, 36, 68, 74, 79, 85, 159, 187, 246
Sebba family, 30
Security Service of the Reichsführer S.S., *see* S.D.
Seidl, Siegfried, 196
Sephardic Jews, 168, 190
Serbia, 23, 24, 181-82, 184-85
Servatius, Robert, 3, 4, 9, 19, 20, 21-22, 23, 34, 56, 62, 69-70, 90, 93, 94, 108, 120, 122, 131, 145, 164, 208, 209, 221-22, 238-39, 241, 243-44, 247-48, 250

Sevastopol, 232
Shimoni, Yad, 238
Siberia, 52
Sicherheitsdienst, see S.D.
Siemens-Schuckart Werke, 79
Silber, Gershon, 228
Six, Alfred, 281
Slawik, Alfred Joseph, 281
Slovakia, 81, 82, 85, 138, 139, 142, 144, 174, 181, 195, 196, 198, 202-05, 225
Slutsk, 15
Smolensk, 256
Smolevichi, 15
Sobibor, 109, 170
Sodom and Gomorrah, 278
Sofia, 186, 187
Sofia, the Chief Rabbi of, 187
Solingen, 27
South America, 103, 160
Soviet Army, 33, 72, 111, 138, 140, 145, 183, 188, 193, 195, 201, 202, 205, 234
Soviet Intelligence service, 238
Soviet prisoners of war, Nazi-held, 95, 158
Soviet Union, 15, 53, 73, 76, 78, 83, 94, 96, 100-01, 106, 107, 109, 122, 130, 138-39, 163, 184, 185, 191, 225, 226, 255-56, 258
Spain, 156-57, 168, 176, 177, 200
Speer, Albert, 40
S.S. (*Schutzstaffeln*), 11-12, 15, 16, 28, 29, 30, 31, 32, 33, 34, 35, 37, 40, 49, 50, 60, 68-69, 71, 75, 79, 84, 91-92, 95, 99, 101, 103, 104, 105, 107, 109, 114, 115, 119, 121, 123, 129, 139-40, 141-42, 143, 144-45, 151, 158, 159, 165, 167, 174, 178, 187, 190, 197, 203, 205, 212, 214, 220, 229, 236, 238, 246, 287; *see also Einsatzgruppen* (mobile killing units); R.S.H.A. (Head Office for Reich Security); S.D. (Security Service of the Reichsführer S.S.); *and* Bureau IV, R.S.H.A.; Subsection IV-B-4, R.S.H.A.
S.S. *Wirtschafts-Verwaltungshaup-tamt, see* W.V.H.A.
Stahlecker, Franz, 73-74, 75, 79
Stalin, Joseph, 176
Stalingrad, 99, 116
Stauffenberg, Klaus von, 99
Stephan, Metropolitan of Sofia, 187
Stern, Der, 22, 238
Stern, Samuel, 197
Stettin, 155
Stone, Julius, 258

Storey, Robert G., 254
Storfer, Bertold, 50-52
Storm Troopers, *see* S.A.
Strauss, Franz-Josef, 58
Streicher, Julius, 30-31, 39, 69, 80, 258
Stuckart, Wilhelm, 113, 129, 159
Sturm Abteilung, see S.A.
Stürmer, Der, 30
Suarez (suburb of Buenos Aires), 237
Suarez, Georges, 266
Subsection IV-B-4, R.S.H.A., 31, 70, 72, 147, 155, 158, 188, 217
Sudetenland, 101, 102
Summa Iniuria, 296, 297
Supreme Court of Israel (Court of Appeal), 8, 26, 69, 143, 147, 210, 222, 238, 248-49, 284
Sweden, 170-71, 172, 174, 200
Switzerland, 30, 85, 129-30, 143, 156, 167, 172, 177, 200, 237, 263
Szalasi, Ferenc, 201
Sztojai, Dome, 176

Talaat Bey, 265
Taylor, Telford, 261
Tehlirian (Armenian assassin), 265, 266
Thadden, Eberhard von, 151, 281
Theresienstadt, 47, 60, 64, 65, 80-81, 82, 85, 117, 119-20, 123, 125, 133, 134, 145, 146, 156, 158, 159, 173, 174, 196, 225, 226, 234, 244, 284
Thierack, Otto, 157-58
Tiso, Josef, 202, 205
Tohar, Zvi, 238
Torrès, Henri, 266
Tramways and Electricity Company, 28, 29
Treblinka, 15, 87, 89, 109, 187, 225
Trianon, Treaty of, 182, 195
Tuka, Vojtek, 204
Turner, Harald, 23, 184, 185
Twenty-five Points, 43

Uebelhör, Regierungspräsident, 94
Uganda, 76
Ukraine, 154, 206, 265
Ulbricht, Walter, 13
Unit 1005, 207-08
United Nations, 262, 270, 271
United States, 98-99, 215
Upper Austrian Elektrobau Company, 29
U.S.S.R., *see* Soviet Union
Utashe, the, 183, 184

Vaadat Ezra va Hazalah, 198
Vabres, Donnedieu de, 257, 274
Vacuum Oil Company, 28-29, 30, 31, 33, 34
Vallant, Xavier, 162
Vatican, the, 85, 187, 196, 200, 204
Veesenmayer, Edmund, 139-40, 141, 147, 195, 199, 201-02, 205, 281,
Versailles, Treaty of, 33, 37, 182
Vichy France, 130, 155, 162-65, 167, 169, 172, 176
Vienna, 30, 34, 42, 43, 46, 56, 60, 63, 65, 73, 74, 75, 85, 117, 120, 137, 167, 196, 199, 200, 244
Vilna, 121
vom, von, von dem: *for names combining one of these elements, see that part of the name following the element*

Wächter, Otto, 179
Wade, E. C. S., 93
Wagner, Gerhard, 108
Walloons, 166
Wandervogel, 32
Wannsee Conference, 53, 112, 129, 133, 137, 151, 159, 160, 170, 216
Warsaw, 12, 15, 73, 107, 118, 119, 121, 213, 215
Wartenburg, York von, 100
Warthegau, the, 87, 95-96, 127, 154, 164, 206, 213, 217
Wechtenbruch, Dieter, 145, 146
Weimar Republic, 38, 43, 185
Weisenborn, Günther, 104
Weiss (of the Austrian Vacuum Oil Company), 29-30
Weiss, Manfred, steel combine, 142
Weizmann, Chaim, 122, 125, 248
Weizsäcker, Ernst von, 171
Weltsch, Robert, 59, 297

West Germany, 13-14, 15, 16, 17, 24, 34, 58, 128, 162, 248, 250, 264, 286; *see also* Adenauer, Konrad
Western Regions of Poland, *see* the Warthegau
White Russia, 15, 87, 107, 206
Wilhelm I, 101
Wilhelm II of Germany (the Kaiser), 255
Winkelmann, Otto, 139-40, 141, 281
Wirth, Christian, 87
Wisliceny, Dieter, 124, 144, 145, 146, 188, 190, 195, 196, 197, 198, 203, 204, 205, 213, 236
Wolff, Karl, 15
World Jewish Congress, 271
W.V.H.A. (*S.S. Wirtschafts-Verwaltungshauptamt*), 68, 71, 79, 81, 86, 152, 200

Yad Vashem, 44, 207, 221, 222, 225, 230
Yahil, Leni, 179
Young Men's Christian Association, 31
Yugoslavia, 22, 23, 61, 138, 176, 178, 182-85, 196, 198, 225, 245, 258

Zagreb, 183
Zbaszyn, 43, 229
Zeisel, H., 261-62
Zionism, 10, 40-41, 58, 75
Zionists and Zionist organizations, 20, 30, 39, 40, 41, 57, 58-60, 61, 63, 65, 122, 143, 197, 198, 199, 200, 204, 209, 266
Zöpf, Willi, 14, 167, 168
Zuckerman, Itzhak, 122
Zuckerman, Zivia Lubetkin, 121-22

EICHMANN IN JERUSALEM

A REPORT ON THE BANALITY OF EVIL

"A brilliant and disturbing study of the character and trial of Adolf Eichmann." —STEPHEN SPENDER, *The New York Review of Books*

"The task she sets for herself far transcends the crimes of one man since it deals with the greatest problem of our time...the problem of the human being within a modern totalitarian system.... Our best protection against oppressive control and dehumanizing totalitarianism is still a personal understanding of events as they happen. To this end Hannah Arendt has furnished us with a richness of material."
—BRUNO BETTELHEIM, *The New Republic*

"Highly personal and impulsively written, this book...reflects great courage, great independence of mind, and...a shining humanity.... Far from being 'soulless,' it reflects not only its author's brilliant analytical gifts, but compassion, outrage, and a true sense of tragedy."
—FREDERIC S. BURIN, *Political Science Quarterly*

"It is the great merit of this book that it shows, through a profound and documented analysis of the issues and the historic background of the Eichmann trial, what evil really is.... This book... is bound to stir our minds and trouble our consciences."
—HANS MORGENTHAU, *Chicago Tribune*

*Selected as one of the 50 Notable Books of 1963
by the American Library Association*

Hannah Arendt covered the Eichmann trial for *The New Yorker*, where her report first appeared as a series of articles in 1963. For this new edition of *Eichmann in Jerusalem,* the author has added further factual material that has come to light since the trial, and a Postscript commenting on the controversy that has arisen over her book.

Dr. Arendt, now a Fellow of the Committee on Social Thought at the University of Chicago and University Professor of Political Philosophy at the New School for Social Research, is also the author of *The Origins of Totalitarianism, The Human Condition, Between Past and Future* (revised and expanded edition, also available in a Viking Compass edition, C237), and *On Revolution* (C166).

THE VIKING PRESS · 625 Madison Avenue · New York 10022

$1.95